SETTUP

A Detective Evans & Dr. Murray Series

TK THOITS

Second Edition

ASA PUBLISHING CORPORATION

AN INNOVATIVE OUTSOURCE BOOK PUBLISHING HYBRID

ASA Publishing Corporation
1285 N. Telegraph Rd., PMB #351, Monroe, Michigan 48162
An Accredited Publishing House with the BBB
www.asapublishingcorporation.com

Book Title: The SETTUP *A Detective Evans & Murray Series*
Date Published: 08.01.2025
Book ID: ASAPCID2380929
Edition: 2 *Trade Paperback*
ISBN: 978-1-960104-81-6
Library of Congress Cataloging-in-Publication Data

This book was published in the United States of America.
Great State of Michigan

Acknowledgment

After years of writing, SETTUP was submitted to Mr. Hill who welcomed it to the fold as a commercially viable project. Many thanks to Charlie Vrainian who educated me on all things related to venture capitalism. Michael Ranville offered critical information on style and content. Steve Jaqua, of Pinstripe Publishing, offered essential literary insight and encouragement. Uncle Rog, Diamond Dave, 2YMD, Mad Dog, Skeeter, Shorty, BJ, Swazy, Fuzzy, are wonderful betas who deserve to have no criticism rain down on them. I am responsible for all manuscript errors, holes, mistakes, and misinformation.

Please join my Readers Club to hear about the next thrilling edition of the Detective Evans and Dr. Murray Series by replying to DetectiveEvansDrMurray@outlook.com. My readers are the best and I willingly accept all feedback, comments, and suggestions.

Book clubs and reading groups- I would love to join your discussions via zoom or telephone. Email me at DetectiveEvansDr.Murray@outlook.com and we can work out a date and time.

Table of Contents

SETTUP

A Detective Evans & Dr. Murray Series

TK THOITS

Chapter 1

December 9, 2022. Blanchard Hospital. Grand Rapids, Michigan.

An EMT transporting an unresponsive teenager burst through the Emergency Department entrance crying out, "Seizures, where do you want us?"

A tall, muscular thirty-year-old charge nurse wearing ED-designated black scrubs pointed and directed them, "Over here, I've got you in Trauma One."

The EMT's partner said, "Eighteen-year-old with a history of epilepsy who's in status epilepticus. He's already had two fifteen-minute seizures. The second one ended as we got off ninety-six. We gave him ten of midazolam after the first one. He's hypertensive at 166/92, 118, pulse ox holding at 93%."

"Let's get him on the gurney," the ED nurse said, unbuckling the straps that held the motionless teen on the stretcher.

The nurse said, "On three. One, two, three, . . ." and without further direction, the transfer became a well-coordinated effort between the nurse, two EMTs, and a nurse tech as they pulled the young patient off the EMS stretcher onto an ED gurney.

"I just spoke to Neuro, who wants him loaded with three thousand of Keppra. They've got a study going for treating status epilepticus, which they think he'll qualify for. We're gonna need pharmacy if he enrolls," said Dr. Wright, the Emergency attending working in the Trauma Bay.

Suddenly, the teenager's eyes popped open and the eerie, expressionless look on his face was replaced by lip smacking and chewing movements. He curled his right hand awkwardly and raised his right arm while deviating his head and eyes to the right. He cried a frightening cry, more like a prolonged gasp, stiffened his arms, then legs. A third seizure started. The patient was sweating profusely as the jerking and shaking progressed at a sickening pace. He bit his tongue and spewed blood-tinged saliva through clenched teeth.

"Get me two of Ativan and the crash cart. I'm gonna

intubate," Dr. Wright said.

The nurse pulled the crash cart parallel to the gurney in preparation for the procedure.

Dr. Wright administered two sedating meds, then said, "Give me a number six tube."

Using a laryngoscope, Dr. Wright pulled the teen's tongue up, visualized his vocal cords, and placed the endotracheal tube. Removing the stylet, he listened for, and heard, breath sounds over the patient's chest. "Let's get a chest X-ray to make sure we're okay. Is pharmacy here yet? We need to get him the study drug."

"Pharmacy's talking with the parents, but they haven't consented, so we can't give it," the nurse said.

The eighteen-year-old's head sagged to his right. A rumpled, urine-soaked sheet covered his waist and right leg; IV, nasogastric, and endotracheal tubes were in place. The respiratory tech was no longer bagging him. Instead, she configured the ventilator to the settings which Dr. Wright ordered.

"Where's Neuro? I need them *now*," Dr. Wright demanded of everyone in the room.

"She's here," the nurse said, nodding toward the Neurology resident entering Trauma One.

Carrie Hildebrandt was a senior Neurology resident who matched to start a Neurocritical Care Fellowship the following year. She arrived in blue scrubs and an overused, white, lab coat with her golden hair pulled back in a tight, high ponytail. She carried a stethoscope and ophthalmoscope in her left coat pocket; the right housed a reflex hammer and tuning fork. "Have you given him anything since we spoke?" she asked.

"He just had another one, so I gave him two of Ativan. I had to intubate. Keppra's going," Dr. Wright explained.

"Okay, good. Has EEG been called? He needs it for the study," Carrie said. She had treated numerous cases of status epilepticus during her residency and felt comfortable managing one more.

Dr. Wright said, "We called EEG, but haven't seen them. Pharmacy's trying to get consent from the parents."

"They just consented," a registered ED pharmacist said, run walking into the Trauma Bay with a syringe in her hands. She swabbed the IV port with alcohol. There was a hush of anticipation as the colorless study drug was pushed into the teen's IV.

Carrie performed a neuro exam, which was limited due to the number and volume of sedating medications the teen had received. "Let's get him upstairs. Has the Neuro ICU charge nurse been called? Can you have EEG meet us up there?"

The nurse threw a urine-soaked sheet on the floor saying, "Dr. Hildebrandt, I'll call report in a sec, I want to get him cleaned up a bit. He peed the bed with the last one."

"Great, thanks. Thanks, everybody. I'm gonna talk to the parents, then head up to the Unit," Carrie said, walking toward the ED Family Conference Room.

The young patient lay motionless on the gurney, unaware of the aftermath generated by his ED encounter. A whooshing sound announced each ventilator-assisted respiration. A med tech stuffed soiled sheets into a red, plastic laundry bag. The nurse placed fresh linens on the unresponsive teen, then locked the side rails at transport height. Dr. Wright took a phone call about a heart attack en route. A premed, undergrad scribe stood off to the side, silently entering a note in the EMR. The distinct ammonia odor of urine enveloped Trauma One.

Chapter 2

Four million sheltered animals are adopted each year in the U.S.

Stella received a text late, after midnight, informing her that a patient enrolled in SETTUP (Status Epilepticus TreatmenT UPdate) had been admitted to Blanchard Hospital. She had been enrolling patients in the drug trial for eight months. She wasn't looking forward to going in on a Saturday, she wasn't on call. She didn't want to miss taking Charlie, her eight-year-old third grader, to his swim meet.

She was pretty and popular when she entered high school. Her friends were too numerous to count and included more than one bestie. She dated often, but never enjoyed the dating game, certainly not as much as her friends. Maybe it was the guys that she accompanied, but Stella sensed that her escorts were prouder to be seen with her, than be with her.

Her competitive nature was evident with her studies. She viewed exams and standardized tests as an opportunity to stand out. Stella graduated number one in her class before following her brothers to Hope College.

It was an uncharacteristically warm April day during her freshman year when Stella, reading Bible passages for her Great Books course, first met Ashley Hayes. Ashley was not accustomed to seeing a co-ed reading scriptures on campus and struck up a conversation.

Stella found Ashley, a communications major who was a year older, to be warm, kind, and insightful. Their initial conversation lasted well into the night; they agreed to meet the next day. Their conversations, which lasted for hours and followed no agenda, flowed from topic to topic like a meandering stream. As days and weeks passed, a friendship blossomed. Dating followed.

Stella dressed in their bedroom closet so as not to wake Ashley, but always notified her wife when she was leaving for the hospital or clinic. Sitting on the side of the bed, she said, "I'm off."

"Where to?" came from under the sheets.

"I gotta go in. The ding I got at midnight was a text notifying me of a study patient who came in."

Ashley covered her eyes with her arm. "K. Did you feed Billy?"

Billy was rescued from the local animal shelter two years before. Billy intentionally refrained from jumping on Charlie, which endeared him to the entire household. A deal was struck, and the Hayes-Murray roster expanded by one.

Billy was housebroken within a week and moved right in, sleeping on Charlie's bed at night. Using 23andMYK9, a canine DNA kit, he was identified as part Lab, part Shepherd, part Beagle, part Corgi, and part Chesapeake Bay retriever, which accounted for his luscious brown curls. The energetic puppy enjoyed jumping on people, chairs, and beds. He was loved by family, friends, and neighbors. Charlie declared Billy the best dog ever. "Nope, I managed to dress and eat without waking him."

Ashley said, "Guess I'll feed him."

"Thanks. I won't be long, we've got Charlie's swim meet today," Stella said.

"Then walk him," Ashley mumbled.

"And that's why I love you so much. He loves your walks," Stella said, caressing her wife's shoulders.

Ashley pulled the covers over her head and said, "I know you do. Now, how about if you get out of here so I can get some more sleep?"

"Will do. Love you." Walking into Charlie's room, Stella paused and stared at her sleeping son. She pulled the covers over his shoulders and planted a gentle kiss on his forehead.

Sensing an intruder, Billy opened his eyes. Recognizing Mom's scent and movements, he announced his desperate need for attention by thumping his tail on the bed.

Stella kissed Billy's wet nose and whispered, "Yes, you're a big sweetie."

Not enough. The thumping intensified.

She petted his stomach. "I don't have time for cuddling, you big baby."

Satisfied with the smooch and belly rub, the thumping ceased. Billy yawned, stretched, and exhaled an audible 'back to sleep' sigh.

The moon descended over the high-rise skyline as Stella arrived on the Neurocritical Care Unit in Blanchard Hospital. The NCC team huddled at the opposite end of the hall. She opened a desktop computer, then EPIC, the electronic medical record (EMR) used by Triumphant Health. She found Danny, the eighteen-year-old SETTUP patient volunteer who went into status epilepticus the evening before, had been admitted to Room 16. He suffered three seizures, two of which lasted fifteen minutes, thus meeting criteria for status epilepticus. Standard medications did nothing to quell his seizures. Status epilepticus was broken, the avalanche of seizures stopped, only after the experimental drug was infused. This is good stuff. She couldn't recall more than a few patients who failed to respond. If this keeps up, we might have something good going on here. She read in the medical record that Danny hadn't been extubated.

The glass door to Danny's Neurocritical Care room was decorated with snowflakes and candy canes. Stella turned on the room lights and put the IV infusing sedating meds on hold. She pulled the sheets off his arms, legs, and feet to observe for spontaneous movements. Seeing none, she called out, "Danny, Danny," and observed no response. She shook Danny a little harder and saw his eyelids flicker.

"Danny. Danny. I'm Dr. Murray," she said, rubbing Danny's sternum. Danny gagged, then coughed five deep coughs, bucking the vent. Well, he's awake now.

"Danny, I'm Dr. Murray. You're in Blanchard Hospital because you had a couple of seizures last night. You're on a ventilator. I'm going to ask you to do some things, I want you to do the best you can. Open your eyes. Danny, open your eyes," Stella said, vigorously rubbing his sternum with her knuckles. Danny's eyes were wide open, giving off a scared-shitless look. He coughed harder, continuing to buck the vent.

"Danny, blink your eyes fast, fast, fast. Blink, blink, fast, fast."

Danny blinked slowly.

"Good. That's good. Danny, I want you to pick up your right hand." Nothing, no response. Drifted off or couldn't do it, she needed to know which. She rubbed his sternum even harder.

"Danny, pick up your right hand." After a five second delay, he picked up his right hand, to the extent the restraint on his wrist allowed.

"Good, great. Danny, that's great. Danny, I want you to pick up your left hand."

Nothing.

"Danny, pick up your left hand," Stella repeated, tapping his left forearm. He struggled to move his arm along the bed before it rose a few inches.

"Danny, pick your right leg up," she commanded. He lifted his right leg off the bed.

"Good. Now pick up your left leg." After a short delay, Danny managed to hoist his left leg an inch off the bed. The blinking rate was slower on the left, and his left arm and leg were weaker than their counterparts on the right. Damn it, he's got left sided weakness. Subtle, but it's there.

Stella looked in EPIC and saw that a progress note had not been entered for the day. There was no documentation of the left sided weakness in last night's nursing note.

She walked to the end of the hall anxious to learn whether Carrie, the Neurology resident who admitted Danny to the Neuro ICU the night before, had noted the asymmetric exam. Her least favorite neurologist was leading Neurocritical Care rounds. She waited until the team finished their conversation before speaking.

"Sorry to interrupt, but sixteen was entered in a study last night and—"

"Yeah, we know," the NCC attending interrupted.

Stella never got along with the Neurocritical Care attending. Smart enough, but she, along with most of her colleagues, found him to be an irritating little runt with a caustic personality. His lazy nature made him the least popular faculty member among their peers. The residents, however, loved this particular attending because he allowed residents rotating through the NCC to see his patients, thereby reducing his daily workload.

"Well, he's never had documented weakness after a seizure

before, so can you order an MRI to rule out stroke?" Stella asked.

"How do you know the weakness isn't because of the seizures?" the NCC attending said in a challenging tone.

"As I said, he's never had documented postictal weakness before, and he's had epilepsy for ten years or so. It'd be kind of unusual for him to develop the weakness now," she replied, applying reason to her argument.

"It's because of the seizures. MRI's a waste of money," the attending insisted.

"Study protocol says we have to do one."

"That's bullshit. Hildebrandt, order the MRI. Enough of these damn interruptions, let's get back to rounds," the NCC attending said, turning his back on Stella. Carrie subtly nodded toward Stella as the NCC attending addressed the three Neurology residents rotating through the Unit.

Stella nodded and whispered, "Thanks" to Carrie, co-signed the note which her research nurse entered in EPIC the night before, then signed the SETTUP consent form. She documented the neurological exam findings and left the floor.

Stella remembered being told during the SETTUP Investigators Meeting that the most common side effects from the investigational drug were: rash, edema, headache, dizziness, and low sodium levels. There were no cerebral vascular red flags, no mention of stroke, or warning stroke (TIA) during Phase I or Phase II trials. There was no mention of liver damage, cancers, or infections associated with the study drug.

Stella went home and took her son and wife to the swim meet. It was difficult to concentrate on Charlie's races because she kept thinking about the teenager's weakness, which shouldn't be there. She wondered if Danny had had a stroke, which triggered status epilepticus. Maybe status epilepticus caused a stroke. Had a brain tumor caused the left sided weakness and seizures?

Stella disliked working on the weekends when she was not on call. However, the unusual case bothered her so much that she broke the lifestyle wellness covenant–no work on the weekends–that she'd brokered with her wife. After returning home from the meet, Stella checked emails from Solutions & Synergy, the company administering SETTUP. There were none with stroke in the subject line. She logged onto the SETTUP website, searched for stroke, and found nothing. Was this the only stroke reported?

After reading medical articles which summarized the results of the early trials involving the investigational drug, Stella researched the authors of the manuscripts. Interestingly, they were part of a private business, not affiliated with academia. She looked for an email address and sent off an inquiry, wanting to know if the scientists' drug caused clots, strokes, or TIAs during preclinical work.

Stella discovered the Medical Director for SETTUP was Roy Abernathy, M.D. She recognized Abernathy's name from the Investigators Meeting. She had not previously noted that he was employed by Solutions & Synergy. She asked Abernathy via email whether stroke or TIA had been reported in any SETTUP patient volunteers.

She didn't wait for a reply, knowing it wouldn't come until Monday. She found it difficult to think about anything other than the teenager's weakness for the remainder of the weekend. She'd check with her research nurse to find out when Emily Naismith, the Solutions & Synergy Site Monitor who oversaw the Grand Rapids site, would be in town to check patient logbook binders. Stella intended to ask Emily whether she had heard of stroke occurring at other Clinical Sites.

That evening, Stella received a text from Carrie, the Neurology resident. Danny, the teenage patient, completed his brain MRI. He suffered a stroke.

Stella called the resident, "Was it a big stroke? I can't pull up the images here for some reason."

"I'm so sorry to bother you at home Dr. Murray, but I thought you'd want to know. You were right, the status patient had a small stroke."

Stella said, "No, I'm glad you did. Have you finished his stroke workup yet?"

"I put orders in, but he hasn't had everything done," Carrie replied.

"Good, thanks. Smoking was his only stroke risk factor, right?" Stella asked.

"Yup."

"I appreciate it, Carrie. The stroke is so unusual. I reviewed the literature on the study drug again today. I found no evidence of stroke or cerebrovascular disease in the preliminary studies," Stella said.

Carrie said, "We talked a little bit about him on rounds this morning after you left. My attending thinks it's a cryptogenic stroke, which isn't unusual in the young. I saw one in a forty-year-old last month."

"I know it happens. I'm more than a little sensitive about the study drug. I've reported the stroke as a serious adverse event."

"I documented that we don't know the cause of the stroke, just like he told me to," Carrie said.

Stella said, "Well, that makes sense. He knows everything, doesn't he?"

"Um . . ." Carrie said hesitantly.

"Don't answer that," Stella said, smiling toward the phone.

"Thanks, Dr. Murray," Carrie said, laughing. "I'll talk to you later, I gotta run."

"Thanks for the call and Merry Christmas, Carrie," Stella said, discontinuing the call.

Emily Naismith, Site Monitor overseeing Grand Rapids patient logbook binders, needed to know about the stroke. Stella texted Emily and asked if she could come to GR within the next day or so. Emily replied that she could be there on Monday.

***

Stella had a full schedule of patients on the first day of the following work week. Ten minutes before five, her Medical Assistant told Stella that there was a woman in the waiting room who said she had an appointment to see her, but wasn't on the schedule.

"It's Emily, the research Site Monitor," Stella said.

"Ahh, okay. That makes sense."

Stella brought Emily into her office and showed her EPIC

progress notes, which documented Danny's left sided weakness. Stella showed Emily the brain MRI images which confirmed the stroke. Stella told Emily that the stroke was scored as serious and unrelated to the study drug.

Emily confirmed it was the first stroke she'd seen in a SETTUP patient and would report the stroke to her supervisor, Dr. Abernathy, the Medical Director of the drug trial. After checking her calendar, Emily told Stella that she was scheduled to return to Grand Rapids in four weeks, on Monday, January 9. Emily hugged Stella, wished her a Merry Christmas, and left the office.

Chapter 3

The NIH allocated eighteen billion dollars for Clinical Research in 2022.

He phoned Solutions & Synergy. "Dr. Abernathy, please."

"Hi there, long time," Dr. Abernathy said.

"How's it going?"

His parents never asked for much, so it wasn't hard to comply with their wishes. He was encouraged to study and thrived in the classroom. He was offered academic scholarships at colleges and universities along the East Coast. He was interested in Boston University, but Roy Abernathy's parents decided that Roy should remain closer to home and selected Bowdoin College for him. Bowdoin was good enough for Roy because his parents were Bowdoin graduates. His mother died of metastatic ovarian cancer during his final undergraduate year.

Abernathy replied, "It's all good, all good. You know, I've heard from several physicians participating in the trial, and they're all saying the same thing. Your drug works great."

He said, "Fantastic. So, no issues?" After pushing him into sports, his father taught him that winning matters. He tolerated athletics, but craved his father's attention. Sure, competing and winning was fun, but the fatherly praise? Pure gold.

"One of my Site Monitors recently reported a side effect, a bad one," Abernathy said.

"How bad?"

Abernathy replied, "Bad, bad. Serious bad. Bad enough to immediately report it. I just wish she had talked to me before putting it in the books."

"What's going to happen now? Is she going to report more side effects?"

Abernathy said, "If anything shows up, yes, she needs to report it. All it takes is for one person to complain of a symptom and we're obligated to report it. In triplicate. The FDA demands transparency. Everything must be documented, recorded, then documented again. More importantly, going forward, I now know that she can't be trusted to follow my directives. Trust is so important in my job. I can't work with people that I don't trust. It just doesn't work."

"What does that mean for us? I mean, we're screwed, right?" he said.

"Not necessarily. If someone in the reporting position were to be replaced with someone who I can trust, someone who will listen to me and evaluate side effect symptoms the way I want them evaluated, then the problem goes away. The drug works well. I mean, everything is trending toward a successful trial. One day, this stuff is going to earn someone a huge paycheck," Abernathy said.

"What other drugs are looking good right now?"

Abernathy said, "You know, I respect you and everything you've done in your little hipster world. You've obviously surrounded yourself with talented people, who've helped you realize noteworthy success. But you should have listened to me when I suggested that you work with West Coast Medical. Their new migraine med has done amazingly well. Every Doc and their mother is prescribing it. They had something like a billion dollars in sales last year."

Abernathy just stirred up painful memories. "Goddamn it. I remember, we all remember. Anything else going on?" he asked.

"No, not unless you want to get into antibiotics or antihypertensives. You know, those things can make millions, just like your drug will someday," Abernathy said.

"Not interested. Let's be in touch. Talk to you soon," he said, disconnecting the call.

He walked circumferentially around his office contemplating his next move. The group demanded transparency. Dilemma time. He could either bring up the serious side effect during their next meeting or inform everyone now. He landed on today.

He intended to take a deeper dive and registered to attend a national conference in Los Angeles. He wanted to hear for himself what the doctors involved in the clinical trial were saying about their drug. While in California, he'd make an unannounced visit to Northern Biotech. He'd see what they had going on in their research and development pipeline. Opportunity. He'd emphasize opportunity. Was Northern Biotech open to looking into a collaborative effort that may lead to a profitable and long-lasting partnership.

Chapter 4

Ancients believed that the epileptic was unclean and whoever touched him might become prey to the demons that caused the spells.

A college buddy first told him about the dark web. Classrooms weren't the only place where he learned many lifelong lessons. The right college friends were an endless source of helpful information and offline resources. His informal education, although unpublished, had been verified through many life experiences and had proven to be more useful than traditional classroom-based schooling and internet searches.

As instructed, he set up an encrypted email account. He accessed the dark web after normal business hours because he didn't want anyone at work to know about his project. Even if his efforts were successful and put millions in the pockets of everyone involved, he anticipated that his partners wouldn't support his methods. Sometimes having the loudest voice in the decision-making process didn't matter.

He was appropriately paranoid and took precautions to assure that no one discovered his dark web communications. Before dirtying his hands, he assessed the integrity of the encryption program by sending an email to an old college roommate, DB. DB was Chief of IT at a San Diego advertising firm. He asked DB to break the encryption, not telling him what it was about, other than to say it was work-related.

Three days later, DB replied.

> Dude,
>
> *You win. That is some professional shit. I couldn't decrypt it as I'm not, and never will be, a cryptographer. Your best bet is to ask Big Brother (FBI or CIA) for help, and good luck with that.*
>
> DB

Confident in DB's computer skills, he believed that the encrypted email wouldn't be read by anyone other than the person for whom it was intended. He didn't think his dark web activities fell under the purview of the FBI. He couldn't think of a scenario where the CIA would be involved in his project.

He first became acquainted with "KFAP" through David, a high school friend who served with KFAP in the Marines. Per David, KFAP was just the kind of maniac he was looking for.

While fighting in the desert, KFAP was generally allowed to live by the motto "survival by any means," ramped up to the *n*th degree. His rationalization that "these guys are trying to kill us and it's my job to kill them first" wasn't always in keeping with the intentions or wishes of his Commanding Officer. KFAP had a reputation in the 2nd Battalion as a killer among killers. It was his understanding that it was "us against them" and his job was to eliminate as many of the enemy, by any means possible. He viewed every person not wearing USMC camo fatigues as the enemy. He showed no remorse, none, for culling the local tribes.

KFAP was viewed as an anomaly. Older than every other enlisted Marine, he was well spoken, intelligent, and entertaining. When he had his game face on, the rest of the troops knew to stay away. Off duty was another matter. The guys flocked around KFAP as he made each of them seem like he was their new best friend. It was well known that after he had a few beers, he was more entertaining than the sanctioned USMC entertainment. His offbeat humor helped make their tours more tolerable. Maybe a little.

It was a cold, dolphin-gray overcast Tuesday when he decided he couldn't do it alone, he needed help. David was as solid as they come, and if he recommended KFAP, that was good enough for him. He wouldn't take the next step until the office emptied out. At five-thirty, he circled through the interoffice messaging system and discovered everyone had signed off for the night. Satisfied that he was alone, he sent an encrypted email to KFAP.

> KFAP,
> I'm requesting your assistance regarding a
> career issue. I'm on the verge of something big
> at work and don't appreciate a co-worker

jeopardizing my position or advancement. You
may decide whether to disable or eliminate
this person. This is a time sensitive assignment,
this person must be taken off the job within
two weeks.
Emily Naismith, Site Monitor,
Chicago, IL.
Anonymous

They say travel is tiring. KFAP wasn't bothered by the travel fatigue that came with his comedic career. He took well-timed naps and was able to approach each day with unbridled enthusiasm. Finding the brick-and-mortar environment too confining, he specifically chose a non-office job after ending his military career. The freedom that his post-military career offered worked out perfectly; he harbored no regrets about giving up the imprisoning office life.

He recently finished a gig in Charlotte. He intended to ask his agent for a return performance in a few months. He received mostly supportive comments from the North Carolina crowds. Reviews included, "Almost died laughing." "He killed it." After leaving the military, KFAP changed his acronym from 'Kill For A Purpose' to 'Kill For A Price.'

KFAP checked his email. He read, then reread, the email from Anonymous. Well, well, well, Anonymous. You're an interesting one and propose an even more fascinating job. Who are you, and why can't you manage this career issue by yourself? KFAP knew what he needed to do that morning, and it wasn't writing. His socially acceptable career, his shit-for-money career, his comedic career would have to stand down for the moment.

Using the dark web was a two-way street. After a little internet digging, KFAP was able to ascertain, with confidence, his employer eighty percent of the time. So far, none of KFAP's clients had unmasked his identity.

He replied to Anonymous:

Ho, Ho, Ho,
Merry Christmas to you and yours. Your timing

is perfect. I have not earned enough PTO for a vacation, which means I'm available to address your career issue. You'll need to make up your mind as far as the intended outcome. Currently, I'm offering two packages. The Cadillac is offered for the reasonable price of $50K and culminates in elimination. For the budget minded shopper, the Yugo was recently added for $25K and involves removal from the job. There are no Bluelight Specials this month. Thank you so much for reaching out.

Wishing you and yours Happy Holidays,

KFAP

He wondered if he had just made a colossal mistake. He wanted to hire a hardcore mobster, not a freakin' oddball. Bluelight special? Happy Holidays? He thought about what he wanted, what he needed, and how much he was willing to pay. He could afford elimination. If Emily Naismith were removed from her job, the fear of getting caught would hover over his head for a few years. Elimination, on the other hand, had no statute of limitations, and meant a lifetime of looking over his shoulder.

While thinking about how he'd reply, he called home, said he was working on an urgent project, and hoped to be home within the hour. He further delayed making the KFAP decision by checking his phone for text messages and emails.

Elimination. After struggling with the decision for several minutes, he decided to eliminate the threat. The potential benefit elicited by elimination outweighed the risks. He read on Facebook that she was single, with no children. Her family would get over it. She lived in Chicago, where the urban lifestyle came with risks. He hoped KFAP would make it look like an accident. Without suffering. He'd demand that she not suffer. The last thing he wanted to do was to upset KFAP. But it was his money, his job. He read, then reread, his reply twice. Satisfied that the email struck a balance of expressing his conviction without desperate begging, he pushed the Enter key.

> KFAP,
> I want elimination. Having said that, I have two requests. Please make it look like an accident and she must not suffer. I know I'm not in a position to tell you how to do your job, but $50K should allow me these two requests.
> Anonymous

He paced around his office anxiously waiting for a reply. How would KFAP take the suggestions? Should I have mentioned the accident scenario? Although it seemed like hours, he waited minutes for a reply.

> Season's Greetings,
> 'Tis the season for giving. Elimination requires that $50K be given (wired) to account number CH93 4456 1382 2312 9990 7 within the next thirty minutes.
> Thank you for the suggestion of making it look like an accident. I'm embarrassed that the whole unlucky scenario never occurred to me. Please go to my website and click on the Helpful Hints link to leave more step-saving ideas. There will be no further communication between us once the transfer is complete.
> Wishing you a Happy New Year,
> KFAP

Two weeks before, he spoke to a banker who walked him through the process of making a wire transfer. He didn't recognize CH93, which must be the code for Switzerland. He was told GN70 was the code for the Grand Caymans. Logging off the dark web, he opened the bank app on his phone, sent the money, then waited.

He repeatedly checked the time to see if he would arrive home when he said he would. Why, at a time like this, he was worried about getting home on time was beyond explanation. Feeling a bit paranoid, he listened for sirens. He went to the bathroom and nervously peed. He ran back to his office to find a reply.

> Hoping your heart is full of Holiday Cheer,
> I think we're going to get along just fine. The deposit has gone through. As such, you have successfully signed the contract. There will be no further communication between us. You must submit a new work order for each new request. It was a pleasure working with you.
> Hoping your dreams come true,
> KFAP

Holiday Cheer? Dreams come true? This guy is a certifiable nutcase. He didn't want to be confrontational, but felt compelled to ask.

> KFAP,
> Will you be incorporating my requests in your plans? They're important to me, maybe as important as the end result. Accidental, without suffering.
> Anonymous

KFAP was thrown off by Anonymous's latest email. Hadn't he just said no more communication? Understand English much? KFAP sent off what he intended to be his final reply.

> Joyous Noel,
> Effective communication makes for good times, don't ya think? Perhaps you should watch my Theodore Talk about Effective Communication in the Workplace. My fee buys you a contract and nothing more. I am a professional who expects to partner with similarly qualified personnel. You may offer feedback on how the contract was fulfilled. You may or may not utilize my services going forward. Do not ever, even accidentally, tell me how to do my job. Accidents have a way of suddenly affecting suggestioners (adjective. səg-jes-chen-ers. Anyone named Anonymous who offers unwanted and unwarranted suggestions).

Warmest Holiday wishes,
KFAP

What the hell. He can't find me. He doesn't know who I am and, according to DB, never will. He wanted to scream or hit something. He slumped in his chair. What's done, is done. He felt dirty; his shirt clung to his sweaty skin. He went to the bathroom and splashed water on his face. He brushed his bangs off his mug and straightened his tie.

He was expected home sooner and ate a cold dinner. Alone. Family movie night was cancelled.

KFAP looked up the target. Interesting, she lived in Chicago, was employed by an Indianapolis company, and worked in Grand Rapids. Chicago offered two advantages–it was closer to home and would be easier to work anonymously in the larger city. After some internet digging, he found out that the targetess had made an upcoming hotel reservation in Grand Rapids. That sealed it. KFAP was scheduled to perform at Dr. Funny Bones in Grand Rapids on January 6 and 7. Nurse Naismith, I'll see you in Grand Rapids. What? You're free? Fantastic, I'll leave a ticket for you at the will call window. I hope you enjoy the show.

KFAP announced to no one that the KFAP Games had been awarded to Grand Rapids. Chicago and Indianapolis were encouraged to put in bids for future Games. KFAP eagerly awaited the Opening Ceremonies.

Chapter 5

One month later. Grand Rapids, Michigan.

KFAP walked into Devries Place, hidden within a growing crowd of Cottage & Lakefront Living Show attendees. Owning a second home, cottage, or cabin on water, whether it be on one of the Big Lakes (Superior, Michigan, Huron), a stream, a river, or an inland lake, was common in Michigan. The sheer volume of second homes in Northern Michigan made the Cottage and Lakefront Living Show, which ran in Grand Rapids the first weekend in January, one of the most well-attended shows year in and year out.

As a high school junior, KFAP applied to several colleges and accepted an academic scholarship from Butler University. Without studying excessively, he received a Bachelor of Science degree, then a Master's in Computer Science. He rose to VP of Information Technology at TW Financial Holdings Corporation. He used his computer savvy to the benefit of every partner at TW. Even with extra money in their pockets, TW's Board members didn't care for KFAP's methods and placed him on probation. KFAP, acknowledging that his moral compass was not aligned with other business leaders, felt unappreciated. He resigned and signed up for a hitch with the Marines. After completing boot camp in Oceanside, California, he was sent to Afghanistan where he completed two tours. The killing began overseas.

Upon returning to the States, KFAP was approached by David, an old friend from the 2nd Battalion, about a problem he was having at work. David worked construction and had a "real asshole" for a foreman. David worked hard, there was no doubt about that. He was troubled because there was nothing he could do to satisfy Brian the asshole. With mounting bills, he wanted the job, needed it really, but didn't appreciate Brian constantly hounding him. It got to the point that David hated going to work, knowing he'd get his balls busted. He asked KFAP if he could get Brian to back off a little.

David texted KFAP a description of Brian and KFAP was able to pick out the short, bearded, balding foreman from the others on the construction crew. He followed Brian the asshole after work for several days. Brian liked to drink beer, a lot of it, which contributed to his being overweight and terribly out of shape. He planned to approach Brian at his apartment after he'd stopped at his favorite haunt, the Glory Days Bar. No sense calling him out in front of his work crew or beer buddies.

KFAP parked across the street from Brian's apartment building and approached him as he exited his rusted, 2015 navy Taurus. "Brian, a word?"

"Who the fuck are you?" Brian said, slurring his words. He balled up his hands. He stood with his feet close together, his balance off.

"Friend of a friend. Word is that you have been leaning hard on the guys at work, even though those same guys are giving you a full day's work."

"What the fuck do you know about my work?" Brian said, his cheeks reddening. He started swaying.

"I've watched you, Brian. I know you don't do shit, other than give your guys a hard time. How 'bout if you back off a little bit and let them do their jobs without jumping on their asses every day."

Brian was having none of it. He sure didn't like this A-hole calling him out. "I don't know who the fuck you are, or why you're here, but you better back off, fuck head."

"No need to get upset, just lighten up on the guys. You've got to admit they're doing good work."

With his face and neck now crimson, Brian replied, "I don't have to admit shit, fuck face. It's time for you to get out of here."

KFAP held his hands up as if stopping traffic. "Dude, no need to get upset. All I'm asking is that you back off on your crew."

"Who the fuck are you trying to tell me how to do my job? Listen pal, I've heard enough from you." Brian took a couple steps and clumsily threw a roundhouse swing. KFAP easily sidestepped the punch, and, grabbing Brian's right arm, pulled him to the ground. As Brian struggled to get to his knees, KFAP punched his jaw, fracturing it. He then viciously thrust two fingers at Brian's exposed neck. Brian grabbed his throat, coughed, gasped, and collapsed while making no effort to brace himself. His skull cracked loudly when it slammed the pavement. His eyes were closed, he wasn't responding. Blood seeped from his nose, ears, and scalp.

Shaking Brian's shoulder, KFAP said, "Brian. Brian, open your eyes. I didn't hit you that hard. Come on, dude wake up. Open your eyes." Damn it, he couldn't have known that Brian would go down so easily. He reached and felt a pulse, albeit a weak one, and noted that Brian was still breathing. At least he's not dead. Hopefully, he'll remember my message and stop constantly criticizing his crew. KFAP called David and, without emotion, told him about his interaction with Brian. He warned David that he may need a new foreman.

Brian was discovered later that evening by an apartment complex resident, who immediately called 9-1-1. The EMS crew found Brian unresponsive and transported him to the closest Emergency Department. Brian suffered a traumatic brain injury when his head hit the concrete street. The resultant massive brain swelling couldn't be controlled with medications or surgery. With no chance of making a meaningful recovery, Brian's family made the difficult decision to take him off life support. His organs were harvested for donation two days later. KFAP recorded his first civilian kill as serious, unexpected, and related to a crucial conversation gone sideways.

***

KFAP took the stairs up one flight and walked on the skywalk around Devries Place toward the Three Fires Hotel. He purposely kept his head down, his face hidden underneath a red baseball hat.

He entered the hotel via the Plaza Necessities, a men's clothing store. He nodded, but did not speak, to the young salesman behind the counter. Wanting to appear as if he were an interested shopper, he strolled the aisles, even trying on a pair of pants. He purchased nothing and after spending twelve minutes in the boutique, walked over to Modern Floral. He didn't nod or acknowledge the salesperson, who wrapping up a bouquet of long stem roses for a teenager. The youngster paced nervously. KFAP wondered if the tuxedoed teen was attending his first prom.

Ostensibly, while shopping, KFAP kept an eye on the elevators. Fifteen minutes later, he saw his target enter The Dining Room, the hotel's feature restaurant, and knew it was safe to make his way to her room.

KFAP stared at his shoes and walked purposely through the concourse. He intentionally avoided exposing his face to the hotel security cameras. At the end of the day, it wasn't a big deal, because he had plans for the CCTV tapes. KFAP was joined at the elevator bank by a group of seven, who wore identical name-tag lanyards. Several had earbuds in; all focused their attention on their phone.

Perfect. The group won't remember anything about the nondescript middle-aged guy, other than he pressed 11. They were so mesmerized by their phones that they probably hadn't even noticed which button he pushed.

Holiday muzak played as the elevator rose so quickly that KFAP felt a sinking feeling in his stomach. After everyone departed on the seventh floor, he pressed 16, his true destination.

The elevator doors opened to a foyer centered with a glass top table with fresh flowers in a red glass vase. An oblong mirror in a wood frame was situated over the middle of the table. Signs with an arrow pointing right for rooms 1610-1624, and left for rooms 1625-1639 were attached to the walls. KFAP went left, south, and made his way quickly to Room 1633.

Each door in the hotel was secured with a Maglocks magnetic card lock system. He pulled a device, which was the size of two decks of cards, out of his backpack and placed it above the door handle. The device read and copied the magnetic code for the door. He put a blank card in the bottom of the device and copied the code onto the card. He put the card in the door, saw the green light, and heard the familiar *click*. Love the click! KFAP removed the card and entered the room.

The accommodations were smaller than he envisioned. The floor was covered with wall-to-wall plush, even bouncy, bark-gray carpeting. There was a flat screen Sony TV centered on a laminated dresser at the foot of a queen-sized bed. There were no Christmas decorations in 1633. He opened the forest green drapes and the white lace curtains underneath, and peered out over the west side of the city and the Grand River. KFAP remembered reading that in the 1600s, the Grand River dropped seventeen feet over a four-mile stretch, which led to roaring rapids and the naming of the city as Grand Rapids. As the years passed, the river leveled out, and the rapids largely disappeared.

Who the hell named them the Grand River and Grand Rapids? Neither the river nor rapids were all that "Grand" in their appearance. Peering to the south, he noticed the Pearl Street Bridge and saw no rapids to speak of, certainly not enough that would qualify as Grand. He looked north and saw a six-foot drop in the river leading to a casual Grade IV rapids. He decided his definition of "Grand" did not align with that of his forefathers.

He opened the small minibar refrigerator and saw that it was stocked with bottled water, two IPAs, and two single-serving-sized bottles of chardonnay. On top of the refrigerator was a basket holding a bag of honey roasted peanuts, a single portion of trail mix, and a bag of chocolate covered raisins. The December issue of Grand Rapids Magazine lay on the table.

He went into the bathroom looking for Emily's toiletry bag. Opening it, he removed her pill bottles. After hacking her pharmacy account, KFAP discovered that she took melatonin for sleep and a thyroid medication. Several years before, he incorporated hacking his target's pharmacy as part of his preparation. Once again, he found the medication information helpful. He emptied Emily's melatonin bottle in the toilet. He remembered his primary care physician telling him to never throw drugs in the toilet, because the ingredients eventually made their way into the city water system and allergic reactions popped up. Guess no one told Nurse Naismith that.

He filled the melatonin bottle with roughly the same number of self-compounded tablets. Before arriving in Grand Rapids, he crushed fentanyl tablets, then shaped and scored them to look like Emily's melatonin pills. He knew that Emily took three 3 milligram melatonin tablets for sleep and decided 4,800 micrograms of fentanyl ought to give her a good, no Grand! night of sleep.

Nurse Naismith, before I go, I think a Thank You is in order. Thank you for going to work every day with a sense of entitlement, which forced Anonymous to address his career issue with the Cadillac package (yay for me). Oh, I agree. If it comes up again, I will speak to Anonymous about making "requests." Anyway, thank you for giving me the opportunity to master my pill compounding skills. Thank you for being you, so easy to work with. Hugs and kisses. Love you. Miss you.

Noting that he placed her toiletry bag on the wrong side of the sink, KFAP corrected it. He walked out of the bathroom and examined the room. Closing the heavy drapes and lace curtains, he perused the room looking for anything out of place. Satisfied that the room looked undisturbed with everything in its rightful place, he walked to the door.

He pulled on a white T-shirt and a generic white knit skull hat, and stuffed the red hat and black shirt in his backpack. Gloves were returned to the backpack. Stepping outside, he allowed the door to Room 1633 to close and lock. He took the stairs to the lobby and left the hotel through the front entrance. He overheard a conversation from a family that he guessed had just returned from the Cottage & Lakefront Show. They were excitedly talking about how their newly purchased jet skis would make for an especially fun summer.

KFAP lived by several rules: Be prepared. Research thoroughly. No repeat business. Know your limits. Improvise. Adapt. Overcome.

He was struck by the sight of so many people out and about on the sidewalks. Having changed his outward appearance, he was confident no one would remember him from either the hotel or the Cottage & Lakefront Living Show. He smiled while waiting for the crosswalk light to change.

So easy. It was so easy.

Chapter 6

January 9, 2023. Grand Rapids, Michigan.

Opening his office door, Lieutenant Jefferson cried out, "Evans, get over to the Three Fires Hotel."

Troy Evans was one of the younger detectives in the Grand Rapids Police Department. After spending eight years as a patrol officer, he did well enough on the Detective Exam to earn a promotion. He kept his brown hair short, neatly trimmed above his ears. Always clean shaven, he never dabbled with a mustache or beard. He wore a tie with either a sport coat or two-piece suit to work every day.

Evans admitted that he was obsessed with a few things, including thoroughness. When his intellect and dogged determination were combined with thoroughness, he was an efficient and effective investigator. He did his job well, with an above average closure rate in his fifteen years as a Major Cases Detective. "Hey, Lieu, did someone skip out on paying their bill?" he asked.

Mason Jefferson had been employed by GRPD for forty-five of his sixty-four years. He spent two years in the Army before joining GRPD. Jefferson's baptismal patrol beat covered the Southern Section of the city, including his old high school, South High. He loved the people on his patrol, and they loved him right back. Crime in the Southern section was plentiful, but after a few years under Jefferson's watch, serious crime dropped. After spending ten years on Patrol duty, Jefferson was promoted to Sergeant. The men and women working under Jefferson respected him, admired his work ethic, and appreciated his leadership style. Jefferson and his team received accolades from the City and GRPD leadership.

Jefferson, had been the first to suggest that Evans take the Detective Exam. After he easily passed it, Jefferson mentored him for several years and felt good about the way he was maturing professionally. The one thing he didn't like about Evans was his tendency to question everything. Absolutely everything.

"Hardly. Emily Naismith didn't skip out on anything. Cleaning staff found her dead at the Three Fires."

"What makes you think it's a homicide and not suicide?" Suicide wasn't a major crime; Evans wanted to know how or why it had been ruled out. He was currently working on a meth distribution network, a gang shooting, three assaults, and a tax fraud; his caseload was full and sought clarification.

Jefferson said, "I don't think I said homicide. She was found dead in bed, which makes it a suspicious death that we are obliged to investigate. The Three Fires people said she was from out of town and didn't appear to be depressed when she checked in. She's apparently here for business, something to do with Triumphant Health."

Evans wasn't satisfied with the story. How could the staff at the Three Fires tell that she wasn't depressed? And why was a Triumphant employee at the Three Fires?

Jefferson's office was small, with filing cabinets against the wall, a desk, with two uncomfortable wooden chairs situated in front of it. When he was first named Lieutenant in the Major Case Division, he faithfully decorated his office for the Holidays. For the last two years, his Christmas trappings remained in a cardboard box, gathering dust like memories stuffed in an attic corner.

With less enthusiasm in his voice than when he first handed out the assignment, Jefferson leaned back, and locking his fingers behind his head, said, "I don't think she's a Triumphant employee, but she missed a meeting there today. She has something to do with research or something. Please get over there and take a look around. Rule out homicide, rule in suicide, whatever. I want boots on the ground, and you're the next one up."

Evans headed to his desk to do a little research before visiting the crime scene. He found a LinkedIn page for Emily Naismith. She was employed at Solutions & Synergy, Inc. as a Site Monitor. She had many LinkedIn contacts in Chicago and Boston, fewer in Jacksonville and Cleveland, and surprise, surprise one in Grand Rapids. Why was she communicating with Dr. Stella Murray?

Well, that's interesting.

Delving into her social media life, he found Emily maintained Instagram, Facebook, TikTok, and Snapchat pages. She was not particularly active on any of the sites. She had 306 friends on FB, twelve followers on Instagram. Emily didn't post often, only a few photos.

Walk or drive to the Three Fires? The hotel was a short, three-block walk from GRPD Headquarters. The cost of parking and required valet tip clinched it, he'd walk. It'd do him good to get out; snow was not in the forecast.

Giant ornamental tree balls, six-foot red bows, and Christmas lights decorated four sides of the hotel. The west side of the Three Fires Hotel bordered the Grand River, which unofficially separated the west from the east side of the city. The hotel was built in 1902 and took its name from the Indigenous inhabitants of the area. Around three hundred years ago, the Ottawa tribe established several villages along the west side of the river. Their camps were bordered on the north by the Ojibwa/Chippewa while the Potawatomi tribes settled to the south. Together, they were called The People of the Three Fires.

Evans saw a GRPD cruiser parked in front of the hotel and wondered which patrol officer he'd see at the scene. The expansive lobby was warm and basked in gold-tinted lighting. A ten-foot diameter glass chandelier hung over the Registration Desk. A twenty-foot Christmas tree was located next to the Concierge's Desk. Holiday decorations consisting of Santa Clauses, snowflakes, and candy canes were taped to walls, and strategically placed on tabletops. Nine reindeer hung from the ceiling.

He rode the elevator in silence and stepped out onto the sixteenth floor to a small lobby. A sign directed him to rooms 1625-1639. He walked nearly to the end of the corridor to find a GRPD patrol officer standing outside the door, which was crisscrossed with a yellow tape warning – Police Line Do Not Cross.

"Jonesie, good weekend?" Evans asked.

"Absolutely. Lotta laughs," Jones said. Standing an

impressive six feet five inches tall, he equally filled the doorway and his navy GRPD uniform. Mohammad Jones assumed his Serve And Protect posture–feet shoulder width apart, knees locked, thumbs hooked on his service belt. Evans surmised it was Mohammad's cruiser parked in front of the hotel.

"Hey, Gordie, nice to see you," said Spencer Cracken. Spencer, who never seemed to have a bad day, was a Forensic Services Unit Specialist with whom Evans worked often and well. He was a pleasant, rotund fifty-two-year-old Irishman whose strawberry-colored hair was framed by red glasses. The only thing Spencer loved more than his job was assigning nicknames. Uncoordinated as a youth, Spencer was targeted for bullying. He took revenge on the smug and arrogant of the world by giving them unflattering nicknames. While Evans tolerated the whole nicknaming thing, he found Spencer's work to be exemplary.

Spencer was the first person to call Evans "Gordie" after the most famous Detroit Red Wing of all time—Gordie Howe. He couldn't remember who told Spencer that he played hockey, but once Spencer heard that, he only referred to Evans as Gordie, Mr. Hockey, or Number 9.

Spencer, standing at the foot of the bed, was his usual enthusiastic, smiling self while packing his bag. "Frankly, there's not a lot for you or me here. I took pictures of the vic, the room, the closet, the bathroom, her bags, and that's about it. Oh, I dusted for latents in the bathroom, her luggage, doors, windows, and counters."

"Hey Spence, did you pull the sheets down, or were they this way when you found her?"

Taking a few steps towards the head of the bed, Spencer said, "Always with the sharp eye, Mr. Hockey. I took several pictures before pulling the sheets and covers off. The sheets weren't messed up at all."

"Phone, laptop?" Evans stared at the young lady on the bed. She was lying on her left side wearing a Pearl Jam T-shirt and yellow panties. The sheets on the other side of the bed were not messed up, she hadn't struggled. He noted a dark discoloration below her eyes.

"Yeah, her purse was on the table and her suitcase was over there," Spencer said, motioning toward the dresser. "Her phone was charging and the alarm was blaring when housekeeping found her. You know, I've always maintained that the evidence doesn't lie. Having said that, it's unclear to me what brought the young lass to her unfortunate and untimely death, but it doesn't appear to be related to trauma," he said, closing the latchet on his case.

"Suicide?" Evans asked.

Spencer nodded. "Possibly."

"Anything else?"

"Again, not really. Nothing out of place, no weapon, no needle tracks, no blood, no superficial signs of sexual assault. Even the sheets were still creased. It looked like she went to bed planning on going to work in the morning and never woke up."

Evans asked, "What's your best estimate on the time of death?"

"Wilma, our distinguished ME guesstimated, based on her core temp, ten to twelve hours ago."

Evans looked toward the door. He had worked with Mohammad on a few cases, which was easy to do as it was a small department. Mohammad had the patrol beat for the downtown section of Grand Rapids. "Jonesie say anything?"

"You mean Strahan? Not to me, but ask him yourself," Spencer said, walking toward the windows.

"Strahan? Where'd that come from?"

Spencer turned, saying, "Large football player with a gap in his front teeth. How could I not? Number 9, you need to work on your Detective skills."

Mohammad shaved his head while maintaining a goatee that never seemed to grow. Four years ago, he was playing defensive end for Western Michigan University. Never drafted into the NFL, he joined GRPD after graduation. His imposing physical stature, baritone voice, and interest in team-based policing made him a GRPD favorite.

Evans walked to the door and asked, "Jonesie, you found her?"

Mohammad, who rarely showed emotion, gestured with his hand toward the bed, stating, "That's right. Someone from Triumphant called the front desk when she didn't show up for a meeting or something. They wanted to see if she had checked into the hotel. The front desk had housekeeping check her room. Housekeeping let herself in after knocking, heard the alarm, and saw the vic in bed. The poor woman said she shat her pants and ran out of the room after determining the vic was unresponsive," Mohammad said, grinning. "She immediately called the front desk, who called us. I found no sign of foul play. I found nothing that appeared suspicious or out of line. No alcohol or drugs in the room. I called it in and have been waiting outside since."

Evans turned toward Spencer. "Before you go, did you find any medications or pill bottles in her things?"

"I checked the bathroom, her toiletries and her suitcase, and only found a bottle of melatonin, which is an over-the-counter sleep product and levothyroxine, which my wife takes for thyroid," Spencer said. He started off every morning with his hair parted on the right and spent the rest of the day pushing his ruby-colored locks off his face.

"Ever heard of an accidental melatonin or thyroid overdose?" Evans asked. He leaned close to the victim and took a portrait picture with his phone.

Spencer replied, "Nope, but I'm only a lowly Forensic Unit Service Specialist or FUSSy."

"Do you know if Wilma is backlogged?"

"I don't believe so. I think the distinguished Dr. Death will treat this with the expediency it deserves, like she does for all your cases. In other words, I'm sure Wilma will put it at the top of the pile."

Evans stared at Spencer. "Dr. Death? That's a new one."

"Not really, but it's a good one, if I do say so myself," Spencer said.

"Spence, I need to see her contacts, texts, and emails from her phone and laptop, as soon as you can."

Spencer said, "Sarah will need warrants."

"I'll take care of the paperwork, just get the vic's stuff to

Sarah. I've only been here a few minutes and already I'm feeling anxious about this one. Suicide looks unlikely. Her profile doesn't exactly fit with an overdose, other than she was a health care worker who may have had access to opioids," Evans said. Young woman dies in the middle of the night. He was getting a sinking feeling in the pit of his gut, which traditionally had been an accurate barometer for some nasty shit.

He replayed the story as he returned to Headquarters. A healthy young woman dies suddenly. It didn't make sense. Overdose? Spencer had never heard of an overdose on melatonin. Evans was eager to see what the tox screen showed. If it was an overdose, was it accidental or intentional? Tox screen and autopsy may tell him the how, but not the why. He needed to find out more about Emily. Specifically, what did she do at Triumphant Health? He intended to speak with people at the hospital who worked with her and knew her well. But first, paperwork. Filling out the death report was his way of delaying that which he dreaded the most. Notification of the parents.

Chapter 7

The first writings on epilepsy, written in 400 B.C., were found in the book of Hippocratic collection of writings On The Sacred Disease.

Yi bounced into the Conference Room to find Gwen talking to Albert. "Hi guys."

Albert immediately diverted his attention toward the approaching researcher saying, "Hi, Yi. You're looking nice today."

"Hey, Yi," Gwen said.

Yi Zhang was a tiny ball of energy who apparently didn't need the same amount of sleep as everyone else, averaging four hours a night. She maintained a lithe figure while snacking before, during, and after meals. She kept her hair in a shoulder-length bob, never wore a skirt or dress, even outside of the lab. Her spoken English, an amalgam of Oxford English idioms and urban slang, was acquired during a five-year stint of post-doctoral work in London. Yi came to the States to work for Palladium Pharmaceuticals, a large international conglomerate based in the Midwest.

"Nice?" What's so nice about a tee shirt and jeans? Albert gave Yi the creeps by focusing on her personal life while ignoring her contributions in the lab.

Albert Brasston was the CFO of SGY Bioengineering who maintained his self-described hipster appearance by shaving once a week and wearing untucked shirts with a sport coat. Albert's long, black hair was combed back and held in place by too much styling gel. He wore John Lennon glasses.

Albert made Yi feel uneasy, was tolerated by Gwen, and admired by Scott. Scott, Gwen, and Yi were the lead scientists that made up SGY Bioengineering.

Ignoring Albert, Yi asked, "Gwen, how's it going with the nanoalkylating agent?"

Gwen Hopkins grew up in the Midwest, the oldest of six children. Never venturing beyond Iowa's borders during her first eighteen years, she moved to Iowa City after graduating high school in three years. She obtained a Bachelor of Science in biochemistry from the University of Iowa, then continued her education at Stanford, where she earned a PhD in Bioengineering. After spending fourteen years in academia, Gwen found the work environment at Stanford's Jane M. Clarke Center too West Coast. Missing the homey roots of the Midwest, she transitioned to a position in Research and Development at Palladium Pharmaceutical, where she thrived as mentor, scientist, and nurturer for the Neuroscience Division. She first met Yi at Palladium Pharmaceutical. The motherly fifty-one-year-old researcher replied, "I'm embarrassed to say not well. I'm frustrated that even at ten nanometers, I'm having trouble getting it into viral particles."

"A former colleague of mine works with viral vectors. I will text you his contact information. Although he does not have your experience, maybe he can help you to solve your challenges," Yi said.

"Merci, Yi. You're a never-ending source of resources," Gwen replied.

Albert jumped in. "I couldn't agree more. I think it's great that you're willing to help your less cultured peers, if I can even say that."

"Nice try, Albert, but Yi and I are having an adult conversation here, and she still isn't interested in you," Gwen said with a gentle smile.

"I was addressing Yi, who is clearly capable of speaking for herself. I think it has been well established that you are not the mom of Yi," Albert smirked.

"Afternoon, ladies. What'd I miss?" Scott said, sauntering into the room. Scott Williams was a brilliant, distant, divorced scientist. He maintained a pear-shaped habitus since high school. Never fitting in with the cool kids because he wasn't athletically inclined, he earned an academic scholarship to the University of Wisconsin-Madison and breezed through undergraduate studies, majoring in Biochemistry. Remaining in Madison for his postgraduate studies, he obtained a PhD in Immunology. Scott formed SGY Bioengineering after enticing Gwen and Yi to leave Palladium Pharmaceutical. He sat in "his" seat at the head of the table.

Albert said, "Thank you for making yourselves available for our little impromptu sit down. I'll get right to it and tell you I need more money. Actually, it's Solutions & Synergy who needs money for SETTUP, the trial involving your seizure drug. Enrollment has been poor, and they're looking to hire more nurses."

Gwen spoke up, "Albert, I know you're the numbers guy, but that doesn't make any sense. Why do they need more nurses if they're struggling with enrollment? They should be letting nurses go, not hiring them. I know we have some money now, but it's not right of them to ask us for funding."

Albert replied, "Look, it wasn't my idea, Gwen. I received a letter, I mean an email, stating the trial was going well, but they needed money."

"How much are we talkin' about? Hundreds, thousands?" Scott asked. He evenly aligned four scientific journals on the table.

"Two hundred and fifty thousand."

"I'm not buying it, Albert. That's not how it works in the real world. They should be asking anyone other than us. I'm not in favor of giving them any money," Gwen said.

"Maybe they've asked others, I don't know. What I do know is that they've asked us for dough, and I want to give it to them. If your seizure drug does well in the trial, it will mean more money for each of you. A lot more," Albert said.

"Why don't they go after a venture capital group, like Great Lakes VC. They paid us a lot of money for Seizural," Scott said. He turned the stack of journals forty-five degrees so its long side ran parallel with the side of the table.

"It doesn't work that way. They'll only invest in a drug after it's been approved by the FDA," Albert said. He stood and paced, retracing his steps like a screen saver. He'd been kind and complementary toward Yi, knowing that one day he may need her in his corner. He desperately needed the money. He lost thousands with that last hit. If he couldn't secure the funds, there's be no payments. If he wasn't able to settle up, he'd be in deep shit.

Albert said, "Yi, you've been awfully quiet. You want the trial to succeed, don't you? I know you're on board with me. Let's give them the money so they can finish the trial."

Yi replied, "I'm down with Gwen and Dr. Scott. While I don't want to see the seizure trial fail, financing it is not our fiscal responsibility. Solutions & Synergy should not have asked us for funding support. They may ask a university or a Big Pharmaceuticals company for capital because they have bigger bucks in their money coffers than we do."

Albert altered his negotiating tact. Facing the scientists, he opened his arms as if leading a prayer and said, "Wow, all of a sudden, we're too good to help our colleagues in need. Hear me out. Helping Solutions & Synergy is the right thing to do and I think, deep down, you agree with me. How about if we tell them that our limit is a firm two hundred thousand? And I'll tell them it's a loan. After the trial is a tremendous success, and the FDA approves your drug, which I'm sure they will, then they'll pay us back and then some." His stare pleaded for support.

"A loan? Yeah, I guess I can go along with that," Scott said.

"Wait a minute, Scott. Have you heard anything that we've said?" Gwen said, looking at Yi, then Scott.

"My lab, my decision," Scott replied. He ran a finger along the binder edge of the journals.

"Hold on there. We're all equal partners here. It says SGY Bioengineering on the front door, remember? I'll agree to a loan, but you don't get to make unilateral decisions. It's our money, too," Gwen said.

"Albert, tell them we can loan them some money, but two hundred thousand is too much. Tell them it's a hundred and twenty-five or nothing," Scott said.

"I'll take it. I mean they'll take it. On behalf of Solutions & Synergy, many thanks to each of you. I'll write up the loan agreement and you guys can sign it."

Yi wondered why the creepy bloke couldn't stay seated for an entire meeting.

Gwen rubbed her temples, trying to thwart a ripening stress headache. Walking to her workstation, she questioned what just happened back there.

Often, and this was one of those times, Scott had trouble focusing on the big picture while ruminating over past regrets. His thoughts were currently directed toward his ex. Never should have married that woman, never should have agreed to the divorce. Never, never, never. He dreamed of the day when he could wave goodbye to her fat ass while riding off on his new Harley.

Chapter 8

One quarter of epilepsy patients have seizures resistant to medications.

Koral Roberts used his key card to enter the parking ramp off Pearl St., descended two levels, then pulled into the first open space. He was oblivious to the cooing pigeons perched on the infrastructure girders. His hurried walk caused his shoes to click loudly, causing several of the birds to take flight. The abrupt sound of beating wings startled him, eliciting a "duck and cover" response. When he was safely past the drop zone, he noted no avian excrement on his suit or head. He recorded the final score as: Roberts 1- Goddamn Filthy Pigeons 0. Another win.

Sixteen years before, Roberts invited several financially savvy, ambitious friends from Michigan to join him on the yellow brick path of venture capitalism. Prior to forming COR Venture Capital Group, the partners made their money in finance, real estate, and tech. COR's startup funds paled in comparison to the $375 million they raised during their initial fundraising endeavor. COR specialized in purchasing, then infusing money, operational guidance, and managerial assistance, in startup bioengineering, pharmaceutical, and other healthcare related manufacturing companies. COR fast-tracked the development of medications, catheters, and other medical devices. Once a product did well on the open market, the manufacturing company was sold. For considerable profit.

He rushed past the COR receptionist without an exchange of greetings.

Hampton Xavier was a short, gruff, and generally intolerant sixty-six-year-old CEO of COR. Xavier challenged COR's younger minds to find groundbreaking products and generously rewarded those who succeeded. He had his favorites within the Group, and right now, Roberts wasn't on the list.

Xavier wore a charcoal-colored pin-stripe Brooks Brothers suit, with a red and navy striped tie bound in a tight Windsor square knot. Precisely one-half inch of a similarly colored handkerchief stood at attention in the left breast pocket of his coat. He was the only Ivy Leaguer in the group, having graduated from Dartmouth, then Harvard Law School, before the others seated around the table had finished high school.

Xavier harshly welcomed Roberts by grunting, "Glad you made time for us tonight, Roberts. Now take a seat."

"Evening, everyone," Roberts said, joining the other COR Board members around a nine by six-foot Brazilian cherry hardwood table. Black, leather COR coasters were strategically placed in front of each chair.

Koral Roberts was conceived while his parents were exploring the atoll reefs off the shores of Belize on a scuba diving excursion. They agreed to name their first child after the reefs, regardless of its gender. Although he was not particularly fond of his given name growing up, largely because of the name-calling, he learned to appreciate it. Once he grew a slightly red-tinged beard, added pearl-colored glasses, and gained unbridled academic success, the confidence he held in his name grew to its current level.

Xavier opened the meeting by asking, "Bull, where are we with your cancer drug?"

Brock "Bull" Zemanski was a physically intimidating six feet three inches, 215-pound partner who was first dubbed "Bull" in high school. His friends told him they called him Bull because of his physique; the truth was that he bullied his diminutive classmates. He wrestled at Michigan and stayed in good physical shape following graduation. He learned early on in life that size matters. He used his height as a threatening advantage when negotiating deals. With his intimidating physical presence and tendency to raise his voice, he usually got his way. Usually. His partners recognized his proclivity toward bullying and uniformly stood their ground. He enjoyed a monthly movie night with his family and was COR's self-designated film expert.

Bull said, "I won't bore you with a long presentation. The monoclonal antibody trial for pancreatic carcinoma is going well. As you may recall, there's no good treatment for this particular cancer. The average five-year survival rate for all stages of pancreatic carcinoma is terrible, less than ten percent. The study I've been following involves giving patient volunteers a monoclonal antibody which selectively binds to, and kills, cancer cells. The selectivity of the antibodies is key. Because the antibodies don't affect normal cells, the side effects haven't been too bad. We signed up thirty-five clinical sites across the country. Enrollment started slowly, but it's picking up. We're on track. The drug is kicking ass."

Three years ago, Roberts recommended that COR purchase a startup pharmaceutical company that was in the initial stages of developing a drug for Alzheimer's Disease. The drug failed to improve memory, or even slow memory loss, in patients with Alzheimer's. The experimental drug was a bust, which he viewed as an embarrassing personal defeat. Recognizing an opportunity to agitate Bull, Roberts asked, "Why's enrollment so bad when there's no treatment for pancreatic cancer? Is there a treatment option which we weren't told about before we jumped into this drug?"

"I don't know why enrollment started slowly, but it's fine now. Remember, there are about 57,000 new cases of pancreatic cancer diagnosed in the U.S. each year. I expect the study will meet its targeted goal of 2,000 patients fairly quickly," Bull replied.

Xavier said, "Nice presentation, Bull. You're recommending that we purchase?"

"Yeah, I think we should," Bull said.

"What about that side effect. It sounds bad," Roberts said.

Xavier looked at Bull and said, "I agree. Encephalitis sounds dangerous. Maybe we should cut bait. If we bury the side effects and get out now, we could probably sell to Pharma and mitigate our losses."

"I think we should stay with it, sir. It's only been the one patient, and the Phase I and Phase II data looked great. I know the one case means the drug carries a certain risk, and it may not get FDA approval, but this is what we do. Gamble with high risk to achieve high reward. I say we give it a little more time," Bull said.

"Fine, I hope to hear good news next month. Roberts, you wanted to tell us about a seizure drug," Xavier said.

Roberts stood, opened his laptop, and projected his presentation on the south wall. "These slides come from an old roommate of mine who happens to be a Neurologist. To remind everyone, seizures are common in the U.S. With an incidence of five or six per 1,000, epilepsy is more common than Parkinson's disease and MS, together. There's a life-threatening condition called status epilepticus where seizures don't stop, they keep coming and coming. Approximately 145,000 cases of status epilepticus are diagnosed every year, with a mortality rate of about twenty percent. Doing some quick math, that's 29,000 lives that we may be able to save each year. It's an important public health issue which I'd like to address by investing in the company that made this new seizure drug.

"The drug has a novel mechanism of action, which is a bonus. It's well tolerated at therapeutic doses and doesn't interact with other drugs, which is another bonus. When seizure medications interact with each other their efficacy may be compromised.

"Solutions & Synergy had trouble signing up Clinical Sites because university neurologists asked to be compensated a thousand dollars for each enrolled patient and Solutions & Synergy was only offering two hundred bucks. They were forced to change their strategy and started recruiting community neurologists. Unlike university faculty members, local neurologists happily accept a couple of Benjamins for every patient volunteer. The private practice neurologists initiate treatment of status epilepticus, then transfer the patient to the closest university for definitive treatment. We might want to think about using anyone other than Solutions & Synergy to conduct future trials."

Xavier said, "Solutions & Synergy has a great reputation, I don't want to make any changes there, but let's watch it."

Bull rolled a pen between his fingers and asked, "What do the preliminary results show?"

Roberts replied, "The drug works well, it stops the seizures cold. I told you that the drug uses this cool nanotechnology.

Because there's nothing like it on the market, I think the FDA will look at it favorably. You talk about high reward Bull, and no offense to your cancer drug, but I think mine is the real deal. And it doesn't cause meningitis or encephalitis. It's going to be a killer once it hits the market. I think we should consider purchasing the bioengineering company that created it."

The room became still upon hearing Roberts's recommendation. Xavier contemplated COR's next move. Xavier and Roberts maintained steady eye contact throughout the exchange. The veil of silence stood tall until Bull's pen clinked on the table after slipping through his fingers. All eyes shifted to the pen, then Bull.

After a minute Xavier stated, "Roberts, I don't want another dumpster fire like that Alzheimer's drug you got us into. I'm not ready to talk about purchasing yet, but let's watch it closely. By that, I mean frequent updates. Monthly, even if they indicate that we should dump and run. I don't want any more disasters."

"Good enough," Roberts said, closing his presentation and taking his seat.

Bridgett said, "Are we ready to hear about the GI bleeding study? It's fascinating, cutting edge stuff. The study's going well, we're nearing the end. I think we can start looking for a buyer."

Xavier said, "Finally. I could use some good news. Go."

Bridgett had rehearsed her talk so often that she had no prepared notes. "About four years ago, we purchased a company called Biofabricating Solutions. As you all know, I currently sit on their Board of Directors. Tissue engineering is a new field that applies the principles of engineering to the human body at a cellular level to develop biological substitutes, which restore or maintain tissue function. Our company has been working on vascular tissue biomaterials and the preliminary results are great. Alcoholics end up with paper-thin esophageal veins which hemorrhage spontaneously, even to the point of bleeding to death.

"The organization is involved in a study which has fifty-nine Clinical Sites around the U.S. and India. With no shortage of alcoholics in either country, the study has been filling quickly. The biosynthetic veins are super strong. We're seeing less bleeding and fewer deaths in study patients. I'm anticipating that we'll complete enrollment in a couple of months, followed by a statistical analysis. When that's finished, I propose we start looking for a buyer."

Xavier said, "Sounds promising. Let's get word out that Biofabricating Solutions is for sale."

"I can do that," Bridgett said.

Xavier opened the floor for questions or general discussion. Hearing none, he announced the meeting was adjourned and wished everyone a Merry Christmas.

Chapter 9

Physicians in six states are required to report patients who have seizures to the DMV.

Evans listened to his car's ticking slow down while sitting in the driveway next to the house where Emily grew up and where her parents currently reside. A plow service had pushed the white, powdery, four-letter word from the driveway into a pile across the street. The walkway to the front door was shoveled.

He dreaded the conversation he was about to have. Unbuttoning his overcoat, he strode to the front door. The house was a boxy, red brick two-story colonial with black shutters and an unattached garage. Strings and strings of small, white Christmas lights lined the gutters and circled the forsythias genuflecting under the weight of a recent snowfall. A wreath, protected by a glass storm door, hung on the front door. A black mailbox with a swinging door was situated to the left.

He was about to ring the doorbell when he heard footsteps, the door opened, and found himself face-to-face with a middle-aged woman. She wore black slacks, a white Oxford blouse, and white athletic shoes. Her brown hair hung on her shoulders. Behind the door stood a tall, gray-haired gentleman wearing a black suit, white shirt, and red tie. "Detective Evans?"

"Mrs. Naismith?"

"Yes, and the gentleman behind the door is my husband. I have to tell you that you scared us to death when you called earlier."

"Sorry about that. May I come in?" Evans wiped his shoes on the outdoor Christmas doormat.

"Yes, please. Let's have a seat in here," Emily's mother said, pointing toward the living room. A Christmas tree stood in a corner of the room. Christmas cards lined the bookshelves.

"Thank you. You have a lovely home," Evans said, following the Naismiths out of the foyer. Emily's parents sat on the couch; Evans chose the floral pattern armchair situated at the end of the davenport. The Naismiths held hands as if anticipating unwelcome news.

"I'm a Major Cases Detective of Grand Rapids PD. This is not the . . . ah, not the easiest part of my job. I'm afraid it's um . . . about your daughter, Emily. Emily, your daughter, she was found dead in Grand Rapids earlier today."

"Noooooooooooo," Emily's mother said. Tears morphed into wailing. Evans said nothing as Emily's father hugged his wife and joined her crying. Evans sat silently, wringing his hands for the longest three minutes of his life.

Emily's dad broke the silence, asking, "Are you sure? Sure, that it's our Emily?"

"Yeah, I'm sure. The whole world is on the internet these days, as you well know. I found her driver's license in her wallet and compared that picture to the picture on her LinkedIn account."

He removed his phone from his right breast suit pocket. He had taken a picture of Emily at the scene for this reason. "I'm afraid I have to ask for confirmation by having you look at a picture I took this morning," he said, holding his phone in front of the Naismiths.

Emily's father took the phone and, looking at the photo nearly dropped it, confirming that Evans took a picture of his daughter in the hotel earlier that day.

Evans waited silently until one of them, it was Emily's father, looked up. "Is that Emily?" Evans asked, seeking verbal confirmation.

Emily's father managed a quiet, "Yes." Emily's parents struggled to compose themselves. It would be years before they accepted her death.

"What happened to her?" Emily's mother asked. She asked for her husband's handkerchief.

"I don't have all the answers for you, I've only been on the case for a few hours. She checked into the hotel and was acting normally, according to the Registration Desk. I found nothing unusual or out of place in her room. I don't even know the cause of death right now." Evans accepted his phone from Emily's father and said, "Unfortunately, I have to ask you some difficult questions. Did Emily do drugs?"

"No, she's a good girl. Why would you even ask that?" her mother shot back.

Because many "good" girls ended up abusing drugs. "An accidental overdose is one possible cause of death. She worked in health care, and we occasionally see overdoses in nurses and doctors. She was found in bed, with no sign of a struggle, and no weapons around. The scene raised the possibility of an overdose. How about her mood? Was Emily depressed?"

Emily's mother replied, "Emily? You obviously don't know her. She's the most positive person I know." Her eyes were red; she dabbed at a stream of tears with her husband's hanky.

"I'm sorry for these questions. I didn't see a ring, was Emily married or engaged?" Evans asked.

"No."

"Is there a boyfriend in the picture?" He knew that females were murdered by an intimate partner nearly thirty-five percent of the time.

Emily's father remained quiet, allowing his wife to answer. "She's seeing someone, a guy named Tyler Bright."

"Were they serious?" Evans asked.

"Yes," Emily's mother said.

"Really?" Emily's father asked. "I only saw him at dinner that one time."

"Yes, dear, they're close. Emily liked him a lot and was thinking about moving in with him," her mother said for clarification.

"She never said anything to me about moving in with him," Emily's father whined.

"We can talk about that later, hon. Detective Evans, I'm certain that she didn't commit suicide, so how'd she die?"

"As I said, I'm not sure. Nothing stood out at the scene. I should get some results from the autopsy over the next several weeks, which I'm hoping will shed light on the exact cause of death. Do you have a phone number for this Tyler fella?" Evans asked Emily's mother. It was apparent that she was closer to Emily than her father.

"I think I might have it, let me find my phone," she said, retreating from the room. She returned punching her passcode on her iPhone. Scrolling through her contacts, she found Tyler, "Here it is, ready?"

Evans took out his notepad and said, "Yup, go ahead." He recorded the number and asked, "Is that a local area code?"

"No, it's not. I'm not sure where it's from," Emily's father said.

"What can you tell me about Tyler? Did they have any problems as far as you know?"

Emily's mother blew her nose and cleared her throat before saying, "Emily never said anything like that. I think she said he grew up here. Went to Loyola, works in Evanston. Seemed like a nice enough guy."

"Do you know where he works? I mean, do you know the name of his company or business?" Evans asked.

"Let me think. Global . . . Global something. I don't remember, I'm not sure. I looked them up once. They're a nonprofit, interested in making non-traditional healthcare services or something, available around the world," Emily's mother said.

"That's all right, I'll search the net for them. You don't have a photo of this Tyler on your phone, do you?" Emily's boyfriend had a common name. A picture would help confirm that he'd found the right guy.

"I'm sorry, I don't. No pictures . . . of him," she said, looking at the floor. The tears had not stopped falling.

"Is Tyler the same age as Emily?" Evans asked, wondering if the boyfriend was older. The larger the age discrepancy, the more jealous the male became. Having investigated numerous spousal murders, Evans had noticed a trend–older men who married younger wives were usually control freaks.

"I wasn't struck by an age difference between them. When will you have the results of the autopsy? When can we bring her home?" she asked.

He said, "The preliminary autopsy results will be completed by our Medical Examiner in two or three days and the final report will be available in several weeks. I'll let you know the results as soon as I get them. The body will be released once the autopsy is complete."

Their faces held a look of horror as the crying ramped up several notches. Fuck me. Had he just blurted out "the body?" You moron. Emily's not a body, she's their daughter.

"Um . . . sorry. Emily's body will be released once the autopsy is complete. You'll be the first to hear about any updates or progress that I make. Again, I apologize for delivering such horrific news. I'm sorry for your loss. Here's my card, it's got my cell number on it," Evans said, standing and handing his card to Emily's father.

"Thank you for driving over, Detective. Please let us know as soon as you know anything," Mr. Naismith said, holding his wife's arm.

Evans left the house and walked slowly toward his car. Well, that was a shit show. Not a complete cluster, but close. It killed him to hear the Naismiths refer to Emily in the present tense, while he referred to her in the past. It's never a good thing when parents are forced to bury a child. Death was one of life's five great stressors. He hoped Emily's death wouldn't strain their marriage too much. Fuck me. What a waste.

He drove to a nearby school parking lot, turned off his car, and looked up Emily's boyfriend on Linkedin. Tyler Bright worked at the Institute for Global Strategies Inc., just like Mrs. Naismith said. Twenty-eight years old, nice-looking kid. Better check him out before returning to Grand Rapids.

He entered the building through the revolving door and found the Institute for Global Strategies on the wall-mounted directory. Second floor it was. He didn't see a stairwell, so he rode the elevator. He exited to a narrow hall lined with worn gray carpeting and tan walls. His wife would call the walls taupe. She was like that.

The frosted glass door to Suite 218 had Institute for Global Strategies Inc. stenciled on it. Evans entered and found himself staring at a pleasant-looking receptionist.

"Hi there. You must be Dr. Runquist."

"Afraid not. Detective Evans, Grand Rapids Police Department," he said, reaching for his shield. I'd like to speak with Tyler Bright if I may."

"Sorry about that, I was expecting someone else. I can take you to Tyler." She opened the door behind her and motioned for Evans to join her. "He's not in any kind of trouble, is he?"

"Not that I know of." He followed a couple of steps behind. He recognized Tyler, even with his full beard, which was not present in the company directory picture. The beard made Tyler look older than twenty-eight.

"Here you go. Detective Evans, this is Tyler."

"Thank you." Evans turned toward Tyler, introduced himself, and offered a handshake. "Detective Evans."

"Pleased to meet you, I think. I'm Tyler."

"Is there a room where we could have a little privacy?"

"Ah, sure. Let's go to the break room. What's this about, have I done something wrong?" Tyler sat in the middle of an oblong table.

Sitting across from Tyler, he said, "No, not that I'm aware of. You're dating Emily Naismith, correct?"

"Yeah, for a couple of years now."

"How's it going?"

"Fine. We're good, all good."

"Emily thought it was going well, also?" Evans asked.

"Yyyeeeees," Tyler said, hesitantly. "She's the one who brought up moving in together."

Evans said, "I'm afraid I have some bad news for you. Emily was found dead in her hotel room this morning."

It didn't take years of experience to read Tyler's reaction, he was visibly shaken by the news. Right then, either Tyler deserved an Emmy, or he cleared himself of any wrongdoing. He had no clue. Evans said, "I'm sorry for your loss. Not the best part of the job, I'm afraid."

"What happened to her? How'd she die? How could this have happened?"

"It's early in the investigation, so I don't have all the details for you. She was found in her hotel bed. The preliminary autopsy results should be available over the next few days, and the final report in several weeks. I just notified Emily's parents, who told me the two of you were going out."

"Yeah, it's been almost two years now," Tyler said, reaching for a napkin, unsuccessfully fighting back tears. "Sorry."

"That's all right. I know how upsetting it is to receive news like this from a stranger," Evans said. Leaning back in the uncomfortable plastic chair, he continued, "Were you and Emily having any problems with your relationship?"

"What? No, not at all. She was going to move in with me. We were fine," Tyler said, blowing his nose in the napkin.

Evans asked, "Okay, had to ask. How about her job, did she like her job?"

"She loves it, loves working in research with patients and stuff. What she didn't like was the travel. But yeah, she loves it."

"No issues at work?"

"She mentioned there was some frustration a couple of times."

"Frustration? Frustrated as in depressed? Frustrated as in things weren't going her way. What was she frustrated about?" Evans asked, leaning forward.

"She said that she was frustrated, but wouldn't say anything else about it. If she told me once, she told me a thousand times, 'patient information is protected by confidentiality, and my research work is confidential also.'"

"How about her work peers or her supervisor. Any issues there?"

Tyler said, "She said her boss was kind of a dick. But in the same breath, she always said she respected him."

"Did she ever say anything about the performance reviews that she was getting from the dick? Did she ever say anything about leaving Solutions & Synergy, maybe looking for a different job?"

"No, she never mentioned anything about that. I speak to her every day. I called her last night after dinner. We talked about work and the move."

Evans made notes of Tyler's answers. "Do you know who her

boss was? And how about his or her name?"

"I think it's a guy, but I've never met him. She rarely spoke about him."

"Could he have been the source of frustration?"

"I'm not sure. Again, she wasn't very specific about any of it. She just wanted to vent," Tyler said. He wiped tears away with the balled-up napkin.

"I understand. Any chance Emily was depressed?"

"Absolutely not. She's the most positive person I know," Tyler said, using the exact same words as Emily's mother.

"Anything else you can tell me? Nothing's too small, nothing's too inconsequential. I need to find out who did this to Emily, because I don't think she did it to herself," Evans said.

"No, but I can't think right now. I don't think there's anything else I know."

"Tyler, I'm sorry for your loss. I'll be informing her parents of any updates, so I suggest you remain in contact with them."

"Sure. I can do that. Thanks."

Evans wanted to examine Emily's phone and laptop, which required three warrants: one for each device and the third for her phone company. He asked Stella to delay their meeting. She confirmed they'd meet at her office after five.

Chapter 10

Babylonians classified the seizure type according to the evil spirit that invaded the body during it.

After arriving back at GRPD Headquarters, Evans wrote up his interviews with Emily's parents and Tyler. He then filled out a warrant to enter and search Emily's apartment. He asked Chicago PD to serve the warrant and conduct the search. He got back in his car and headed to Triumphant Health.

Repeatedly checking the time, he saw that he was going to be late. He greeted Stella in the spacious Neurology waiting area. "Sorry I'm late, traffic was a bitch."

Stella said, "No worries, you're rarely on time."

"Oh yeah? How long did your patients have to wait for Dr. Murray today?"

"Listen PD, I wait for my patients, they don't wait for me. Come on, I finished with my last one," Stella said.

"PD?" Evans asked as he stood. He waited for clarification before pointing out that Police Detective was redundant. Detective would suffice.

"Pencil dick," Stella said as her face lit up with a bright smile. "Let's head over to my office."

"Ouch."

"What's this about, are you missing the game or what?" Stella said, still smiling. Evans and Stella had played on a men's league hockey team for years. Every team in the beer leagues was looking for a goalie. Stella had offers to join several when she was looking to get back in the game. She opted to form her own team and filled the roster with guys she knew from school, the Triumphant Health Medical Staff, and her brothers's friends. Stella named the team Murray's Manons, after Manon Rheaume, the first woman to play in an NHL game.

Stella first met Evans when she consulted on one of his criminals, who passed out while he was housed at Kent County Jail. She told Evans that the guy likely had a seizure, but hospitalization was not required. She scheduled the prisoner for the First Seizure Clinic, and the felon was promptly returned to jail. Eventually, their talk turned to the common ground of hockey.

Stella invited Evans to join Murray's Manons, and he brought a new dynamic to the team. He was a skillful player who could skate, pass, and score. He elevated the play of the other Manons, such that they started winning regularly.

"No, it has nothing to do with the game, which I hope to make by the way," Evans said, sitting in a chair in front of her desk.

"Good, the others like it when you show up," Stella said.

"And you don't?"

"Sometimes."

"Whatever. What can you tell me about Emily Naismith?" Evans asked.

Stella said, "Emily, the Site Monitor? Not much, other than she's smart as hell and does a great job. She was a no-show today. She was supposed to review our books." She glanced at her desktop monitor.

"What books?"

Looking at Evans, Stella said, "I'm involved in a research trial looking at a drug for treating status epilepticus. Emily's my Site Monitor. She goes over our patient logbook binders, where we document on every patient that's enrolled in the trial. You know, blood test results, EEGs, MRIs, clinical outcomes, adverse events, that sort of thing. Emily doesn't show up for work and now you're grilling me. What's really going on here, Gordie?"

"I'm afraid I have some bad news. Emily was found dead this morning in the Three Fires," Evans said.

"Dead? What do you mean, dead? She was fine. What happened to her?" Stella asked with tears forming.

"When was she fine?" Evans asked.

Stella reached for a tissue, saying, "It was in Miami, at the Investigator Meeting."

"What meeting? When was this meeting? Have you seen her recently?"

With her ears and face flushed, taking on the same red hue

as her eyes, Stella said, "It was a meeting for the Neurologists participating in SETTUP. I remember it was in Miami because some business guy's murder hogged the headlines that week. I haven't seen her recently."

"What's set up?" Evans asked.

"That's the acronym of the status epilepticus study I'm participating in. It stands for Status Epilepticus TreatmenT UPdate. Everyone tries to come up with a witty, catchy name so it will be easier to remember the trial after the results are published. So what happened to her?" Stella asked.

"You know I can't give you anything. Tell me more about Emily. What was her job in this research trial thing?"

Stella composed herself and said, "As I said, she's my Site Monitor. She makes sure we follow the study protocol and goes over our patient logbook binders in great detail. She documents serious and non-serious adverse events, makes sure we cross our T's and dot our I's with the paperwork, which is unbelievably detailed."

Evans asked, "What are adverse events? Did you get the sense that Emily did drugs or alcohol?"

"Adverse events are side effects, which the experimental drug may or may not have caused. And absolutely not. There's no way she could have done her job as well as she did if she were drunk or high. Listen, Emily wasn't some party frat boy. She was professional in every sense of the word," Stella said.

"Okay, all right, I get it. What about this trial thing? What can you tell me about it?"

"As I said, it's a drug study for treating status epilepticus. A seizure is a sudden hypersynchronous discharge of electrical activity within the brain. You're probably aware that we see different kinds of seizures. The worst of the worst is called status epilepticus, which is when a seizure lasts for more than five minutes, or someone has multiple seizures without waking up between them.

"Status epilepticus is a neurological emergency, which puts patients at risk of dying. SETTUP involves giving people in status an experimental drug that hopefully stops their seizures."

"How's it going, the trial?" Evans asked.

"Fine, it's going well. The drug works great. I enrolled two more patients last week."

"Can you think of anyone who would want to hurt Emily?"

"No, no one. No one working on SETTUP, that's for sure."

"What happens to the trial now, with Emily gone?"

Stella answered, "Nothing. Emily will be replaced, and the trial will keep going. SETTUP involves a novel agent created by a local biotech company called SGY Bioengineering. They're not unlike all the other small biotech companies who can't afford to run a clinical trial, which can cost up to a billion dollars from start to finish.

"The FDA requires rigorous trials to be conducted before approval of a medication is granted. Because the trials are heavily weighted in personnel, and require a lot of testing, the cost of running a study like this rises rapidly. The small biotech companies either sell out to Big Pharma or hire companies like Solutions & Synergy to run the trials."

"You said the trial is going well, what does that mean?"

Stella said, "Going well means the investigational drug is working, it stops the seizures without causing a lot of adverse events."

Evans probed, "Have you heard about side effects from Solutions & Synergy?"

"No. They run the study, but don't directly see any of the patients."

Evans asked, "What happens next, you know, if the trial is successful?"

"If it keeps stopping seizures, the FDA will approve the use of the drug. Then I can start writing orders for it, giving me another avenue for breaking status. Oh, and eventually it may put millions in the pockets of SGY Bioengineering."

"So why would anyone want to slow down or stop the trial if there's so much money to be made?" Evans asked.

"Good question. No one on my side of things would ever want to stop a successful clinical trial. It's all very preliminary, but the drug has been working great so far. Pharma would never want to stop a trial which could end up being their next cash cow," Stella answered.

"What would it take for this drug to *not* be the cash cow that you say it could be?"

"A failed trial. Either the drug wasn't effective or it proved to be unsafe. You know, adverse events start cropping up and the FDA doesn't approve it. I've only seen one bad side effect so far."

"One side effect, that's it. What was it?"

"No, I've seen plenty of adverse events, but only one serious one. One of my patients had a stroke. But I can't be sure the stroke was from the study drug because he had a stroke risk factor," Stella said.

"Back up. I thought you said it was Emily's job to record side effects," Evans said.

"I did, SMs monitor our records including adverse events, which we tell them about. I told Emily about the stroke, and she reported it to her boss. She also checked with her colleagues to see if anyone else had seen stroke, but I haven't heard back from her," Stella said.

Evans asked, "What's an SM?"

"Site Monitor."

"You could have just said that. Do you trust Solutions & Synergy and Emily to tell you about side effects? Do they ever hide stuff from you?"

Stella said, "Yes, I trust them. And no, they can't not report an adverse event. Our drug trials are highly regulated by the FDA these days, for everyone's safety. You know, I sent an email to Emily's boss, a Dr. Abernathy, the other day telling him that I saw a stroke in one of my patients. He still hasn't gotten back to me. I also sent an email to the company that made the investigational drug being evaluated in SETTUP. One of their scientists replied that they hadn't seen stroke in their preclinical work."

"Okay, good to know. Who benefits from Emily not monitoring the trial?" Evans asked.

"No one that I can think of, because, as I said, she'll be replaced."

"Two more questions. Who do I talk to at Solutions & Synergy about Emily, and what's the name again of the drug company that's involved in your trial?"

"The person you want to talk to at Solutions & Synergy is Dr. Abernathy. He's the Medical Director of SETTUP and, I believe, their Chief Medical Officer as well. It's SGY Bioengineering that made the drug. They're on 37th Avenue, just south of town," Stella said.

Evans said, "Let me know who they replace Emily with, I need to talk to him or her."

"Do you want me to do all your work? Where are you with finding the guy who killed Emily?"

Evans said, "Same place as I was twelve hours ago."

"That's not very encouraging."

"These things take time. Thanks again, Stells. See you Wednesday." Walking to his car, Evans reviewed their conversation. Stella provided wonderful insight into the inner workings of clinical trials and the vast sums of money involved in medical research. He wasn't expecting her to be so upset after hearing about Emily. Stella shed an abundance of tears, real tears, and was genuinely upset. Too upset?

Sex, money, power.

Sex. There's no way Stella was involved with Emily. Unless she was.

Money. Was Stella in line to make some money if the trial was successful? She constantly complained that her salary was lower than her male coworkers. Was she looking to even out the bottom line?

Chapter 11

Gordie Howe scored an average of thirty-four goals a year during twenty-one consecutive NHL seasons.

Evans checked his emails and found what he was looking for—notification that Forensic Unit Services was able to access Emily's phone and laptop. He walked to the stairwell, the forensic guys were located two flights above.

He walked directly to the office of his favorite Forensic Unit Cyber Specialist, Sarah Chaudry. Although diminutive in stature, Sarah's intelligence towered over others. She obtained a PhD in computer science at the University of California-Berkley and worked at an internet search company for several years. Sarah followed her soon-to-be husband to Grand Rapids before joining GRPD.

Officer Chaudry was the first and only member of the GRPD Forensic Cyber Unit. Sarah's computer skills were superior, which meant that she could easily access phones and computers. The privacy firewalls that protected financial institutions, governmental agencies, and personal systems were a fleeting hindrance for Sarah. She loved her job and always stayed within the boundaries of the law. She accepted the position after receiving assurances from GRPD's top brass that she wouldn't have to deal with blood, bodily secretions, or any evidence not connected in some way to the World Wide Web. Any contact with hoarders was a hard stop.

Evans waved to Sarah while she completed a phone call. He asked, "Can I see Emily Naismith's phone and laptop?"

"Fine, how are you?" Sarah said, standing and moving in for a hug.

"My bad. How's Officer Chaudry today?" Evans said, giving her the hug she sought.

"Officer Chaudry is fine, as I said. Gordie, we miss seeing you in the Tower." Sarah thought her Unit represented the Ivory Tower of the Department and told anyone and everyone that the Forensic Unit Specialists were Top Dogs in the Ivory Tower.

"I miss you, too. You know that I know that I've been riding your coattails for years, right?"

"I know, but it's nice to hear you admit it every once in a while."

"How's the old man? You going to let him get back on the ice with us?" Evans asked.

Sarah said, "Get your games to start during daylight hours and maybe you'll see him again. I can't have him playing after midnight when he has parental obligations."

"How is little Sammy?"

"Not so little anymore, he weighs twenty-five pounds," Sarah said, opening her phone's photo app to show Evans pictures of her eighteen-month-old toddler.

"Very cute, takes after his father. You know, hubby's a big boy. From what I hear, engineers can function with or without sleep. They don't really do anything, do they?"

"Jerk!" Sarah said, slipping her phone back in her coat pocket. "Her things are over here. You know it took me all of eleven seconds to get in her phone and thirty seconds for the laptop." Sarah walked to a shelf with an Evidence basket that held Emily's laptop and phone, and handed them to Evans. "Here you go, hot shot."

"Ten seconds? Hubby will be looking for a trophy wife who isn't so slow."

"You really are a dick, aren't you? Have at it, Detective Hockey Player. Who is this Gordon How anyway?" Sarah asked, crossing her arms.

Evans said, "Who's Gordie Howe? Did you just tell me to go to hell?"

"Whatever."

"Later. I'll return these to Evidence and save you a step," Evans said. He maintained the line of evidence by signing out the phone and laptop. He took the stairs to the second floor and his desk.

Emily had 429 emails on her phone. He realized it would take hours to get through all of them and shouldn't have promised Sarah that Emily's things would be returned any time soon.

He started with emails and saw SETTUP was the subject heading of most of them. There were several communications centered around recruitment, including suggestions on how to improve signing up patient volunteers.

Stella told Evans that Dr. Abernathy, Emily's upline, was the person at Solutions & Synergy to talk to regarding Emily. Evans saw that she had received many emails from Abernathy discussing enrollment, updates, and general news. Emily sent frequent updates to him, most often after enrolling a new study patient.

Evans found a group email that Emily sent on December 19 to Randy Walker, Tricia Wilkinson, and Stephen Cohen. A quick check on Linkedin showed that Randy, Tricia, and Stephen were Solutions & Synergy employees. Each held the title of SETTUP Site Monitor and worked in Chicago, Boston, and Jacksonville, respectively. They agreed that the experimental drug worked great and people tolerated it well. Emily said she'd seen a stroke in Grand Rapids, and the doctors felt that the investigational drug was probably not the cause of the stroke. None of the three had seen stroke at their sites, but vowed to watch for stroke-like symptoms in the future. They'd make certain that a stroke evaluation was completed before blaming the symptoms on migraine or something else. Emily asked the other Monitors whether they had heard about stroke at sites other than their own, because she hadn't. Stephen hadn't heard about stroke from any of his Site Monitor buddies. Tricia said she knew people who worked in other cities and promised to find out what their experiences were. They all complained about having to review patient logbook binders, as records for every other trial were now online.

Emily asked Abernathy in an email for patient identifiers on all of the patients who suffered a stroke during SETTUP, as she wanted to read about the strokes in EPIC, the electronic medical record. He told Emily that she couldn't look at records of any patient not enrolled in Grand Rapids, the Clinical Site she monitored. Interesting that Abernathy didn't ask about or comment on the stroke. His reply to Emily said, in effect, "we'll talk." Evans admitted that he didn't know much about research, but he thought stroke was a big deal which could terminate a study.

He then found an email that was completely different. It was an isolated email, not part of a trail, to which Emily never replied. He wondered if this was what he was looking for. The email, Abernathy's last to Emily, was sent on December 19.

> Emily,
>
> Why have you stopped responding to my emails? I hope you're not jeopardizing your career over the incident. For the sake of clarity, let this serve as a reminder that you have a performance review coming up next month.
>
> Dr. A

Fuck me, first the stroke, now an incident. It was as if Abernathy no longer cared about the stroke, and wanted to focus on the incident. What was this event or episode, and was it significant enough to kill Emily?

Emily received emails from multiple doctors, including Stella. Interesting. Evans had no idea who the others were, but assumed they worked on the drug trial. There were not as many emails from Stella as the other physicians, but there were some. Emily received a flurry of electronic communications from Stella the week before. One stood out; it was unrelated to work.

> Emily,
>
> What did you do over the weekend? I hope something fun. When do you arrive in GR? Text me as soon as you check in. Let's have dinner.
>
> S

Hmm. Evans acknowledged that he couldn't read emotion in Emily's response, but it didn't seem to be strained. Emily was genuinely excited about seeing Stella. The content of Stella's email was distinctly different from those composed by other physicians, all of which were work related and professional in content.

He wondered if Stella was having a relationship with Emily outside of work, which suddenly went south. He was determined not to let their friendship get in the way of his investigation.

After reviewing Emily's emails, he checked her phone for text messages. Texting was Emily's preferred form of communication. She had hundreds of conversations going, most of which involved family, friends, and her boyfriend, Tyler. In recent texts, Emily and Tyler discussed moving in together. Emily had not shared anything about the Abernathy incident with her boyfriend.

Abernathy sent a text message to Emily on December 19, the same day as his final email to her. He asked her a second time if she wanted to risk her career and jeopardize her position at Solutions & Synergy. He reminded Emily that she'd received the top rating, a high performer, during her last annual review. He referred to her as a "rising star," and recommended her for Solutions & Synergy's Leadership Skills Program, which was offered to their Best and Brightest. Emily had not replied to his text.

Emily asked Randy, Tricia, and Stephen via a text message about their performance reviews with Abernathy. Some respected him, they all feared him. No one had anything particularly positive to say about their supervisor.

Evans found a text message from Stella dated January 7.

> Text me when you arrive, we'll have dinner.
> Can't wait to see you.

He moved to Emily's phone log. He noted that she called her mother and Tyler daily, sometimes twice. Evans focused on December 19. Emily received a call from Abernathy on that day; their conversation lasted twelve minutes. Emily immediately called Tricia Wilkerson and they spoke for fifteen minutes. Emily called her boyfriend Tyler next, but must not have gotten through as the call lasted nine seconds. Emily's last phone call with Tyler was on January 8 and lasted thirty-four minutes. Tyler may have been the last person to have spoken with Emily.

Evans intended to ask Stella if it was normal to communicate with a research assistant using a personal email account? He texted Stella and asked if they could meet at The Store when she was through with patients.

Stella replied, "Of course."

He called Solutions & Synergy and scheduled a Zoom call with Abernathy for the following day.

Chapter 12

During the Antiquity period there was a widespread belief that epilepsy was contagious.

He was puzzled as to why he hadn't been able to sleep the night before. Work was going well, kids were doing great in school, and his wife wasn't complaining about anything. He'd made good business decisions recently. Hadn't everyone struggled through a dry spell now and then? Sure, one of his partners went through a slump during their initial round of investments. One associate recommended that COR purchase a company which was later sold at a loss. Another guy was recently handed a company run by his father-in-law, despite never having developed a relationship, not one, with Big Pharma, a university, or anyone. It was a manufacturing company that was bringing a recently FDA-approved cardiac catheter to the market. Sale of the company could mean billions for COR. Then there's Bridgett, who stumbled on her biofabricating company and was now looking at a financial godsend. He had never been handed anything. Seldom blessed with business luck, he'd prospered with self-determination, effort, and grit.

Stephanie Van Huissen was a forty-three-year-old nurse whom he and several of his business partners developed a friendship with during their collegiate days. She started her undergraduate education at Michigan. After her mother died unexpectedly during her sophomore year, she transferred to Rush to be closer to her father. He remembered Stephanie as a straight shooter who'd be a perfect fit for the recently opened position at Solutions & Synergy. Stephanie wasn't an agitator, she'd do her part to keep SETTUP on track.

He'd loosely stalked her on FB over the years. After receiving her nursing degree, she worked on med-surg floors, then moved over to the ED. She transitioned to research three years before. It looked like she had become a health nut, participating in marathons and Iron Woman contests. Since she already worked in research, she'd be a natural fit, damn near perfect, for the open position in the seizure trial. He'd reach out to her to gauge her interest. He sent an email to her from a "remember me" angle.

Stephanie replied quickly. Yes, she remembered him. She wondered if he married the Alpha Delta Pi sorority girl who he dated while they were at Michigan. Wow, her memory was better than his.

He sent a follow up email asking if she was interested in a career change. Stephanie replied maybe, what was he proposing? He touted Solutions & Synergy as a company on the rise and encouraged her to read about them. Stephanie asked if she could call him to discuss it further; he replied that a phone call sounded like a good idea.

He called that evening. "Hey, Steph, long time."

"Hey right back at you. Wow, seeing your email was a flash from the past. How'd you know my address?" Stephanie asked.

"Social media, how else? I don't remember who posted it, maybe Bridgett. But I saw you referenced the other day and told myself 'I know her,' I should reach out."

"That's amazing, I'm glad you did. I've tried to keep in touch with Bridgett, but haven't done a very good job of it. Did you just want to tell me about the position, or were you stalking me?" Stephanie asked. She opened her laptop and searched for him on Facebook.

"Oh, heavens no, nothing like that. I wanted to see how you were doing, and to let you know about the career opportunity," he said.

"I'm in nursing, how about you?"

"I was in finance after school. About sixteen years ago, Bridgett, myself, and some of the others from Michigan formed this small venture capital group. We invest in drug or medical device manufacturing companies, that sort of thing. Did Bridgett tell you that we work together?" he said.

Stephanie said, "No, I don't remember hearing that. But that's so interesting that we all ended up in health care." Not seeing anything about Bridgett or a venture capital group on the social media site, she believed he needed to update his account.

"Yeah, the financial stuff had become routine, even boring. I'm happy and not the least bit bored with what I'm doing now. How about you, do you like working with patients?"

Stephanie said, "I love working with patients. It's so satisfying when we can help them. Mostly, I work with people who haven't responded to standard chemo or radiation therapy." She searched for the Michigan ADPi chapter.

"Now that's interesting. Must be rewarding when they're helped by your research," he said.

"It is when they respond, that is. Not so much when nothing helps. Overall, I like what I'm doing. I'm happy."

"Yeah, I imagine that can be devastating if they don't respond. My main reason for reaching out was to gauge your interest in a career change. Have you ever thought about, like, something different?"

"Maybe, but nothing in business. Like I said, I don't do financial stuff," Stephanie said, laughing. Not seeing his old girlfriend in any of the ADPi photos, she closed her laptop.

"It took a while, but I found out that I'm not wired for finance, either. The opportunity is with a company called Solutions & Synergy. They administer clinical trials."

"Now, that I'm good at. What kind of trials?"

"I heard that they needs to replace a Site Monitor for a drug trial, but they get involved in all kinds of trials and studies. They say the drug, and I'm definitely talking out of my ass when I say this, works great," he said.

"That's what I do now, I can handle that in my sleep. Would I be working with you guys, or for you guys?" Stephanie asked.

"No, not for us. You'd be a Solutions & Synergy employee. You'd have no contact with any of us. We partner with Solutions & Synergy financially, but we don't get involved in any of the clinical stuff. They run the trials and we provide financial backing," he said.

"Alright, I get it. I think I've heard of them. Have they ever run any Oncology trials?"

"Yeah, absolutely. I know they've got one going for pancreatic cancer. Listen, Solutions & Synergy is a good group, which is why we partner with them so often. They're based in Indianapolis, will that be a problem for you?"

"I'm not looking to move. Would I be able to work from home and visit sites virtually?" Stephanie asked.

"I don't know about that. If you want to hear more about the position, I'll send your contact information to HR."

"Wait, tell me again what your interest is in filling the position?"

He glibly stated, "It's two-fold. I think you'd bring a lot to the table, and it's all about making connections. Making sure the right people are talking to each other, developing relationships, networking. That's a huge part of what I do. As I said, I heard they needed someone and quickly. I don't know any details, but I think they're worried that if they can't replace the Site Monitor, the trial might be put on hold."

Stephanie said, "Makes sense. What do you get out of it?"

"If the trial doesn't finish as expected, my group might not be able to assist with getting the drug to the market: lose, lose. But if we can assist them in any way, you know, to help keep the trial open and moving forward, then it becomes a win for everyone involved. I don't want to see the trial fail because of a manpower issue. Plus, it's an opportunity for you to, you know, advance your career by moving to a new position or whatever."

"Well, your enthusiasm is certainly contagious. But I need to do my due diligence before we go any further," Stephanie replied.

"I would expect nothing less. How about if you call me once you've finished your deep dive into Solutions & Synergy? Does that work for you?"

Stephanie said, "Yes, but it won't be today. I'm kind of busy right now. We enrolled two patients yesterday."

"I understand. In addition to a good interview, you'll need good references, and we wouldn't want you to leave your current job in the lurch."

"Right, but I thought you said they needed help right away."

"I did. But I don't want you to ruin your reputation at Rush by quitting without giving adequate notice. When I was growing up, okay, when I was raising hell, my dad must have told me a thousand times that 'there's a right and a wrong way to go about things.' My dad didn't get everything right, but that philosophy has been good to me over the years," he said.

"I hear you. Well, it's been nice talking to you. You've given me something to think about, that's for sure. I'll be in touch."

"Great. It was great catching up. I hope to hear from you soon."

"Bye. Thanks again for reaching out. Say hi to Bridgett and the others."

Chapter 13

Venmo processed $244 billion USD in payment volumes in 2022.

Normally, he asked his admin assistant to place his calls, but not today, not this one. Nobody at work needed to know about this conversation. After three rings, the call went through. "Good morning. How are things in your neck of the woods?" he asked.

"Indianapolis is not exactly surrounded by a forest," Abernathy replied.

Roy Abernathy had done well in his career at Tufts. He authored several pivotal articles on gynecological cancers, including novel chemotherapeutic approaches for metastatic ovarian carcinoma. He was awarded enough grant money to employ three research assistants. He believed applying for the Department of Oncology Chairperson was the right thing to do; it would be a feather in his career cap.

Abernathy obtained an Executive MBA by virtually attending classes at night and on weekends. He was confident that he had positioned himself to be the next Department of Oncology Chairperson. Everyone of any importance at Tufts knew Abernathy and his work. He made no enemies during his time there, at least none of importance.

A junior faculty member vigorously touted an outside candidate, an experienced woman as the better qualified applicant. The junior faculty member reasoned that the outside contender was in the twilight of her career and would merely keep the Chairperson's seat warm for himself. After the first two rounds of interviews, two candidates separated themselves from the field: Abernathy and the outside candidate. When the votes were tallied, Abernathy lost by one. The Search Committee met behind closed doors where concerns were expressed that a member of their own Department lobbied, lobbied hard, against their peer. The outside candidate was offered the position of Department of Oncology Chairperson. The following day Abernathy hired an executive headhunter firm.

He was growing weary of Abernathy. Maybe it was time to sever their relationship. He said, “Okay. How are things in Indy?”

“I have good news and bad news, which do you want first?” Abernathy asked.

“I don’t want news, I need results,” he said.

“The latest is good, genuinely good. The drug works great. Patients are doing well with it. The side effects that have been reported were anticipated and not too disturbing,” Abernathy said.

“That sounds promising. Nothing bad?”

“I didn’t say that,” Abernathy said, raising his voice. “What I said *is*, the drug works great, side effects were anticipated, and not too troubling. Look, I’m being fully transparent here. All the common side effects such as rash, nausea, dizziness, lightheadedness, shortness of breath, and headache have been reported.

“We’ve seen more serious side effects including kidney damage, liver damage, edema, a pulmonary embolus in Miami, meningitis in Cleveland, and now a stroke in Grand Rapids. The stroke was small, and the patient had multiple stroke risk factors. We can also argue that the stroke symptoms were part of a migraine or high blood pressure or some such bullshit. The best news is that they can’t disprove our claim that the drug didn’t cause the stroke. The other side effects cannot be causally related to the drug,” Abernathy said. He was glad that only one stroke had been reported at that point. Boston’s SM called him asking if she should push the doctors to get an MRI on a patient who, after receiving the drug, had trouble speaking. Abernathy told the SM to leave it alone.

He didn’t like the idea of serious side effects, whether they were attributed to the drug or not. He asked, “Hearing about stroke and meningitis threw me off. Will the doctors and other research people fall in line and stop reporting those things?”

Abernathy replied, “You couldn’t be further from the truth. The FDA has too many reporting regulations. There was nothing that could be done on their end of it. Having said that, our late Grand Rapids Site Monitor sent an email to Site Monitors in

Boston and Chicago telling them to be on the lookout for stroke-like symptoms without considering other plausible diagnoses. One possible solution is that if whatever happened in Grand Rapids were to happen to Chicago and Boston, then all of your little problems would go away." He'd purposely left out Jacksonville. He had plans for Jacksonville, who had done the right thing when he forwarded Emily's stroke email to him.

"My little problem! Are you out of your goddamn mind," he screamed into the phone.

"No. There are two potential problems to address, which you can do by looking into Boston and Chicago. I told you that I need people that I can trust. You know, people who will work with me when it comes to reporting adverse events," Abernathy said.

"How about if you take care of those issues yourself."

Abernathy sighed, "Nonsense. I'm not involved in any of this. I'm the lowly middleman who supplies information. This is your study."

"My study! When the hell did it become my study?" he asked. The conversation was not going his way, he needed to turn it around.

"You sound upset, was it something I said?" Abernathy asked.

"Screw you, Abby."

"How about if you stop acting like a bull in a china store. Look, you obviously see something that I don't. If you want to address them, go ahead, that's fine with me. If you don't want to handle whatever, that's fine too. It makes no difference to me if your trial is successful or not. Is there anything else I can help you with? Do you need any more information?" Abernathy asked.

He replied, "While I think about my next steps, get me the names of the people on that email thread, the ones working in Chicago and Boston."

"Easier said than done. We at Solutions & Synergy value our employee's personal information."

"Cut the crap. Get me their names and contact information," he said.

"Not so fast. Information is power, and power means money.

A lot of it. The information that you desire will cost you," Abernathy said.

"This is bullshit."

Abernathy said, "I know you're used to getting your way, but raising your voice doesn't cut it with me. I mean, it doesn't even sound like you value my services. You know that you're not exactly negotiating from a position of strength, right? If you want the names, you're gonna have to pay for them."

"I've already paid you enough. I'm not shelling out any more for a couple of names."

"If the drug that your group's looking at hits it big, which I expect it to, you stand to make millions. I'm the poor schlep who makes nothing while doing the heavy lifting. The names will cost you ten grand, and the contact information to make sure you get the right people behind the names, is another ten."

"Like I said, screw you Abernathy. Were you bullied as a kid? Did you feel abused when you couldn't get in a surgical residency?"

"Careful with those veiled threats. It's twenty grand or nothing."

"Twelve and no more."

"How well positioned will you be without this information? Eighteen."

"Fifteen."

Abernathy said, "Tell you what I'm going to do. Because it's the Holidays, I'll give you the names and contact information for fifteen. That's a pretty sweet deal for you."

"I'll have a check for you next week."

"That's more like it, I'm glad we were able to settle our little disagreement. I don't take checks. Venmo it to me," Abernathy said.

"I'm not going to Venmo you anything, I don't do Venmo."

"The name on my account is Doc Abernathy. When the deal's completed, you'll get the names and their information."

"When do I get more clinical information?"

"I hear from my Site Monitors every Thursday. I should have more information next week."

"Keep it coming."

Abernathy chided him, "No regrets, you made the right decision."

"I haven't decided on anything yet. Just get me those names." After disconnecting the call, he left the office and drove to Ted's Sport and Bait Shop. He walked past displays of hiking gear and camping equipment. He wasn't interested in the ocean kayaks that were on sale. Approaching the back counter he said, "Ted, I'd like to look at your guns."

Chapter 14

Autopsy is derived from the Greek autopsia, meaning "the act of seeing for yourself."

Evans anxiously awaited the autopsy results. Despite the narrative sold in movies and TV, he rarely, as in never, attended autopsies. He never felt the need to see more dead bodies. He did, however, enjoy listening to Kent County Medical Examiner, Dr. Wilma Colson-Brown, summarize the salient features of an autopsy. She never limited herself to only presenting the medical facts; she made a production out of her reporting, a performance that Evans found entertaining.

Evans said, "Wilma, can I stop by to hear about Emily Naismith's autopsy?"

"Gordie, I was just going to call you. She's an interesting case with a couple of things that I think you'll find fascinating."

"What's up with Gordie? Have you been talking to Spencer?" he asked.

"Who else, but our elephantine Forensic Specialist. I'm impressed, I didn't know you played hockey like Gordie Howe himself."

"I don't. Can I come over now?"

"Now's as good a time as any."

"See you in a few."

Evans drove to Kentland Hospital, parked, and walked to the basement. The Medical Examiner's Office was housed in the Department of Pathology, which was buried in Kentland's lower level.

Wilma Colson-Brown was a five feet eight inches introvert, whose parents named her after Wilma Rudolph, the Olympic track star. Wilma loved her name, but wished more people knew she was named for the runner. She grew weary telling people that she was not named after the wife of a fictional cartoon caveman character. Wilma shunned organized sports as a youth, and instead focused her attention on the theater. Her acting career began in high school. She starred in two shows during her undergraduate studies at Wellesley. Her love of the stage yielded to her academic demands during med school and residency. She joined the local Civic Theater shortly after moving to Grand Rapids. She was well aware of the paradox between her personal and professional lives. Her introverted shyness led her to a career in pathology, but once the curtain rose, she loved to perform. She was never sure why she asked her parents to sign her up for acting lessons in the first place.

One would never know it was the Holidays, there were no seasonal decorations on display in the basement. Evans entered the Medical Examiner's office to find an empty reception area. "Hello? Dr. Colson-Brown," he called out. Hearing no reply, he stepped behind the desk and said louder, "Dr. Colson-Brown?"

"I'm here, I'm here. Come on back," Wilma said.

He walked along a corridor with green linoleum flooring and sandy colored tiles on the walls. He saw light coming from an office and knocked on the half-open door.

Wilma stood and greeted Evans with a big smile and a hug. "Long time no see, Detective."

"Yeah, my bad. But you know it's a good thing if we don't see each other." Saliva gushed into his mouth as soon as he eyed a bowl of bite-size chocolates on Wilma's desk. "May I?"

"Please do. But I still miss seeing you. You know, Smitty never shirks his duty. He's always standing right next to me during his autopsies," Wilma said, passing the bowl to Evans.

He opened the holiday-colored red, green, and silver packaging and popped the chocolate in his mouth. "Mmm, delish. You know, Smitty's deranged." Smitty was Evans's old partner.

"It is my professional opinion that Smitty has full control over his faculties."

"No receptionist any longer? Wasn't there a Suzanne or something, the last time I was here?"

"Yeah, no. Budget cuts. Samantha was with us for years, but with the cuts, we only have one admin assistant for the entire Department. We don't make the big bucks like the surgeons do. Have a seat," Wilma said, pointing toward a chair in front of her desk. "Seriously, how are things going, I never see you anymore."

"Fine, I'm good. Same old, same old. Go to work, catch the bad guys, then head home. What can you tell me about Emily?" Evans said, reaching for a second chocolate morsel.

"Emily's very interesting." Wilma clacked the keyboard, opening Emily's autopsy report. She rotated her monitor toward Evans so he could see what was on her screen.

Evans finished chewing and swallowing before saying, "That's twice that you've said that, which can't be a good thing."

"No, you never want to be an interesting case. I imagine she was even more lovely in life than in death. Tragic, really. On gross exam, Emily was five-six and weighed 123 pounds. No scars, or distinguishing features other than a small tattoo on her left wrist. Did you know that if something is found in twenty percent of the population, it's considered a normal finding. For the last ten years, I've seen tattoos on more than twenty percent of the people in her demographics, so I don't consider the tattoo to be an abnormality."

"Interesting," he said, unsuccessfully stifling a smile.

Wilma brought Emily's report up on her monitor and scrolled down to the Toxicology section. "Anyway, her tox screen showed a blood alcohol level of zero. We detected no cannabinoids in her blood or urine. Emily had not used cocaine during the twenty-four hours prior to her death."

"Okay, she was clean. You said something about a couple of interesting things."

"Patience. There was no meth in her blood or urine. Now, what's interesting, I mean, one of the interesting findings, was this little baby right here. She had a serum fentanyl level of 10 ug/ml." Using a wireless mouse, Wilma repeatedly circled the lab results with the curser.

"All right, now we're getting somewhere. What's a normal fentanyl level?" Evans asked.

Wilma smiled, formed two circles using her thumbs and index fingers, and while making circling motions with her arms said, "Nothing, zilch, nada. A normal fentanyl level is zero."

Evans said, "Whatever, smart ass. What I meant to say is, is a fentanyl level of ten high enough to kill her?"

"Now you're catching on. And yes, it's a lethal serum level. You could put Secretariat down with a level of ten, let alone a person of her size.

"The other unusual thing, other than the fentanyl level, was that she was a healthy thirty-one-year-old woman. No heart issues, no athero, no cerebrovascular issues. I found no evidence of sexually transmitted diseases. Serology showed no evidence of Hepatitis B or C. As you know, about a third of opioid abusers also abuse alcohol. Her liver showed no signs of cirrhosis." She brought up a slide of an H&E-stained section of Emily's liver. Pointing at the monitor Wilma said, "Looking at that thing of beauty. She had the liver of a normal thirty-one-year-old."

"You know, I have no idea what that pink and purple blob is. And I didn't understand anything that you just said. How about this time in English."

"Smitty knows all my jargon. But the normal liver thing is important. When we chronically give opioids to rats, it causes liver damage. Emily's liver was perfectly normal."

"Did she abuse opioids or not?" Evans asked.

"You're a quick study there, Detective Gordie. She definitely died from a fentanyl overdose. After seeing her fentanyl level, I asked myself the same question—was this a one off, or did she chronically abuse opioids? In other words, and from now on I'll only use one-syllable words so that even you can understand, opioids take a toll on the liver of an abuser. There's no pathological evidence that Emily abused opioids in the past." Wilma scrolled back up to the Chemistries section.

"Thank you, that I understood. So, we're looking at an overdose. Was it an unintentional overdose, an intentional overdose, or a suspiciously intentional overdose? Bottom line, was her death accidental or intentional?"

"Yes. All I can say is that I'm one hundred percent certain that she OD'd. It could have been accidental. It would have to have been one of her first uses because, as I said, I didn't see any evidence of chronic opioid use. Could have been suicide, and of course, I can't rule out homicide.

“We’ve mentioned suicide. The problem with that is that I reviewed her medical records. Her primary physician was a GYN in Hyde Park of Chicago. Emily was completely healthy with no chronic medical issues. Her gynecologist never discussed depression or anxiety with her. There were no documented concerns of drug use,” Wilma said.

“Yeah, there were already problems with suicide on my side of things, too. There was no note. She set her alarm for the next morning. She was charging her phone. She laid out the clothes she was going to wear that day. Not exactly the behavior of a suicidal person,” Evans said.

“And that’s why I need you here observing my work. It’s the details of her history like that, which help me interpret my findings and allow me to give you accurate information. I’m sure you know that sometimes suicide is spontaneous. They don’t always leave a note,” Wilma said.

“I know, but you’re putting suicide at the bottom of the list,” Evans said, dropping his right hand downward.

“Yes, I am,” Wilma said.

“Well, this one gets more interesting by the day.”

“That’s what I said. Now, the other thing, which you may or may not find interesting, is that her beta HCG level was 139,931 mIU.” Wilma smiled, underlining the lab result with the curser. She sat back, waiting for him to react.

Evans had no clue as to what the beta whatever level meant. He pointed at the monitor and said, “Yeah, so. What does this beta stuff you were jabbering on have to do with Emily?”

“Jabbering? Really? Beta HCG is a test for pregnancy. Emily was about nine weeks pregnant.” She scrolled to the conclusion of her report.

“Well, fuck me. Pregnant. That’s horrible, awful. She had a boyfriend, who’s probably the father. Having said that, sex can be a powerful motive for murder. Are you going to do DNA analysis on the fetus?”

“Do you want me to? Yeah, I guess I can, to help establish paternity. Get me a buccal swab,” Wilma said.

Making teeth-brushing movements, Evans said, “Is that the

cheek thingy?"

"Yes, a smear of his inner cheek will suffice," she said, smiling.

"Ah, okay, I guess. What else have you got for me?"

"Medications. You should know that Emily was prescribed one medication and took one supplement—levothyroxine and melatonin, respectively. Her GYN documented that she used melatonin for trouble sleeping. Probably related to job stress."

"Is melatonin ever used for depression?" Evans asked.

"No, it's strictly used as a hypnotic, to help people fall asleep. The GYN wasn't aware that Emily was pregnant. Office records show that she was sexually active and using a diaphragm for protection. I'll have the final path results for you in several weeks."

"As always, Wilma, thanks a million."

"My pleasure. I hope to see you for the complete autopsy next time."

"That ain't gonna happen. Later," Evans said, walking out of the basement and the ME's office.

This case keeps getting worse and worse. Now it's a pregnant nurse who died from an overdose. Didn't see that one coming. He'd seen hundreds of ODs due to fentanyl, but Emily didn't exactly fit the profile of an addict. Nurses? Not unusual for a health care worker to overdose. It's not an every day occurrence, but it happens.

Chapter 15

Mistletoe was recommended as a remedy for the falling sickness by English and Dutch medical authorities into the eighteenth century.

Evans entered The Store a little before six P.M. The neighborhood bar was located on the west side of the Grand River and was expectedly crowded, even on a school night. After their beer league games, some of the guys on Murray's Manons went to The Store to decompress.

The bar walls were painted light green, the flooring black linoleum. Both bartenders wore Santa hats. Christmas lights decorated the top shelf, liquor bottles. The store theme was emphasized by hanging a sign above each booth, listing items which were found in that aisle. Mistletoe hung from each sign.

The Store was filled by a nice balance of students, people enjoying a drink after work, and couples. After allowing his eyes to accommodate to the dimness, he spotted an open booth on the east side of the horseshoe-shaped bar. Beans, canned vegetables, rice, and soup were listed on the sign above the open booth. Men's Big Ten basketball was on the TV.

Evans played football, hockey, and lacrosse growing up. He was recruited to play hockey and lacrosse by DI schools and received scholarship offers for both. Hockey was his first love, so he signed to play with Lake Superior State. Unlike some of his teammates, he harbored no illusions that his hockey career would continue after college, so he regularly attended classes. He majored in Criminal Justice. He considered minoring in computer science, as it seemed that the entire world had gone digital, with everything one click away. Entering his sophomore year, he changed his minor to psychology after admitting that people, not computers, committed crimes. By studying psychology, he hoped to better understand the mind and psyche of criminals.

"I'm glad you bumped it back, clinic ran over," Stella said, taking off her coat and sliding into the booth opposite Evans.

"Ran late? I recall something about you waiting for your

patients, Dr. Murray," he said. "I'll get our nurse over here for you."

Evans ordered a beer, Stella a glass of chardonnay. The server hastily put paper coasters on their table before moving on to take orders at a nearby table.

"Why the urgency, what's going on, Gordie? I get the sense this isn't related to our game tomorrow," Stella said, taking off her mittens and scarf.

"You guessed right, it's not. I went through Emily's phone and found the emails and text messages that you sent her."

"What about them?" She stacked her winter accessories on her coat.

Evans said, "Why didn't you tell me that you knew Emily?"

"I distinctly remember telling you that we worked together."

Evans said, "Am I wrong, or did the emails and texts imply that you were friendly with Emily outside of work?"

"I don't know about that. We first met at the SETTUP Investigator Meeting. Nice, pretty, enthusiastic, smart. I heard we'd be working together and asked her to dinner. She agreed and we had a great time. The next day we had lunch. Now I make a point of seeing her whenever she's in town. I admit it, I was looking forward to seeing her," Stella said.

"Nothing more than that, a few isolated meals? I saw the emails asking about her last weekend, when would she arrive, wanting to have dinner with her."

"I saw Emily Sunday. We had dinner at Gerhardt Puck's restaurant, and then parted ways. She went to her room, and I went home. She was alive and well when we said our goodbyes," Stella said.

The server hurriedly set a bottle of beer and glass of wine on the coasters before moving on.

Stella said, "Why the third degree? Am I a suspect or something?" She looked embarrassed, maybe even a little remorseful.

Evans had to know if she was having a relationship with Emily, and felt the need to ask because Stella wasn't offering up any pillow talk. "Stella, were you having an affair with her?"

"An affair! What, do you get your jollies off thinking about two women together. God, you're unbelievable. I don't deserve this. How about if you skip tomorrow's game, we don't need you after all," Stella said. Still agitated, she stood and nearly knocked over a nearby chair. Holding her mittens and scarf in one hand, she tried to put on her coat but couldn't find the sleeve and stormed out of The Store holding it under her arm.

That went well. Was Stella protesting too much? Probably not, she seemed genuinely embarrassed when he mentioned the messages. But, and it was a big but, she never denied having an affair. Stella, Stella, Stella, what have you done?

Their server stopped by the booth and said, "What was she so pissed about? I've seen you guys here before, but I've never seen her so upset. What'd you say to her?"

"Nothing, just a little misunderstanding. She's probably already forgotten about it."

"In your dreams, that was one pissed off woman. Oh, and that'll be eight bucks for the drinks."

He paid the bill and left. He wasn't ready to cross Stella off his suspect list, not yet.

Chapter 16

Galen, a Greek physician and philosopher, described one case of a boy who felt a cool "breeze" feeling rise from his leg to his head prior to a seizure.

He was tired. The fatigue was probably brought on by a lack of sleep. Or stress. Or death. Death was so final. He hadn't thought much about death, not even when his grandparents died. They were old and expected to check out.

It was a beautiful, breezy day with wisps of clouds scattered across the endless blue sky. The thermometer peaked at ten degrees. The ambient temperature had no influence over the making of life-or-death decisions.

He turned to his laptop and logged onto the dark web. The intrigue, the illegality, the anonymity of using the dark web caused tumescence. It was safe to craft the brief email during daylight hours. He didn't anticipate a lot of back and forth. Replies were returned quickly.

He sent an email.

> KFAP,
> I have a request. Two people need to be taken off their respective jobs. Killing is not necessary.
> Tricia Wilkinson, Massachusetts Central Hospital Boston, Site Monitor.
> Randy Walker, Rush Lutheran Hospital Chicago, Site Monitor.
> Payment goes to the same account?
> Anonymous

KFAP paused after reading the note. He had done a research assistant a few days before and didn't like doing jobs that were related in any way. This latest request made it three people with the same job description. However, the fact that they're in different cities, even states, might make it okay. On the positive side, the same job title drove the price up. Another positive thing about the new jobs was that they were in Boston and Chicago, two cities where he liked performing.

He had two careers which he equally loved. One paid well, the other not so much. One, he was constantly refining, the other had become routine, hardly ever changing. One temporarily improved the life of others, one ended life. The well-paying job began when he was in the Military. The comedy began after he received an Honorable Discharge from the Marines.

Growing up, KFAP never imagined a stage career. It took him many years and several bad experiences before he was comfortable speaking in public. He paired the two careers by accepting lucrative assignments in cities where he performed. He believed it was safe to conduct both jobs in one city, knowing the authorities would never associate a comedian with his second, villainous career.

Comedy gigs typically ran Friday through Saturday, allowing him to research and prepare for his well-paying job Sunday through Wednesday. Preparation for his alternative career was meticulous, precise, and thorough. He never failed to complete an assignment, and never crossed paths with the local police department.

KFAP replied.

> Happy New Year, Anonymous,
> Thank you for thinking of me as you contemplate your career plans. I must confess, I'm surprised to hear from you so soon. After our last interaction, I thought your career would have taken off. A career issue, isn't that what you called your last request? Do you need my assistance directing you on a different career path? Perhaps one without competition?
> Warmest,
> KFAP

What the hell. Different career plans? Without competition? So, you're a funny guy now. He wasn't going to put up with KFAP hijacking the conversation. There's only one person in charge here, and he's not named KFAP. He replied.

> KFAP,

I'm interested in only one thing- utilizing your services. Will you accept the assignment or not?

Anonymous

You're no fun. How about some back and forth? A little negotiation never killed anyone. He tried another approach.

New Year's Salutations,

Hit a nerve, did I? Remember, if you need help advancing your career, I'm here to help in any way possible. I've counseled many people on their career choice. Well, yes, if you're a stickler for detail, I mostly help them to end their careers.

I think it's fascinating that you worded your ask as a request. Not a hit, not a contract, not a job, but a request. It's almost as if you've requested cheese on a hamburger, or time off from work, or a book from the library. For clarification, I accept or decline assignments. Not unlike the Fab Four, I don't do requests. Once we come to an agreement, I will decide when and how to complete said assignment. You will not offer suggestions on how I should do my job, remember? I must remind you that there are deal breakers on both sides of the aisle.

I will never accept an assignment involving children or families. On your side, there will be *no* repeat business. For a price (everyone has a price, no?), I'm willing to overlook the last one. As you have challenged the repeat business clause by making additional requests, the risk of doing business has gone up. My fee structure is a bit of a moving target. Your latest request will cost you $200K. You will not contact me once the payment has been made, unless you have another proposition. It has been a pleasure doing business with you.

Sending you warm New Year wishes,
KFAP

After reading KFAP's reply, he marched to the whiteboard in his office. He wrote pluses and minuses in columns. There was only one plus. The negatives were more numerous, impactful, and emotional. He didn't like seeing elimination written under minuses. He was not that kind of a person; he had been raised right. Thou shall not kill. Thou shall not take the Lord's name in vain. Thou shall not covet thy neighbor's wife. Okay, he came close to that one, but only because his neighbor's wife coveted him. She was depressed after her divorce and approached him at the end of a neighborhood New Year's Eve party. The relationship ended without consummation.

Yes, there was a single positive, but it was huge. Game-changing huge. Life-altering huge.

What a mess. Does KFAP think I'm made of money, because I'm not. Well, I kind of am. Sure, I might be able to come up with some cash, but he doesn't know that, and that's not the point. I can't let KFAP believe he's in charge. And I can't come across as being weak. Used to controlling conversations at work, he vowed to take charge. He erased the whiteboard and continued the electronic conversation.

KFAP,

You have proven yourself capable of completing an assignment. While I acknowledge that every job carries risks, there is very little associated with this one. The people involved do not know each other. They live and work in different states. I would be grateful if you were to complete the job as proposed. Times are tough and I cannot afford your asking price. I think $100K is a reasonable fee for this straightforward assignment. I've wired the money.

Anonymous

He hadn't wired the money but wanted KFAP to believe he had. As he hit Send, he was overwhelmed by a sense of elation.

Done. Still the Big Dog.

A reply came immediately.

> Kind Anonymous Sir,
> Thank you for your speedy reply. Buoyed by the New Year, I am feeling charitable and will accept $150K. I don't think anyone will question that you've made the right decision. After all, it's your career we're talking about, amirite? Don't forget to visit my website and leave a performance review. Remember, people on the receiving end of my assignments are never in a position to offer any kind of a review, leaving me with poor likelihood to recommend scores. You will not contact me again, unless you have another job.
> I hope you can make it a great day.
> Warmly,
> KFAP

What a frigging weirdo. Does this nutcase think he is a comedian? I don't suppose a normal person goes into this line of work. Well, it's a done deal.

He logged off the dark web then wired the money. He needed to get away. Go to the gym, work out, pump some serious iron. It'll feel good to break a sweat. He put on his coat, closed his office door, and said goodbye to his admin assistant.

He hummed his victory song while walking to the elevator; a tune that he insisted be played after every one of his winning matches.

Chapter 17

Aura comes from Latin aura, "a breeze, air in motion."

Decorations at the Three Fires Hotel had changed from Christmas to a New Year's theme since Evans last walked through the door. Approaching the Concierge Desk, he saw that "Katie, Rockford, MI." was on duty. Showing her his credentials, Evans stated, "I'm Detective Evans and I need to speak with Security."

"Very well, sir. I'll call over there and have them meet you here. Thank you for your service."

"Thank you, Katie. I appreciate that."

During his junior year in high school, Evans was interested in dating a classmate who had been elected to the Student Council the year before. He figured they'd see each other more often if they served together, so he ran for, and was elected, President of Student Council. He started dating the future Mrs. Evans after the election.

Evans stepped away from the concierge to meet the approaching head of Security, whose name badge read "James, Grandville, MI."

"Troy Evans. I'd like to look at some of your CCTV footage," he said, initiating introductions.

"Nice to meet you. James Brandon, but everyone calls me 'Bud.' Been Chief of Security here for a few years now. Worked for twenty years with Grandville PD before coming over. The job's a little soft, but comes with good benefits, nice hours, and no weekends. The salary's not very good, but three out of four ain't too bad, right? Let's get to the office and bring up the tapes. I'm assuming this is related to the other day."

"It is indeed. Were you here on Sunday?" Evans asked. He was trying to recall if he had ever crossed paths with Bud when he was a member of Grandville PD.

"Nope, no weekends. I start every Monday morning at six-thirty sharp."

James "call me Bud" led Evans to the elevator and the fourth floor. The door to the Security office was unlocked. Bud sat in a chair positioned in front of a bank of a dozen fifteen-inch TV monitors.

Evans said, "I need to see the entrance to the hotel, the elevators to Emily's floor, and her room, which was 1633, from Saturday night through this morning. That's January 7 through today."

"No problemo, let's start with the front entrance," replied Bud. Tapping on the keyboard with his index fingers, he accessed the system archives. Images from the evening of January 7 breezed through the center monitor.

Evans saw by the time stamp that Emily arrived at the hotel at 12:34 P.M., right before a hotel van dropped six people at the Pearl Street entrance. The people from the van look like, well, normal people. No one appeared anxious, no one studied other guests. Emily went from Registration to the elevators, and then likely, to her room. Emily traveled with a purse, laptop bag, and a small rolling suitcase. There was no CCTV footage of her room, only a view of the sixteenth floor's corridors. Emily stayed in her room until around 5:25 P.M. when she took the elevator to the ground floor. She exited to the left, which took her to The Dining Room, a Gerhardt Puck Restaurant, which faced west, toward the river. Ninety minutes later, Emily left the restaurant with a woman.

He knew Stella was Emily's dinner date that night. The tape shows Emily and Stella left the restaurant together, confirming what Stella said. However, he saw the two of them go from the restaurant to the elevators and presumably Emily's room. Stella told him that she left after dinner, but the tape proves she stopped by Emily's room before exiting the hotel. The next time Emily was seen, she was lying toes up on the Medical Examiner's gurney. Stella may have been the last person to see Emily alive. Not good Stella, not good at all.

"Can you tell me how many times the key card was used to open her door?" he asked.

"You bet. Room 1633 was opened three times on Sunday, at 1:01 P.M., 5:43 P.M., and 7:02 P.M. But I can't tell you how many times it was closed, only opened."

"Wait a minute, she was still in the restaurant at a quarter to six. Let's look at the CCTV tapes from the floor again."

Evans saw no one on the sixteenth floor from the time Emily left her room for dinner until housekeeping arrived the next morning. There were no images of Emily and Stella returning to Emily's room after their meal. The CCTV had been altered or erased, presumably removing images of someone other than Emily entering and exiting her room.

"Who has cards to get into rooms?"

"Housekeeping and Security. Oh, and Registration can make room cards. So technically, they have access to every room as well," Bud said, shifting his seat and leaning over the desk.

"But all of those people would have shown up on the film, right?"

"Yes, we can see when our staff enters a room," Bud replied hesitantly. He paused the tape and stared at Evans.

"Whose card was used to enter 1633 at five forty-three?"

Bud looked at the computer screen and replied, "I don't recognize it. It's not one of ours."

Evans said, "It looks like the tape, or part of the tape, was erased or altered."

"You can't erase it. This is the top of the line as far as video systems go. I upgraded a few years ago," Bud interjected.

"Is your system online?"

"Yes, we are. We use TFH.net. But no one can view it without a passcode, which changes daily. I'm telling you this is the best that money can buy," Bud said, feeling his body temperature rise.

"You might want to upgrade, Bud. You've been hacked."

Bud stared ahead and said softly, "What the hell."

Chapter 18

The Aztecs and the Incas strongly associated epilepsy with magic and religion.

Evans was upset that the Three Fires Hotel CCTV tapes had been altered. He didn't think Stella was capable of such sophisticated hacking. He needed to see all the hotel tapes from January 8, the day Emily died. He hoped there would be other views, which the perp had overlooked, that showed someone, anyone other than Stella, had been in her room.

"Thanks for showing me when Emily entered the hotel and registered. Now I need to see all the tapes, everything you have, from the time she checked in until the following morning."

"All of it? You want to see all of our CCTV footage?" Bud asked, turning his chair toward Evans.

"Yes, all of it. I need to see every restaurant, bar, store, bathroom, door, window, vent, duct, sewer, gutter, fire escape—any way that the unsub could have gotten into the hotel."

"Make yourself comfortable, it's going to take me a minute to bring all of that up," Bud replied. He turned back toward the monitors and started pecking at the keyboard. The system asked him to enter the date and time that he wanted to review. He asked, "Are we starting with Sunday?"

"Yes, please. Sunday, January 8, around noon thirty through eight the following morning." Evans heard several dings from his phone indicating the arrival of new emails.

"Okay, I've cued up the film from the Monroe Street entrance. We just looked at the Pearl Street entrance," Bud said.

Evans opened an email from Lieutenant Jefferson on his phone and asked distractedly, "I'm sorry? What about Pearl Street?"

Bud said, "There are two entrances to the hotel, off Pearl and Monroe Streets. Don't forget that you can also enter through Devries Place, via the crosswalk."

"Hadn't thought about that. Do you have a camera showing people entering the hotel from Devries?" Evans asked, returning his cellphone to his coat pocket.

"Not exactly, but there's a camera inside The Plaza Necessities."

"Alright. Let's start with Monroe and we'll leave the Plaza Necessities for last," he said. He focused his attention on the screens in front of Bud, knowing Jefferson's email did not require an immediate reply. Realizing there wasn't anything for him to touch or adjust while leaning forward, he sat back in the chair.

"Here's noon at the Monroe Street entrance," Bud said, pointing at a monitor.

Evans stared at the screen. People coming and going through the entryway with nobody acting suspiciously. More foot traffic moving in and out of the hotel than he expected. After reviewing the two entrances, it was time to look at the Plaza Necessities, where people could enter the hotel from the Devries Place Convention Center.

Browsing. Mostly, people were browsing through the store. He didn't see anyone actively shopping. More importantly, he didn't see any suspicious looking people entering the store from the skywalk.

"Can you speed up a bit, at this rate it'll take forever."

Bud said, "You got that right." He fast forwarded the tape two times, then four times.

He stared at one screen while Bud monitored twelve. There was little talk between them, the speed of the tapes forced them to concentrate on the monitors.

Bud asked, "Say, is Mason Jefferson still on the force?"

"He sure is and he keeps me on a damn short leash, if you ask me," Evans said, smiling.

"I only worked with him this one time, but he seemed to be a straight shooter."

"Yeah, he is. I give him a hard time, mostly when he's not around. But he's been good to me."

After about an hour, Evans stood and pointed at the screen, crying, "There! Stop it right there. No, can you back it up a minute to where that guy in the hat first enters the store. He came from the Convention Center."

"That guy" appeared to be a male, roughly six feet tall, not stocky, not overweight, with short, dark hair. Evans guessed he was twenty to fifty years old, wore black pants, a dark T-shirt, and a red hat. The person of interest had a backpack draped over his left shoulder and wore no glasses. There were no visible distinguishing scars or tattoos on his body. No labels, patches or other identifiable features on his clothes or backpack. Evans watched him walk through the clothing store and even try on pants. The guy hadn't bought anything. He was in the store for maybe twenty minutes, before walking into the Floral store.

Evans watched Red Hat guy pick up a few items and put them right back on the shelf. He kept his head down and as such, Evans never got a good look at his face. He blended in while ostensibly shopping, and subtly looked towards the elevator bank every fifteen to thirty seconds. A casual shopper? Possibly. A hotel resident? Maybe.

"Will you print out a picture of the guy right there, that's probably the best view we have of him. Bud, thanks for your help." Evans was pumped, and inadvertently crumpled the picture as he grabbed it off the printer.

"Don't you want to see any more of the tapes?" Bud asked.

Evans returned to his chair saying, "You know what, I'd better. I'd like to know how long that guy was in the hotel. We'd better go back to the Monroe and Pearl Street entrances now that I know who I'm looking for. I'd like to see every image of that guy in the hat that we can find." He ran his hands over the picture, trying to smooth it.

Bud sat up straighter and replied, "Coming right up."

An hour later, Evans left the hotel with a printed picture of a male who actively hid his face from the security cameras. The behavior of the guy in question was not that unusual, and only a little suspicious. Evans was certain that somebody hacked the system and erased images of Emily leaving her room before dinner and accompanying Stella back after their meal. He wasn't certain whether the male was a person of interest, or just a guy shopping. One troubling aspect about the guy was that Bud couldn't find any other images of him. He just magically disappeared.

Seeing the suspicious man was positive news for Stella, she was no longer at the top of Evans's suspect list. Maybe Stella experienced a lapse of judgement, but she wasn't a killer. At least he hoped not.

Chapter 19

Fentanyl is a synthetic opioid that is fifty to one hundred times more potent than morphine.

Fentanyl. Damn it, Evans needed to tell Emily's family about the fentanyl. But before that, he wanted to talk to Stella about the health care side of the opioid crisis.

He called her, who didn't pick up, and left a voice mail, "Stells, it's me. I need to talk to you about something medical. Give me a call, will you? Maybe we can talk after the game tonight. Thanks. See ya."

He went back to reading about the opioid crisis. Opioid consumption had spiraled completely out of control. From use to abuse in sixty seconds.

Stella returned his call. "Gordie, I got your message. Let's talk tonight after the game."

"Perfect, see you then."

"See you tonight," Stella said.

Stella grew up wanting to follow in the medical footsteps of her grandfather. Following her training in major universities in the Midwest, she joined the Triumphant Health Medical Group. Word that an empathetic and compassionate Neurologist had arrived in town spread throughout the community. Her patients loved her as much as she cared for them. Patients started asking to see Dr. Murray by name. Despite having little free time, she applied to be a Principal Investigator (PI), or supervising physician, for a clinical drug trial investigating the efficacy of an experimental epilepsy drug. Enrollment was good, the study met its primary end point. She was one of several co-authors for the study manuscript that was published in *JAMA Neurology*. Because of her excellent work, she was invited to be a guest lecturer at universities across the country. She applied to be a PI for other drug trials. Stella flourished as a clinician, educator, and researcher.

After the game, Stella dressed and left the female-only locker room. She was not in the mood for Evans and intentionally left without looking for him.

Evans caught up with her in the parking lot. "Hey, Stells wait up. I thought we were going to talk."

She hadn't zipped up her coat and didn't stop walking. "It's not always all about you, you know. I need to get home."

"You've been in a pissy mood all night, what gives?" Evans asked.

Talking in the cold sent puffs of smoke from her mouth. "What gives? What gives? I'm not allowed to have a bad day once in a while? That's not allowed in your pissy little detective world?" Stella said, putting her bag and goalie stick in her SUV.

"Hey, Stells, talk to me. What's going on?" Evans said, setting his bag in the middle of the parking lane.

She stood next to her vehicle and sighed. "Look, I'm in a shitty mood. I just want to get home."

"What's going on? Anything I can do to help?"

"No. It's Charlie, he's acting out," Stella said. Shivering, she zipped up her coat and put on mittens.

"How's my favorite nephew acting out?"

"Godson, you're still not his uncle. At home he's fine, but at school he's been acting out. You know, shitty behavior stuff. But he knows better than that. He wasn't raised to be a little jerk, or to pick on other kids."

"You can't be a jerk at his age. It's probably typical boy stuff." Evans made a smiley face in the snow with the toe of his boot.

"Well, he's never done it before, and I feel terrible about it. I'm a terrible mom." She hugged herself, trying to stop shivering.

"Hey, come on. Charlie's a great kid, and you're not a terrible anything. You know that, right?"

She looked down and stomped her boots. "I know, it's just that I've got a lot on my plate right now."

Evans asked, "Anything I can do to help out?" He kicked snow on the circular mug, covering it.

"No, I can handle it. I just want to get home."

"I know you can handle it, you're the best. Charlie knows it, Ash knows it. Everyone knows it."

"What did you want to talk about anyway?" Stella asked,

reaching for her car door.

"Can you give me two seconds on opioids?"

"Opioids? What do you want to know about them?" She removed a snow scraper from the car and stomped her feet again.

"Who, why, what, where?"

"Oh man, it's a problem, a huge problem," Stella said, scraping snow from the rear window. "About ten percent of the seventy-six million Americans who were prescribed opioids in 2016 misused them. This means the general public and health care workers alike. The why is easy, opioids control pain."

"First off, who's in that ten percent of abusers?" Evans used his stick to shoot snow at Stella's car.

She stopped scraping and said, "What, are you twelve now? It's men more than women, although women are catching up."

"Okay, mostly men. Why do they use opioids?" Evans asked.

"Abuse or use, there's a difference. Use is for pain, and that usually means cancer. When cancer metastasizes to the liver or bones, it causes a lot of pain. Abuse, that's a different story. You know more about street use than I ever will."

"Yeah, I know about the addicts. What about health care workers?" Evans asked.

"You know we're in an opioid crisis right now, right?" Stella said.

"I'm aware."

"Well, it's a big problem. It's estimated that 760,000 people died from an opioid overdose between 1999 and now. Think about that for a second. More people have died from opioids than died during the Civil and Vietnam Wars, combined.

"I can't tell you exactly how often I see overdoses. They fry their brain when the opioids shut down their respiratory center, causing them to stop breathing. The lack of oxygen results in brain damage. Poor bastards don't know what hit them. They fall asleep and never wake up. It's a shame," she said, scraping the snow off her car's passenger side windows.

"I hear you. But why do health care workers get addicted?" Evans asked.

"Right, you asked about that. Nurses and physicians, probably because they can. I mean, we have access to the drugs, nurses more than us. We can write scripts, but we can't write them to ourselves, and we can't write scripts for family members, either. All healthcare workers are under a lot of stress these days. Nurses are getting sued too, you know. The stress is getting worse as the general population attends Medical School on the internet. You know, the lay public thinks they know more medicine than we do these days," Stella said. She cleaned snow off the roof and hood.

"Shit, I've known that for ten years."

"Not in the mood for any of your crap tonight."

"I know, sorry. Tell me about nurses who abuse opioids."

"What do you want to know? Maybe ten percent of docs and nurses have an addiction issue. Mostly it's alcohol, but some will get hooked on opioids. It's commonly nurse anesthetists, oncologists, floor nurses, and ICU nurses. They administer opioids to patients daily and therefore have the easiest access," Stella said, clearing snow off the windshield.

"Do nurses die after their first use? Is that typical?"

"I don't know the statistics on that. But I'd guess no, not with their first one. They probably start with a low dose and increase as needed."

"What's the end game, why increase the dose?" Evans asked, using his stick to wipe snow off the driver's window.

"Stop that, I don't want you scratching my windows. Opioids produce a euphoria. If a low dose doesn't do it, then they increase the dose to get them to where they want to be," Stella said, walking around her SUV to the driver's side.

Evans stopped scraping. "This is good stuff. Which nurses are at greatest risk for abusing opioids?"

Stella said, "It's probably nurse anesthetists."

"How about non-clinical nurses. Do they ever get hooked?"

"I guess anything's possible, but they wouldn't have access to a Pyxis, which is a machine that dispenses drugs to nurses working in hospitals. Meaning they'd have no access to opioids. Now, if someone worked in a detox center, they'd have access to methadone," she said.

"Methadone, that's nasty stuff, isn't it? But I want to get back to fentanyl. What's a fatal dose of fentanyl?" Evans asked.

"It depends on the person's height and weight."

"Well, roughly how much fentanyl does it take to kill someone?"

"A dose of two milligrams will usually do the trick."

"Do you give out prescriptions for fentanyl?" Evans asked.

"I can, but don't. I don't even think our headache guys write for fentanyl. You never told me why we're having this discussion."

"I'm working on an unusual case. An overdose, but the person doesn't fit the profile of an addict. I want to be certain before I call it a homicide," Evans said, using his stick to scrape snow off the side mirror.

Stella said, "Hey, I told you to put your stick down. Scratch my mirror and you're buying me a new one. Physician or nurse?"

"I have to be careful here. You guys aren't the only ones with confidentiality, you know."

"Wait, does this have anything to do with Emily?"

"I can't say," Evans quickly replied.

"It does, doesn't it. You think Emily overdosed?" Stella asked, returning her scraper to her back seat floor.

"I don't think I said that."

"No way. Emily didn't abuse drugs. Look, she wasn't clinical, she had no access to a Pyxis or opioids. She didn't abuse drugs."

"I see people on the street using drugs every day without access to a pixie. That doesn't mean shit to me."

"Pyxis, PD. Non-clinical nurses have no access to opioids through the system," Stella said.

"I'm not saying this has anything to do with Emily. But, hypothetically, hypothetically speaking, in hindsight, did you ever wonder whether Emily was using drugs?"

"Never. She wouldn't have been able to do her job while she was high. Are you saying Emily died of an overdose?" Stella asked emphatically.

Evans pointed his stick at Stella saying, "Can't say."

"Can't or won't?"

"Both. Look, I wanted to pick your brain on opioids, but I've already said too much."

"You need to look at Emily as a homicide," Stella said, opening her car door.

"Thanks, Stells, you're the best. See ya."

"Homicide," she said, closing her door and starting her car.

"Later," Evans said. He waved goodbye. Homicide. Hmm. He noticed that Stella hadn't cleared herself of wrongdoing when she acknowledged that she could write a prescription for fentanyl. And she knew exactly how much fentanyl it takes to kill someone.

He wanted to talk to someone at Solutions & Synergy about Emily, but talking to her parents and boyfriend would have come first.

Chapter 20

Galen considered untimely intercourse among the causes of epilepsy.

KFAP had seen and heard enough for one night and returned to the motel. His ears were still ringing when he entered his temporary lodging located a few miles from the Charles River. He paid cash for five nights knowing he'd be sleeping in his own bed in a couple of days.

Tricia Wilkinson took the stage around eight, which allowed him to finish his gig at Nick's Comedy Shop and still arrive at Tricia's preferred venue, The Flying Bulldog, before closing. His performances at Nick's were successful, he'd received a positive reception and favorable reviews.

From the back of the Bulldog, KFAP was able to observe the restrooms, the bar, and the stage where Tricia's cover band, The Best of You, performed. He surmised that grunge was an apt descriptive of the bar, the group, and the night in general. He left after Tricia's last set. He set his phone alarm and turned out the lights. With his plans finalized for the following day, he had no trouble falling asleep.

KFAP awoke feeling good, no, Grand! He had a light continental breakfast while Tricia followed her morning routine of visiting a coffee and bagel store three blocks from her apartment.

He put on latex gloves. The locked front door to building 484, which housed Tricia's apartment, didn't slow him down. Using a bumper key set, he picked open the front door and entered Tricia's apartment, which wasn't large. Shoes and black, leather boots were scattered on the floor to the side of the entrance. A coat was thrown over a loveseat. Tricia, you need to have your apartment cleaned. I'm sure your mother told you more than once that a clean apartment is a happy apartment.

A small living room was located to the left of the front door. A framed print of what looked like two kayaks copulating hung on one wall. A thirty-two inch flat screen TV sat on an aged entertainment table. A worn, brown paisley throw rug slept in front of the loveseat. Two barrel armchairs, each covered with different shades of red floral patterns, bordered the loveseat. Two Holiday cards stood tall on the entertainment center. Tricia, you've got to send them to receive them. Maybe you can mail more cards next year. Oops. As you were. There might not be a next year.

KFAP moved to the bathroom.

Tricia, I'm sorry it must end like this. You know it's not you, right? And it's nothing personal. You and I, we've got a lot in common. You work two jobs, I work two jobs. You do whatever your boss asks you to do, I do what my bosses ask me to do. You help people and I help people, kind of. Look on the bright side. Without having to lay out a few shekels, you've got a brand spanking new inhaler. And it's one that packs the kind of punch that you've been looking for. You're welcome. Still friends?

He preferred to break up the monotony of killing by altering his approach. Guns (acute lead intoxication), poison, trauma, knife, garrote; he was proficient and comfortable with all modes of death. He'd had so much fun in Grand Rapids that he decided to roll with it. He'd take advantage of the drug crisis and use the tools in hand.

A litter box sat on the floor to the left of the toilet. Hmm, hadn't seen a cat. KFAP opened the medicine cabinet and found what he was looking for. He removed Tricia's Spiraval canister from its blue and gray plastic holder and replaced it with a self-compounded cannister. He placed the faux Spiraval inhaler on the shelf, shut the medicine cabinet door, and walked out of her bedroom.

He enjoyed compounding pills but found preparing an inhaler to be a whole new level of challenge. He successfully won the battle on his fourth attempt. He thought about filling the canister with a combination of fentanyl and cocaine, giving Tricia her own Hot Shot. Wanting to avoid the duplicity of two researchers overdosing on fentanyl, he filled the cannister with cocaine.

KFAP froze when he heard a scratching noise, which didn't sound like Millennial feet shuffling across the floor. The cat. He stuck his head out and saw a Maine Coon cat standing near the front door, arching its back. He approached the feline who rubbed herself against his leg. A name tag was cut in the shape of a guitar and read "Cream." Scratching her head KFAP said, "Cream, I don't think mommy's going to feel good after she gets home. Would you like for me to foster you until we can find you a suitable replacement?"

He left Tricia's apartment, then the complex. Goodbye Boston, I shall return. Reviews from the Friday show included "He left them in stitches." Hopefully, nobody will need medical attention during his return engagement.

Sir, yes sir. Assignment completed, sir. Sir, yes sir, I am dumber than a toad when I say my assignment was completed. Sir, yes sir, I can count to two if I am given two tries, sir. Sir, yes sir, I'm aware that another assignment needs to be addressed. Sir, yes sir, I am the dumbest goddamn human being on the face of God's green earth when I say an assignment needs to be addressed and not completed. Sir, yes sir, I will complete the assignment without acting like the goddamn idiot that I am, sir. KFAP fondly recalled his time in the Corps.

After breakfast, per her habit, Tricia took two puffs from her inhaler. The uncut cocaine was rapidly absorbed into her lungs, then bloodstream. Within seventy seconds, the cocaine had circulated and triggered a fatal arrhythmia. Tricia collapsed with the compounded inhaler still in her hand. Her body was discovered two days later after a neighbor asked the police to perform a wellness check.

The arrythmia prevented Tricia's heart from pumping an adequate volume of blood to her cranium, causing global ischemic damage. The police called for an EMS team, who transported Tricia to the ED. She was pronounced dead at 8:26 A.M. on January 16, 2023. The Emergency attending physician called Boston PD after her tox screen showed a lethal serum level of cocaine.

Chapter 21

In 1956, eighteen states provided for the sterilization of people with epilepsy.

Evans drove to Emily's parents' house in light traffic. He parked in the empty driveway and slowly walked to the front door. Déjà vu all over again, plus. Tell them about the pregnancy or not, he hadn't made up his mind. How much pain can they tolerate? How much misery did they deserve? The walkway had not been cleared of an overnight snowfall.

Emily's mother greeted Evans after opening the door and saying, "Nice to see you again, Detective. We're looking forward to hearing whatever news you have."

"Thank you. Will Mr. Naismith be joining us?" Evans asked. He sat in the same chair as he had three days earlier.

The Christmas tree, along with every other holiday decoration, had been taken down. Shades half covered the windows. A void echoed throughout the living room. The sadness was palpable.

Emily's mother sat on the couch. Showing Evans her phone, she replied, "No, not directly. He's at work and wanted me to call him so he could listen in on our conversation. Do you mind if I call him?"

"No, that'd be fine." Not having Emily's father in the room would make the second half of the conversation more difficult.

She called her husband who answered on the second ring, "Hi, hon. Detective Evans is here with me. I'm going to put you on speaker phone. Can you hear us, okay?" She tapped the speaker icon.

"Yes, I can hear you. Can you hear me, okay?"

"Loud and clear," Evans said. "Let me begin by saying again how sorry I am that we have to meet under these circumstances. Nobody should have to go through what you're going through."

"Thank you, Detective. It's been devastating, but I think we're doing okay, given the circumstances. What do you have for us today?" Emily's mother set her phone on the cherry coffee table, next to a box of facial tissues. She dabbed her teary eyes with a tissue.

Evans faced the table when speaking. "I'm glad you're handling it as well as you can. I told you that I received the preliminary results of Emily's autopsy. I wanted to tell you about it in person because I wasn't anticipating the results."

"What does that mean?" Emily's father asked.

"Remember a few days ago when I mentioned that Emily may have died of an overdose? I wasn't wrong. It looks like that's what she died from."

"Overdose, like drugs?" her mother asked. "That's not our Emily, she's no drug addict."

"The ME is certain at Emily died of an overdose. Fentanyl. Emily had a lethal dose of fentanyl in her system."

Emily's father spoke up, "I don't believe it. We know our Emily, she didn't do drugs, or anything like it."

"I know this is terribly hard to hear. This is what I meant when I said, 'I wasn't expecting the results.' I was floored when she told me about it," Evans said, holding his hands together, as if praying.

"She?" Emily's mother asked, clutching a tissue.

"Dr. Colson-Brown, the Medical Examiner. She's the one who told me that blood and urine toxicology reports confirmed that there was a lethal level of fentanyl in Emily's system," Evans said.

"I don't care what those tests showed, she didn't do drugs. The blood must have been contaminated. Maybe they looked at someone else's blood. The fentanyl got in her system some other way, or you looked at the wrong blood sample. Maybe she was poisoned," Emily's father insisted.

"So, you're not aware that Emily ever did any drugs. No pot, no cocaine, no meth, no drugs, nothing?"

"Nothing. She told me several years ago that she smoked pot in college one time with her boyfriend. She didn't like how it made her feel. She never did it again and broke up with the boyfriend because he wouldn't give it up," Emily's mother said.

"Smoking pot one time doesn't make her a druggie, Detective. I bet most college kids have done it more often than that," Emily's father stated.

"You're probably right about that," Evans said, reflecting on his collegiate days. "So, you're certain that Emily never did drugs."

"Never," her father emphasized.

Emily's mother replaced her damp tissue with a new one. "Yes, we're certain," she confirmed.

Evans continued, "Okay, all right. I hear you. I asked you the last time I was here, but I'm afraid I have to ask again. How was Emily's mood? Ever see signs of depression?"

"Mood? She was fine," her mother said.

"According to a neurologist friend of mine, depression is underdiagnosed in young people."

"That may be, but Emily wasn't depressed. She was happy, very happy," her mother said as tears welled up.

"Never upset over a breakup with a boyfriend? No friends that upset her? Any work problems that got her down?"

Emily's mother replied, "She was a little sad when she broke up with her old boyfriend, the one before Tyler. They'd been going out for a couple of years, so yeah, she was sad when they ended it. But it wasn't bad and didn't last all that long. Emily called him a 'hot head.' Apparently, he had a bit of a temper. Emily told me that when they started spending more time arguing than enjoying themselves, she had had enough and called it quits."

"Do you recall the hot head's name, or have a phone number for him?" Evans asked. He took a pen from his shirt pocket and a notepad from his coat.

"Max Wainwright was his name and yes, his number is on my phone. I can give it to you after our call," Emily's mother said.

"That's fine. Have you seen this Max since the breakup?" Evans asked, rolling his pen between his thumb and index fingers.

"I haven't seen him, but Emily told me he became engaged shortly after they broke up. Obviously, he wasn't upset by their breakup. Then Emily met Tyler, and they've been happy ever since."

He asked, "Did Emily feel safe around Max? Did he ever harm or threaten to harm her?"

Emily's mother said, "I don't think so. Emily never said that she felt endangered by him. She just said that at times he was more interested in himself, and that he had a little temper."

"How sad was Emily after the breakup?"

"It never got to the point of clinical depression, if that's what you mean. It never got that bad," her mother clarified, while wiping away tears.

"Was Emily ever suicidal?"

"Never," Emily's parents said in unison.

"Over the years, fentanyl has been used as a means of suicide, which is why I had to ask."

"You're way off base, there. Emily would never have considered suicide," her father said.

"Okay, had to double check. The autopsy showed no heart attack or signs of a stroke, which means that the so-called natural causes of death have been ruled out. Dr. Colson-Brown said she was signing it out as a 'suspicious death.' If Tyler tells me the same story, that Emily never used drugs, then I'll treat her death as a homicide."

Her mother cried into the rapidly disintegrating tissue.

Emily's father asked, "Anything else you can tell us, Detective?"

Evans looked at Mrs. Naismith. He hesitated. "There is one more thing. I don't know if Emily told you, but she was pregnant," he said, wondering if he had just made a huge error.

"Pregnant?" Emily's mother said, picking her head up with a surprised look on her face.

"Yeah, about nine weeks."

Emily's mother shook her head in disbelief, "That's horrible. How could they do that? How could they murder Emily and her little baby?"

"I'm afraid there are a lot of bad people out there."

"That's two, isn't it? Two murders?" Emily's father asked.

Evans said, "Yeah, I'm sure the prosecutor will consider their deaths as homicides."

"Detective, you've got to get them. Murdering a poor baby," Emily's mother replied. She blew her nose.

"I know, it's a terrible, horrible thing. Believe me, I'm going to do everything I can to find out who did this."

"You find them, and you make them pay. They don't even deserve to even live in prison with our baby taken from us at such a young age. And pregnant. We're counting on you for that," Emily's father demanded.

"I understand and I'm also very upset by all of this. Again, I'm going to do everything I can to find the person or persons responsible for her death."

Emily's mother sobbed softly.

Her father asked, "Any chance it's related to her work? Any new leads for us, anything at all?"

"I don't think it's work related, but nothing has been ruled out. I was wondering whether the pregnancy had anything to do with it, but no. No new leads, I'm afraid. I'll talk to Tyler and confirm that there was no drug use. And I want to talk to her old boyfriend, Max, as well. Thank you for everything. I can let myself out," Evans said, standing and walking toward the front door.

Emily's mother said to the phone, "I'll talk to you tonight, hon," then ended the call. "Detective, I've got that phone number for you, Max's."

"Oh, good. I would've left without it," Evans confessed.

He called Tyler from the car. "Tyler, I just spoke with Emily's parents and want to know if I can stop by for a quick update on where we are with her case."

"Um, yeah, I guess so. You remember where my office is?" Tyler asked.

"I remember. See you soon." He entered Tyler's office address on his phone's GPS program, selected it as his next destination, and drove to there. The receptionist recognized that he was not Dr. Runquist.

"Hi Detective. Let's go to the conference room," Tyler said.

"Thanks for seeing me today. Oh, before I forget, I need to get a swab from your cheek," Evans said, pulling an Evidence bag, which held a test tube, from his left breast coat pocket.

"What for?"

"Just being thorough. Open wide," Evans said, holding a large cotton-tipped swab. He swabbed Tyler's cheek then returned the specimen to the test tube, before placing it in the Evidence bag.

"I just told Emily's parents that she died of a fentanyl overdose," Evans said.

"You're lying."

"Yeah, the Medical Examiner confirmed it. Her heart was clean, no signs of stroke or anything else. She was healthy, other than the tox report. Did you ever see Emily do drugs?" Evans asked.

"I already told you no, never," Tyler said.

"You never thought she was high?"

"No, because she never was."

"Did she ever smoke pot, use cocaine, ecstasy, or PCP?"

"No, no, no, no, no, no. Are you even *listening* to me? You've asked me that, like, ten times. She might have one glass of wine a month, and that was it," Tyler said.

"Okay. Last time I was here, I asked you about Emily's mood. I'm afraid I have to ask you again. Was Emily depressed?"

"No, she was incredibly upbeat. Never down, no crying. Last time I told you that she got frustrated with some work stuff, but she was never, you know, depressed."

"Did she ever talk about suicide?"

"Never. She went to church every Sunday. She liked her job. We were getting along great. I think I told you last time that we talked about moving in together. She wasn't depressed or suicidal. Not in the least bit."

Evans asked, "Do you know her old boyfriend, this Max guy?"

"Never knew the dude. Again, she didn't dwell on the negatives, and told me next to nothing about him. They argued and that was it," Tyler said.

"In the little that Emily did say about Max, did she ever mention feeling threatened by him?"

Without hesitating, Tyler said, "No."

"Did she say anything about the breakup with Max, like it was contentious or anything?" Evans asked.

"No, not really. She heard Max became engaged after they broke up and that was that."

Evans was at ease informing Tyler about the pregnancy. Giving unexpected news to a mother and soon to be grandmother was a whole different level of hurt. "Okay, thanks. One more thing, Emily was pregnant."

"Emily was?"

"Yeah, about nine weeks."

"Holy shit. She never said anything about that. Are you sure?"

"Yeah, the ME is positive. I'm sorry to tell you this," Evans said, uncertain why the sight of Tyler crying was less upsetting than watching Emily's mother weep.

"Detective, that's horrible news. Why didn't you say something the first time you were here?" Tyler asked, wiping his eyes and nose.

"I'm sorry, but we had no idea until she completed the autopsy."

Tyler said, "Pregnant. Wow."

"I don't mean to dump all of this on you, but I thought you'd want to know."

"Man, this keeps getting worse and worse," Tyler said.

Evans said, "Yeah, I know. It sucks."

"This is, like, completely way worse than sucks. It's horrific," Tyler said, with his face buried in the crook of his elbow.

"You're right, it's terrible."

"Will you excuse me, I need to think about this some more," Tyler said, standing.

"Absolutely, I can show myself out," Evans said. At that point, he was happy to allow Tyler to process the deaths of Emily and her unborn child alone.

Sitting in his car, Evans searched the internet for Max Wainwright and found there were two who resided in Illinois. One was seventy-eight-years-old, the other twenty-nine. The younger Wainright was an attorney, who worked in a downtown office. Evans drove to the city.

He took the elevator to the ninth floor and spoke to the receptionist, "Good afternoon. I'm Detective Evans from Grand Rapids PD and I'd like to speak to Max Wainwright, please."

"Um . . . let me see if he's in today," she said, clicking her mouse. "He's here." She picked up the phone and said, "Max, there's a detective here to see you. All right."

Addressing Evans, she said, "He'll be right here."

"Thanks so much," Evans said.

Max didn't look anything like what Evans imagined he would. He was several inches short of six feet, skinnier than skinny, looking like either a marathon runner or a chemo patient. Without needing to shave his scalp, Max's head was as shiny as a cue ball; he was entirely bald. He dressed in business casual attire.

"Hi, Max Wainwright," he said, extending his hand. "Let's go back to my office. What'd I do to deserve a meet and greet with a detective, Detective?"

"Just a routine chat, nothing serious," Evans said.

"So, I don't need my attorney present," Max said, gesturing for Evans to sit in the chair in front of his desk.

"No, I don't think so, unless you've done something wrong. Have you done anything wrong?"

"Nope, not me."

Evans said, "I'm investigating the death of Emily Naismith."

"She's dead?" Max said, showing no emotion.

"Yeah, I'm afraid she was found in a hotel room. I spoke to her parents who told me you went out together."

"Yeah, we went out for a while."

"I'm sure you can appreciate that a scorned lover is near the top of my suspect list," Evans said.

"Yeah, I can imagine. It's true, what the Naismiths said. I dated Emily. But it didn't work out, so I moved on. Or we moved on, I should say."

"Simple as that?" Evans asked, cocking his head slightly to the right.

"Yeah, pretty much so," Max said, holding his hands in his lap and speaking without gesturing.

"Well, Emily's parents had nothing but good things to say about you. They went on and on about how great of a guy you are. Did you ever see Emily use drugs? You know pot, cocaine, or ecstasy."

"Yeah, I knew they liked me. I don't do drugs, so Emily didn't either," Max replied with a stone face.

"Were you ever concerned during the breakup, or at any time, that she was depressed?"

"I never let her affect *my* mood, that's for certain," Max said.

"You sure about that? Depression is underdiagnosed."

"No, she never said anything to me about depression. I've certainly never been diagnosed with it. So, if that's all you have, thanks for coming over today," Max said, standing.

"How."

"I'm sorry?" Max asked, staring at Evans.

"You never asked me how Emily died. People who aren't criminally involved in a case always ask me how? How did they die? Was it suicide? Was it an accident? You never asked me what happened to her."

"Well, I . . . ah . . . assumed she died of an accident or something."

"You assumed. Hmm. Assuming isn't the normal response when I tell someone about the death of a woman that they wanted to marry."

"I thought it would be, I don't know, kind of morbid for me to ask," Max said, looking lost.

"Interesting choice of words," Evans said.

"Maybe inappropriate would have been better. I didn't want to appear out of line since, you know, we weren't going out anymore." After a prolonged pause, he said, "Well, if you need anything, like, I don't know, information or whatever, you know where to find me."

"I certainly do. How about if you don't leave town for the next few weeks while I sort everything out," Evans said. He clicked his pen twice, before returning it to his shirt pocket.

"What? You can't do that. Am I a suspect?" Max asked.

"Maximus, everyone's a suspect at this point. Can you tell me where you were on January 8?"

"The eighth? Coming home from Grand Rapids. We were at a Cottage Show that weekend."

Max had just placed himself in Grand Rapids on the day Emily was killed. "Who's we? And what show?" Evans asked.

"The Cottage & Lakefront Living Show. We have a cottage on Lake Charlevoix, so my fiancé and I went to the Show last weekend. We ate breakfast then hit the road afterward."

"I need your fiancé's full name and phone number," Evans said, removing his pen from his pocket.

"Sure, it's Brie Driesbach." Max gave Brie's phone number to him.

"Max, you just confirmed that you were in Grand Rapids on the day that Emily was killed. We'll be in touch," Evans said, returning his notepad to a coat pocket, still holding his pen.

Max said, "You know, I haven't even *seen* Emily in two years."

"We'll be in touch."

Evans drove back to Grand Rapids while reviewing his conversation with Max. Interesting. Death usually elicits raw emotion: anger, despair, fear, desperation, none of which Max displayed. Mad Max wasn't the least bit upset hearing about his former lover's death. Maxy Boy, you're not at the top of my list, but you're not off it, either. Interesting. Max seemed to be herding him out of the office. Hiding something, Maxster?

Chapter 22

Nearly 795,000 strokes occur in the U.S. each year.

After a light workout and breakfast, Stella found three of her patients on the Blanchard Hospital inpatient Neurology list, two of whom had been enrolled in SETTUP the night before. One went into status epilepticus due to non-compliance, failing to take his antiseizure medications. The other was admitted due to stupidity. Nice to get two more enrolled in the trial, but come on guys, take your meds and don't screw up.

Stella drove downtown and turned in to the dedicated physician area on the first floor of the parking structure. Not wanting to get her shoes wet walking through a fresh snowfall, she took the overpass above Michigan Street to Blanchard Hospital.

She was stopped by a bedside nurse before entering Room 3024.

"Dr. Murray, did you hear that he had a stroke last night?" she said, nodding toward the room.

"No, no I hadn't heard anything. I'm not on service this month. I'm only seeing a couple of study patients this morning. How's he doing?" Goddamn it. Kenny came here for seizures. He's only in his thirties, how could he have stroked out?

The nurse said, "He's okay. When he buzzed me to pee, I noted facial drooping and slurred speech, so I called a Stroke Code. The Rapid Response Stroke Team performed an NIH Stroke Scale at bedside and gave him a score of four. He started getting better so quickly that he wasn't given anything."

"Thanks, Mary. Great pick up on the stroke."

Stella checked Kenny's record in EPIC and saw that a Stroke Code was called eleven minutes before midnight. His blood pressure was elevated and had since normalized. Kenny scored four on the NIH Stroke Scale, one for orientation (the disorientation wasn't related to the stroke; he'd always been a few elephants short of a parade), one for face, one for arm, and one for speech.

"Kenny, you had quite a night," Stella said, noting the flattening of his right face. She pushed aside the bedside table and stood on the right of his bed.

"Yeah, but I'm better now Dr. Murray."

Stella noted Kenny's slurred speech and asked, "Did the weakness start suddenly or gradually?"

"Dunno. My old lady said my face looked crooked, I jess thought it was swollen," Kenny said, kicking the sheets off his legs. His left leg did the majority of the kicking.

"Any visual changes? Numbness or weakness in your arms or legs?"

"Nah, just my face. My talkin's better now."

"Headache?" Stella asked.

"Nah, just my face felt swollen."

"Is it true you missed taking your seizure meds? You know that not taking your pills will bring on seizures."

"Yeah, but it was only one dose."

Stella asked, "Any more seizures last night or today?"

Kenny looked perplexed. "I dunno."

"Okay, that probably means no. Good. Kenny, we've talked about how you can't forget to take your meds. You have to make up all missed doses, because not taking your pills is probably why you had the seizures.

"And thanks again for entering the trial. We had to give you an experimental drug because multiple meds didn't stop your seizures. You know, the last one wouldn't react to anything that we threw at it. We almost intubated you. The good news is that the experimental drug worked great. How are you doing with it by the way? Any reactions to the new one?"

"Nah, I'm good Dr. Murray, no problems with your med— medicar— medicartions."

She returned the table so it was aligned parallel to his bed and placed the call light on the table. "All right, then. The stroke was small, you won't need rehab. If you can go another day without any seizures, I hope the inpatient team will get you outta here. Either my research assistant or I will see you in the clinic."

"Thanks, Dr. Murray, I'm down for that."

"Take care Kenny. I'll call your wife and give her an update. I'll see you tomorrow. Oh, one more thing, I want you to get out of bed. You should be walking in the halls with your nurse or PT."

"I want to get out of bed, but they won't let me. The alarm goes off every time I want to pee or go for a smoke."

"I'll talk to the nurses about the alarm, but I need you up and walking in the halls. And Kenny, you can't smoke. Smoking is probably why you had the stroke," Stella said.

"You're funny, Doc. I've tried to quit, but can't."

"Well, if you keep smoking you might have a big stroke and you don't want that, do you? I'll give you a patch to take away the urge to smoke."

"You trying to scare me, Doc?"

"No, I'm being completely honest with you."

"Take 'er easy," Kenny said, laughing. His spoken words were slurred, the laughter was not.

Stella walked to the end of the hall to see the second patient enrolled in the drug study the night before. Jacob was an angry nineteen-year-old who, after having seizures for ten years, still hadn't accepted his diagnosis. Jacob blamed his parents for his seizures, Stella for the driving restrictions, Stella for the work limitations, and Stella for everything else that was wrong in his life.

"Hi Jacob, how are you doing?" Stella asked.

From under the covers, Jacob said, "Jake. It's Jake, not Jacob."

Stella moved the bedside table aside and asked, "Jake, have you had any more seizures, even small ones?"

"No."

"How about the seizure meds, any reactions to them?"

Jake ripped the covers off his face saying, "Don't give me any of that experimental shit anymore. I'm not a fuckin' rat you know."

"Jake, please stop swearing and sit up. I'm not one of your buddy boys. You're here because you went into status epilepticus, which is a neurological emergency. When it was apparent that standard meds weren't working, we had to give you the experimental drug. Which, by the way, worked great. It says in EPIC that the seizures stopped as soon as the drug was given. Any reactions to it?"

Jake said, "Yeah, my back hurts like hell and my leg is numb."

"Did you fall when you had the seizures? Which leg is numb? Is it numb and weak, or just numb?"

"I didn't fall on anything. My left leg is numb. Numb, numb. Dead numb. It hurts to move it. I've never had back pain like this before, you gotta give me something for it. Something strong, it's killing me," Jake said wincing, trying to convince Stella that he was in extreme pain.

"I want to go through an exam." Stella found Jake's speech was unchanged, and he had no cranial nerve deficits. His strength in the upper extremities was normal. Jake gave a poor effort when she assessed the strength in every muscle group in his legs. Sensation was intact, upper and lower extremity reflexes were symmetric.

"I'm going to ask the inpatient team to order an MRI of your back. You have a lot of weakness in your legs, but it seems to be related to pain," Stella said.

"I ain't doin' that shit unless you give me something for pain."

"They'll give you pain pills. Did you take your seizure meds before coming in here? Any missed doses?"

"*No*!" Jake shouted. "You always fuckin' accuse me of not taking my fuckin' pills."

Stella never cared for Jake's foul mouth or the lack of respect which he showed her. She authoritatively replied, "Watch your mouth, Jake. Not taking your meds is the number one reason why you have breakthrough seizures. I had to ask about missed doses because I know you've missed them in the past. The chart said you were at a party when the seizures started. You hadn't missed even one dose?"

"Dude, it was an awesome party."

"Awesome or not, you need to make up each and every pill that you miss, remember? And what about cocaine?"

"I don't do that shit," Jake said defiantly.

"Well, there is a problem then, because your tox screen

showed cocaine in your system."

"Your frickin' test is frickin' wrong."

"Jake, the tests don't lie. I know you were exposed to cocaine." Stella had had the same cocaine conversation with Jake a year ago.

"It wasn't crack or heroin, only coke," Jake rationalized, while pulling the covers over his head.

"Not taking your medications and doing cocaine will bring on seizures. Having a seizure means no driving for six months. Your back pain may be from a fracture in your back caused by the seizure. No driving and back pain are two reasons for you to do everything you can to avoid having seizures."

Jake rolled on his left side, facing the wall, away from Stella. "I don't drive because of you. I can't work because of you."

"Jake, we've been over this before. No driving is a State of Michigan regulation because of your seizures. I've told you that you can get a job, but with some restrictions. My number one rule is to always make up missed doses. All right, then. The inpatient team will let you know about the MRI and give you pain pills. I'll see you tomorrow and in clinic by either myself or my research nurse in a couple of weeks."

"Can I get out today?" Jake asked.

"No, the inpatient team needs to make sure you don't have any more seizures before they let you go. And I want the MRI of your back."

"This place sucks."

"Don't miss taking your meds, don't do cocaine, and you won't have to be admitted."

Stella looked in EPIC and saw that a psychiatry resident rotating on the Neurology service was assigned to Jake. She texted the resident, who didn't reply immediately.

Noting that she was running behind, Stella walked swiftly toward the elevators. She made her way through the hospital and across Michigan Street to the Triumphant Heath Medical Group Clinic building. She walked into the fifth floor Neurology Clinic minutes before her first patient had checked in.

Stella finished her day fifteen minutes behind schedule. She loved patients and their families. Acknowledging that it was impossible, and strategically a faux pas to pick favorites, she enjoyed epilepsy and dementia patients the most. She was constantly amazed at how supportive the families were. She wondered if she would do the right thing when her parents started to decline. She couldn't imagine her older brothers stepping up.

Chapter 23

In the time of Talmud (2-5th century B.C.), Jews referred to a person with epilepsy as a "nikhpe," meaning "one who writhes."

After his last meeting of the day, he logged off from his desktop and opened his laptop. A private matter needed his undivided attention. Despite being proficient with computers, it took him nearly an hour to hack the Northeastern Florida-Jacksonville's system. He went to the Department of Clinical Research, then clicked on a link to Neurosciences.

He confirmed that Stephen Cohen's name was in every Northeastern Florida-Jacksonville SETTUP patient's record in EPIC, the electronic medical record. He hacked the Northeastern Florida-Jacksonville's email system and thirty minutes later, created a folder in Stephen Cohen's account titled "Private." He downloaded thousands of pictures, depicting every form of pornography, involving all genders, races, and ages, then included pictures of bestiality for good measure. The images were shockingly disgusting, which would repulse all but the most hardened sex offenders.

After signing out of Stephen's email account, he set up an account with PornHub. He altered the account to make it look as if StephenTheStud had established the PornHub account in 2010. Stephen's cell phone number and email addresses, personal and professional, were listed on the porn account. He uploaded photos from Stephen's Northeastern Florida-Jacksonville personnel file and FB account to the StephenTheStud's profile. He then opened a second file, titled "Private2", and downloaded several articles from various Neo Nazi groups located across the country.

Satisfied that he had created a sufficiently appalling background that would ruin the career of a promising researcher, he composed an email. The electronic letter was sent on Northeastern Florida-Jacksonville letterhead to a twenty-one-year-old SETTUP patient who was recently discharged from the hospital. The email was a reminder that the patient, as a volunteer in the Status Epilepticus TreatmenT UPdate Trial, needed to make a follow-up appointment with the Department of Neurology. Attached were a map of the Northeastern Florida-Jacksonville campus, directions to the Neurology Clinic, files of repulsive pornographic pictures, and Neo-Nazi literature hailing the coming of the Fourth Reich.

He then hacked the Northeastern Florida-Jacksonville Philanthropy Department and identified a benefactor. The gentleman, with his wife, had donated millions to the University, which were used to establish the Northeastern Florida Epilepsy Clinic. He logged onto Stephen Cohen's email account a second time and constructed a note which thanked the benefactor for his ongoing generosity and support. Files of pornography and articles promoting the eradication of Israel were attached.

Satisfied that Stephen Cohen would not be employed at Solutions & Synergy for more than a few hours, he clicked on the Send button. Other than the amount of time invested, it had been a good night. Definitely a win. He circled the office, and when he was satisfied that he was alone and not being observed, headed home for a late dinner.

The next day, the Dean of Research at Northeastern Florida-Jacksonville took phone calls from an upset benefactor and a Neurology patient. The Dean promptly called Abernathy.

"Dr. Abernathy, I can't tell you how upset I am right now. I just had a scathing call, my second of the day, regarding one of your employees. A Stephen Cohen."

"I'm not familiar with the young man," Abernathy said.

"That doesn't matter. What matters is that he's been sending pornography and Nazi information to patients and donors. What kind of a twisted mind does that? I don't have to tell you how many personal conduct policies he's violated."

"Pornography? That doesn't sound like any of my people. Are you sure about this?"

"Positive, I'll forward the emails so you can see for yourself. It goes without saying that he's done here, finished. He's not allowed on my campus. I can't believe this is happening," the Dean said.

"I understand completely. I'll have my HR team reach out to him and let him know that Solutions & Synergy is done with him as well," Abernathy said.

Chapter 24

Godfrey Hounsfield, an EMI researcher, invented the CT scan with profits earned from a more famous EMI client–The Beatles.

KFAP checked his bank account. The Swiss account was rising nicely. Time to think about retirement? No, he enjoyed getting paid for telling stories. Beats a poke in the eye with a sharp stick, according to his mother. Dear, sweet Mom was full of such simple nonsensical sayings. Rest in peace, Mom.

He had two email accounts, each through a different server. He used the primary address to communicate with his agent regarding all things related to his comedic career. A dark web account was reserved for his self-satisfying, not-so-funny career.

Finally, they want me in Montana. His agent arranged for gigs in Boston and Portland, Maine for the spring. That made sense, he'd killed every set the last time he was in Boston. Shout out to Tricia for providing me with the opportunity to "kill it" while in Boston. Love you. Come on, I told you it wasn't personal. It never was for KFAP.

Reading "Boston" reminded him that he hadn't fulfilled his latest contract. Site Monitor Randy Walker was still out there.

He read that Randy Walker worked at Rush Presbyterian but was employed by Solutions & Synergy. Interesting. KFAP wasn't aware that there were many contractors in medicine. This challenged his belief that nurses and doctors worked for hospitals. Strange new world. This foray into medicine has provided him with an opportunity to diversify, to expand his professional horizons. Randy, what you're hearing is a window opening. You know what that means, don't you? Don't let the door hit you on the way out. Ha. Contributing to the global nurse shortage has offered a nice, new income stream, don't ya think, Randy? KFAP drove to Chicago.

He reviewed the map of the Rush Medical Center and surrounding neighborhoods. He knew what his route would be, where he'd park, and where to best observe Randy Walker. He set his phone alarm for 5:05 A.M., his habitual palindromic wake up time, and went to bed. The faulty thermostat refused to warm the room. With no worries, nothing on his mind, and the blood in his veins as cool as the room, KFAP slept soundly.

At six-thirty the following evening, he drove to the Medical Center. Most of the street parking spots were filled by the time he arrived, but managed to find a parking spot three blocks south of the Rush employee entrance. The employee door was across the street from a construction site. One crane suspended a Christmas tree two hundred feet in the air; a second dangled a U.S. flag. KFAP watched Rush employees arrive and depart from campus on foot or via a van. Rush must have an off-site parking lot and ferry employees to the hospital. He needed to check out the off-site parking.

Randy Walker walked out of the employee parking lot onto S. Wood Street and jogged to catch up with a short woman, probably a nurse or nurse assistant, wearing navy scrubs. They appeared to know each other and engaged in a conversation that had them shaking their heads and laughing. Good to know Randy has a sense of humor, it may serve him well in the future. Yeah, he was sure Randy would need it.

Thank heavens for Chicago. What does the Chicago PD call fifty shootings and fourteen deaths? A slow weekend. The ugly reality of the rising crime rate meant no one would notice the mugging of a hospital contractor.

Most of the staff at Rush had emptied out and were on their way home by the time KFAP returned the following evening. The construction crew departed before five due to darkness. KFAP broke the street light in front of the construction trailer which offered him a little additional darkness. The broken light bulb and gray skies kept viewing limited, at best. It wasn't the middle-of-the-night black that he preferred, but he could work with it. Hadn't he been told to "improvise, adapt, overcome" a thousand times when he was stationed in the desert.

He sat in his car with the radio off, parked in the northwest corner of the construction site with a worn, yellow hard hat sitting in his lap. Looking at his rearview mirror, he saw Randy leave the Roberta and Barry Coen Research Building, cross S.

Wood Street, and make his way toward the employee parking lot, east of the construction site. KFAP put on the hard hat.

Before leaving the hotel, he removed the dome light from the car ceiling so Randy wouldn't notice the door opening. After Randy walked past the construction site, he silently slipped from his car holding a crowbar next to his right leg. He closed on Randy after a few strides. Randy, with his undivided attention focused on his phone, was unaware of his surroundings when the five-pound iron bar hammered his head. He dropped immediately. KFAP removed Randy's wallet from the right back pocket of his scrubs and picked his cell phone off the sidewalk. Randall S. Walker was lying silently still with his eyes closed. Randy wasn't complaining, not one bit, about how unsafe the streets of Chicago were. Shallow respirations caused a minuscule rise of his chest. Sticky blood matted his hair as a stream of blood flowed toward a growing pool surrounding his head.

KFAP picked up the crowbar and while walking toward his car, started singing "Bang, bang, KFAP's silver hammer came down upon his heeeaaad, do do do do." The silence of the night was broken by enthusiastic barking, which caused him to scan the street. His attention was attracted to a light near the exit of the Cohen research building, where he saw a lone figure dressed in scrubs fifty feet from Randy. KFAP could not make out the hospital employee's facial features, even with their face highlighted by the glow of a phone.

He kept his gloves on and set the crowbar on the floor in front of the passenger seat. He was sweating in twelve-degree weather. He heard no sirens and knew he'd made a safe escape. It had gone as expected. Yes, witnesses occasionally pop up and complicate life. No, he wasn't too worried about the hospital employee that stumbled on Randy. Studies show most witnesses were neither reliable nor accurate.

His assignment was to get Randy off the job. If he wakes up, he'll have the worst headache of his life and will, without a doubt, call in to work tomorrow. If he doesn't wake up, he'll need that sense of humor. Lighten up, buddy. You live in the big city where these things happen.

Randy was nearly stepped on by a radiology tech who had just left the Cohen Research building. The tech recognized the scrubs and ID badge as "one of ours" and called 9-1-1. Randy's head CT showed a skull fracture, subarachnoid blood, and a small subdural hematoma. The growing cerebral edema caused a two millimeter right to left intracerebral shift. Randy was admitted to the Neuro ICU where a fifth year Neurosurgery resident placed a ventriculostomy tube, which drained bloody spinal fluid from his swollen brain. None of the nurses or physicians recognized Randy, even though he had enrolled a Neuro ICU patient in SETTUP the week before.

The ED social worker found Randy's emergency contact, his mother, in the Employee Handbook and summoned her to the hospital. Randy's mother hesitated when she first entered Room 5, uncertain whether the person in the bed was her son. Randy was intubated, his eyes swollen shut. Bloody fluid drained into a small bag that the nurse secured to the side of his bed. EEG leads protruded from the gauze that mummified his head. Randy's mother questioned everyone wearing scrubs, some more than once, whether the brain damage was permanent.

***

KFAP spent the next fifty minutes on the Eisenhower expressway contemplating drop sites. The hat, gloves, phone, wallet, and crowbar needed disposal. He dropped the crowbar and phone at the bottom of the lake in Forest Hill Park. What, Randy, you're not into recycling? Think about all the starving kids in China who would love to have your phone. The hard hat was left in the trash can in the Men's Room at a Rapidway gas station and Convenience store. The gloves were deposited in the dumpster behind Bow Wow Meow Animal Hospital. He removed thirty-two dollars but left a credit card in Randy's wallet, which was dropped in a trash can that stood in front of Free Range, Illinois's largest shooting range. "Yes, Randy, I'm taking the cash. We agreed to split the gas, remember? No, I'm not taking your credit cards. What, do you think I'm a thief, now?"

KFAP reflected on the night during his drive home. Randy, I don't know how you missed it, the sign was right there for everyone to see. EVERYONE BEYOND THIS POINT MUST WEAR A HARD HAT. I had mine on. Live and learn, I guess. First thing tomorrow, I'm gonna swing by the obits to see if you're still with us. If you're not listed, can I use you as a reference?

Chapter 25

Hippocrates stated: "The releasing factors of seizures are cold, sun, and winds, which change the consistency of the brain."

Cole Smart walked into his office and booted up his desktop. He had worked at Solutions & Synergy for thirty-six years, while holding the title of VP of Human Resources for the last ten. He rose through the ranks due to his excellent work. He was efficient and effective at writing company Policies. He outlined the Roles and Responsibilities for every salaried position at Solutions & Synergy. He did his due diligence before deciding on the company's health care plan. He thoroughly vetted financial advisors before selecting the company who he thought had the best personnel. The CEO appreciated Cole's work and respected his ability to make difficult decisions.

The recent opening of several Site Monitor positions provided Cole with an opportunity to shine. Historically, it had been difficult, for many reasons, to replace one, let alone four, Site Monitors. There was the embarrassingly low salary, having to work with prima donna doctors, endless travel, and volumes of FDA-required paperwork.

He decided to buff the job description to make the position sound more exciting than it was, thus speeding up recruitment. A title. People loved having a title. He needed to come up with a strong one, the likes of which Site Monitor simply could not compete. Director of Clinical Research. Salary? You will be handsomely paid, as you are now a Director. He planned to conduct the interviews virtually as there was no reason to bring candidates to Indianapolis for face-to-face interviews.

He sipped his coffee and remembered that he had recently been sent a resume for someone with a research background. It took him a few minutes to find the email that was sent by Dr. Abernathy. After rereading it carefully, he noticed that it had not originated from Abernathy. The original email, and attached resume, was sent to Abernathy from someone outside the corporation. Abernathy forwarded the email to Cole and recommended that the candidate fill all of the open spots.

Reviewing Stephanie Van Huissen's resume, he noted she was from Chicago, which should help as she's probably heard of us. She obtained her nursing degree from Rosalind Franklin University of Medicine and Science more than a decade ago. Good, not a newbie. She'd worked in research at U of Chicago for a few years. Perfect. She had mostly been involved with Oncology trials, which shouldn't be an issue. Cancer, seizures—semantics.

He had gone to war with his CEO to get access to social media sites which were blocked for every other employee. Cole reasoned that he needed to view the webpages as a way of initiating background checks on prospective hires. It didn't take him long to find Stephanie on FB, TikTok, and Instagram. He liked what he saw.

He was able to compartmentalize his work and personal lives, which satisfied Solutions & Synergy's HR policy. His personal Dating Policy placed no restrictions on dating fellow S&S employees, as long as *she* could separate personal relationships from her professional life. First Impressions Matter. It was imperative that he make a good first impression with Stephanie. Carry the conversation, ask about her job, family, and career goals.

Cole spoke with her for ten minutes. She said all the right things, everything he wanted to hear, before agreeing to a face-to-face interview. After hanging up, he determined she deserved the works: a navy suit, silk tie, fresh haircut, Cole Haan shoes, followed by dinner at the hot, new restaurant called The Elements. He hoped that her status hadn't changed. According to FB, she was currently not in a relationship. He sent an email to his admin assistant.

> Barb,
> Please set up a sixty-minute interview with
> Stephanie Van Huissen with reservations
> at The Elements to follow.
> Cole Smart
> Vice President, Human Resources Solutions
> & Synergy.

Chapter 26

People with epilepsy were prohibited from marrying in seventeen states until 1956.

Most victims knew their killer. Intimate partners were always one through ten on Evans's list of suspects. Work peers were on the list, but in the lower half. With Tyler, Emily's current boyfriend, all but cleared and the old boyfriend, Max, remaining low on his list, Evans considered whether any of Emily's work peers should be investigated. And Stella. Damn you, Stella. He read about Solutions & Synergy.

Solutions & Synergy incorporated in 1984 and grew to become a multibillion-dollar company. The "Our History" section on their website described their humble beginnings when the owners, as graduate students, reviewed case studies regarding marketing strategies employed by Big Pharma. The students realized there was an opportunity to contract with Big Pharma to operationalize clinical trials.

Their marketing pitch was that Solutions & Synergy allowed Big Pharma to focus on drug development, while Solutions & Synergy conducted the FDA-required, multicenter clinical trials. Big Pharma realized cost savings by eliminating the growing legal and logistical nightmares associated with running clinical trials. A niche industry was created.

As Solutions & Synergy's reputation grew, they expanded from conducting multicenter pharmaceutical trials with large universities and healthcare systems, to working with Small Pharma and small businesses.

He found an email address and a phone number under the "Contact Us" tab on their website, which seemed to be the logical place to start.

He asked for the HR person in charge of SETTUP and was forwarded to Cole Smart, the VP of HR.

Evans began the conversation, "Mr. Smart, I'm Detective Evans from the Grand Rapids PD. I want to ask you about Emily Naismith."

"Hello, Detective. I have to stop you right there because I can't discuss employee personal information without a warrant," Cole said.

"This is an ongoing investigation, and I would certainly appreciate your cooperation." Evans hated it when people who were not involved in any criminal activity refused to cooperate without seeing a warrant. He pinched his pen tightly and doodled the outline of a traffic STOP sign.

Cole said, "Sorry, but I don't report to you. Our Policies are what they are, and they're clearly written. I can't give out employee contact or personal information."

"I understand, but this is a murder investigation," Evans said. He crossed out the doodle.

"Murder? I thought she died in her sleep."

"Where did you hear that?" He wondered how 'died in her sleep' entered the office rumor mill. He wrote sleep in his notes.

"I . . . I don't know," Cole stammered. "That's what's going around the office, I guess. I must have heard about her from an account manager. We have HR specialists who oversee each account or study, like SETTUP."

"Well, that's interesting, Mr. Smart, but you were misinformed. I'm afraid I can't go into any details with you as this is an ongoing investigation. Suffice it to say, with Emily being dead, there's no reason for her personnel records to remain private."

"That's not true. I wrote the Solutions & Synergy Employee Confidentiality Policy. I'm obliged to maintain confidentiality for seven years after an employee terminates their contract with us," Cole said.

"Look, I can get the warrant if you insist, but that'll take days, and I don't want to delay the investigation any longer than necessary. You want me to find who killed her, don't you?"

"Yes, of course I do."

Maybe the boss's tact will help. "Do you want me telling your supervisor how uncooperative you were?" Evans asked.

"Go ahead, that would be our CEO, and he's the one who approved the Policy, which I wrote, by the way."

"Unbelievable. How do you think being uncooperative with the police will go over with your investors? Huh? Look, I just need a quick peak in her personnel file. In and out. I haven't received this much pushback in a murder investigation in, forever," Evans said.

"I'm sorry, but as I said, rules are rules. Get me the warrant and her file's all yours."

Evans hung up. Who is this guy? Hiding something or just being an asshole. The one interesting thing that he took from his conversation with Cole Smart was that the word on the street at Solutions & Synergy was that Emily died in her sleep. Where'd they come up with that? Who was pushing the whole sleep narrative? With Dr. Abernathy up next, Evans read about the doctor online.

Dr. Abernathy was a fifty-seven-year-old Oncologist by training, who went to medical school at Boston University, where he matched to do an Internal Medicine Residency. He then went across town to Tufts University where he completed an Oncology Residency and Fellowship. He stayed on at Tufts as a junior faculty member before joining Solutions & Synergy thirteen years before. Nothing out of the ordinary about him on the internet.

Evans called Dr. Abernathy's office and spoke to his admin assistant. "Hello, this is Detective Evans from Grand Rapids Police Department. I believe I have a Zoom call scheduled with Dr. Abernathy later on today."

"Yes, you do, in . . . let me see here. It looks like your meeting is in about two hours."

"I unexpectedly have an opening in my schedule and wondered if he's available now? It won't take long, a minute or two, at most," Evans pleaded.

"He has a meeting in, let me see . . . fifty minutes. Let me see if he's free to speak with you."

"Thanks, I appreciate it." Evans waited for a couple of minutes before the admin assistant returned his call. Dr. Abernathy was available, and she rescheduled their Zoom meeting.

"Dr. Abernathy will call you at this number, Detective."

"Thanks, again," Evans said, hanging up. Two minutes later, his phone rang.

Evans said, "Dr. Abernathy, thank you for taking my call. I'm Detective Evans from Grand Rapids PD, and I need to talk to you about an employee of yours, Emily Naismith."

Roy Abernathy accepted the position of Chief Medical Office and Director of Clinical Research at Solutions & Synergy after leaving academia. The positives of the job were there. He was well compensated. He no longer took night or weekend call. He didn't have to deal with insurance companies and their insistence on obtaining prior authorization before he could prescribe name brand medications or order expensive imaging studies. He managed a large Department, almost the entire organization. He received excellent yearly performance reviews.

Despite feeling mentally and professionally prepared for the new career, doubts lingered. It was a leap to go from the fast pace of clinical work, research, and teaching to a desk job. The unconscious angst woke him around two-thirty every morning, which forced him to start his day earlier than when he was a practicing oncologist, and made for long days. The sedate office schedule made time stand still. He was bored in his new job, which led to depression, which manifested itself with anger.

When Abernathy first began working at Solutions & Synergy, he wasn't prepared to be hit in the face by a faceless enemy. Over many years, the culture at Solutions & Synergy had morphed into a business-like approach of "we do a lot of work, most of which is okay." Reports arrived on his desk days after deadlines had passed. Budgets were hard stops, not guidelines. Freedom of thought was discouraged. He missed patients, missed teaching, missed his Tufts colleagues.

Thirteen years ago, when superficial reports were handed in late, when people sauntered into meetings unprepared, when he was not allowed to implement progressive initiatives, he fought the culture. The infighting caused his temper to flare, regardless of who stood in front of him. He cemented a reputation of Danger! throughout Solutions & Synergy. People knew to stay off his lawn. Solutions & Synergy wore him down. Tired of the fighting, the arguing, of not being intellectually challenged, he began to toe the line. Boredom became omnipresent, depression deepened, and anger simmered.

Abernathy negotiated deals honestly and mentored subordinates. He never compromised his medical integrity. He carried a conscious bias and intentionally signed up to operationalize oncology drug trials. Focusing on GYN oncology studies was the right thing to do, because there was still no cure for the malignancy that had taken his mother. Studies came and went with little progress being made toward finding a cure for cancer. Bored by always doing the right thing, for the right reason, without seeing substantial results, he peeked behind the curtain hiding the road less traveled.

One day while reviewing his finances, Abernathy thought about generating a new revenue stream. He wondered whether someone might pay for the results of a successful, unpublished, clinical trial. The sale went smoothly, nobody blew a whistle after the information leak. Months later, a coding error in Solutions & Synergy's accounting program allowed him to determine his own end-of-year bonus. He looked right, left, right, and with no one peering over his shoulder, gave himself a sizable perk. No one at Solutions & Synergy discovered the error. He enjoyed spending time on the road less traveled. Boosting his income should have lessened the anger. It had not.

"Detective, I'm sorry that you contacted me without a warrant. I can't give you any information without it."

Evans was visibly frustrated by the overwhelming privacy concerns at Solutions & Synergy. He was thankful for the TV show *48 Hours* and tried a different approach. "I understand, but it's a murder investigation. I'm sure you're aware that the first forty-eight hours are crucial to solving homicide investigations."

"She died in her sleep. When did this become a homicide investigation?" Abernathy asked.

He noted Abernathy had a full head of gray hair and was a few pounds overweight. "I'm sure you understand that I can't go into the details of her case. Suffice to say, her death is suspicious, and it's being considered a homicide at this point. Tell me about

Emily."

"She was nice. She showed up, did her job. I don't know what else I can tell you," Abernathy said.

"Was she a good employee?" Evans asked.

"As I said, she did her job."

"Well, would you say she was an adequate employee, a good employee, or a great employee?"

Abernathy replied, "She worked here. Look, she was fine, she did her job. I'm not sure where you're going with this."

"I'm just trying to get to know Emily. No hidden agenda here, Doctor. Did she have any performance issues?"

"Not that I'm aware of."

"And you'd know because you were her supervisor, correct?" Evans asked.

"Yeah, she reported to me. She was a . . . good employee," Abernathy faltered. He stared and reached for something on the right side of his desk.

"Any concerns about drugs or alcohol use?"

"No, none. She had to have passed a drug screen before she was hired on here."

"Would you consider Emily's job to be stressful?"

"I don't know, maybe a little, I guess," Abernathy replied. He studied the document.

"I'm asking because maybe Emily was clean before joining you, then turned to drugs or alcohol under the stress of the job. Did you have any concerns that she started using drugs or alcohol after joining you?" Evans asked.

Putting the paper down, Abernathy said, "None. She didn't abuse drugs. Is this going to take much longer, Detective? I have a meeting in a couple of minutes."

Abernathy had at least forty-five minutes before his meeting. "No, not much longer. Any behavioral issues?"

"No, no behavioral issues since she started."

"Was she depressed?"

Abernathy saw an opening. A smirk developed as he said, "I wasn't going to say anything, but since you brought it up, yes. I think she may have been depressed. I think you're right. Maybe she was depressed and that's why she killed herself."

Evans was startled by the turn the conversation had just taken. "Suicide. Do you think she could have committed suicide?"

"Of course she could have. Even *I* know that you don't have to be majorly depressed to commit suicide, and I'm not a psychiatrist," Abernathy said.

"This is helpful, very helpful indeed. Hmmm. Suicide. Tell me about this SETTUP trial thing."

"It's a multicenter seizure trial. It's a comparative study, so we don't know if the drug is working."

"Did Emily have any issues with the trial?"

"Issues? I have no idea what you mean by that."

Evans asked, "Well, like side effects or patients reacting to the drug. Or maybe the drug wasn't working well, that sort of thing. Could she have seen any of those things?"

"Emily did her job when she documented adverse events which occurred during the trial. As I said, we don't know whether the investigational drug is working or not."

"Had she reported unusual side effects or, you know, a lot of them?"

"Detective, SAEs of any ongoing clinical trial are strictly confidential, and I certainly cannot get into any details surrounding the study with you or anyone else, probably not even with a warrant."

"What are SAEs?"

"Serious adverse events," Abernathy said.

"That helps, thanks. Do you know of anyone who would want to hurt Emily?"

"No, certainly no one here at Solutions & Synergy."

"Do you know anyone who would want to stop the SETTUP trial?" Evans asked.

"No one would ever want to terminate a successful clinical trial. There are many, many seizure patients who stand to benefit from the drug that's being tested. A lot of good comes from our research. We're not ending it. We're ramping up interviews for Emily's position as we speak and hope to replace her soon," Abernathy said.

"Will Cole Smart do the hiring?" Evans asked, noting that Abernathy first claimed to not know how the study was going before describing it as a successful clinical trial.

Abernathy said, "I don't know who hires the Site Monitors, I'm not in charge of HR. Any more questions, Detective? I'm extremely busy today," he said, gesturing with both hands.

Evans changed his line of questioning. "You were an Oncologist before joining Solutions & Synergy, correct?"

"Am. I still am an oncologist, I've maintained my license."

"A neurologist that I know told me that oncologists prescribe narcotics and opioids fairly often," Evans probed.

"Not nearly as often as neurologists, I imagine. But yes, I used to prescribe narcotics. Detective, you have no clue how painful mets to the bones are," Abernathy said, raising his voice.

"Mets?"

"Metastatic disease, spread of cancer throughout the body."

"You're right about that. I can't imagine how painful that must be. Knock on wood, I've been healthy my whole life. Because you still have a medical license, that means you can still write a prescription for fentanyl, correct?"

"Yes, I can, but I haven't."

Evans said, "Did you ever give Emily a prescription for fentanyl?"

"That's absurd. She wasn't my patient. Are you saying she committed suicide by overdosing on fentanyl?"

"I don't think I said that, and I'm not going to say anything like that because it's an ongoing investigation."

"Well, what can you tell me about her passing?"

"Passing? Do you think Emily passed you on the highway? Do you think she passed you in the hallway? She was murdered. Murdered in cold blood. I wouldn't call her murder a passing. Not at all," Evans said curtly.

"Passing is commonly used vernacular for death in health care, Detective. I meant no harm or insult by it."

"Apology accepted. Thank you for your time. I'll talk to you later," Evans said, abruptly signing off the video call.

Evans sat back in his chair. Damn it. Forgot to ask about the incident. Next time. There would be a next time. He wondered whether the incident between Emily and Abernathy involved sex. Maybe Emily spurned Abernathy's come on. Men do not tolerate rejection well; it may have provided him with a motive for doing something stupid.

Stella told Evans that the people behind SETTUP stood to benefit financially from a successful outcome, like a five or six figure benefit. That's not chump change. People were killed for a lot less money than that. Evans moved Abernathy to the top of his suspect list.

Evans made a note to get a warrant for Emily's Solutions & Synergy personnel file. He called Forensics, "Hey Spence, will you check on something for me?"

Chapter 27

Jean Fernel (1497-1558) speculated that seizures were caused by poisonous vapors affecting the brain.

Stella looked at Kenny's MRI, twice. He had a stroke in his left brain. Smoking was his only stroke risk factor. If cigarettes had caused the stroke, she expected to see more changes consistent with small blood vessel disease on the MRI.

Jake's spinal MRI showed an acute compression fracture of the T7 vertebral body. Oh man, those hurt. Jake wasn't kidding when he said he was in pain. Stella wondered if he would be scared from using cocaine when she suggested the fracture was related to cocaine use.

Stella left the Physicians Work Room and went directly to Kenny's room, asking, "Kenny, how're you doing today? Any seizures last night?"

"Nah. I'm doin' good, Dr. Murray."

"How's your speech and arm?" Stella noted that Kenny's speech had improved, less slurred.

"Just fine. My old lady says my talkin's good. My face don't feel swollen anymore," he said, with the left half of his face displaying emotion.

"I agree with her, your speech sounds better today. Your face still looks a little flat on the right. How are you doing with the experimental medication, any reactions to it?"

"Nah, I'm doin' good, Doc. Am I going home today?"

"I looked at your MRI, it shows you had a stroke in your left brain."

"The MIR showed a big stroke? Did it show seizures, too?" Kenny asked.

"No, it doesn't show seizures, but it does show you had a small stroke in the left brain, which is why your right face is droopy, your right arm and leg are weak, and your speech is off. You need to quit smoking because that's probably what caused the stroke. Smoking causes the arteries to narrow and, once an artery closes off completely, that's when you have a stroke."

"Doc, I told you I'm gonna try to quit, but I don't know if I can."

"At least you're willing to try. The inpatient team has you on Keppra, Vimpat, and the new one. No driving for six months, and either my research nurse or I will see you in the clinic in about four weeks."

"Are you gonna make me touch my nose, put the vibrator on my toe, scratch the hell out of my feet, and watch me walk?"

Stella smiled. "No, I'm going to let the inpatient team do all of that."

She found the Neurology resident assigned to Kenny and said, "You were correct. Kenny had a lacune, possibly from small vessel disease. Say, do we have a meeting scheduled for next week?"

"Yes, a mentoring session Wednesday afternoon."

"Good. I want to talk to you about work-life balance." Stella had been approached by two faculty members with concerns that the resident was falling behind with her reading. The resident's boyfriend was the problem. He insisted that she spend less time looking at journal articles and more time catering to his needs.

She walked to Jake's room, the last room on the east wing. "Jake, Jake. Wake up. It's Dr. Murray. Have you had any more seizures?"

Receiving no reply, Stella shook Jakes shoulder a little harder, turned on the overhead lights, and pulled a blanket off the patient. "Jake, have you had any more seizures?"

"Did you know they got me out of bed at two frickin' A.M. for that effing MRI?" Jake said with his eyes closed.

"Jake, open your eyes, I need to tell you about the results. You've got a fracture in your spine. I'm not sure why your left leg was numb, the fracture isn't affecting your spinal cord. You'll need pain pills when you go home. You may be a candidate for a procedure where they inject a glue-like material into the fractured bone, which strengthens it and relieves your pain.

"Oh, and Jake, inhaling cocaine is nasty and may have caused your seizure and spinal fracture. You need to stop doing cocaine so that you don't have more seizures or a big stroke, which is the last thing you need right now."

"That's so random. You sound like my parents. My buddy's been doing coke for years and never had a stroke. What about him? Huh?"

"Jake, this is serious. I don't want you to stroke out. The inpatient team will have you talk to an IR specialist to see if you're a candidate for the vertebroplasty procedure that I just mentioned. It's where they inject the cement-like material to strengthen the fractured bone. They have you on Keppra and the new medication. I want you to stay on both meds until I see you in the clinic in a month or so."

Jake slammed his fists on the bed, yelling, "No more effing shots. When am I gonna get my pain pills?"

Stella said, "As soon as the nurses can give them, you'll get them. Jake, I hope you're treating your nurses better than you treat me. They do a great job, even though they're understaffed and overworked. Please do whatever they say. If you don't have any other questions, I'll see you later."

Stella noted that the psychiatry resident documented in EPIC that a migraine caused Jake's leg numbness, and included warning stroke, damage to the spinal cord, and a pinched nerve in the differential diagnosis. Warning stroke? The resident hadn't even ordered a brain MRI to look for it.

Stella hurried to the elevator. She crossed Michigan Street wondering how one, and possibly a second, epilepsy patient had suffered a stroke.

Chapter 28

The Fourth Amendment of the U.S. Constitution offers protection against unlawful government searches and seizures, and is the basis for obtaining a search warrant prior to searches.

Something was off with Abernathy, and it didn't appear to be as simple as haters gonna hate. He was hiding something. Evans prepared warrants to search his financial records, computers, email accounts, and cell phone. Probable cause was shaky at best. He had nothing other than a hunch, unconnected dots, which never played well with judges. Play the game, get the warrant. Evans had obtained a warrant with less evidence of wrongdoing and suspected he'd be successful again.

A crime had been committed, Emily was dead. Motive? Money, lots and lots of money. Means? Abernathy was wealthy and could afford to hire a killer if he didn't have the balls to do it himself. He was a physician who knew the exact dose of opioids required to kill a 123-pound Site Monitor. As a licensed physician, he could easily procure enough opioids to kill someone. Opportunity? Abernathy could have traveled to Grand Rapids under the guise of monitoring the trial and killed Emily.

Probability that Abernathy was dirty? Evans put it barely above fifty-fifty. He was so damn arrogant, Evans hoped to embarrass him by serving the warrant while he was at work. Evans wished he was as good a wordsmith as his wife. She worked in marketing and was an excellent writer who, when she put pen to paper, could sell a timeshare to a death row inmate.

Evans planned to write the warrants then drop them off at the Prosecutor's Office after it opened. The Prosecutor would edit them, but the majority of work would already be done. After revisions, he'd submit them to the judge that afternoon. He opened his laptop, printed, then filled out form MC231: Instructions for Preparing Affidavit and Search Warrant. It took him twenty minutes to write the first one.

Evans wanted to know more about the seizure drug that Emily was involved with and the people that made it. And Max.

What to do about the old boyfriend, Mad Max. Although Max didn't have a clearly stated motive, he had the means and opportunity to kill Emily.

Chapter 29

It is likely that no medieval doctors read On the Sacred Disease from the Hippocratic collection of medical writings as no translation in their language has been found.

Stella told Evans that SGY Bioengineering made the drug that was being evaluated in the SETTUP trial. He walked along a shoveled, brick walkway that led him to 5556 37th Avenue. He took one step up to enter the one-story, deep but not wide, elongated, brick building with no windows in front and only a few in the back. SGY Bioengineering was displayed on the façade. There were no holiday decorations on the exterior of the building.

Evans looked around the eight-by-ten-foot foyer, which was certainly different. The walls were covered with navy and dark green checkered wallpaper. On each wall hung a framed black and white scenery photograph. Navy upholstered side chairs were pushed against each wall. The room was decorated with four signs, one on each wall. He noted a pattern of four. He pushed the button and heard a bell ring behind the door.

The door opened and he was greeted by a twentyish young man with long, greasy brown hair wearing a white lab coat with SGY Bioengineering embroidered on the left chest.

Evans introduced himself. "I'm Detective Evans, and I have an appointment with Dr. Williams and the others."

"Oh, okay, come on in," the Gen Z said, motioning for Evans to follow him through the door. The lab assistant led Evans into a completely different environment. The floors were sterile, white linoleum. The walls and ceiling were painted off white. Bright fluorescent lights were directed upward. Without counting, Evans estimated there were fifteen people working, each wearing a white lab coat with a blue SGY Bioengineering logo stitched on their coats. The exterior of the building gave no clue as to what went on inside. The young lab assistant walked through a center aisle, then turned right, and approached, Evans guessed, Dr. Williams.

"Hey, Dr. W., there's a policeman by the name of Tom Evans to see you."

"Close enough. Dr. Williams, I'm Detective Evans," he said, offering his hand.

Scott stood six feet three inches and replied with a surprisingly high voice, "I'm Scott. We're going this way." He began walking without making eye contact or returning the handshake. Scott was an avocado-shaped forty-two-year-old scientist with thick-lensed tortoise-shell glasses. He wore a Grateful Dead tee shirt under his lab coat, which had his name sewn on the upper right chest. He led Evans through the main lab and out a door.

The corridor took them past four offices to a conference room. The room was large enough to accommodate three wood-laminated tables: two circular, one elliptical. Inexpensive, steel and blue plastic chairs circled each piece of furniture. A coffee maker and microwave sat on a counter, next to a refrigerator. Scott unbuttoned his coat before sitting. After his divorce, he shaved his scalp and allowed his weight to balloon. He rubbed his pate, expecting to feel a full head of hair. "Have you met my partners, Gwen and Yi?" Gwen and Yi sat on opposing sides of the table, knowing Scott had a preferred chair at the end.

"I've not had the pleasure. Detective Evans," he said, looking at Gwen, then Yi.

Gwen spoke up, "I'm Gwen Hopkins, and this is Yi Zhang. Pleased to meet you."

Scott said, "Well, Detective, what's the purpose of this meeting?"

Evans sat at the end of the table opposite Scott. "I'm investigating the murder of Emily Naismith. She worked on a clinical trial that's looking at your drug."

"Ah, okay. You want to talk about SGY140008-12," Scott said.

"I guess. But specifically, Emily Naismith, who worked on a seizure trial. Is that SGY1400 thing that you mentioned a drug for seizures?"

"Yeah, SGY140008-12 is our latest creation that's going through a clinical trial for status epilepticus," Scott said.

"Do any of you know Emily?"

Scott leaned back in his chair and sighed, "Can't say that I do."

Gwen leaned forward, wondering why he was asking about Emily and not the study drug.

Scott asked, "What was her involvement in the trial?" He looked distant, or vacant. Maybe it was sadness. His face looked hollow, his eyes blank.

"Emily was a nurse who worked as a Site Monitor in Grand Rapids."

"No, I don't know her. I'm not involved in the clinical side of things. I'm a scientist. I create drugs which are then tested in clinical trials," Scott said.

Gwen spoke up, "Because we all worked on SGY140008-12, we're familiar with it . . . the drug, that is. But I personally don't know anything about the trial or trial personnel. Yi, do you know anyone working on the trial?"

Yi replied with a soft voice, "I do not know any study personnel."

Scott's use of "I create drugs" was an odd choice of words. Evans came up with formulating, pioneering, and biosynthesizing before creating. "You said that you create products. How do you make a drug?"

"Better life through chemistry," Scott said in a monotone voice.

Gwen said, "It's a little more complicated than that. It took us years to get the drug to where it was safe for human exposure."

"Fair enough. Do you make things other than medications?" Evans started looking at the scientists differently. Smart, but if they're creating drugs, that's a whole new ballgame. As soon as that thought appeared, his admiration of the scientists vanished. He was here to determine if one or all of them had anything to do with Emily's death.

"Yeah, no, just medications. I worked in drug development at Fitzer for a number of years before I got tired of working for The Man. I took Gwen and Yi from Palladium, and we formed Scott,

Gwen, Yi, or SGY Bioengineering. Much happier working for myself than the money grubbers at Fitzer. I like working with Gwen and Yi. We're good at what we do. I have more than twenty-five patents." It was twenty-six, but Scott decided that saying "more than twenty-five" was more impressive than a number.

He continued, "I've always been in drug development, but when Fitzer shifted me in a direction where I didn't want to go, I left. Being a detective, I'm sure you know all about working for The Man and being told to do something which doesn't align with your moral compass. Their focus was solely on making money, and not necessarily for the good of mankind. I'm happy. I have a roof over my head. I'm pursuing things which I find interesting."

"Yeah," Evans chuckled, shifting in his seat. "I do know what it means to work for The Man. So, only medications for seizures?"

Gwen spoke up, "Oh no, not at all. We cover a broad spectrum of disorders. Yes, mostly involving the CNS, based on our background. Scott has always been interested in immunology and I've worked in nanotechnology for several years. I'm so glad he was able to poach Yi, with her BBB expertise, from Palladium Pharmaceutical. Are you familiar with nanotechnology or the BBB?"

Evans said, "I don't think we're speaking the same language right now. It's fair to assume that I know nothing about nanotechnology, seaness, or bees."

Scott said, "CNS stands for central nervous system, which is the brain and spinal cord lumped together. BBB stands for the blood-brain barrier, which represents a major obstacle for the delivery of drugs into the CNS. You see, the BBB selectively allows tiny, small individual molecules to pass through to the brain while limiting the passage of larger pathogens and toxins.

"Unlike other organs in the body, more than ninety-eight percent of small molecules, and nearly one hundred percent of large therapeutic drugs, can't reach the brain because of the BBB. Our search for a novel approach to get molecules to cross the BBB led us to nanoparticle-mediated drug delivery, a process which we've nearly perfected. Getting pharmaceuticals into the

CNS has led to the development of precision therapies for a number of brain disorders. We've carved out a nice, not so little, niche with our expertise, which as I said, has led to several patents."

"Thank you for all of that, of which I understood only a few words. Have you guys heard how the trial is going?"

Scott said, "We heard it's going well, so well, that they asked us for money." He never took his eyes off Evans.

Gwen spoke next, "That's not exactly true. We were told the trial was *not* going well, which led them to ask us for money."

Evans leaned forward. "They asked you for money? Who asked you for money? Is that normal?"

Scott said, "Solutions & Synergy did the asking. Yes, it's unusual for them to ask for it. And Gwen's right, Albert told us they needed it to complete the trial. He said that if the study ended up being successful, it would mean more money for us. So, we agreed to give them a loan."

"Who's Albert?" Evans asked, looking at Scott, then the others.

Scott gestured with a hitch-hiking motion over his shoulder. "Albert Brasston, our CFO. We walked past his office. Albert and our attorney negotiated a sweetheart deal with a venture capital group for this patented ligand that we made. It's a molecule which binds to certain receptors in the brain, so that when it's given during a PET scan to a patient who has just had a seizure, it highlights the active receptors, thereby telling physicians which network of neurons was involved at the onset of the seizure.

"This venture capital group wanted to buy us, all for that one contrast agent. You know what I think of The Man, no way I was going to sell out to them. We negotiated with this group so that they'd give us enough money to bring the contrast product to the market for a small percentage of its sales."

"When we're through I'd like to talk to your CFO. Who's your contact at Solutions & Synergy?" Evans asked.

Scott said, "No idea, that's Albert's bailiwick. Albert's as nutty as a BabyRuth, but I love him. He's invested well for us over the years and helped our attorney negotiate several contracts."

Gwen spoke up, "Not everyone loves him as much as you do, Scott.

Evans sat back, made notes, and asked, "How about a Dr. Abernathy? Do any of you know Dr. Abernathy? He works over there."

Scott said, "I don't. You guys? Albert probably does, he handles all that administrative stuff while we crank out therapeutics."

Gwen said, "I don't know him personally, but I believe he's the Medical Director for SETTUP."

Yi spoke up, "I do not know Dr. Abernathy."

"What about side effects during the study? I heard there were stroke side effects associated with SGY400000," Evans said.

Gwen interjected, "It's curious that you ask that. Yi received an email from a neurologist working on the trial, telling us about a stroke that one of her patients had. She wanted to know if we'd seen stroke in our preclinical work."

Scott said, "Gwen's right, we were contacted by somebody from Triumphant Health wanting to know if we'd ever seen stroke. Yi correctly replied that we hadn't seen anything like that. I can confirm that we saw no strokes during our preclinical work, Phase I, or Phase II studies. Our drug does not cause stroke. Period. End of story. Anyway, Albert never said anything about stroke. He just said they needed money."

"What are Phase I and Phase II studies?"

"Phase I trials are open label, everyone gets the experimental drug, no placebo is used. They start with a small number of patient volunteers focusing on pharmacokinetics. Basically, seeing how the body reacts to the drug. Is the drug broken down in the liver, or is it removed from the body in the gut or kidneys. If there are no red flags during Phase I, then you move on to Phase II studies, which are also open label."

Scott placed his hands on the desk. Apparently, talking about drugs excited him and caused him to raise his already high-pitched voice further, nearly to the point of yelling. "In Phase II they start with maybe a hundred patient volunteers receiving the drug and look at tolerability, adverse events, and an effective dose. They always start with a low dose, then increase it based on efficacy and tolerability. If all goes well with Phase II, then you move to Phase III trials, which involve a large number of patients to see if the drug can withstand the test of numbers, thousands of patients, and to confirm you have the right therapeutic dose.

"Basically, we need to prove our drug's results are statistically significant and better than the standard of care, which is everything already on the market that's used to treat whatever disease or disorder. During Phase III trials, the study drug might be compared to placebo, standard of care, or added to standard of care." He sat back and rubbed his scalp with both hands, seemingly satisfied with the lengthy explanation.

Evans marveled at the path that medicines followed to get to pharmacy shelves. He asked, "How much does all of that cost? It must take a pretty penny to get something new on the market."

Gwen answered, "Hundreds of millions of dollars, often topping out at a billion. But remember, if one of these drugs hits it big, the initial investment will be recovered, and then some, often in the first year or two that the drug is on the market. There are meds which have yearly sales in the billions. That's billions with a capital B. We hope that's where SGY140008-12, which we are *not* convinced causes stroke, takes us. But we'll see where it ends up."

Evans found himself liking the scientists more and more. All straight shooters. All a little different. "So, if your thing hits it big, how much money are you guys looking at? In general, no specifics—six, seven, eight figures?"

"We won't know that until the trial ends and we see how successful the drug is at stopping status epilepticus. Oh, and assuming no more strokes are reported," Scott said.

Evans stared at his notes and crossed off Solutions & Synergy, Emily, Abernathy, and side effects. "You've confirmed a few things, including the massive amounts of money involved in pharmaceuticals, drugs, or whatever, and medicine in general. Thank you for taking time with me today. How about if I have a chat with your numbers guy."

Gwen spoke up, "Thank you for talking to us, Detective. Do

you know who killed the researcher?"

Evans said, "I'm afraid not yet, but I'm working on it."

Scott stood and walking toward the door said, "Follow me." He knocked on the door frame of the CFO's office saying, "Albert, will you talk to the Detective. Thanks." He stepped aside, allowing Evans to enter.

Remaining seated, Albert looked up at Evans and asked, "You're a Detective?"

Evans offered his hand while responding, "Yes, I am. Detective Evans with GRPD." Albert reciprocated with a limp, childlike grip.

"Thank you for taking the time with me. How'd you get hooked up with the SGY Bioengineering?" Evans asked. He wasn't offered a seat, so he dragged a chair in front of Albert's desk.

Albert sat back in his chair and pulled his cell phone out of the left breast pocket of his shiny, sable blazer. The sheen indicated the coat was made of silk. Evans already didn't like the CFO because of his teenager handshake, shiny coat, and cell phone, which appeared to be glued to his hand.

"I've worked in finance my whole life. Several years ago, I was looking for a change, a new challenge, you know. They were looking for a finance person and found me through a headhunter." Albert swiped his phone and entered a passcode using his thumbs. He appeared to be reading text messages or emails.

Start with generalities. "How's it worked out? That's pretty heavy stuff. They tried explaining their work, which I didn't understand at all. They lost me at nano."

"Of course you didn't understand, you're not a scientist. Anyway, I focus on the finances."

Evans wondered why he bothered acting like the good cop. He was no good at playing the good cop. Now, Smitty, his former partner, he was the perfect good cop. He asked, "What was the deal that you negotiated for that PET scan stuff?"

"I wasn't involved in the negotiations. We have an attorney for that," Albert said, staring at his phone.

Evans's smile turned into a frown. What's up with this

pretentious asshole? Come on, all he does is invest someone else's money and watch his 401K grow. First question and he's blowing smoke up my ass. He's either hiding something or being a dickwad. He intended to find out which one. "You weren't involved with the negotiations surrounding that PET scan stuff?"

Albert typed something on his phone, saying, "What difference does it make who negotiated the deal. There was a good outcome for all parties involved. Our guys did very well at the end of the day. I helped our attorney negotiate a small slice of the pie for the engineers. You know, a bite of the apple."

Evans asked, "Who asked SGY Bioengineering for money?"

Albert stopped working on his phone and looked at Evans for the first time. "Well, it's . . . it's ah, complicated. You have no idea how much money it takes to run a clinical trial."

"You're right, I don't know how much it costs. Care to enlighten me?"

"Hundreds of millions of dollars, far more than the budget of GRPD Major Cases Division," Albert said.

Well, fuck me, the asshole searched me on the net. "Millions. Wow, I had no idea it took that much. Why did they ask you for money?" Evans asked, repeating his question.

"You don't know how these things work, do you? They ask everyone for money. Remember, it's hundreds of millions, up to a billion dollars."

"You said the engineers stand to earn a nice paycheck if the drug does well, once it's on the market. What about you?"

"I'm a salaried employee, and my paycheck is none of your business. Any more questions, Detective?"

Evans asked. "How did you know Emily? Was it through her work?"

"I don't know who you're talking about. I don't know any Emily's." He bounced his leg.

Evans asked, "You sure you didn't know Emily? She was murdered while working on the SETTUP trial."

"Like I said, I'm positive I don't know her," Albert said, his eyes glued to his phone.

"Where were you on January 8?"

"Not sure. Here or there." His leg bounced faster.

Evans wasn't going to let him off that easily and said, "Can you be a little more specific?"

"Not really. I don't know, around, I guess." The knee bouncing slowed.

"Who do you communicate with at Solutions & Synergy?"

That got his attention. Albert put his phone in his pocket and said tersely, "That's privileged information. We all signed an NDA before SETTUP, and I can't divulge that information to you or anyone."

"Why all the secrecy, Albert? The scientists had no issues answering my questions. They obviously have nothing to hide. I've often wondered why people don't answer my questions, or better yet, answer my questions with another question, which you've done repeatedly. What are you hiding?" Evans asked, staring at the CFO.

"It's nothing like that. Unlike the scientists, I'm familiar with the law and know the details of the NDA. I've got nothing to hide. Now, if you'll excuse me, I have to take a conference call," Albert said, standing.

"I don't need permission to ask you again, where you were on Sunday?"

Albert grabbed the office door brass handle, turned, and said, "No, you don't." Evans heard Albert walk down the hall and close the door to a restroom.

What an asshole. Evans noticed that Albert hadn't answered his questions. A salaried employee could still receive a bonus. He wouldn't say where he was on January 8, the day of Emily's murder.

Evans needed to check with Abernathy to find out whether Solutions & Synergy asked SGY Bioengineering for financial support. If so, why had they asked for money. The look on the scientists' faces when he mentioned that their drug may cause a stroke was interesting. They're obviously aware of how much money they stand to make if their drug doesn't cause serious side effects. If no more strokes were reported, they could rush their drug to the market and start earning millions. Evans needed to check financial records for SGY Bioengineering, Albert, and each one of the bioengineers. There's a lot of money floating around this SETTUP thing, certainly enough to kill Emily over.

Based on today's interviews, Albert had inserted himself into the conversation. Could Emily have been involved with him, then called it off when she realized that he's a complete douche? Probably not, Emily's parents never mentioned Albert. Nevertheless, Alberto, the whole evasiveness is not a good look for you. Move over Abernathy, you've got company at the top of my list.

Chapter 30

"Gossip is the opiate of the oppressed."
—Erica Jong

Stephanie was excited walking into Solutions & Synergy Headquarters. It was a beautiful, but cool, sunny day in Indianapolis. A new day, a new start. She exited the elevator on the sixth floor to find a friendly face sitting behind a desk.

"Hi there, how may I help you?"

"I'm Stephanie Van Huissen. Today's my first day and I was told to report to HR to fill out some paperwork."

The receptionist picked up a bulky manila folder and, walking around the desk, greeted her, "Welcome, I've been waiting for you. Come on, we're going this way. Can I get you anything? Water? Juice?"

"No, thanks."

The receptionist pushed open the door to a windowless office, saying, "Here we are. I've reserved it for the next two hours, but I'll get you out of here well before that." Six chairs surrounded a rectangular table. Two boxes, each containing a Lenovo ThinkPad, were stacked on the table. "Go ahead and take a seat, and we'll get you set up."

Stephanie sat at the head of the table, where the computer boxes were situated. The receptionist placed the manila folder in front of Stephanie and sat next to her.

"Here's the book of company Policies. Read it carefully, cover to cover, you don't want to miss anything. I'm kidding. As far as I know, no one has ever read it," she giggled. "Then, I need you to sign these forms. How much you want to put in your IRA, how to fill out your time sheet, how to submit your expenses, that sort of thing."

It took Stephanie an hour to sign and initial the forms which were required of every new hire.

"IS is next on your itinerary. They'll meet you here to set up your laptop and email, things like that. They can sync your email with your phone if you'd like. Sure I can't get you anything?

Water?"

"No, thanks. You've been tremendous. I wouldn't have known how to complete everything without your help."

"Of course. Now, it's a matter of hurry up and wait. Why don't you stop by my desk after you're done with IS."

"Will do," Stephanie said. It was a minute before there was a knock at the door.

"Hi, there. Does someone need an email set up?" a thirty-year-old said, entering the room. His navy striped, button-down shirt was untucked. His hair was nearly completely shaved on the left side of his head and his remaining jelled hair was combed to the right. He wore opaque glasses and black jeans.

"I certainly do and hope you can help me out."

"I can try. I'm Nate by the way. I was told to be here for a new hire, but they never told me your name."

"Pleased to meet you, Nate. I'm Stephanie."

He set up her email, and synched her phone with the email account.

"You'll need to change your password every three months," Nate said sheepishly. "S&S is careful with their data."

"I can do that. Say Nate, will you do me a favor? I'm a new Director of Clinical Research and was hired to take over for Emily Naismith. I'd like to see her emails. Can you get me in . . . to her account?"

"Emily? You're taking over for Emily? No way. That totally creeps me out."

Raising her eyebrows and cocking her head, Stephanie asked, "What do you mean 'creeps you out'? I was told she moved on to a different position."

"Different position? Are you crazy? She was murdered. I heard she was shot, like, fourteen times."

"Seriously? Now you're creeping me out. Is this for real? She was shot dead?"

"It's true. She was murdered in Grand Rapids. They haven't caught the guy yet. You'd never catch me doing her job," Nate said, shaking his head.

"That's bullcrap. The head of HR told me she moved to a

different position."

"Consider the source. Nobody talks to HR," Nate said, picking up the empty Lenovo box.

"Was she murdered because of her work? You're seriously upsetting me," Stephanie said.

"This, I do not know," Nate said, standing. "Emily was in research, so probably not. I thought she just filled out a lot of paperwork. I can't let you see her emails by the way, according to Dr. Abernathy."

Stephanie perked up. "Do you know Dr. Abernathy? He's my supervisor. But, he's the one who said you can't see her emails? Maybe I should ask him what happened to her."

"Yeah, he sent out a memo stating that no one can access her stuff," Nate said, putting the packaging and the empty box in the plastic trash can.

Stephanie said, "Well, that's odd. I think that's odd. Don't you think that's odd?"

"I don't know, Stephanie. You're talkin', like, way above my level. And yes, everyone around here knows Dr. Abernathy. He kind of stands out when he tells you that he's the smartest guy in the organization."

"Nate, you've been soooooo helpful. First, for getting my email set up, then for telling me about Emily. I hope I see you around," Stephanie said.

Grinning, Nate said, "That's what I do. Well, I'm off to the C-suite. I'll tell you what, other than Dr. Abernathy, the rest of those guys up there are, like, so lame. They can't do anything on a computer. But, hey, at least they keep me employed. Later, Stephanie Marie Van Huissen."

"Bye, Nate. Thanks, again," Stephanie said, gathering her paperwork, phone, and laptop. She left the office and walked to the receptionist's desk. "Nate, the IT guy, just told me that Emily was murdered. Did you know this? Am I the only one who didn't know about her?"

"Yes, poor Emily. Such a sweet thing. An email went out telling us about her death. They offered counseling, but I don't know anyone who's done it. I heard she was raped and strangled, but they haven't caught the guy yet."

"Raped? Nate said she was shot. How sure are you that she was raped, because Nate said she was shot. He never said anything about rape or strangulation."

"I'm sure it's true. I heard it from my friend, Dani, who works in cancer research and knew Emily."

Stephanie set her laptop on the counter and said, "That makes me feel better. I was afraid her death was work related. Rape wouldn't be work related, would it?"

"No, not at all. Oh, Stephanie, I'm sorry that I upset you. Her death had nothing to do with our work here."

"Thanks. Say, I need to talk to Dr. Abernathy. Can you direct me to his office?

"I can do better than that. I'm gonna take you there. Dr. Abernathy's on your itinerary for eleven. We're a little early, hopefully he's free."

"That's okay, I can wait."

Together, they walked down the hall. Stopping in front of two chairs outside an office, the receptionist said, "Here we are, hon. Now, remember call me any time for anything."

"Will do," Stephanie said with less enthusiasm than when they first met.

Chapter 31

Seize is derived from the French sacire, "to take possession, take possession of."

Evans walked to his desk, turned on his computer, and opened his email. His Inbox was full, but his eyes went directly to one from the Sixth Circuit Court. The warrant. He read that The Honorable William P. Glenn approved the warrant to search Abernathy's financials and laptop, but only for emails sent to or from Ms. Emily Naismith pertaining to SETTUP. Further evidence proving the results of the SETTUP trial had a bearing on her death was required before approval would be granted to view confidential trial results.

Fuck me. The judge didn't give me what I wanted. But it's a start. Maybe Abernathy screwed up somewhere and bragged about doctoring the books.

Evans walked to the Lieutenant's office and saw that he was on the phone. He sat when it became apparent that Jefferson was not ending the call anytime soon. Moments later, Jefferson hung up and turned toward Evans. "Mayor's barking up my ass, Evans. She brought you up, you know."

"What have I done to upset Her Honor this time?"

"Let me count the ways. What'd you need to see me about?"

Evans explained, "I need to go to Indy for the Three Fires case."

"Can't you do it virtually?"

"Nope, need to see their smiling faces. I don't trust them to give me everything I asked for."

"Who is it that you don't trust?" Jefferson asked.

"I'm worried that Abernathy and his buddies at Solutions & Synergy will hide stuff from me. During a video chat the head of HR claimed confidentiality and wouldn't answer any of my questions."

Jefferson asked, "Remind me again, who's Abernathy?"

"Sorry. He's the Medical Director of Clinical Trials at Solutions & Synergy, the company that ran the research trial that Emily was involved in. He was her boss and stands to make a ton of money if the trial has a good outcome. I'm wondering if she saw something in the trial that meant Abernathy would lose out on an early retirement. Also, I found an email describing some sort of incident between the two of them, and another where he threatened her. I'm guessing that Abernathy came on to her, and when she blew him off, he resorted to threats. And, *and* he refused to answer most of my questions," Evans said.

"You're coming back tonight?" Jefferson asked.

"That's the plan, Stan."

"Where are you on the fraud case?"

"Working on it."

"How about the assault?" Jefferson asked.

"Goes to trial in two months."

"Keep your expenses down. I'm sure you heard the Mayor ripping me a new one. They're setting the City's budget in a few weeks, and I don't want to give her a reason to make any more cuts."

"No problem, Lieu. You know I'd never do anything to leave you or the Department in the red."

According to Evans's phone GPS app, the drive to Indy would take him four hours. He called his wife and told her he was coming home before a quick trip to Indy. Yeah, work related. A four-hour drive, he wanted to take off soon. Yes, he'd be home for Troy Jr's game and Eva's meet on Saturday, he'd be home tonight.

He found his wife in their bedroom, putting away laundry.

"Those mine? Thanks," Evans said.

"Yes. Laundry isn't your strong suit, Detective."

"Well, aren't you the nicest wife."

"Yes, I am. Now, do you have time for some afternoon delight?"

"You read my mind, Mrs. Evans," he said, taking off his coat.

***

Driving to Indianapolis, he thought about his wife and how much he loved her from the first day that they met. He was still proud of his ingenious plan to get to know the future Mrs. Evans better by running for the High School Student Council.

Evans notified Indianapolis PD that he was serving a warrant at Solutions & Synergy and requested that an IPD Patrol Officer accompany him.

Solutions & Synergy headquarters was a modern, large, spacious facility settled in a somewhat industrial neighborhood. It was a sunny, windy day with the mercury topping out at twenty-eight degrees when Evans arrived in Indianapolis. He was looking forward to summer.

A female officer wearing Indianapolis PD blues stood in Solutions & Synergy's lobby. Evans straightened his wind-blown hair during introductions, then walked with Officer Burton across the expansive foyer. They approached a young man at the reception desk whose name badge read Oliver.

"Oliver, just the man I'm looking for. Will you please direct us to Dr. Abernathy?"

"I can help you with that. But before you see him, you'll need to stop at Legal first, which is on the third floor. Elevators are on your right. I'll call ahead for you. You'll need to display these," Oliver said, handing them badges which identified each as "Visitor."

Evans and Officer Burton rode the elevator in silence while he rubbed his thumb over his key fob, a habit that he was having trouble breaking. Stepping off the elevator first, he held the door open for Officer Burton, allowing her to enter Suite 321 first. The receptionist greeted them with a welcoming smile, "Hi there, how can I help you today?"

"I'm trying to execute a search and seize warrant," Evans said, waving the warrant in front of her. "We're supposed to meet someone from your Legal Department up here."

"Let's come to my office and talk about this warrant," an approaching attorney said.

"Detective Evans, Grand Rapids PD, and Officer Burton, IPD. Lead the way," Evans said, more harshly than he intended.

None of the three spoke as they walked to the attorney's office. "Seat?" He gestured for the law enforcement representatives to sit as he walked around his cherry wood desk.

"Can I look at it, Detective?"

"You may. It's a warrant for Dr. Abernathy's laptop and phone," Evans said, flipping it on the attorney's desk. Evans doubted a corporate attorney had looked at a warrant for years, if ever.

After perusing the legal document, he looked up, "Everything seems to be in order. May I ask why you want to look at his things?"

"It's part of an ongoing investigation."

"Care to elaborate?" the attorney asked.

Evans said, "I do not. You know I can't talk about ongoing investigations, counsellor."

The attorney returned the warrant to Evans and said, "Dr. Abernathy's up on six."

The three of them stared at the elevator door as they rode up. They walked up to an administrative assistant, and with an unenthusiastic wave, the attorney said, "Hi, Kathy, Legal. Need to see Dr. Abernathy."

"He's on a Zoom call at the moment."

"We'll wait."

The attorney and Officer Burton sat, Evans stood. They could hear Abernathy speaking, at times yelling, but could not make out the content of his conversation. He ended the Zoom call, came out of his office and glared at the attorney. "What do you want? We're not meeting today."

The attorney pointed at Evans and said, "It's the Detective, he has a warrant for your laptop and phone."

Evans complemented his grin with a finger-wiggling wave.

"What about them?" Abernathy asked.

"He has a warrant for them, sir."

"I'm not giving up my phone and laptop. Are you crazy?" Abernathy said.

Evans jumped into the conversation, "It's not up to him. A judge signed the warrant, I'm afraid you need to hand them over."

"Evans, I don't care what you say, you're not getting my phone or laptop. There's privileged information on them.

Confidential stuff that nobody can see," Abernathy said.

"It's either hand them over or face obstruction charges. I don't think you want to do that, do you, Doctor?" he replied. He enjoyed seeing Abernathy squirm.

Abernathy looked at the attorney and said, "Can't you do something about this?"

"I looked at it. He's right, my hands are tied. The judge signed it, it's all legal."

"Lot of good you are. What's with no warning, Evans? You show up and take my things just like that," Abernathy said.

"Unfortunately, that's how it goes," Evans said.

"Bullcrap. That's not how it goes in my world. That's not how most people would do it. No respect." He stormed into his office without closing the door.

Evans noted a defeated tone in Abernathy's voice. He wasn't going to win the argument and was pissed.

Evans followed Abernathy into his office saying, "Look, we can argue all day about your rights, the right and wrong way to serve a warrant, but at the end of the day, it's a signed, legal document, and I've got a long drive ahead of me. Will you just hand them over, so it doesn't get any uglier than it already is?"

Evans could hear Abernathy screaming at the attorney as he and Officer Burton walked to the elevator with Abernathy's laptop and phone in hand. He thanked the Indianapolis PO and set his sights on Grand Rapids.

***

After arriving at GRPD headquarters, Evans walked up two flights and dropped Abernathy's electronics on Sarah's desk with a note:

> Sarah,
> Call me when you're able to access Dr. Abernathy's email and text messages.
> Evans

Seeing Abernathy in person, Evans knew he wasn't the suspicious guy that he'd seen on the tapes from the Three Fires Hotel. Abernathy stood several inches short of six feet and the guy on the tape didn't carry his paunch.

Chapter 32

The probability of two individuals having identical fingerprints is one in sixty-four billion.

Stephanie could hear Abernathy yelling and saw animated arm gestures through the frosted glass office door. She used her phone to search the internet for information regarding Emily's death. An article on MLive said Emily Naismith worked as a nurse for Solutions & Synergy and died under suspicious circumstances at the Three Fires Hotel. The article said nothing about murder, gun shots, strangulation, or rape. The investigation was ongoing according to Lieutenant Jefferson of the Major Cases Division of GRPD. Can't trust the gossip tree at Solutions & Synergy, every one of them had it wrong.

Abernathy opened his door at ten minutes after the hour and greeted Stephanie with a flushed face. "Stephanie, I'm sorry to keep you waiting. Please come in," Abernathy said, motioning her in.

She stood and said, "It's all right, I'm sure you have more important things to do." She sat in front of his desk and put the laptop and folder on the chair next to hers.

"How's your day going so far?" Abernathy asked, looking across his oversized desk.

"Fine, eager to get started."

Abernathy said, "Good. I wanted to meet with you and outline the details of your job. You'll be working on SETTUP, a status epilepticus study. You should be able to log on to our website and find the SETTUP folder. Everything you'll need, including, most importantly, the protocol, is in that folder. It's a standard Institutional Review Board-approved protocol. Obtain consent, enroll, randomize, give the drug or not, record outcomes, record AEs, obtain follow up labs, EEGs, etcetera. As a Site Monitor, you're responsible for strict adherence to the protocol for every patient enrolled at each of the four sites you've been assigned to."

Director. I was hired to be a Director of Clinical Research.

"What do you mean four sites? I was initially told that I'd be monitoring Grand Rapids. Now everybody is talking about four sites. There aren't four sites in Grand Rapids, are there?"

"Four sites in Grand Rapids? Are you kidding me? No, the four are Boston, Jacksonville, Chicago, and Grand Rapids. Was it the head of HR that you met with? I'm told the guy's apparently brilliant but he's kind of weird and lacks certain social skills. He knows nothing about the clinical side of things. Anyway, something came up. I'm sure you can handle it."

Leaning back in his chair, Abernathy continued to outline Stephanie's roles and responsibilities. "As you know, following the protocol is job number one, followed closely by data entry. Was the consent thoroughly explained to the patient, did they sign the consent, details like that. You've been through The Collaborative Institutional Training Initiative (CITI Program) training, haven't you?"

"Yes, sir. I went through all of that at the University of Chicago. That's where I learned that study volunteers should not incur any increased risk of harm, beyond the normal risks inherent in everyday life, when they participate in our trials," Stephanie said.

"That's correct. Our reputation is based on following protocols and CITI training is key. It goes without saying that adverse events are critical with this, and well, every trial. At Solutions & Synergy, we let the data speak for itself and want every clinical trial to be successful. Effective and safe, that's kind of my motto around here. As always, I need to know about serious adverse events. With SETTUP, it's tricky. We saw a stroke in a patient that was incorrectly ascribed to the drug. That was a mistake on our part, which will *not* happen again," he said staring at her.

Stephanie wasn't sure if he expected a reply, so she broke the silence. "Sure, all serious adverse events are to be reported immediately. And no strokes." Wow, what have I gotten myself into? Can't report an adverse event. That's a new one.

Abernathy continued, "The patient smoked, which I'm sure caused the stroke. Hypertension and diabetes are the top two risk factors for stroke, with smoking right behind. Anyway, I want you to start off by visiting each clinical site. You know, introduce yourself to the Principle Investigators (PIs), review the logbook binders, get to know the lay of the land, so to speak. Did they go over how to itemize your expenses? You'll be traveling a fair amount."

"Yes, she showed me how to maintain an expense account. I'll probably mess it up the first time around," Stephanie said.

Without smiling, Abernathy replied, "I hope not. I don't want to hear about any mistakes in your reports, expense accounts, or anything else. Are we clear on that?"

What an A-hole. "Yes sir, all clear. I'll make sure I do it right the first time and every time." She was pissed at her friend for recommending Abernathy. Technically, he recommended Solutions & Synergy, but still.

"Good, that's more like it. As you know, the PIs are responsible for the conduct of SETTUP. In Boston, the PI you'll be working with is El-Mandi. A good man, smart as hell, but English isn't his first language. In Jacksonville, it's Sureshyihjani. I guess he's okay, but a terrible recruiter. They're at the bottom of the pile as far as enrollment goes. I've known Howard in Chicago for many years. He's all right, I guess. Finally, in little old Grand Rapids it's Daaaaaactah Murray, who can't recruit to save her life and isn't smart as hell. And who has already left her nosey little fingerprints all over the trial.

"I'm sure the PI's assistants arrange their schedules. You'll find the name and contact info for the research assistants in the folder, under sites, then PIs. I suggest you contact the assistants first, then the Docs. Questions about who you will be working with or what I expect from you?" Abernathy said, looking at his desk monitor.

"No, thank you. You've been very thorough," Stephanie replied. What a pompous douche. She thought about the quickest way out of his office.

"Any final questions for me then?" Abernathy asked, without looking away from his monitor.

"Yes sir, I've got a couple. What happened to Emily Naismith?

I was told during my interviews that she left to take another position, which apparently isn't the case at all. I read that she died under suspicious circumstances."

Abernathy glared at Stephanie. "Emily was a victim of a random assault. It had nothing to do with her work here. Just a damn shame too, she was one of my better employees. But her death had nothing to do with our work. What other questions do you have for me?"

Random assault? That's not what it said in the paper. Stephanie asked, "Where do you think I should start? I was thinking of starting in Grand Rapids."

"That's easy, you don't need to see Jacksonville any time soon. Sureshyihjani can't recruit for shit and has only enrolled a few patients. Not Grand Rapids either, you should start in Boston."

"I was thinking about starting in Grand Rapids, because I believe that's where Emily was working when she died. Maybe start there?" Stephanie asked, shifting in her seat.

Abernathy stared at her with scalpels and replied, "Boston. I believe I said Boston is where you will start. Grand Rapids will be after Chicago and Jacksonville. It's in the middle of nowhere, for Christ's sake. Don't waste your valuable time starting at the smallest site in the entire trial. I'm still not even sure how Grand Rapids ended up in SETTUP. Other questions?" he said, returning his gaze to his monitor.

"Yes sir, Boston it is. One more thing, can I see Emily's notes and emails, that sort of thing? Having access to her notes will help my preparation. I would like to know what issues or challenges she was having. I want to, you know, be prepared for success," Stephanie said confidently.

"Be that as it may, reviewing her emails will not be necessary. They're private and do not fall under your line of duties. I can't even see them, for Christ's sake, and she reported to me. Anything else?"

"No, I guess that's all for now. I'm sure I'll have more questions as soon as I walk out of here and delve deeper into the SETTUP folder. You know how that goes."

Abernathy said, “I guess that’s all for now, then.”

“Thank you so much for meeting with me today,” Stephanie said, standing. “Everyone has been so welcoming. I look forward to seeing you again.”

Abernathy stayed seated and forced a compulsory smile. “Sure. I need to hear from you every Thursday.” He wondered what her game was, and why she was asking about Emily. She might not be long for this job, after all. She’d better not be playing me.

Stephanie walked out of Abernathy’s office frowning. Pushing the elevator down button, she started crying. She had an asshole for a supervisor and was hired by a creepy VP. Her predecessor died under questionable circumstances. Why hadn’t her friend told her that Emily died on the job? She wondered if it was too late to back out of the employment agreement that she’d just signed.

She pushed the down button a second, third, fourth, fifth time with increasing urgency.

Chapter 33

Epilepsy was thought to be caused by evil spirits and was called the Sacred Disease in ancient Greece.

Evans's list of leads to follow up on and alibis to rule out was too long, he needed to prioritize. He didn't want to spend more than a few minutes verifying Max's story. Removing Emily's old boyfriend from the suspect list would allow him to focus his time and energy on his top suspects. Evans called Showspan, the company that organized the Cottage & Lakefront Living Show.

"Welcome to Showspan, how may I help you?"

"This is Detective Evans, GRPD. Let me begin by telling you that I'm holding a warrant in my hand as we speak (it was blank). I'm interested in a visitor that recently attended one of your shows. I believe the Cottage & Lakefront Living Show ran in Grand Rapids from January 6 through January 8. I need to verify that this guy attended your Show and on what days."

"I can do that for you. Let me bring the Cottage Show up. What's his name, again?"

"Wainwright. Maxwell Wainwright."

"Wainwright, Wainwright . . . here he is. Maxwell purchased two eTickets on November 13 for January 7."

"That's it? He didn't attend on Sunday, the eighth?"

"Nope, just the two tickets for January 7. Guess he didn't want our more economical weekend package. If he had attended on the eighth, he would have had to purchase tickets at the door. Anything else I can do for you?"

Evans said, "Nope, that's it. Thanks."

Okay, fine. Max was cleared for Saturday, but not Sunday. He checked his notes and found the name and number of Max's alibi and fiancé. He called her and she answered on the first ring. "Hello?"

"Brie Driesbach?"

"Yes. Who is this?"

"Detective Evans, GRPD."

"Oh, hi. Max said you'd probably call. You know this is lame, right?"

"How so?"

"Max wouldn't hurt a fly. He's not capable of killing anyone."

Evans asked, "How long have you known Max?"

"It's been more than two years now. I'm a court reporter. He was taking a deposition and we started talking afterwards. We got along and I started seeing him. And the rest, as they say, is history."

"Nice. You've met a lot of attorneys on your job, right?"

"Yes, Detective, I work with attorneys every day."

"I don't think I'm disparaging an entire profession when I say, from the little interaction I've had with attorneys, they all seem to be a curious lot and detail oriented. Do you think that's a fair assessment?" Evans said.

"Yeah, to a certain degree, I guess."

"That wasn't the impression I had when I first met Max. He wasn't the least bit curious about the devastatingly tragic news which I just gave him. He had no questions for me, none. It was as if he wanted to rush me out of his office. I don't know, it was different, he was different. The whole interaction was different."

Brie had worked with attorneys and police often enough to know the answer, but asked her question to make a point. "What would you have said if he had asked you about his old girl friend's death?"

Evans hesitated, then smiled at his phone. "I would have told him that I can't comment on an ongoing investigation."

"Exactly. He's a former litigator. He knew you wouldn't comment on an open investigation. He thought you were there to tell him that a former girlfriend died. Through his eyes, once you delivered the news, you were done. There was nothing more to discuss.

"Look, he is different. I love him dearly, but he's not perfect, no one is. He started off as a litigator in a large firm. Every day it was big pressure, high stakes. It wasn't life or death, but his clients faced either freedom or jail time. His world is black and white, right or wrong.

"Another quirky thing about Max is that he's a bit self-centered. We've had many difficult conversations about how his focus has always kind of been on himself. He's come a long way over the last couple of years. I think he's doing better, but changing your focus like that is hard to do, and remains a work in progress. He ended up changing his area of interest when he joined a smaller firm. He's doing taxes and financial planning, which is a better fit for his black and white outlook. He still focuses on himself too much, but that's okay in his new position. If he does well, his clients do well. They love him and he's thriving."

Evans asked, "I'm glad to hear he's doing well. Were you recently at the Cottage & Lakefront Living Show in Grand Rapids?"

"Yeah, last weekend. His family has owned a cottage on Lake Charlevoix for many years. We've gone to the Cottage Show for the past couple of years. It's a nice weekend away for us," Brie said.

"Did you go both days?"

"Oh, heavens no. We go over on Saturday and come back on Sunday."

"Which hotel did you stay in?"

"Hotel? We haven't stayed in a hotel in years. We rented an Airbnb," Brie said, laughing.

"Right. I don't suppose you have a phone number for that place, do you?"

"It doesn't work that way. We get instructions on how to get into the condo or house. We never see the owners. There are no phones where we stay."

"Fine. When did you leave?"

"Detective, I was with him all weekend. We got to GR around ten Saturday morning and left Sunday around, I don't know, maybe eleven. He was by my side all weekend. The only thing we killed was a bottle of Pinot."

Evans said, "Being a court reporter I'm sure you understand. His reaction was so different that I had to check him out."

"I understand. I know you're used to dealing with the scum of the earth. Max is admittedly a little different, but being different doesn't make him a killer. I've seen a lot of evil in court and that is not my Max."

"Brie, you've painted a nice picture of your fiancé and I understand him a little better because of it. I won't be bothering Max or you, again. Thank you for your time."

"Glad to help," Brie said, disconnecting the call.

Evans crossed Mad Max off his suspect list.

Chapter 34

The lead pencil was first mass produced in Nuremberg, Germany in 1662.

Evans was frustrated at not being able to tie everything together in a nice, neat bow. If Abernathy wasn't at the Three Fires Hotel, and it did not appear to be him in the picture that Evans took from the hotel security tapes, then maybe he hired out. He was shrewd, so nothing was off the table.

Forensic Cyber Specialist Sarah Chaudry was a tremendous computer sleuth. Always staying within the boundaries of the law once she held a valid warrant, she could access hidden files and dig up critical information which Evans couldn't.

Evans arrived at the Ivory Tower on the fourth floor of GRPD Headquarters to see Sarah holding a phone and staring at a large screen attached to the wall. He said, "You know you'll get in trouble if anyone sees you playing video games on company time."

"Don't you ever shut it off, Mr. Hockey guy. Seriously, what have I done to deserve your presence?" Sarah said, smiling.

Evans said, "I need your help. I'm missing something. I'm thinking this guy murdered Emily. It's a long story, but he couldn't have been the killer. He must have hired out."

"Maybe he didn't pay for it. Could he have sold something, like information, perhaps? Or, maybe he's not your guy."

"I've thought of that and you're right. He has access to drug trial results, which could be worth a lot of money. I know he's not the only one who'd benefit if the drug trial goes well. However, he's the one who stands to benefit the most if goes well. So far, all roads lead to Abernathy."

"Who is this guy?" Sarah asked.

"Roy Abernathy. He's a doctor that works for a company that runs drug trials. He was Emily's boss. I left his laptop and phone on your desk."

Sarah said, "Okay, yeah, I saw them, but haven't gotten to them yet. Interesting. So, he sells results to someone, who, with that data or those results, kills Emily?"

"Maybe."

"So, who else benefits from the trial? Any chance you're overlooking someone?" Sarah asked.

"I've talked to most everyone involved. The only other people who stand to benefit like this schmuck are the scientists who made the seizure drug. But Abernathy is still my main guy. I know something's missing and need your help finding it. Will you root around his financials, texts, and emails?"

"Root around? Seriously? And what specifically do you want me to find while I'm rooting around?"

"Find evidence that he's my killer. Or prove that he's the one who had Emily killed. I'm certain he's involved, but I need objective evidence before I can make an arrest."

"Is that all?"

"You up for it?"

"Always. If I'm being totally honest, this is the kind of thing that gets me going. Find the bad guy in a haystack," Sarah said.

"I'll owe you," Evans said.

"Big time. I'll add it to the list."

"Right. Say hi to the old man for me."

"Will do. Want to see the latest pictures of Sammy?" Sarah asked, bringing up the fifteen photos that she took of her son over the past forty-eight hours.

"Love to. Say, Sarah, do you know what a PD is?"

Sarah brought her hand to her mouth, hoping to hide her flushing face. "Is this a confession? A new pet name perhaps?"

Evans said, "Oh, hell no. There's no PD, none. No PD at all. I don't even know what PD is. Asking for Smitty."

Chapter 35

Romans called epilepsy "the morbus comitialis," attributing the name to the fact that an epileptic attack spoiled the day of the comitia, the assembly of the people.

Sarah finished a fraud case and returned the phone she was examining to the case file container in the Evidence Room. She returned to her desk and opened the laptop that Evans had dropped off. She gave him a hard time but admitted that she enjoyed working with him. She appreciated that he didn't have the personality of a stump, which was so common in the tech universe. And a sense of humor, to boot. Evans sealed the deal when he invited Sarah's husband to play hockey with him in the beer leagues.

Four years ago, Sarah hesitated before accepting the job offer from GRPD. She had had enough working for a large, national corporation. In hindsight, the Forensic Cyber Unit position had worked out well for her. She was happy with the new job and confident that she'd made the right career choice when she joined the Force.

Sarah started with Abernathy's bank accounts. The savings account held $36,091. It had earned no interest over the last three years. Must be his rainy-day fund. The balance of his checking account stood at $90,165. Sarah expected to see a larger bottom line in his checking account. He must invest his paychecks as soon as the bills are paid.

Abernathy had a steady stream of income coming in from several avenues. His biweekly $11,589 paycheck was automatically deposited in his checking account. Multiply that by twenty-six pay periods puts his base salary above three hundred thousand. Holy shit. He earns sufficient money to procure enough fentanyl to kill half of Grand Rapids, let alone poor Emily. Sarah made a note to ask Evans about the relationship between Emily and Abernathy. People would do almost anything to keep their job if they were being paid as much as he was.

For the last two years, Abernathy received an end-of-year

bonus of $65,000. The bonus was deposited in his account on the third Friday of December. Sarah wondered what criteria was used to determine whether he had earned the perk.

His home in Carmel, Indiana was valued at $838,000. That's interesting, he's paying property taxes in Indiana and Florida. What do we have here, but a second home. Sarah located the Florida address in Saint Augustine, and noted it was an hour drive from Jacksonville and two hours from Gainesville and Orlando.

There was a one-off deposit of $50,000 made to his checking account on December 29. Similar deposits were not made during the previous two years. The deposit looked different. After a little digging, she discovered it was made through Venmo. There was a second deposit, also completed through Venmo, of $15,000 made on January 10. The depositor was kept confidential for both deals.

Sarah found no large, unexplained payments made by Abernathy. He wrote no checks, made no withdrawals, and had not initiated any transfers above $2,000. Money only moved in one direction, toward his bottom line. Unless the isolated deposits were the result of Abernathy selling information, the lack of sufficient expenditures required to hire an assassin was problematic for Evans.

Sarah read many emails that focused on whether Solutions & Synergy should get involved with SETTUP. The back-and-forth communications centered on the feasibility, potential financial risks, and anticipated monetary gain of running the multicenter trial. Their Board of Directors seemed to bow to the demands of Abernathy; he was the driving force behind the company signing the contract to operationalize the seizure trial.

She found nothing incriminating in the emails filtered to include Emily + SETTUP. After spending hours going through his accounts, she was sure there was nothing of significance to see; his Inbox was clean. She ran a restore program while saying, "Come out, come out, wherever you are," and found herself staring at a trove of deleted files, folders, and communications.

Hours later, after separating the mundane from the germane, Sarah stared at the intentionally deleted, erased, and destroyed potentially compromising files. Now we're getting to the nitty gritty. What have you got in here that you don't want me to see, Dr. Abernathy?

She searched every IP address which his computer had communicated with. Most were part of the Solutions & Synergy network. That made sense, email was the preferred form of communication in most businesses these days. Sarah searched for IP addresses that weren't used often and found two that stood out. One was part of the Northeastern Florida-Jacksonville network. Why was Abernathy communicating with a university in Florida?

She followed the IP address and found out that someone, presumably Abernathy, had sent emails through Stephen Cohen's Northeastern-Jacksonville account to a SETTUP patient, and another to a benefactor to the University. They were sent from Abernathy's IP address, but through Stephen Cohen's email account. Who was Stephen Cohen? Why would Abernathy communicate with anyone under the name of Stephen Cohen? The only way it made sense was if he hacked Cohen's account and sent the emails himself.

She then discovered that Abernathy's device had electronically walked through Northeastern-Jacksonville Human Resources website, specifically personnel files. This may have been how he gained access to Stephen Cohen's email account. What the hell. Abernathy searched Northeastern-Jacksonville's EPIC records, too. Sarah recognized EPIC, because her MyRecord accounts for Kaiser Health and Triumphant Health were EPIC based. Had he searched the medical records of patients who were not his primary patients?

Abernathy had not documented anything, he only reviewed EPIC records and results. He stayed in EPIC for over thirty-six minutes before leaving the web page. Was he fishing for SETTUP results? Could he have been searching Solutions & Synergy employee medical records? Bad boy, Dr. Abernathy. It was evident why Evans said that he was dirty.

The second IP address which he sent emails to was associated with an organization called COR VC Group. Sarah searched COR on LinkedIn and saw that they were a venture capital group, based right here in Grand Rapids. After a little more digging, she found they invested in, then purchased, companies which produced health care products, drugs, and devices. Interesting. Wonder if COR was involved in the SETTUP trial? The COR website didn't list any specific companies which they currently had a vested interest in. Maybe COR was significant, maybe not.

Sarah was able to retrieve from the cloud a few deleted emails which Abernathy had sent to COR, which were sent to one device, or one IP address. There were communications sent before and after Emily's murder. Holy shit. Maybe this is what Evans was looking for. She placed the information she had on COR in a side folder. She had enough information for Evans that warranted a call.

"Abernathy had money coming in, a lot of it."

"Is that right? What's his salary?" Evans asked.

"Well over three hundred thousand, plus bonuses. You should also know that he received two payments that I can't explain. They weren't part of his base salary or part of a bonus system, as far as I can see. These two random payments just suddenly appeared. Say, is there any way that Emily posed a threat to Abernathy? With that salary, I could easily see him fending off any and all competitors for the corner office."

"Yeah, maybe. I read in one of Emily's emails where Abernathy described her in a performance review as a rising star. Maybe he was afraid that Emily was climbing the corporate ladder a little too quickly. Did he have any money going out?"

"No, and I looked in all the right places. He hadn't made any sizable payments, nothing that a murder-for-hire scheme would command."

If Abernathy hired out, there would be a money trail. If, and it was a huge if, he did the deal himself, he would have left an electronic footprint in Grand Rapids. Evans asked, "Was Abernathy in town on the day Emily was killed?"

Sarah said, "No, none of his credit cards were used in Grand Rapids on or around January 8."

"Fuck me. Does he have any offshore accounts?"

"Negative. All of his banking is based in the good old U.S. of A.," Sarah said. "But I'm not surprised. There were no withdrawals which could have been used to build up such an account. There's one more thing. Abernathy communicated with a venture capital firm called COR, which is based in downtown GR. Have you heard of them?"

"No, and what does a venture capital group have to do with any of this?"

"No idea. I'll dig into them some more after my Departmental meeting and get back to you."

"Thanks for all of this," Evans said.

"Any time, PD. Any time."

"Not funny."

Information means power. What intelligence was so powerful that it could be used to bartered for Emily's death? Sarah confirmed that Abernathy wasn't in town on the day of the murder. So, who *was* in town?

Chapter 36

Hans Berger reported the results of the first EEG in 1929.

Stephanie checked into her hotel room and took a thirty-minute nap. Feeling refreshed, she called her contact at Massachusetts Central Hospital and confirmed their one o'clock meeting and the location.

After a quick ride, Stephanie met the local research assistant in the lobby of MCH. "I've brought the logbook binders to the conference room," the researcher said.

"Great, time for me to dig in," Stephanie said, sitting at the table and opening her laptop. MCH had enrolled twenty-eight people, so she had twenty-eight binders to make her way through, a full day. She opened Streamy, a popular music streaming service.

She put sticky notes on forms 122-1007-922 and 122-1007-1003 in binders # 4, 11, 22, which needed to be initialed by Dr. El-Mandi. She noted one protocol violation. She tagged #17 to remind herself to ask the research assistant why #17 was discharged before the follow up EEG was obtained.

Interesting, binder #17 had speech difficulties when she came out of status epilepticus. The speech cleared up the following day and it was never looked into further. Apparently, the patient complained of a headache upon awakening and the Neurology resident's note said he treated the patient for migraine with aura. Stephanie was glad they hadn't considered stroke as the cause of #17's speech disturbance. The patient's symptoms lasted several hours, overnight, and Stephanie feared an MRI might have shown a stroke. Dr. El-Mandi filled out an event report on that one, listing the migraine as an adverse event. That was his right, to say it was a migraine. After all, the Neurology resident diagnosed and treated the patient for migraine.

Stephanie found little things missing in the logbook binders–an initial here, a signature there. She dreaded telling Abernathy about the protocol violation. She stood and went looking for the research assistant. "Knock, knock. Do you have time to look at a few things for me?" Stephanie said, peering in her cubicle.

"Sure thing, let me finish up with this email and I'll join you in the conference room."

Stephanie walked back to the conference room and opened logbook binder #17 to the Results tab. When the assistant joined her, she pointed to the logbook and said, "Dr. El-Mandi needs to initial here, here, here, and sign the next page. Oh, and I can't find the follow up EEG on this one."

"That's not a problem, he comes over once a week to sign everything. I think the EEG was obtained a day prior to discharge. Yeah, here it is. Where else did I mess up?"

"You didn't mess up at all," Stephanie said. "Do you remember this one? She complained of difficulty speaking when she woke up. The Neurology resident treated her for migraine but didn't investigate the speech difficulties any further. I'm wondering if a stroke could have accounted for her abnormal speech? What do you think?"

"I specifically remember that one. Your predecessor, Tricia, recorded the migraine as an adverse event. I remember it because we both have migraines. We laughed about how if a guy had complained about a migraine, he would have insisted it was a serious adverse event."

"Too funny," Stephanie said.

"The resident said something about an MRI, but Tricia checked with her superiors and was told an MRI wasn't necessary."

"Really? That's unusual, to not report all adverse events, even migraines. Do you know who said it wasn't necessary?" Stephanie asked.

"No, I don't know who it was. Now that I think about it, I'm not sure she said who talked her out of getting the MRI."

Stephanie said, "I'm asking because I was told we have to be careful about reporting TIAs or strokes. Anyway, I only have one more question. Do you mind me asking you about Tricia?"

"What about her?"

"You said she did great work, and I can see that she did. I was hired to replace her, but I don't know what happened to her."

The research assistant lowered her voice and said, "I heard she ran a crack house and OD'd on Oxy and crack."

"For real? Are you telling me I was hired to replace a crack addict? I can't believe that. There's no way they'd let her work with patients," Stephanie said.

"I know, right? That's exactly what I heard, in a crack house. I didn't believe it at first, either. I mean, a crack head at Mass Central?"

Stephanie said, "Wow. I guess you never know. Anyway, the rest of the logbook binders look like they're in order. Where do you want me to put them?"

"That's fine, you can just leave them here. I'll get them back to storage later this afternoon."

Stephanie returned to her hotel and kicked off her shoes. Sitting on the bed, she opened her laptop. She reflected on her conversation with Abernathy. She didn't care for his bullying, but was hesitant to argue with him on her first day. Damnit, as a Director she should have some say in how she interacts with the Clinical Sites. He's a big picture guy who shouldn't be the one to set her schedule. She found a direct flight from Boston to Grand Rapids. Thinking the fifty-dollar fee wasn't too much, she changed her flight.

Tricia, the Site Monitor that Stephanie replaced in Boston, had not reported that a patient's speech change might have been due to a stroke. Abernathy clearly said a stroke occurred, so maybe the stroke hadn't occurred in Boston. Pressing him on where a stroke occurred was the last thing she wanted to do. She wouldn't report a stroke unless the MRI screamed, "Look right here at this stroke caused by the investigational drug SGY140008-12."

Chapter 37

Revenue from online gambling in the U.S. was $12.4 billion in 2022.

Albert, the CFO of SGY Bioengineering, acted squirrely when Evans spoke to him a few days before. He wondered if Albert was jealous of the money the scientists made off that PET scan contrast stuff. He wondered if Albert's potential financial windfall following the successful completion of SETTUP would provide him with enough incentive to see that the study proceeded without a hitch. The judge approved Evans's warrant to search Albert's laptop and seize his phone. The warrant for reviewing his phone records and text messages was similarly approved.

Evans went to SGY Bioengineering to serve the warrant. He rang the bell and waited in the stark lobby. He recognized the lab tech as the same one who greeted him the day before. The young man addressed him with a soft, "Hello," and led him through the lab to Albert's office. Albert was sitting behind his desk looking at his phone.

Evans said, "Albert Brasston, it is with extreme pleasure that I am authorized to serve you with this search warrant."

"What about a warrant?" Albert asked, looking up.

"You can stay seated Alberto, no need to get up. It's part of my investigation into the murder of a young woman. I've asked to see your electronic communications for the last three years," he replied.

Albert asked, "Wait, why do you need my stuff? Am I a suspect?"

Evans dragged the same chair in front of Albert's desk as he had two days before. "At the moment, I have 600,000 suspects. Pretty much anyone who was in or around Grand Rapids on January 8 is a suspect."

"Bullshit. I'm not giving you anything."

"This little baby says you will," Evans said, dropping the legal document on Albert's desk. "Or you'll be charged with obstruction, fraud, and as many other charges as I can think of.

Read 'em and weep because right now, I'm holding all the cards, Albertosan. If, for any reason, you choose to not play nice with me, I promise you that this will not end well for you."

Albert said, "I know my rights. I want my lawyer to go over the warrant before I give you anything."

"No, you don't get to have a lawyer look at it, or advise you, or any other bullshit. It was signed by a judge, which gives me the right to see everything I asked for. Let's find your laptop."

"What gives you the right to read my personal emails?"

"The law, Einstein."

Albert pushed his laptop toward Evans. "That's it, you have my entire life right there."

"I highly doubt it. I'm gonna look through your emails and while I'm at it, social media too. Are you on those Instagram, Facebook, or TikTok things?"

"I'm not on Facebook or anything. None of them," Albert said.

"Hip guy like you? I don't believe it," Evans countered.

"I told you, I don't do any of that shit."

Evans picked up Albert's laptop and stood. "Okay, I'll check it out at the Department, and if I find you're on any of those things, you're in deep dodo, Alberto."

"Okay, okay. I have a couple of accounts, but I never go on them. You're wasting your time looking there."

"Trust but verify. Let me have your phone," Evans said, enjoying seeing the CFO turn red with anger.

"You know this is BS, right?"

"Right. Let me see it," he said, reaching for Albert's cell.

"You can do that, just take my phone like that?"

"Yes, Albert, I can. We'll be in touch. Don't leave town without letting me know."

"Are you shitting me?"

"I'm not shitting you. You can't go anywhere for forty-eight hours, or maybe it's seventy-two. I can never remember," Evans said, smiling. He had no authority to keep Albert in town, but doubted Albert was aware of that.

He returned to GRPD HQ and thought he'd take a quick look

at Albert's things before handing them off to Sarah.

He started by examining Albert's work emails, most of which centered on finances, which made sense as he was the CFO. Evans found several old emails dealing with a contrast material called Seizural. Eventually, they negotiated to sell the patent to a venture capital group while maintaining a portion of Seizural's sales. Praises all around for Albert.

Albert asked the scientists for a bonus after reminding them that he negotiated the sweetheart deal. Albert reasoned that, although he didn't own the patent or develop the contrast material, his work led to a considerable profit for the scientists. The partners appreciated his effort and gave Albert a $250K bonus. At the end of the day, he did well from the sale; he shouldn't be hurting for money.

Evans searched for emails sent from a financial institution and found one of interest. Albert's bank inquired as to whether he had recently withdrawn a significant amount from his account. Albert verified that he made the withdrawal, and he appreciated the bank's monitoring for fraudulent activity.

Evans found one email in Albert's Junk folder from an online gambling site and followed the link to the website. They offered legal online betting, with opportunities to bet on any sport. Wagers could be dropped on revenue and non-revenue collegiate sports. There were opportunities to lay money down on every major pro sport, opportunities which did not end at the borders. He found it amazing that over 2,000 different bets could be placed on the Super Bowl alone.

Evans found no emails sent to or from Emily on Albert's computer or phone. He couldn't find any emails having to do with SETTUP. He had not communicated with anyone at Solutions & Synergy. Evans checked Albert's phone records to see if he had made any calls to Abernathy. Nothing, not one damn call. It got worse. Albert had made exactly zero calls to Emily and had not received any from her. He was struck by the lack of communication between Albert and Emily. How would Albert have known to go after Emily? Who gave her up? While Albert's communications hadn't provided Evans with a direct link between Albert and Emily, the absence of electronic dialog hadn't cleared Albert of any wrongdoing.

Follow the money.

Chapter 38

Egyptians documented a case where direct stimulation of the brain in a man with "a gaping wound in his head" caused him to "shudder exceedingly."

After setting aside Albert's phone and laptop, Evans wrote out a warrant. Having reviewed Albert's electronic communications, he wanted to see all of the CFO's savings and checking accounts, investments, and retirement accounts. All credit card expenditures needed to be accounted for.

Evans went to Albert's bank to review his accounts and credit card expenses. An associate banker reviewed the warrant, then took him to a room where clients could examine the contents of their safe deposit box. She got Evans in their system, specifically Albert's accounts, and left the room with the warrant face sheet in her hand.

Albert's biweekly $6,323 checks were directly deposited in his checking account. His current savings balance stood at $901. His checking account held $1,105. Albert's last direct deposit was five days ago, and he currently had $1,014 remaining in his account. Damn. Good old Albert burned through money like shit through a tin horn. Evans wondered if Albert was spending money on a special female friend. Or a special guy. Maybe Albert was into drugs. Albert had an IRA through Vanguard. He couldn't see the Vanguard account or transactions and vowed to amend the warrant.

He noted that Albert's credit card use had been steady over the prior three years. His line of credit with American Express was $20,000. Albert's monthly Amex balance ran between $4,000 and $6,000. For as far back as Evans could see, he paid off the entire balance on time, every month, until last summer. In June, he made three payments to Triumphant Health. The charges didn't say what he was seen for, or what his diagnosis was. Three office visits over six weeks wasn't related to a yearly physical.

In July, Albert stopped paying off his entire debt; his monthly payments dropped to $200. His biweekly paychecks weren't used to pay off his Amex balance. August was the first month that Albert's condo rent wasn't automatically deducted from his checking account; that's not where his money was going.

Evans looked back at Albert's savings and checking accounts and saw that prior to July, he maintained a savings balance of around $11,000. His checking account moved up and down, but it never fell below $20,000. July was a turning point for the Big A.

He found Albert's credit card was used often during a July trip to Las Vegas. He spent $7,000 over a three-day weekend. Evans found credit card evidence that Albert took one, and only one, trip to Las Vegas. He had no credit card charges in Nevada after that weekend. Had Albert hit rock bottom in July? What happens in Vegas, eh, Albert.

Evans remembered seeing an email from a gambling site in Albert's personal email account but couldn't remember if it was in his Junk folder, or the primary Inbox of a good customer. Maybe Albert wasn't spending his hard-earned money on women or drugs after all. Had Albert gambled his money away and was now up to his ears in debt? Evans wondered if Albert was at risk of losing his job, car, or condo due to burgeoning financial obligations. Maybe Albert removed, or had Emily removed, from working on SETTUP, allowing the trial to proceed, thus assuring himself of a get-out-of-bankruptcy card.

Sure enough, on September 23, $6,000 was withdrawn from Albert's checking account. After that day, he made regular payments to an online casino. The payments started small and by the middle of October, he was making them regularly. Daily. The renumerations ranged from one hundred to $7,000. The gambling started abruptly and escalated quicky. Within three months, Albert was underwater. Good God. He had a serious gambling problem.

Evans searched Albert's checking account to see if he made any Venmo payments. Bingo. Albert made a $5,000 payment in late December, right before Emily was killed. A shiver ran down his spine.

Evans searched further and saw that Albert used Venmo for two large purchases or payments. A $5,000 purchase was in late

November and the other in December for $6,500. They were made to the same person or account. He wondered if Abernathy was the recipient and made a note to ask Sarah about it.

Albert was clearly a lousy gambler and in serious financial trouble. But how does Emily get involved? Maybe he heard the trial wasn't going well because Emily reported a stroke, and believed that murdering her would position SGY Bioengineering for success. Once the trial ended and the scientists started reaping financial rewards, they'd cut him a big, fat Thank You check.

When Evans first met with the scientists, they told him that Albert had asked for money under the guise that it was needed to keep SETTUP going. But maybe Albert intended to use the money to pay off his gambling debt. Or maybe the scientists told Albert that they would pay off his debt if he removed stroke-reporting Emily from working on SETTUP. A stretch, but possible.

It was unusual that Albert started gambling late in life. Prior to June, he was saving and investing his money. Who or what caused him to start gambling?

Chapter 39

There are 360 Dutch Reform and Christian Reform congregations in West Michigan.

Stephanie booked a room at the Three Fires Hotel after reading that's where Emily died. She checked in and was given a key card for room 1210. As Stephanie entered her suite, whatever curiosity she had regarding Emily evaporated and was replaced with sadness.

She took a rideshare service to Blanchard Hospital to meet Dr. Murray, the Principal Investigator (PI) for Grand Rapids. Stephanie sat in the Neurology Department's slowly emptying waiting room. Their meeting was scheduled to begin after Stella finished with her last patient of the day. Stella entered the waiting room and, walking around a vacuuming environmental worker, reached out to shake Stephanie's hand saying, "Thanks for waiting, I'm Stella Murray."

Stephanie stood and replied, "Stephanie Van Huissen. You're not late. It's great to meet you."

"It's my pleasure. I'm so glad we'll be working together. Van Huissen sounds Dutch. Is your family from around here?" Stella asked.

"Yes and no. I grew up in Chicago, but my grandparents came from da Neddalands."

"Da Neddalands," Stella repeated with a large smile. "I love that accent. Did your grandparents carry one?"

"Yes, they did. They were great. There are so many wonderful Dutch people in West Michigan. My grandparents told me that when Reverend Albertus Van Raalte immigrated to the U.S. in 1847, he relocated his religious colony in Ottawa County. By 1900, 300,000 people of Dutch ancestry lived here, making West Michigan the largest such settlement in the U.S. at the time. We're no longer number one, but our influence remains."

"That's great. The only history lesson I got from my grandfather was when he told me when the stethoscope was invented. Let's come on back to my office." Stella badged

Stephanie out of the waiting room. They walked past several exam rooms, to her office. She gestured for Stephanie to sit in one of the chairs facing her desk.

"What do you know about SETTUP?" Stella asked, rolling her chair away from the desk and sitting.

"I know it's a seizure trial, comparing efficacy of the study drug versus standard of care for status epilepticus. It's a novel compound that delivers nanoparticles to the seizure focus. It's available parenterally and orally.

"Enrollment locally has been fine. Adverse events include headache, rash, nausea, myalgias, low white blood cell counts, low levels of sodium in the blood, and a reduced platelet count."

Stella said, "Very good. Have you or anyone at Solutions & Synergy heard of stroke or TIA in any trial patients?"

"No, I haven't heard about stroke," Stephanie said, lying for the first time in her professional career.

Stella said, "Well, I had a small stroke in a young patient volunteer this week. He had one stroke risk factor, a twenty or thirty-pack-year history of smoking."

"No, I recently visited my other sites, and no one has mentioned stroke or TIA."

"Other sites? I thought Emily was only responsible for Grand Rapids."

"Lucky me. I'm responsible for Boston, Jacksonville, Chicago, in addition to Grand Rapids."

Stella spoke while staring at a picture of their dog licking their son's face. She smiled every time she looked at it. "What happened to the other Site Monitors?"

"I'm not exactly sure. I accepted the job before I heard I was replacing four people. Apparently, I need to work on my negotiating skills."

Stella laughed, saying, "It would seem so. The drug works great, but two small strokes have shown up. Young people shouldn't have to worry about stroke. The last one smoked cigarettes and pot. He promised to quit cigarettes, but not pot. Big surprise there. Another guy complained of leg numbness, which may have been due to a stroke. Ultimately, the numbness was blamed on a T7 compression fracture which he suffered during a seizure. Remember, I reported a stroke to Dr. Abernathy before this one."

Stephanie realized that the stroke Abernathy referred to had occurred in Grand Rapids and said, "That's interesting. I just haven't seen strokes anywhere else. Can you prove the strokes were caused by the drug? I don't think we want to throw out unfounded accusations which can't be proven."

"As I said, I found an alternative explanation for the first stroke. Fool me once, shame on me. Fool me twice, that's not a coincidence," Stella said.

"Without proof of cause, that's probably all it was," Stephanie insisted. "Remember, the criteria that we're held to before we can say an adverse event is related to the study drug is that the event follows a reasonable temporal sequence from administration of the drug. Okay, that happened. You gave the drug, then a stroke appeared on the MRI. But was stroke a known or expected response to the drug? The answer's no. Stroke has never been associated with SGY140008-12 in Phase I or Phase II trials. No cerebrovascular events or concerns were ever documented in preclinical studies, which means a stroke was not an expected outcome. We have alternative explanations for the stroke, including that it was caused by a migraine or smoking. Look, it's our responsibility to report all serious adverse events (SAEs), but I don't see how the strokes can be related to the drug. I'm just not seeing it."

Stella said, "As I said, two definite and one possible strokes are not coincidental. I don't know if Emily left any notes or anything, but we had great luck, no SAEs, when we first started enrolling patients last summer. It wasn't until the snow started flying that I started seeing strokes, and I'm definitely seeing stroke now."

Reflecting on the Boston case, Stephanie said, "I don't see what the weather has anything to do with any of this. I mean, cold weather isn't a risk factor for stroke, is it?"

"No, it's not. I'm still not certain that the weather is important, but I'm leaving the second one as possibly related to the drug."

"In Boston, they had a patient . . . who had difficulty speaking," Stephanie said.

"Because of a stroke?" Stella asked.

"No, he was diagnosed with a migraine."

"Interesting. Was he imaged?"

"No, never got an MRI."

"I wonder what it would have shown. You know, I told Dr. Abernathy to amend SETTUP's protocol after I saw my first stroke. I suggested that we image everyone who complained of neurological symptoms. I guess he had other ideas. Oh, well. Anyway, welcome to Grand Rapids. It was so nice to meet you, I look forward to working with you in the future."

"Thank you, Dr. Murray. I look forward to it," Stephanie said.

"You know what, Stephanie. I still can't wrap my head around your four-for-one deal. It's just so weird that four of them, four Site Monitors, needed to be replaced mid-trial. I've never heard of that. Do you know why the others, other than Emily, left?"

"I don't know exactly what happened to them. I didn't ask and it didn't come up in my interviews."

"Do you know who I can talk to at Solutions & Synergy about the others?"

"Maybe Cole Smart. He's the head of HR and the guy who hired me," Stephanie said.

"Thanks. Maybe I'll just give him a call to satisfy my curiosity. By the way, have you been in touch with my research nurse? She does most of the legwork around here."

Stephanie said, "We're meeting tomorrow in the lobby of the MSU building." She left Stella's office and waited for the elevator. She didn't feel good about not being fully transparent with Dr. Murray. But Abernathy had said in no uncertain terms, that the wonder drug doesn't cause stroke or TIA. He could not have been clearer.

Chapter 40

The earliest report of seizures is available in the Sakikku, a Babylonian cuneiform medical diagnostic text from 1067 to 1046 B.C.

Stella called Solutions & Synergy and asked to speak with Cole Smart.

"Hello, Cole Smart."

"Cole, I'm Stella Murray. I'm the PI working on SETTUP in Grand Rapids."

Upon hearing Grand Rapids, Emily and Stephanie immediately popped into his mind. "Okay. How can I help you?"

"I still can't get over that Emily's gone. She was so great. We miss her so much. I just met her replacement, who seems to be very nice, by the way."

"Yes, we all miss her. She was a stellar employee. But I think Stephanie will do well for you," Cole said.

"Oh, I agree. She's well read and knows her stuff. But I have to confess that I'm troubled by something that she told me," Stella said.

Cole wondered who had the bigger mouth. Probably Stephanie. "Really? Emily or Stephanie? And what was so bothersome?"

"Stephanie said that she's covering several sites, not just mine." Stella wished she could see Cole's face. Can't read emotion or intent without seeing the eyes.

"Yeah, we had a few spots open up around the same time. Dr. Abernathy said it would be okay to give them to Stephanie. Is there a problem? Is she falling down on the job?" Cole said.

Stephanie's not the problem. Four people leaving in the middle of a trial is the problem, you moron. "No, not so far. But what happened to the others?"

"Oh, I see. Well, I can't tell you everything, but Tricia Wilkerson, she was in Boston, died of a cocaine overdose. Stephen Cohen, the Monitor in Jacksonville, was the nicest guy ever. I still can't believe it, but they found pornography on his company laptop. And Randy Walker, he's in Chicago. He's still in the hospital after getting mugged. I doubt he'll be coming back any time soon, if at all."

"When you hired Stephanie, did you know that you'd need to fill four vacancies?" Stella asked.

"Do you know Dr. Abernathy, our CMO?"

"I know who he is, but we've never met," Stella said.

"Well, he's the one who told me about the four openings. And he was very specific that Stephanie would be the ideal candidate to take over them." Cole said.

"When did the other sites open up? Before or after Emily was killed?" Stella asked.

"After. I first heard about the others about a week, maybe ten days, after Emily . . . died. Or was murdered, I guess."

Stella thanked Cole and hung up. How did Abernathy know about the other Site Monitors? Did he wait to hire Emily's replacement because he knew there would be more positions opening up? And why did Abernathy specifically choose Stephanie? Evans needed to hear about all of this. He might need to expand his investigation.

Chapter 41

In the early Christian church, clergy and synods segregated the possessed from the faithful, afraid that the possessed would desecrate holy objects and infect the communion plate and cup.

Stephanie sent a text to Dr. Murray's research nurse confirming that they were meeting at 100 Michigan Street. After introductions in the lobby, the nurse took Stephanie to a conference room on the seventh floor. The logbook binders were lined up on a table.

Sixty minutes later, Stephanie picked up binder #14, and read that the patient had a twelve-year history of epilepsy. Noncompliance led to two prolonged seizures and enrollment in the trial. He received Keppra, Vimpat, and finally SGY140008-12. The night of admission, his nurse noted facial drooping and called a stroke code. Another good pickup by the nursing staff. He had a brain MRI. He's the stroke guy!

Stephanie noted the MRI report detailed changes indicating that he'd suffered an acute ischemic stroke in the left hemisphere. Dr. Murray graded the stroke as a serious adverse event, unexpected, and possibly related to the study drug, while acknowledging the patient's smoking history. Interesting. It was Stephanie's understanding that Abernathy blamed the stroke on the drug, and not the patient's stroke risk factors.

Stephanie just confirmed what Dr. Murray told her the afternoon before. Binder #14 suffered a stroke, which was possibly caused by the trial drug. She was not looking forward to facing Abernathy's rage.

She moved to binder #15 and read that the study participant was admitted the same day as #14. He was a nineteen-year old, who suffered several seizures at a party. His urine drug screen was positive for cocaine and alcohol. He received brivaracetam, Depacon, then the investigational drug. The day after admission he complained of left leg numbness and severe back pain. An MRI showed a compression fracture of the T7 vertebral body. Ouch. Compression fractures were terribly painful. Binder #15 underwent a procedure which resulted in a reduction of his pain level.

The teen must be the possible stroke that Dr. Murray referred to. What are the odds of two young patients having a stroke. Dr. Murray diagnosed this kid with a possible stroke, while officially blaming the leg numbness on the compression fracture. The patient never had a brain MRI, which would have ruled in or out a stroke. Dr. Murray notified the study Sponsor within twenty-four hours that she had seen a serious adverse event, a thoracic compression fracture. Dr. Murray scored the T7 fracture as serious, unexpected, and not related to SGY140008-12.

Whew, another long day. Stephanie walked out of the conference room looking for Dr. Murray's research nurse, and found her dutifully working in a cubby.

Stephanie said, "I'm done with the books. I was hoping to see Dr. Murray before I take off. Do you know her schedule?"

"I spoke to her this morning, she knows you're here. Want me to message her and let her know you've been through our books?"

"That would be great, thanks."

"It was nice to meet you and I guess we'll see you in a few," the research assistant said.

"You too. And yes, I'll be back. If you have any questions before then, please don't hesitate to reach out to me," Stephanie said.

"Will do. Dr. Murray should be here in about fifteen minutes."

Five minutes later, Stella entered the suite, saying, "Hi there, sorry I'm late. Traffic was a bit heavier than I anticipated."

"You're not late at all. You've enrolled a ton of patients, you've done a great job with your recruitment," Stephanie said, standing.

"Yeah, we're doing well. I'm assuming everything was in order. My nurse does a great job."

"I agree, she seems to be amazing. I just need your signature in a couple of places. I think the books are still in the Conference

Room . . . if you have time," Stephanie asked haltingly.

"Absolutely."

Stephanie led Stella to the room which held the twenty logbook binders. "I don't recall which binders need your signature. We'll have to look for my sticky notes." Stephanie guessed correctly when she pulled out binder #12, then binders # 9, #11, #17. "Can we talk about #14 for a minute? The one that you said had a stroke?"

Stella said, "Sure. I love Kenny and told him to stop smoking the first time that we met. At least the stroke was small. Speaking of stroke, I saw my first stroke, the eighteen-year-old, in follow-up during Clinic today. Thankfully, he has no residual deficits on his exam."

Stephanie said, "I'm glad he's had a good outcome. It looks like you documented the most recent stroke as serious, expected, and possibly related to the study drug, correct?"

"Yes, I said it was expected and possibly related. Why?"

Stephanie said, "I'm having a hard time understanding why you signed off on the first one as unexpected and unrelated to the study drug . . . but this one as expected and possibly related. I don't know, it just sounds like you're disrespecting the entire study by blaming the strokes on the drug."

Stella said, "That's not it at all. We talked about this. Because of the first stroke, when I saw the second MRI, I mean when I saw the stroke on the MRI, I felt compelled to consider the second stroke as not unexpected, which made it possibly related."

"I don't know how you can make that leap, to an expected response with a historical n of one. Remember, I haven't seen stroke in any other clinical sites," Stephanie said.

"I can appreciate that, but I guess we have to agree to disagree. For me, it's not a leap at all. One is not an n of zero. But I appreciate you're being so thorough. You're a lot like Emily and I welcome that."

"It's kind of a big deal to change ascribing the cause of the stroke from smoking to the study drug. I'm going to ask again, do you want to change your reporting and document that the stroke was not related to the drug? Like the way you recorded the first one."

Stella's heart started racing. "*Stephanie. Enough*. I've told you that the stroke could have been related to the drug. It's my call, my decision. End of discussion. Why are you being so persistent?" Stella said forcefully. She relaxed her hands, unaware that they had balled up during the conversation.

Stephanie said, "I'm so sorry, Dr. Murray. I know it's your job and I know you made the right call. It's Dr. Abernathy. I'm under so much pressure from him. He's giving me such a hard time about SAEs. He's insisting that smoking caused the stroke. I have never, ever, in all my time in research, been told so emphatically that a drug doesn't cause SAEs. I'm just not used to that. Before I came here, we recorded everything, every little symptom that came up."

"It's inappropriate for Abernathy to harass you like that. What exactly did he say?"

"It's nothing. You're right, the stroke may have been the result of an exposure to the drug."

"It's not all right. You don't deserve to be treated like that. What'd he say to you?"

"He said that smoking could have caused the strokes. Oh, Dr. Murray, I'm so sorry. This whole mess is my fault," Stephanie said.

"No, it's not your fault. I'll take care of this. You carry on, and I'll deal with Abernathy."

"I'm so sorry that I screwed up."

"No, I'm glad you said something. It'll be okay. I'll take care of it," Stella replied.

When Stella arrived at Blanchard Hospital, she sat in an empty conference room and composed herself. After cooling down, she called Solutions & Synergy. Dr. Abernathy was not available, so she left a message asking him to call her back. The harassment needed to stop. Now.

Chapter 42

In a 1987 ruling, the United States Supreme Court ruled that "a review of the history of epilepsy provides a salient example that fear, rather than the handicap itself, is the major impetus for discrimination against people with handicaps."

Stella had a couple of minutes before her Triumphant Health Medical Group All Chiefs Meeting was scheduled to begin. She called Evans. "Hey, Gordie do you have a sec?"

"Always. What's up?

"I spoke to Stephanie the other day and she shared something odd. Or interesting, depending on your point of view."

"Hang on, who's Stephanie?"

"Sorry. She's Emily's replacement on my status trial. Anyway, she told me that she replied to a job posting for one site. Then they changed it to four centers during her interviews."

"Yeah, so."

"Why four? What happened to the other Site Monitors? We know what happened to Emily, but what about the others? Were they fired? Did they quit? Three people walking out in the middle of a study doesn't happen." Stella said.

Evans asked, "You don't normally see a lot of turnover of those Site Monitors or whatever?"

"Not in the middle of a big study like this, no. They have to undergo extensive training before we can even start enrolling patients. It's hard playing catch-up," Stella said.

"Can you give me her contact information, Stephanie's. I'd like to follow up with her."

"Yeah, but you're gonna want to hear the rest. I asked the head of HR at Solutions & Synergy why they're having so much turnover. Where are my notes? He admitted that it was unusual to have to fill so many spots. I asked why the others left. He told me that this one guy, Stephen Cohen, was fired after they found porn on his laptop. A woman in Boston, Tricia Wilkerson, overdosed on cocaine. The last one was–"

"Randy Walker."

"Yeah, how'd you know?" Stella said, closing the Notes icon on her phone.

"Email. All three of them were included on an email that Emily sent to Abernathy about a stroke patient she'd seen."

"My stroke patient? Are you telling me that Abernathy's involved with Emily's murder?"

"I can't say, but thanks for this," Evans said.

"Wait, wait, wait. I want to hear more about what you've got on him . . . on Abernathy," Stella said.

"Thanks Stells, but no can do. Confidentiality. Will you text me her number?" Evans said.

Evans agreed that something was up. He characterized the latest development as suspicious rather than interesting. What are the chances that the three people on Emily's stroke email are no longer working on the drug trial? He didn't believe in coincidences. His phone dinged, Stella had shared Stephanie's number with him.

***

At seven-fifteen Evans called and left a message when Stephanie didn't pick up. He hadn't had a chance to review his notes when his phone chimed. Must screen her calls.

Evans answered, "Detective Evans."

"Detective, this is Stephanie Van Huissen, you called me."

"Yes, I did. Thank you for calling me back. I'm investigating Emily Naismith's death. Did you know Emily, you know, before she was murdered?"

"No, I didn't. I'm new here. I just started a week ago."

"Oh, I see. What exactly did Emily do on the trial?" Evans asked.

Stephanie said, "Same thing that I do. Monitor sites, document clinical outcomes, test results, adverse events, that sort of thing."

"If Emily had reported a bad side effect, would that have gotten her in trouble with Dr. Abernathy?"

She thought about Dr. Abernathy's stroke rant. Moving the phone to her other hand, she said, "I don't think so. That's a large part of what we do, documentation. Recording an SAE shouldn't have gotten Emily in trouble with Dr. Abernathy or anybody. Nobody would discriminate against us for doing our job."

Evans asked, "What's an SAE?"

"Serious adverse event." Stephanie turned on her coffee maker.

"That's right, side effects. How about if the side effect was a big one, like stroke. Would Emily have been reprimanded if she had reported a big stroke?" Evans asked.

How does he know about stroke? That's confidential information. "Um, no. It shouldn't matter what the SAE was," Stephanie said, placing a single serving pod in the machine.

"I'm concerned that reporting a stroke may have gotten her in trouble with Dr. Abernathy. Is there any way I can see her notes, Emily's?"

That's twice that he's said stroke. Where is he getting his information? Stephanie leaned on her counter and said, "No, you can't access her files. They're confidential."

"How about private, non-confidential emails. Do you have, you know, a secret email account set up for SETTUP?"

"It's interesting that you ask about them. I specifically asked to see Emily's work-related emails and was shot down."

"By who?"

"By whom. Dr. Abernathy was adamant that no one can see them."

"Don't you need to see them to, you know, do your job?"

"It would definitely help, that's why I asked in the first place. But Dr. Abernathy said no. He wouldn't budge," Stephanie said, reaching for her favorite mug.

"Do you know if Abernathy had any issues with Emily? Reading through her emails, I got the sense that she may have been afraid of him."

"Not that I'm aware of, but I've only met him once and I never met her." The coffee maker shushed, indicating the end of percolation. She filled the cup with steaming French Vanilla coffee.

Evans asked, "Do you know if he ever retaliated against someone, anyone, for reporting a side effect?"

Abernathy was pissed when he talked about stroke. Had he sought revenge because Emily blew the whistle? Unlikely. He's a doctor, not a murderer. Stephanie hesitated before saying, "Not that I'm aware of. But he gets upset talking about one side effect." She sat on her couch.

"Was it stroke? Upset or angry? And how angry was he? Tell me exactly what he said." Evans wrote angry on his notepad.

"I can't, confidentiality and all." She blew on her coffee, then took a sip.

Evans changed lanes and asked, "Do you travel for your job?"

"A little. When I was hired for Grand Rapids, they threw in Boston, Chicago, and Jacksonville for good measure."

Well done, Stells. We're gonna make a detective out of you, yet. "What happened to Tricia, Stephen, and Randy?" Evans asked.

Holy shit. He knows about everyone. I bet he knows what happened to them, too. "How do you know about Tricia and the others?" Stephanie asked.

"As I said, I'm investigating Emily's murder."

"Now you're freaking me out. Look, Detective, it was nice when they gave me the title of Director of Clinical Research and a generous salary to go with it, but I didn't sign up for this."

"Slow down. Let's not get ahead of ourselves. You're not in any trouble or danger. Nobody's going to hurt you. Okay?"

"If you say so."

"One more thing before I let you go. How does your compensation work, if you don't mind me asking?" Evans asked.

"I do mind you asking," Stephanie said, as her heart raced. She no longer needed the self-medicated caffeine and emptied her cup in the sink.

"I don't want to know any numbers, I just want to know if you get a bonus if this SETTUP trial does well."

"If the trial goes well, I get to keep my job. Now, I might get a bonus at the end of the year, if all of our studies do well, but nothing's guaranteed."

"Do you know if Abernathy gets a commission, or bonus, or whatever if the drug performs well?"

"Rumor has it that everyone in administration gets a nice bonus whenever we have a good year, Abernathy included."

"Got it. All right, Stephanie, you've been a great help. I'll talk to you later," Evans said.

"Wait a minute, you can't just leave me hanging like that. You ask me all these questions about Dr. Abernathy. You obviously know about the other Monitors. Do I have to worry about being the next one?" Stephanie asked.

"No, and please don't worry. You'll drive yourself crazy if you wake up every day wondering if today's the day. Honest, just carry on doing what you're doing, which, I'm sure, is excellent work. I don't think you need protection or anything like that. It's probably good for you to document all of your communication with him."

"That's not very reassuring, Detective. I already document everything."

"You have my number. If Abernathy says anything that seems a little off or even hints of a threat, you let me know," Evans said.

He hung up and reviewed his notes. Stella was right, Emily was not the only person no longer working on the drug trial. No bonus for Emily or Stephanie, but Abernathy probably gets one. Abernathy wouldn't let Stephanie see Emily's notes. Emily was loved, at least not hated, by everyone at Solutions & Synergy. Emily's stroke email had spooked Abernathy.

Chapter 43

Hippocratic writings of an epileptic seizure included the following description- "the patient is dumb and loses consciousness, being insensible to sound, sight, and pain."

Evans walked into the Lieutenant's office. "Hey Lieu, got a sec?"

Jefferson looked up and asked, "What is it, Evans?"

"The Emily case just took an unexpected turn. I need to track down people in Boston, Jacksonville, and Chicago."

"What's going on?" Jefferson said, tipping his chair back.

"Emily's company replaced people in each of those cities. After she was murdered."

"So?"

"After is the key word here."

"I heard you. What difference does it make when they were replaced?"

Evans said, "Emily was the first to stop working on the study. You're in the middle of a huge drug trial and you don't replace your people right away? Why not? Why wait? I don't know anything about research, but that doesn't make sense to me. The only way it makes sense was if you knew you would have to make multiple hires and waited until the last person was gone before you started looking for replacements."

"Interesting. Do you have four murders?" Jefferson asked, leveling out his chair and resting his hands in his lap.

"No, not all of them were killed. There was a mugging and another guy was fired after they found porn on his company laptop. Guess what the other one died of?"

"I don't have time for this, Evans," Jefferson said.

"An overdose," he said, smiling.

"Fentanyl? Both of them?"

"No, coke. But even that's weird. Two Solutions & Synergy employees overdose within days of each other. What are the chances of that?"

"I agree. But I can't have you investigating the other cases,"

Jefferson said.

"I don't want to. I just wanted to know if you knew anyone in Chicago, Boston or Jacksonville?"

"Nope, can't help you there."

"Thanks, I'll start with cold calls. 'Preciate it, Lieu."

"Evans, I need results on this one, soon."

"And results are what you'll get."

Evans went to his desk and called Sarah. She didn't pick up, so he left a voicemail telling her that she needed to include Tricia Wilkerson and Randy Walker in her diagnostic searches.

He called Boston PD hoping to speak with a Vice Detective. The civilian who answered the phone took his name. She explained that her detective would need to verify Evan's position as a Major Case Detective in Grand Rapids PD before speaking with him.

Several minutes later, Evans received a call from area code 617. *"Henning,"* came booming from the phone.

"Detective, I'm Troy Evans from GRPD Major Case Division."

"*What can I do for you, Detective*?" The shouting continued.

"I'm working on a homicide here, a young woman who was murdered with an intentional fentanyl OD."

"We have opioid ODs every day, what's the big deal?" Henning yelled even louder.

"You know, we recently had a new phone system installed here, you don't have to shout. I can hear you just fine."

"And your point is . . ."

Evans continued, "My vic worked with someone in Boston who also died of an OD . . . within days of each other. They had the same job title and were working on the same research trial. I'm wondering if maybe we should compare notes."

"Maybe, maybe not. As I said, we have a lot of opioid deaths here, probably more than you."

"I'm sure you do, but it's awfully coincidental, don't ya think? Two ODs by two people working on the same project."

"I stopped thinking years ago. Makes it easier to go home at night. What's my alleged vic's name?" Henning's voice thundered through the phone.

"Tricia Wilkinson, date of birth March 6 of eighty-eight. She worked at Massachusetts Central Hospital for Solutions & Synergy."

Henning replied, *"Let's see what we have here. I got a Patricia Danielle Wilkerson who died January 16. Autopsy said she died of cocaine intoxication. Probably a heart attack or stroke. It says here that she used inhalers for asthma, which proved to be a lethal combination."*

"I didn't even know about the asthma. But that only strengthens my argument. Don't you think someone working in health care would know that cocaine and asthma don't go together?"

"Maybe. But kids these days do all sorts of stupid shit. Every day, in fact. I'm telling ya, they're stupid," he bellowed.

"Look, I can tell you're at least a little interested. How about if you ask around, you know, family, friends, see if she had been using for days, weeks, months, years or never. Fair enough?"

"Yeah, I can do that. Twenty bucks says it's a dead end," Henning said with the volume turned all the way up.

"I understand."

"If I find anything, it's going to homicide, understand?"

"I agree. Thanks, again. Let me give you my cell number," Evans said.

He hung up after exchanging contact information with Detective Wilson Henning of Boston Vice. He dialed Jacksonville PD, gave the receptionist his name and title. A call was returned within the hour.

"Detective, this is Tom Worthy. How can I help you?"

"Hey, thanks for retuning my call. I'm with Major Cases in GRPD, and I'm working on a murder that gets more interesting by the day."

"Do tell."

"My vic died of a fentanyl overdose. Problem is that she never used before. Problem number two is that my vic sent an email to three other Solutions & Synergy employees telling them to watch for stroke side effects in this experimental drug trial they all worked on. And the third thing is that one of the recipients of that email was suddenly taken off his job there in Jacksonville, within days of my vic's murder."

"You've got my attention," Worthy said. "What happened to the guy here? Killed? Disappeared?"

Evans appreciated the detective's insight and gave him an abbreviated version. "Neither. He was fired after they found kiddie porn on his work laptop."

"Ouch. But if, ah . . . what's the name of the company? If they don't file a complaint, we don't get involved," Worthy said.

"I know. But that's another thing that's bugging me. Solutions & Synergy didn't make a fuss about it. They fired him and hired someone to fill the Jacksonville, Boston, Chicago, and GR positions."

"Wait, Boston? Chicago? How do they figure in this whole thing?"

Evans explained, "One of the women who received the work email telling everyone to watch out for stroke side effects worked in Boston. She OD'd within seven days of my OD. Another guy, who worked in Chicago, was mugged—two days after the Boston OD and within days of your kiddie porn guy losing his job. All of them worked on this same drug trial."

"Nice work, Evans. Very nice. How can I help?"

"Will you talk to the kiddie porn guy? See if he's a nut-job or, more likely, that if he's been wrongly accused. I'll contact IT at Solutions & Synergy and get working on his laptop."

"All right, I'll take the local employee. What's his name and number?"

"I appreciate it." Evans gave Worthy his cell number, Stephen Cohen's name and contact information, and the cell number of Detective Wilson Henning in Boston.

Out of the hundreds of people working on SETTUP, the recipients of Emily's stroke email were the only ones who were no longer working on the seizure study. Evans could only think of one person who had access to her emails. He wrote a search warrant for the Jacksonville laptop.

Chapter 44

In 1970, a United Kingdom law prohibiting people with epilepsy from marrying was repealed.

Stephanie decided it was better to not delay the inevitable and crafted an email to Dr. Abernathy regarding the Grand Rapids logbook binders and her overall experience there. That Detective had scared the crap out of her and she vowed to mention stroke only if it was absolutely necessary. She wasn't married to the idea that the drug had even caused the strokes after listening to Dr. Murray. Stephanie made sure to include Dr. Murray's decision-making process in the email, which would hopefully deflect attention away from herself.

> Dr. Abernathy,
>
> I wanted to give you an update on Grand Rapids. They've done a fine job of enrolling. I reviewed twenty log-book binders today. The books are in good shape. I found no major protocol violations. There was a missing signature, which Dr. Murray promptly took care of. I found the stroke which you spoke of. Three weeks ago, one of Dr. Murray's patients had a stroke. The patient smoked cigarettes and marijuana. That stroke was recorded as serious, unexpected, and not related to the study drug. This week she saw a second stroke and recorded it as serious, expected, and possibly related to the study drug. I pointed out the obvious discrepancy between attributing only one of the two strokes to the drug. She insisted on leaving the second case as possibly related.
>
> Stephanie

She didn't have to wait long before hearing the familiar ding. He replied.

Stephanie,

Thank you for promptly filing your report. I'm not surprised, Murray thinks she's God's gift to mankind. Please forward the patient identifier numbers for the stroke cases to me.

Dr. A

Stephanie read his reply and sighed. What does Abernathy have against Dr. Murray? She's no dummy, she knows what's going on. Maybe that's the problem; Dr. Murray knows that the drug has been attributed to stroke. What's he going to do with the patient identifier numbers? It's not like he can change the script. Or can he? Would he?

She opened the file containing results of patient #4 who had the first stroke. He was originally Emily's patient and the one that Dr. Murray said the stroke was not related to the study drug. She thought the other stroke patient was #14 and was relieved to find the MRI report documenting the stroke in that same logbook binder. She wrote to Abernathy.

Dr. Abernathy,

I was able to locate the files and patient identifying numbers. The first stroke (which was scored as not related to the drug) was GR11200-04. The second stroke (which Dr. Murray scored as possibly related to the drug) was GR11200-14.

Stephanie

She waited for a ding, but none came. The following day, she decided to contact Abernathy. What started out as none of her business, became her business when she gave Abernathy the patient identifier numbers. He stopped communicating with her and that didn't feel right.

Dr. Abernathy,

I've been thinking about the stroke cases, and the more I think about them, I'm puzzled. I think Dr. Murray correctly interpreted the data. The first stroke was not expected and recorded as such. However, once the first stroke was recorded, then the second stroke was no longer an unexpected event, was it? That's the way every other Clinical Site records adverse events. For clarification, what is the correct way to document multiple examples of one specific SAEs?

Stephanie

Stephanie didn't know whether Abernathy would reply. After all, she was a lowly Director of Clinical Research, and he was the Medical Director of SETTUP. She was leaning toward not receiving a reply as he may not appreciate having his authority challenged. She was certain that he didn't like hearing about stroke.

Later that night he replied.

Stephanie,

Murray's wrong to record the alleged stroke as possibly related to the drug. No one can, based upon an n of one, say a stroke is an expected response.

Dr. A

Hmm. Clear as mud, and not an answer which clarified how the Principal Investigators were supposed to grade SAEs in the future. Stephanie asked for clarification on behalf of the PIs.

Dr. Abernathy,

Thank you for your speedy reply. I still need guidance on how to score SAEs. Per CITI training, each possible reaction is to be handled the same way, each time. How should I guide the PIs?

Stephanie

At seven the following morning, Abernathy called. "Stephanie, this is Dr. Abernathy."

"Good morning, Dr. Abernathy."

"About this stroke stuff. Murray is way out of bounds. Nobody should make that leap, that an n of one automatically means that whatever result or response is now expected."

Stephanie said, "Okay, good. I feel better hearing you say that. During—"

Abernathy interrupted, "I checked EPIC and you were right, there's MRI evidence of two strokes. But there's no way anyone can say they were related to the drug. That's insane. Both of those guys smoked, for Christ's sake."

Stephanie said, "Again, I'm glad to hear that. I'll tell the PIs that the strokes weren't related to the drug."

"You do that, and I'll put something in the February SETTUP email."

"Is there anything that can be done about the one possible stroke case?"

Abernathy replied, "No, and you let me take care of Murray."

"What do you mean take care of her?" Stephanie asked.

"Nothing you need to worry about. Goodbye, Stephanie," Abernathy said, disconnecting the call.

Well, okay then. Stephanie wasn't sure how to interpret his last comment. She felt compelled to document her conversation with Dr. Abernathy, like the Detective told her to. She sent an email the PIs in Boston, Chicago, and Jacksonville and updated them on her conversation with her upline. She copied Dr. Murray on the email, as she was obviously aware of the strokes.

> All,
> Recently, strokes were discovered in two SETTUP patients. The strokes (two definite, a third possible) were felt to be unrelated to the drug. Dr. Abernathy will be sending out an informational missive soon.
> Stephanie

She received replies from three PIs, but not Dr. Murray, expressing gratefulness for the update. She felt good about the open communication and forwarded the emails to the PI's research assistants, as every PI acknowledged their assistants did most of the work.

That Detective really scared her. Stephanie no longer felt bad that she confided with Dr. Murray about Dr. Abernathy's harsh criticism of her. Today, he'd gone too far; he threatened Dr. Murray. Stephanie sent an email to Dr. Murray, summarizing her most recent conversation with Dr. Abernathy.

Chapter 45

Raphael's masterpiece, Transfiguration, depicts a transformed Christ curing a boy of the demons that caused his seizures.

Evans knew something was off when the scientists at SGY Bioengineering told him that Albert, their CFO, asked for money. Albert alleged that Solutions & Synergy, the company that operationalized the clinical trial which their seizure drug was undergoing, and not himself, asked the scientists for a loan. He felt compelled to verify whether the alleged loan had ever left SGY Bioengineering, and if it did, where had it ended up. He wrote out a search warrant to review SGY Bioengineering's financials for the last six months.

Evans received email notification that the warrant was approved, so he immediately drove to research facility. He was met in the lobby and taken directly to the row of private offices behind the lab.

"Knock, knock," Evans said, sticking his head into Albert's office. Albert had his attention focused on his computer and hadn't seen Evans arrive.

Albert received a BA in economics from Notre Dame. He completed his formal education in South Bend after earning an MBA in Finance. With two degrees in hand, Albert had many suitors before eventually joining Goldman Sachs. He was assigned to the Acquisitions Division of their Philadelphia office. He did his job diligently, working seventy to eighty hours a week. He enthusiastically attacked his work and was graded as being "on track" during his annual performance reviews. Goldman Sachs was profitable, which meant his personal finances were in order.

Albert specialized in friendly, sometimes hostile, acquisitions of medium-sized financial institutions. He was comfortable reading accounting reports, spreadsheets, and P&L statements. He was adept at his job and within a day of reviewing an institution's financial information, knew whether the institution was on solid ground or sinking. With time, he became a little too comfortable, which led to cutting corners.

Albert failed to recognize that The Charleston Police and Firefighter Credit Union had not transitioned from the incurred loss model to the expected credit loss model for their allowed loan and lease losses. Which meant the Charleston Police and Firefighter Credit Union made bad decisions based on outdated information. They were going under, and Albert missed it.

The Charleston Police and Firefighter Credit Union was purchased by SunTrust in Virginia Beach, largely based upon Albert's report. SunTrust claimed to have lost fifty million dollars on the deal. SunTrust terminated their contract with Goldman Sachs, who promptly downsized their Acquisitions Department by letting Albert go. Eventually, he signed on to be the CFO of the small bioengineering company.

"Now what?" Albert groaned.

"Now we get to talk. This time I wanna see the latest SGY Bioengineering financial reports."

Albert sat back in his chair and threw his arms up in disgust. "Why?"

"Because I've got this little piece of paper that says I can," Evans said, waving the warrant in front of Albert.

"This is ridiculous, there's no way in hell you'll even understand what you're looking at. What exactly is it that you're even looking for? And when do I get my phone back?"

"Whatever the hell I want," Evans said, pulling a chair behind Albert's desk. "Come on, let's get started."

"I don't have time for this."

Evans said, "What do you mean you don't have time? It looked like you were masturbating on your phone when I came in. Look, the sooner we get this done, the sooner I'll be out of your hair. Deal?"

"You're such an asshole."

"Hey, hey, hey. Slow down, there A-Man. Workplace bullying was yesterday's story. Do you honestly think calling me an A-hole is going to win you any favors at Kent County Jail? How about if we address whether I am or am not a butt hole later. How's that sound? Thought so. Financials," Evans said, lowering his voice.

"What month do you want to see?"

"Let's start with August, then we'll move to September, then we'll move to wherever the hell I want. Capisce?"

"August last year?"

"Yes, genius, August last year."

Albert opened a folder titled Financials, then a folder titled August. "Knock yourself out," he said, swiveling his chair and standing.

Evans pulled Albert's arm down saying, "Sit your little ass down. I'm not done with you, yet. Let's see what we have here. Debits on top and credits on the bottom?"

"Yeah."

"Personnel, rent, utilities, materials, office supplies, fees, miscellaneous. I'm not seeing anything unusual here."

"You're not gonna."

"Okay let's look at September, but keep August open so I can compare them," Evans said.

"Here's September."

"The costs look the same. Now October. Okay, they're similar. Hold on a sec. Miscellaneous expenses took a jump in October. What's that all about?" Evans asked, pointing at the screen.

Albert replied, "I don't remember, all right. That was like, four months ago. Probably some crazy DNA shit or something. Those guys are always ordering stuff that costs me a bundle."

"Costs you a bundle or them? Never mind. Let's see the voucher for that crazy DNA shit," Evans said, without making air quotes.

"I have no idea where it is, they don't always give them to me."

"I don't believe that you'd let them off that easily. And there's no way the scientists would accept anything other than precise accounting from you. Do you have a separate miscellaneous expense folder? Go back to where you opened Financials, maybe we'll find it there."

Albert said, "I know my books, it's not there."

"All right, let's look at November and keep the others open."

Albert opened a November folder, which had a nearly identical debit profile. Evans noted that miscellaneous expenses were back to September's levels. "Okay, now December."

Going back and forth between months, Evans saw that December had a similar bottom line of costs. There were no significant end of year miscellaneous expenses for SGY Bioengineering. "Albert, will you please show me the receipt for that miscellaneous expense?"

Albert said, "I already told you, I don't have it."

"The way I see it Albert, October is a 125-thousand-dollar outlier which needs to be explained. How about your checkbook? Can't I track miscellaneous expenses through the company checkbook? Let's see what you bought for 125 thousand bucks," Evans said.

Albert stared at his desk. He couldn't show Evans the checkbook, because the check in question was deposited into an account which he had set up for himself. The summer before, gambling had entered his life and abruptly overwhelmed him. He had no idea where the urge came from. He had never gambled before and was now obsessed with it. The desire, the passion, to gamble was stronger than anything he'd felt before. It was more powerful than his dalliances with oxy and coke. If only he hadn't asked for that one last hit. He was showing fifteen and drew a seven. Thousands down the drain. The losing streak continued after the Las Vegas weekend and rapidly drained his checking and IRA accounts.

Albert opened the ledger of a checking account no longer used by the company and showed it to Evans. "Here's our checkbook," he said.

Evans perused it and couldn't find a check written for 125-thousand-dollars. "Albert, show me where the damn check is. Where'd the money go?"

Albert said nothing as he closed his eyes and rubbed his forehead. After a moment, all he could muster was, "Don't know."

Evans said, "Well, that's a problem, a huge problem. I'm

going to check with Solutions & Synergy and if they can't confirm receipt of the money, then you are up shit creek. The problem is that it's not just fraud and embezzlement charges that you're looking at. Maybe you used the money to hire an assassin to kill Emily. Maybe I can hang a murder charge on you."

"Screw that shit, I never hired anyone to kill anyone. I don't even know that Emily Smith chick."

Evans stood, knocking over his chair. Scowling over Albert, he yelled, "Naismith. Her name was Emily Naismith and I think you're dirty, Albert. You got in over your head. The losses mounted. You owed some bad people a lot of money. You were desperate. You saw the drug trial as a way out. Who told you that killing Emily was a way for you to get out of debt? Give me a name, you piece of shit."

"No one, man. You're crazy, you know that? I didn't kill anyone."

Evans picked up the fallen chair and slammed it on the floor. "*Who* hired you to kill Emily Naismith?" he said, jabbing his finger at Albert.

Albert said, "No one hired me to do anything."

"Fuck that, Albert. How'd it happen? Who got you to do what you could never do in a hundred years, you piece of shit."

Albert rolled his chair away from Evans and replied through tears, "Take it easy, man. I'm telling you the truth, I didn't do it. I didn't do anything. I needed the money because of the gambling. I lost it all. My savings, my IRA, they're gone. I can't stop. I just can't fucking stop gambling. I'm telling you, I didn't kill anyone. I couldn't ever do that shit."

"Okay Albert, we're getting there, I just need a name. Tell me who it was, and this'll all be over."

"Look, I took the money. I needed it to get out of debt. The gambling was online so I don't owe anyone, other than the casino. That's it. I'm telling you the truth. I'm not going down for your murder."

"A name, Albert, I need the name. You said it, you're in some deep fucking shit, my man. Give me the name and maybe I can get them to cut you a deal," Evans said.

"Don't you get it? I told you that I took the money, but I have no idea who that chick is. I didn't kill anyone. I didn't hire anyone to kill her, and no one hired me to kill her. That's not how it went down, man. You got it all wrong. I used the money to pay off my debt, simple as that. No killing, no insider trading or whatever. I'm telling you the truth."

"All right, Albert, that's all for tonight. I'm going to tell your bosses about the missing funds. If they want to press charges, I'll be back tomorrow with an arrest warrant for your arrest on fraud, misappropriation of assets, and a few other charges which I'll come up with later."

Evans walked to Scott's office, and not seeing him, turned toward the lab. He found the scientist hunched over, pipetting into test tubes. "Scott, I need to tell you something."

"I'm busy here," Scott said, staring at the pipette.

Evans said, "Scott, this is serious. It can't wait."

"What is it?"

"It's Albert, he's been stealing from you guys."

Scott stopped pipetting, and remaining hunched, said, "Really?"

"One hundred percent. That 125-thousand-dollar loan to Solutions & Synergy wasn't a loan after all. He needed it to pay off his gambling debts. He kept the money."

"How'd he get so far under water?" Scott asked.

"No idea. He said the gambling began last summer and spiraled out of control."

Scott rested his right hand holding the pipette on his thigh and sat upright. "What happens to him?"

"If you want to press charges, I'll fill out an arrest warrant and he'll be arrested."

"Should I?"

Evans said, "Should you press charges? Yes, I would. Loyalty only goes so far."

"Okay, let's do it," Scott said, turning back to his work.

"I'll do the paperwork tonight and he'll be arrested tomorrow."

Evans returned to GRPD Headquarters lamenting the busy

work. Late night. He filled out a warrant for the arrest of Albert C. Brasston for fraud, embezzlement and misappropriation of assets.

Albert was guilty, but did he factor in Emily's death? And thanks for the late night, Albert. Perfect timing.

Chapter 46

Around 1780 B.C., the code of Hammurabi stated that a person with epilepsy could not marry or testify in court.

Driving downtown gave Evans a chance to review the facts of the case and prepare for his meeting. Sarah said Abernathy communicated with a venture group called COR. Evans did his own digging into COR and discovered the West Michigan-based venture capital group invested in health care manufacturing companies. If Abernathy communicated with COR, it stands to reason that they're somehow involved with Emily's case. But how?

The Grand Rapids National Bank building at 150 Pearl Street. NW covered the western end of the triangular block. It was located across the street from Rosa Parks Circle and the Grand Rapids Art Museum, and kitty-corner from the Three Fires Hotel. Evans entered the stone structure through the front door, underneath two Roman columns. The lobby was capacious, extended up three flights. Evans found the building's tenants listed in two-inch-tall brass letters and numbers on the far marble wall; COR's office was on seven. He strode to the elevator, which creaked and shifted, first to the right, then to the left, as he stepped in. The elevator rose quickly, and within seconds, he was on the seventh floor. He stepped out onto a marble floor. The elevator shifted left as he exited.

Entering Suite 719, he saw a comely young woman seated behind a faux wood reception desk. She asked, "How may I help you?"

"Hi there. I'm Detective Evans, here to see Mr. Xavier."

"Mr. Xavier told me you were coming. Let me message him to see if he's free." She clicked on her headset and said, "All right, I'll bring him back then. Right this way, please." Evans was led through the reception area to private offices. "Here you go."

"Thank you so much." Evans walked into the office to see Xavier sitting behind his desk, writing. Xavier stood and walked around the desk offering a handshake.

"I'm Detective Evans, Mr. Xavier. It's nice to meet you. Thanks for agreeing to see me on such short notice."

"Hampton Xavier, have a seat," Xavier said, pointing to a chair while walking around his desk.

Evans noted Xavier didn't want to sit in the empty chair next to his. He must like the power associated with the desk, which fits with his power tie, power suit, and power handshake. He's trying to tell me that he's a power kind of guy.

"You're going to have to start, I don't know why you're here, Detective," Xavier said, leaning back in his chair.

"Again, thank you for seeing me on such short notice. As I was driving in, I came up with many iterations of what COR stands for. I'm sure I was way off," Evans said.

"COR stands for Children of Red. Several of our younger partners were friends at Michigan. They took an interest in the hockey team and were all members of the student section known as Children of Red. Apparently, Michigan's longtime coach was some guy named Red."

Evans laughed aloud. "Children of Red. That's pretty funny. I played hockey in college and remember the Children of Red. They made playing in Yost a most unpleasant experience for visiting players and their families. Children of Red, that's pretty funny. How'd you get in the venture capital business?"

Xavier said, "I started off in banking but after twenty-five years, I no longer found it to be professionally fulfilling. It was financially satisfying, but there wasn't any room or place for me to grow. Here, I can invest in ideas which may change people's lives. My mother-in-law died of breast cancer. Chemo kept it at bay for a few years, but there was never any talk of a cure. I thought we could do better than that. We invest in health care companies and in so doing, believe we can make a difference." Xavier's voice was monotone, emotionless.

"I'm sorry to hear about her cancer. How do you choose which products or companies to invest in?"

"We do our due diligence. We consult with several physicians working in the appropriate field. They tell us whether there's a place for the idea, product, or device. One of our partners focuses more on the business side of things and provides us with a valuation of whatever company, its financial stability, that sort of thing," Xavier said.

Evans took notes and asked, "Who makes the final decision on which product or company that you invest in?"

"One of the partners will make a presentation to the Board about whatever drug or device they're interested in. Later, we hear about the company itself and its financial situation. After discussing the product and the company, we decide whether we're going to move forward or not."

"Are you looking at any seizure drugs?" Evans asked.

Xavier looked down and straightening papers on his desk, said, "Confidentially, yes, we are. But it's all very preliminary."

"Which one of your partners presented the seizure drug? Is it a seizure drug that's going through this SETTUP trial right now?"

He focused his steely, blue eyes on Evans. "Roberts. Koral Roberts, one of our junior partners, told us about the seizure drug. He came up with COR, by the way. He didn't tell me the name of the trial, but that's not unusual."

Evans asked, "How's the seizure trial going?"

"Roberts gave us an update last month and said it's going well."

"You've heard the drug is working well?"

"Yeah, Roberts told us that the drug was very effective," Xavier said.

"How does he even know that the trial is going well?" Evans asked, hoping Abernathy's name would come up.

"Roberts has been talking to someone at Solutions & Synergy, which is the company that's been running the trial."

Close, but no Abernathy. He asked, "Who exactly is Roberts in discussions with at Solutions & Synergy?"

Xavier answered, "I'm not sure, you'd have to check with him on that."

"Have you heard of any downside or reactions that people are having to the seizure drug? Xavier had not smiled since Evans had entered the office.

Xavier hesitated, "I've . . . ah . . . heard something about stroke, but that's strictly confidential."

"Stroke? And you're still interested in the drug?"

Xavier said, "Yes. Well, maybe. We haven't made an offer yet. As I said, it's still early in the review process. We haven't heard about the value of the manufacturing company."

Evans asked, "How much will you invest in the drug or the company if you go forward with it?"

"I'm not sure, Roberts hasn't brought up an asking price and, as I said, we haven't heard the valuation of the company."

"Do you know Emily Naismith?" Evans asked.

"I don't know any Emilys."

"Anything else I should know about COR or the seizure drug?"

"I don't think so, Detective. I meant what I said, you can't repeat any of this stroke stuff. It's confidential information," he said, gesturing around the office. He stared at Evans, driving home the message that all talk of stroke must not leave the office.

"I hear you. Thank you for your time, Mr. Xavier. Is Mr. Roberts available? I'd like to speak with him, if I may."

Xavier said, "I think you're in luck. I believe he got back from California last night. I'm going to have you wait in the lobby until he's free."

Evans left Xavier's office and returned to COR's lobby.

Chapter 47

One Babylonian stone slab on medical diagnostics (1067-1046 B.C.) was titled Sakkikumiqtu which translates to "falling sickness."

Abernathy disconnected his call with Stephanie and contemplated his next move. In hindsight, hiring her may have been a mistake. She hadn't turned out to be the team player that he thought she'd be. SETTUP was going well until Grand Rapids. By not silencing the stroke chatter coming out of Michigan, she may have planted her last bulbs. He still wondered how the hell Grand Rapids had entered the trial as a Clinical Site.

He was mulling over whether to be reactive or proactive. Assuming nothing else happened, no more strokes were reported, finish the trial. If more strokes were documented, then get out ASAP. Or take matters in to his own hands, again. From the start, he had not been able to rely on others to do the right thing. The prudent course of action would be to take care of all future problems himself. He needed SETTUP to do well to keep his string of receiving a sizable end-of-year bonus alive.

Abernathy called a contact, who picked up on the first ring.

"It's about time that I heard from you. What have you got for me?"

"An update that I think you'll want to hear," Abernathy said.

"Finally. I could use some good news. Go."

Abernathy said, "You know that I have my Site Monitors check in on a regular basis, right?"

"I'm aware. I believe you said it was every Thursday. What's the latest?"

"Well, I spoke to one and she had good news for me. The drug is working great, it stops status epilepticus in its tracks."

"Already knew that. Anything else?"

Abernathy said, "I've even heard from docs participating in the trial and they love it. I'm being totally honest here, they can't *wait* for the drug to come on to the market. More than one neurologist has asked me to end the study early, which we can't do, by the way."

"I thought you had something new for me."

"I mean, it's so effective at stopping seizures that I think your group should proceed with the purchase," Abernathy said.

"We can look into that. So, no more strokes?"

"I was getting to that. A second stroke was reported in Grand Rapids. Murray, the PI there, is being a pain in the ass."

"Wait a minute, a second stroke?"

"That's exactly what I said. Two strokes reported by one PI, and only in Grand Rapids. Nobody else has recorded even one stroke, which is significant," Abernathy clarified.

"Can't you do anything about it?"

Abernathy said, "I cannot. It's this PI in Grand Rapids. I can't stand her, she's so full of herself. Look, I told you she shouldn't have blamed the strokes on the study drug. Both of those stroke kids smoked cigarettes and pot, which are risk factors for stroke."

"How can they do that? How can they blame the drug for causing a stroke when they smoked cigarettes and weed?"

Abernathy said, "That's my point, she can't. Having said that, that's exactly what she did. The PI in Grand Rapids, this neurologist named Stella Murray, said the second stroke was possibly related to the study drug."

"So, we're screwed?"

"Not necessarily, no. Nothing has been written in stone at this point. The drug works great. It's to our advantage that stroke has only been reported at one site, because I don't think the FDA will interpret the strokes the same way that Murray has. I think the FDA will say Murray is full of it and the strokes were unrelated to the drug."

"What if they don't?"

"There's no way the FDA can say the drug was responsible for a stroke in someone who smokes. It's not going to happen," Abernathy said.

"Looking ahead, how certain are you that the FDA will approve the drug now that two strokes have been recorded?"

"I'm certain . . . it will be approved. But we've got bigger problems than the FDA. The first is the new Site Monitor in Grand

Rapids."

"What's up with the Site Monitor?"

"She hasn't done anything to dissuade Murray from watching out for stroke. She's been useless from my point of view. And secondly, Murray's still a royal pain in the ass."

"Like I said, we're screwed."

"No. How many times do I need to say it. You're looking at huge money when the FDA ignores Murray and approves the drug."

"Don't you get it? I don't care about the money. It's not about the money. It's never been about the money."

"Then what *is* it about?" Abernathy asked.

"You wouldn't understand. Suffice it to say I'm not drawn to money the way you are." He was proud to have impacted his company's financial stability with several eight-figure deals, but he was motivated, driven really, by his personal win-loss record. "When does this damn trial end?"

"Soon, probably days or weeks. But you can't wait for the new Site Monitor to convince Murray that it's time to get off her high horse and stop looking for strokes."

"I understand."

"So, are you going to purchase SGY Bioengineering?"

"You don't know anything about me or my work. The Board of Directors will make that decision. Having said that, they usually do what I say."

"They're going to be thrilled with your decision." Abernathy disconnected the call and leaned back in his chair. The conversation went well. Another win.

Chapter 48

In 1849, Dr. Todd introduced his theory that an electrical discharge in the brain may be the cause of seizures.

Evans read about Koral Roberts while waiting for their meeting. Roberts was a forty-four-year-old who had had a nice run. He was at the University of Michigan from 1989 to 1993 and graduated with honors holding a degree in economics. Evans hadn't played hockey against Michigan until 1993-94, so they hadn't overlapped. Roberts went from Ann Arbor to Virginia, where he received an MBA. Wahoowa. Worked at Fidelity Investments, then COR.

After several minutes, a tall, youthful looking gentleman with garnet-colored hair came in the lobby, extended his right hand, and said, "Koral Roberts. It's nice to meet you, Detective. Thank you for your service. Let's come on back to my office."

Evans was surprised to see the striking pearl-colored glasses and ruddy beard. Roberts wore an open collar, long sleeve, blue pinstripe button-down shirt, no tie, no coat, with gray slacks and loafers.

Evans said, "I understand you went to Michigan."

Roberts turned and replied with a big smile, "Sure did. Go Blue. Did you go there?"

"No, I could never have gotten in. I went to a small school in Northern Michigan called Lake Superior State."

"I'm familiar with LSSU. I went to a lot of hockey games at Michigan and remember playing against the Lakers. I think we did well against you," Roberts said, continuing with the smile.

"Yeah, you did, except for the 1994 Great Lakes Invitational. I think we won in a three to zip shutout."

"Good memory, you a hockey fan?" Roberts asked, entering his office.

"Yes, I enjoy hockey." Evans followed Roberts and sat in one of the dark brown, leather bucket chairs which Roberts gestured toward. No pictures or personal items were visible in his office.

Roberts clasped his hands together, placed them in his lap,

and sat back. "I love hockey, but I can't skate because of weak ankles. So, it was purely a spectator sport for me. How about you, do you play?"

No one has weak ankles, a common misperception. Roberts must have started with bad skates and gave up easily. "Yeah, a little in the beer leagues. These are some nice offices you've got here. How long have you been here?"

"We've been here for about sixteen, seventeen years. Grew up in East Lansing, undergrad at Michigan, and finally UVa for business school. They'd never heard of hockey in Virginia, so it was tough to be away from it for those two years," Roberts said. He chuckled at his assessment of regional hockey.

Evans said, "Kind of funny how that happens. It's huge in Texas, even California, but not in the SEC."

"They don't know what they're missing."

Evans asked, "Koral, that's unusual. Is it a family name?"

"No, my parents named me after they took a scuba diving trip to the Coral Reefs of Belize. They decided on Koral without even knowing that they gave me the ginger gene."

"Well, I guess it turned out all right in the red . . . I mean end. Tell me about COR," Evans said, sitting back and crossing his legs. What was Stella always saying? Don't cross your legs at the knee or you may damage a nerve. He took out his pen and tattered notebook.

Roberts began, "Several of my buddies from Michigan went our separate ways after graduation, but we stayed in touch. We grew weary of our jobs around the same time and started talking about forming a venture capital group. Being members of The Children of Red was our bond and Hamilton Xavier, our senior partner, had no objections to the name, so there you have it. We incorporated in 2006."

"Nice. What do you invest in?" Evans asked.

"At first, nothing. We all had varying degrees of success in our careers, but not enough to start investing or purchasing on day one. We went through a successful capital raising endeavor and then started investing in biotech and health care related companies," Roberts said.

Roberts was comfortable with the easy questions. It was not time to press him. Not yet. "Health care is somewhat open ended, where specifically do you put your money?"

Roberts, keeping his hands in his lap, said with his smile nearly gone, "Devices and drugs."

Not too fast. "That's gotta be a little risky. How often are your projects or drugs successful?" Evans asked.

Roberts uncrossed, then crossed his legs and turned the chair slightly toward the window behind him. He looked over the Three Fires Hotel. "Depends on how you define success. If ten to fifteen percent of our investments meet their projections, then we're able to keep the lights on. We support the little guy, who has an idea and nothing else. At the end of the day, I like to think we've done good work."

Turn up the heat, get some sparks flying. "How about the SETTUP trial, does it look like it'll be a home run?"

Roberts smiled, took off his glasses and wiped them on a handkerchief which he pulled out of his rear right pants pocket. He asked, "Why do you want to know about the seizure trial?"

"I'm investigating the death of a young woman who worked on it. Emily Naismith." Evans wanted to see how Roberts reacted to hearing her name; to let Roberts know that a person, a woman, a daughter, soon to be mother had been murdered.

"I don't know too much about the trial," Roberts said, gazing out the west-facing window. He could only see a sliver of the Grand River, his view largely blocked by the hotel and its parking structure.

Evans noted that Roberts had not made eye contact while avoiding the question. "What was your relationship with Emily?"

Roberts turned and looked at Evans for a second. Putting his glasses on, he wiped off a phantom piece of lint that was not on his pant leg before saying, "I didn't know Emily and know nothing about her. Was she a Laker?"

"You know, I'm not sure where she went to school. But I do know she worked in research, on that SETTUP thing that you're looking at. She was murdered right across the street last week for no good reason. Only doing her job."

With the smile now evaporated from his face and blood rushing to his ears and cheeks, Roberts coldly replied, "That's a shame, but I still didn't know her. How'd she die?"

Fuck me, the bastard's lying; he knew Emily. Evans wasn't buying Roberts's bullshit. His dishonesty wasn't anything that Evans could prove or bring up in court, but what the hell. "Murdered, I think I said she was murdered. Out of curiosity, where were you on January 8?"

Roberts's look changed from bad ass to scared. "Seriously? You didn't just ask me that. I'm not even going to validate your bullshit with an answer. I already told you, I don't know Emily Naismith. Now, I have another meeting, Detective. Thank you for coming in. I wish you luck with your case. Our receptionist will validate your parking ticket on your way out," he said, standing and walking around the desk toward the door.

Evans stood and said, "Not necessary. I left my car on the street. I'm sure we'll talk again, Roberts. Thank you for your time."

Roberts was a money guy. He buys companies, makes a few changes to the org chart, then flips them. After looking him in the eye, Evans was convinced that Roberts was not purely a money guy. He was a dirty money guy. Roberts was involved and Evans needed to prove it.

Chapter 49

Medical student Roger Bannister ran the first sub four-minute mile and later became a prominent Neurologist.

After meeting Roberts, Evans challenged himself to look at the case differently. He had never considered the business side of things. Could corporate espionage have been involved with Emily's murder? Could a competitor in the drug world have sabotaged the trial so their product would be brought to the market ahead of, or instead of, SGY's drug. Need to talk to the scientists again. They're probably aware of competing products or companies. Scott, the lead scientist at SGY Bioengineering, said they'd carved out a not-so-little-niche business. Evans could think of millions, maybe billions, of reasons to develop a competing drug. He needed clarification as to whether SGY had competition in the business of drug development.

Evans drove to the facility, and surprisingly, was greeted by Scott in the lobby.

Brilliant, but socially tactless, Scott made few friends throughout his formative and academic years. His lab tech ex-wife described him as being "on the spectrum." His awkwardness prevented him from initiating casual conversation; they walked in silence to his office. He wore his buttoned lab coat over jeans and a Grateful Dead tee shirt.

"Thanks for arresting Albert. I still can't believe that he stole that money," Scott said, sitting behind his glass and steel desk.

"You never know, I guess. Will the others be joining us?" Evans asked. He sat in the swivel chair in front of the desk.

Scott said, "Afraid not, it's just me this time. We're all grateful for your work with Albert. But I got the impression from your call that you're not here to talk about Albert."

"You are correct, I'm not. I was worried that Albert was somehow involved in Emily's murder. It got me to wondering whether I need to look at this whole deal from a business point of view. In other words, who benefits from your drug *not* getting to the market? What if the trial ends, and you can't get your medication in pharmacies? I guess what I'm asking is, do you have any competitors who might want to get their product out there before yours?"

"Wow, didn't see that one coming. I think we told you that we've largely separated ourselves from other labs by developing a nanoparticle delivery system. You know, I'm super paranoid that someone will steal my ideas. I think on some level, most scientists are suspicious, paranoid, and downright nasty about protecting their ideas and work. Everyone's constantly telling us to share, share, share our ideas with other labs. But I'm telling you, that's not the way it works. I never tell anyone about my projects."

Evans recognized Scott's posture–sitting on the edge of his seat, gesturing. He was jacked up about something.

Scott continued, "We need funding to do our work. Our ideas get us grant money, which keeps the lights on. If I share a concept with you and you get the grant based on my creative thinking, then I'm screwed.

"Without funding, without grants, I can't keep going. I can't pay my bills and my lab closes. Funding is almost as important as our ideas. That's a bit of a hyperbole, but you get the idea."

"Yeah, I'm starting to—"

Scott interrupted, "That's why most labs these days are tied to the deep pockets of a university or Big Pharma. The little guy has a hard time making a go of it alone."

"So, you're saying SGY Bioengineering, or more specifically Albert, had an incentive to get the seizure drug approved by the FDA and brought to the market."

Scott said, "Slow down there, it's not just Albert. Everyone here wants our drug to go all the way. And Albert's not a killer, I just don't see it."

"You didn't see him as a gambler or embezzler either," Evans countered.

"Touché."

"So, let's get back to your competition. Is anyone else working on those nano things?" Evans asked.

"Nanoparticle delivery systems. Yeah, there are other labs

working with nanoparticles. I know Gwen has contacts on the West Coast that work with them. But I'm not aware of anyone using them for CNS delivery."

"Have you ever been approached by a guy named Koral Roberts about purchasing you or your SETTUP drug?"

"No, I don't know any Corals. And remember, I will not sell out to The Man."

"How about a venture capital group called COR. Have you ever heard of them?" Evans asked.

"Nope, never heard of 'em."

"Okay. Only one more. Why four?"

"Four?" Scott asked, staring.

Evans asked, "Yeah, I noticed in your lobby that you have four of everything. Pictures, sayings on the walls, chairs. Not three, not two . . . but four. Four of everything."

"You mean our foyer? Garcia," Scott said, unbuttoning his lab coat.

"Garcia? Who's Garcia?" Evans asked.

"Yeah, Jerry Garcia from the Dead. He was a great musician and only had four fingers on his right hand. To play the guitar as well as he did with four fingers is some amazing stuff."

"I can show myself out."

Scott adjusted his glasses, rubbed his scalp, and said, "Anytime, Detective."

***

Evans walked out of the building thinking that competition or corporate espionage was probably not involved with Emily's murder. He called Stella. "Hey Stells, you got a minute?"

"I've got to lecture some Michigan State med students in a few. What's up?"

"I'm leaving SGY Bioengineering where I just had a nice conversation with Scott Williams, the head guy here."

"Yeah, I know them. I emailed them after I saw that first stroke," Stella said.

"Did they get back to you?"

"Yeah, a Yi Zhang said they'd never seen stroke in their preclinical work."

Evans said, “She’s the quiet one. Anyway, I asked him if he had any competition. I wanted to know if a competitor could have tried to abort your drug trial. You know, stop their drug from getting approved by the FDA.”

“And.”

“He said they have no real competition. What’s your take on that? Are you aware of anyone else making seizure drugs?”

“That’s two different questions. There are a lot of companies making antiseizure meds, there’s a big market for them. Bigger than you’d think. Since 1993, we’ve had something like twenty new antiseizure meds brought to the market,” Stella said.

“Is that a lot?”

“Yes, that’s a lot. To answer your question, yes, there are a lot of people making ASMs, and—”

Evans interrupted, “What’s ASM?”

Stella answered, “Antiseizure medication.”

“Why do you guys complicate everything so much by abbreviating everything? It’s like a different language,” Evans said.

“We just do, okay. So, there are a lot of pharmaceutical companies making ASMs, but I’m not aware of any of them using nanotechnology. That’s one of the things that makes this drug so enticing. There’s nothing like it that’s available now.”

“To confirm, SGY Bioengineering has no competitors in the seizure drug world.”

“They have a lot of competition. There are a lot of people making ASMs, but none that use nanoparticles, as far as I’m aware. You know, I forgot to tell you something. Did you ever talk to Dr. Abernathy at Solutions & Synergy? He’s verbally abused Stephanie and, according to her, threatened me,” Stella said.

“Threatened you? How so?”

“I don’t know exactly. He told Stephanie that ‘he’d deal with me.’ We’ve had a difference of opinion on some SETTUP stuff and that’s probably all it is. Do you think I’m overreacting? I’m probably overreacting. I overreact sometimes. It’s probably nothing,” Stella said.

Evans said, “It doesn’t sound like nothing to me, especially coming from Abernathy. The guy's an asshole. Did you ask him about it?"

"I left a message, but he hasn't called me back."

Evans said, "Hey, one more thing, do you treat addictions?"

"No, we leave that for the psychiatrists. Why?"

"I arrested this guy who said that he never gambled in his life. Never even had an interest in games of chance until last summer. He insists that the urge to bet started suddenly and quickly overwhelmed him. He gambled day and night, all the way to the poor house. Have you ever heard of such a thing?"

"Yeah, kind of, but I've got to jump off. I'll talk to you later," Stella said.

"Later," Evans replied to a dead line.

Stella had confirmed that SGY Bioengineering had no competitors, so Evans crossed corporate espionage off his roster. Albert had been removed from consideration after he showed Evans that he'd written a 125-thousand-dollar check to his favorite online casino.

Evans reviewed his notes. So many moving pieces, none of which fit perfectly together. If neither Abernathy nor Albert pulled the trigger, then who did? Roberts? No, he didn't think the suspicious looking guy recorded on the hotel CCTV tapes was as tall as Roberts. Who was this guy who can slip into four cities, kill, or remove people from their jobs, and leave unnoticed? Blended in? Belonged?

Chapter 50

Around 770 B.C., the treatment of epilepsy in China consisted of herbs, massage, and acupuncture.

Evans stared at the picture of the suspicious shopper that he printed from the Three Fires Hotel CCTV footage. Most perps were dumb as toads. This guy was different. He was clever and prepared. He displayed skills that you don't find in the average street criminal. Unsubs always made at least one mistake. So far, this guy covered his tracks well. Find the mistake.

Evans discovered there were five airlines with regularly scheduled flights to and from Gerald R. Ford International Airport (GRR): United Airlines, American Airlines, Delta, Southwest, and Frontier. He was looking for a male, twenty to fifty years old, traveling alone, who probably arrived in Grand Rapids on either January 6 or 7, and departed between January 6 and 8.

He drove to the airport and approached the United desk. He flashed his ID and asked to speak with a supervisor. He was taken behind the counter, and then to the Supervisor's office.

"How can I help you, Detective?" she asked.

Evans said, "I need to go over some of your recent flight manifests. I want to know if you brought in any males, flying alone, on or around January 6 or 7. Departure would probably have been between January 8 and 10."

"Do you have a warrant that allows you to search our data base?"

"I can get one if you insist, but that'll take a couple of days. I'm kinda pressed for time here. I'm investigating a major crime," Evans explained.

"Without the warrant I probably shouldn't. I definitely shouldn't. But, seeing as how I'm still full of Holiday cheer, let's take a look at what we have," she said, entering something on her keyboard. "We had nine arrivals on January 6. A male traveling alone you said? That would be one, three, two, two, two, one, three, one, three which makes eighteen males traveling alone who landed at GRR on January 6."

"Can you print their names and information for me?" Evans asked.

"You bet."

Fifty-six males arrived on United Airlines over the two days prior to Emily's homicide and eighty-eight departed from GRR in the three days after her death. Of the 144 males who travelled on United, fifty-nine had arrived and departed within a few days preceding and following January 8, the day she was murdered.

Evans made his way through the airlines. After speaking with all five, he found eleven males had arrived and departed on Southwest, one on Frontier, eighteen on American, and twenty-nine on Delta. With four lists in hand, he returned to Headquarters.

Evans attacked the lists of possible suspects starting with the airline that had the highest number first. Fortunately, the flight manifests listed the age of each traveler. He didn't think the killer was a teenager. Using the age limits of twenty to fifty wasn't scientific, but he was able to eliminate more than half of the guys based on their age alone. There were forty-one guys on Evans's final list.

Using pictures and information gleaned from the DMV, he eliminated a few more guys. The male that he'd seen on the hotel CCTV footage was Caucasian, around six feet tall, and not overweight. He eliminated five non-Caucasians, three gentlemen whose listed height was five-eight or shorter, and six who weighed more than 210 pounds. His list was now somewhat more manageable at twenty-eight.

He searched LinkedIn and found the twenty-four guys of interest worked in fields which were related to cottages, water toys or products, watercrafts, home and lawn ornamental junk. He called twenty-four companies and asked if they had a booth or display at the recent Cottage Show in Grand Rapids. All of them confirmed that they had sent a representative to the Show.

Evans called the four guys who remained on his list and inquired as to why they were recently in Grand Rapids. All had viable explanations: work-related visits, seeing ill parents, and a job interview at Triumphant Health.

A dead end, but he felt better having eliminated the obvious. What the hell, better finish this line of investigation and contact Amtrak and Greyhound. His request for passenger lists was met with audible groans and not-so-subtle sighs, which disappeared when he narrowed the arrival and departure dates to January 5 through 8.

Searching the bus and train manifests was truly a dead end. There were only five guys to eliminate, which Evans was able to do quickly.

Evans wondered if Emily's killer could have entered the city under the guise of a Cottage and Lakefront Living Show employee. That worked only if the Cottage and Lakefront Show traveled through Boston, Jacksonville, and Chicago as well. He searched the Show's schedule online and found that it stopped in States with an abundance of lakes, which excluded Boston. He found the Disney on Ice Show held events in Grand Rapids and Boston, but not Chicago. He couldn't find a musical act that played in all three cities.

He was getting frustrated and decided to temporarily step away. He spent nearly an hour on the phone massaging the anxieties of Emily's parents. Yes, he had eliminated a couple of suspects, which was a good thing. No, he was not frustrated. No, he didn't need assistance, he had full command of Emily's case. On a positive note, he had promising new leads to pursue.

Evans finished the day following up on a gang shooting. The gangbangers were always trying to expand their drug territory. The bigger their turf, the more money they made. The problem was that rival gangs never wanted to give up any of their own territory. Dreams of expansion led to property disagreements, which led to war, which led to killings. It was a vicious cycle.

Chapter 51

The oldest written description of a seizure was included on an Akkadian clay tablet that depicted a patient "his neck turning left, hands and feet are tense, and his eyes wide open, and from his mouth froth is flowing without him having any consciousness."

There was a bug on his windshield. Nothing that small, that insignificant, was going to stand in his way. Turn on the wipers, splash a little fluid, seize the day.

He opened his work laptop and signed into the dark web. His concern was that KFAP would refuse the job due to his previously stated proximity clause. He constructed the email.

> KFAP,
> I need your services. The money will be wired once you give the go-ahead.
> Anonymous

KFAP read the email. Really? What the hell is going on with this Anonymous guy? For him to go back to the well this often means he's looking at a significant financial godsend when it's all said and done.

He checked his foreign accounts. Seeing his financial bottom line boosted his mood, which made the decision of whether to accept the job easier. He didn't need the work and had already broken his rule about handling more than one client per project. Time to get a slice of Anonymous's pie. He replied:

> Happy Polar Vortex,
> Welcome back. Thank you for thinking of me in your time of need. Have you finally realized that you're not requesting anything? Like an addict, you crave my services. You cannot pass Go without my services. How fun to be me. I am available to address your cravings.
> Warmest regards,
> KFAP

He expected some funny shit, this guy never fails. But he had to give him credit, he lived up to his end of the deal. KFAP always demanded payment before accepting an assignment. Better confirm it's the same account, same price. He replied:

KFAP,
Good, the sooner the better. Same account, same price?
Anonymous

The damn fool is truly addicted; addicted to being in charge, addicted to getting his way. We can't let that happen, can we? KFAP replied:

Oh, Happy Days,
Those who remain stagnant are soon passed, like the house by the side of the road. Being stagnant in the business of death will be the death of said business. A slice. You will pay me a slice of your pie.
Hungry for some good chow,
KFAP

Still the same nut job. But he's mistaken if he thinks he's getting any more money. Asshole went too far. He replied:

KFAP,
There is no pie. I will transfer the money to the same account.
Anonymous

KFAP expected Anonymous to reply with an authoritarian tone. Good thing I love to do the Negotiation Dance. I like my chances, especially with Anonymous dancing in the dark.

Anonymous,
Thank you for your rapid reply. I've always thought that successful relationships are built on a foundation of trust and honesty. We've had a good thing going, no? I told you that I don't do more than one client per career issue. There must be a sizable pot of gold at the end of your rainbow for you to call me so often. Because I am the one who has been painting your rainbow, you will reward me with a dip in your pot of gold.

Excited about moving forward,
KFAP

He doesn't get it. I control the purse strings, not him. There's no way he knows anything about the end game. He doesn't know shit. Throw him a few bucks and say goodbye for good.

KFAP,
There is no pot, pie, or rainbow. I have a conflict that needs to be addressed, nothing more. I'll pay your standard fee, plus an extra $50K, then we'll say goodbye.
Anonymous

KFAP loved the way Anonymous danced around the issue. Working backwards, KFAP knew every one of Anonymous's career issues involved a Solutions & Synergy employee. He searched their organizational chart and narrowed the list of people who could afford his services to one: Chief Medical Officer, Roy Abernathy, M.D. Well, Roy Boy, it's time to open the checkbook.

Anonymous Doctor,
Your prompt replies are always appreciated. I'm sorry to read that you don't believe that honesty is the best policy. We're partners and partners share. Share information, share goals, share the fruits of their labor.
If you are not willing to share, then I'll be obligated to share with my new partner, JLa (Johnny Law for those of you playing at home). Admittedly, I have an unusual relationship with JLa. I'm willing to change my status because I will not remain stagnant. I'm sure JLa would like to know what Dr. A has been up to lately. You will pay me $1M to solidifying our partnership and prevent me from partying with JLa.
Warmest regards,
KFAP

The dickhead is barking up the wrong tree. By talking to the police, he'd implicate himself, not me. Jack shit, that's what he has on me. I've never killed anyone, I'm not the bad guy here. Nobody shakes me down, nobody. A million bucks? Screw that. I'll throw him four hundred thousand to sink back into whatever shithole he crawled out of.

> KFAP,
> We both know that you're not going to the police any time soon. My final offer is $400K, which if you're willing to ignore, means that we're through.
> Same account?
> Anonymous

KFAP laughed out loud. What an ass. He honestly believes he's in charge. Time for someone to take a seminar on negotiating with the Devil you know.

> Dr. Anonymous,
> I absolutely loved the Dirty Harry movies, and believed that Clint Eastwood was the perfect Detective Harry Callahan. I'd hate for our partnership to end on a sour note. But alas, it's gotten to the point where you've gotta ask yourself a question: "Do I feel lucky? Well, do ya, punk?"
> Fondly remembering DH,
> KFAP

Dirty Harry, my ass. That seals it, this guy is batshit crazy nuts. He needs to get back on his meds. He replied:

> KFAP,
> Old Harry was shooting blanks at that point.
> Four hundred thousand or nothing.
> Anonymous

KFAP tipped his hat toward Dr. A. Well done. No big surprise, he's old enough to have watched all of the Eastwood movies. Guess I'll throw him a bone.

> Dr. Anonymous,
> Allow me to offer you a piece of advice. Be the flame, not the moth. Let's round it off

at $750K and call it a day.

Welcoming in the Chinese Year of the Earth Pig,

KFAP

Game, set, match. Asshole wasn't getting a slice of my pie. Hell, he's not even getting the $1M that he asked for. Take home message: Don't. Fuck. With. Me.

KFAP,

The money was wired. I expect completion by the end of the week and to never hear from you again.

Anonymous

KFAP reflected on the exchange and the resultant deal. He would receive more than ten times his normal rate, which was fantastic. Improvise. Adapt. Overcome.

Emily and Tricia, we are gathered here today to give thanks. Thank you for helping me to perfect the Emily Method, henceforth to be referred to as The Emily. Were you aware that The Emily was instrumental in my securing the most lucrative contract of my fun career? Thank you, you're too kind. Please hold your applause until the end. I have a tiny, small problem with my next contract. I don't have sufficient time for a thorough preparation and the target doesn't take any medications. I know, right? Just when everything was going my way. Anyway, putting aside The Emily for a moment, I want to bounce something off you and don't hesitate to tell me if you think I'm being silly. Acute lead intoxication. What? Give me a break. I know it's boring, but it's effective, efficient, and I'm good at it. Very good. Remember Miami?

KFAP changed his flight plans.

Chapter 52

In 1911, the first modern use of starvation as a treatment for epilepsy was recorded by Drs. Gulep and Marie.

Evans was tired. He'd put in long hours, long days, and traveled extensively for Emily's case. Most of the pressure that he felt to solve it was self-induced. Lieutenant Jefferson and everyone else in the Department were kind of, sort of, fairly understanding.

He looked forward to a good meal and a quiet weekend with his family. He drove home to find that his son hadn't shoveled the driveway as he promised. He was too tired to shovel, but not too tired to remind his son to clear the driveway.

He was greeted by his wife standing by the back door. "Finally, I was afraid you'd forgotten about tonight."

Evans unbuttoned his coat and removed his gloves. "Steel trap, remember," he said, gesturing toward his temple.

She sat on the banquette. "Then what are we doing tonight?"

"Obviously, we're going out. I'm relieved that you hadn't forgotten about going to your mother's."

She pulled on her boots, saying, "Wrong."

Removing his scarf, Evans said, "Parent Teacher Conferences." He folded the neckware.

"What are you talking about. We haven't had a conference with their teachers in years." She removed her coat from the mud room closet.

Evans said, "How could I have forgotten? Happy Anniversary, we're going to the Chop House."

She put on her coat, scarf, and gloves. "You're not very good at this, are you? How do you keep your day job?"

"Hey, I provide a valuable service to the citizens of Grand Rapids, ridding the streets of Major Crimes."

"It's the Griffins game, remember? My office is going, and you promised that you'd take me."

"Promised is awfully strong. Are you sure?"

"I'm positive and you, Troy Fortune Evans, are not getting out of it. I've been looking forward to tonight for weeks."

He buttoned his topcoat and complained, "I don't feel good."

"Cut the bullcrap. Come on, we gotta go. We can take my car, but I need gas."

"If you're on empty, then we're out of luck. Sorry, honey. Maybe another time," he said, putting on his scarf and gloves.

"Move it, Detective," she said, entering the garage.

"So much for my quiet night at home. Why are we leaving so early anyway? The game probably doesn't start until eight," he said, as the garage door rumbled along the tracks hung from the ceiling.

"We're meeting everyone at the Great Big Building for dinner. We talked about this. Honestly, some days I think you're losing it."

"That's funny, most days I think I'm losing it," Evans said.

"Ha," she said, getting into his car.

"Ha, yourself. How come Troy Jr. didn't shovel the driveway?" he asked, backing his car out of the driveway and motoring through the neighborhood.

"He went to Levi's after practice. They're in a gaming competition or something like that. Hey, slow down, it won't do us any good to get in an accident."

Looking at his wife, Evans said, "Would you like to drive?"

"No, I just want you to slow down. Don't give me any of your crap that we're gonna split the ticket. If you get stopped, it's on you. Oh, I'm sorry, how was your day?"

"My day was for shite," Evans said.

"Sorry to hear that. Let's have fun tonight and forget all about it."

"Right."

Evans dropped his wife at the front door of the Great Big Building, then joined her and her work friends after parking the car. They were dining at an Italian restaurant, Trattoria Italiano, located on the second floor of the converted factory. The GBB had four levels with a different restaurant genre on each floor. A comedy club shared the third floor with a pizzeria.

"Hey, everyone, you remember my husband, Troy."

A few guys who knew him yelled out, "Troy!"

"What's it take to get a beer around here?" Evans asked.

She tapped his forearm. "Settle down, honey. Our server will be here in a sec."

"It looks like she's busy, how about if I go to the bar."

"Fine, whatever."

Evans asked if anyone else needed a drink and made his way to the bar with orders for two beers and a margarita. He noted that the GBB was as crowded as the streets. He waited for a bartender to hand off some drinks before placing his order. He said, "Crowded tonight, is this normal?"

The bartender, who seemed to have four hands mixing margaritas and pouring beers, yelled over the crowd, "Yeah, we're usually busy on Fridays. The Griffins are home, and there's a great comic at Dr. Funny Bones, a guy named Mike Lester. He's super funny and rocks the most excellent mullet that won't quit."

Evans accepted the drinks, paid the bill, and made his way back to their table. Dropping off the libations, he said, "I'd hate to work here on a Friday night, our poor waitress is getting slammed."

"Server, honey. We called them waitresses in college, remember? But you're right, it's crazy nuts in here. Let's get our order in so we can see the start of the game."

"You mean the drop of the puck?" Evans said.

"Whatever. I don't know about you, but I'm starving. What are you getting?"

"I was thinking of pizza."

Evans enjoyed himself despite everything. The game was entertaining; the Grand Rapids Griffins beat the Chicago Ice Wolves in overtime. An instant classic it was not. The game took three and a half hours and the Evanses arrived home after midnight. He'd only get five, maybe six hours of sleep, at most.

A nightmare woke him from a deep sleep around three. Ruminating over the content of the nightmare prevented him from falling back asleep. Wide awake, he slid out of bed, upset that a well-deserved slumber was not happening.

Chapter 53

In the Iliad, Homer's description of the Abantes warriors as wearing "their forelocks cropped and long hair at the back" may be the first documented mullet.

Evans felt like a slug for taking the weekend off. He loved the quiet that mornings offered. It was then, before the rest of the department arrived and without interruption, that he did his heavy thinking.

Lieutenant Jefferson, who almost never got to the office early, walked by saying, "Evans, my office."

"Be right there, Lieu." There goes the quiet time. He jotted a note and walked to his superior's office asking, "What's up?"

"I told you I want updates and I haven't heard anything from you on the Three Fires case for days. I need something, anything," Jefferson said.

"There's not a lot to hear. I told you about Albert, the CFO who embezzled money from the Bioengineers. I can't tie him to the actual killing. Abernathy, the Chief Medical Officer at Solutions & Synergy, is the same. He's dirty, he's involved somehow, but I can't pin the murder on him."

"What's next?"

"I was reviewing my notes when you called me in," Evans said.

"This isn't like you. Do you need help?" Jefferson asked.

"I'm fine. Seriously, I have all the help I need. Forensics is looking at financial stuff, laptops, and phones. Dr. Colson-Brown gave me great information from the autopsy."

"But not enough to find the damn killer," Jefferson emphasized.

"Not exactly, but I'm getting close."

"How so? Two seconds ago, you said you can't tie your top two suspects to the killing," Jefferson said.

"No, but they've led me to consider other people. I'm working on it, Lieu. I'm getting there."

"You're talking in circles. I told you I need results and you haven't given me anything. I'm asking Smitty to take over if you haven't made tangible strides by the end of the week," Jefferson said.

"Lieu—"

"Don't."

"Fine, nothing like a deadline to light a fire under my arse. This week it is," Evans said.

Jefferson stated, "Good, I'm glad we were able to come to an agreement. By the way, how was your weekend?"

Evans stood and turned toward the door. "Good, fine. We got out Friday night, went to the Griffins game."

"Nice. They win?"

"Yeah, in overtime. It was a good game."

Jefferson said, "All right, that's all for now. We don't get paid to chitchat, you know."

"Whooooa with the chit chat."

Evans hated interruptions, whether they occurred at night or during the day. He was especially upset when his quiet time was thrown off. His fitful sleep over the weekend was the result of a recurrent nightmare that centered around Lieutenant Jefferson forcing him to grow his hair halfway down his back. Jefferson ordering Evans to do something was easily explainable, he gave Evans orders every day. But the hair, that was different. He kept his hair short, trimmed above his ears, going back to grade school. What was it with the long hair? It suddenly hit him.

The mullet. Mike Lester. Dr. Funny Bones.

Evans wondered whether the killer could have come to town under the cover of a concert or show at the Arena. He ruled out someone who worked on a Show that came through Devries Place, but he had never considered Dr. Funny Bones, the Comedy Club.

He brought up Dr. Funny Bones's January calendar of performers and found one headliner and a feature act who performed on January 6 and 7. The headliner was a guy named Clive Latham and the feature comic was a woman named Juliette Ciccarelli. The picture he had taken from the hotel security tapes was of a male, so he ignored the "Italian Fireball" as Ciccarelli was described in her bio. The comedy club's website listed small blurbs on each performer. Clive Latham's bio listed him as a forty-one-year-old former Marine, whose material includes bits on dating relatives, office bromances, and pet names.

Evans went to Latham's website where he read that Latham graduated from Butler University. Intelligent. Worked in IT at TW Financial Holdings Corporation after college. Proficient with computers. After TW Holdings, he joined the Marines, where he completed two tours. Military background. Other than the whole comedy thing, Latham fit the profile.

His website listed Indianapolis as his home. Evans read that Latham performed on Last Comic Standing in 2016. His act was described by the Indianapolis Star as "A delightful evening. This funny guy came out of nowhere and is now entertaining audiences of all ages and walks of life."

Latham's website indicated that he performed at Nick's Comedy Shop in Boston the weekend that Tricia Wilkerson overdosed, which happened to be two days before Randy Walker was mugged. Evans estimated that it was a three-hour drive from Indy to Chicago. Doable. Latham could easily have flown from Boston to Indy, driven to Chicago, assaulted Randy, and returned home without being missed. He had never performed in Jacksonville, but he had a regular gig in Miami.

Evans searched for images of Latham on the internet and saw that he was a fit appearing male, around six feet tall. A video of Latham performing in a T-shirt revealed no visible tattoos on his arms, neck, or face. There was another video of Latham performing at The Comedy Castle in Royal Oak, MI wearing a red hat. The guy on the Three Fires CCTV tapes wore a similar hat. The height, weight, and appearance were consistent. Evans dug through a pile of papers on his desk. It was him. Latham was the guy on the printed picture the Evans had taken from the CCTV.

Evans excitedly contemplated his next steps. He went to the Evidence Room and signed out Albert's laptop. He searched for Latham on Albert's laptop and found nothing. He changed the search filter to include Clive, CL, comic, Emily, Indianapolis, and the search still came up blank. He returned the laptop to

Evidence. The case file basket which held things from Emily's case no longer contained Abernathy's laptop or phone. Sarah. He forgot that he'd left Abernathy's stuff with her, so he headed to the stairs.

The phone rang before he arrived at the stairwell. "Detective Evans."

"Evans, it's Henning," came booming out of the phone.

Evans wasn't going anywhere soon and sat at his desk. "Right, how're you doing? What have you got for me?"

"I wanted to follow up with you on that overdose," Henning yelled.

"Great, what was in her inhaler?"

"I'll be goddamned, but you were right. She inhaled coke."

"Fuck me. Even a blind squirrel, eh," Evans said.

Smitty motioned for Evans to turn the volume down on the call, because everyone in the department could hear their telephonic back and forth. Evans shrugged his shoulders and pointed at the phone.

"Tell me about it," Henning cried.

"I don't suppose you found any prints on it . . . the inhaler," Evans said.

"Two partials. We think they were Patricia's, but we don't have her prints on file for comparison. The prints didn't match any found in IAFIS (Integrated Automated Fingerprint Identification System)."

"This is great news, I appreciate it, Henning."

"How does it help you? Do you got the shit who did this?" Henning roared.

"I think so. At least, I've identified an asshole of interest. Former military guy, so his prints should be in the system. But you found no others?"

"Right, only on the inhaler. None in her apartment, nothing in IAFIS," Henning yelled.

"How about CCTV? Do you have any tapes from Tricia's apartment, work, where she hung out, or anywhere that she went?"

"Nothing in her apartment. What exactly am I looking for

when I look at every goddamn CCTV camera in the city?"

Evans said, "A male, about six feet tall about 180 or 190 pounds. Short, dark hair, no tattoos."

"You pulling my chain, Evans?" Henning bellowed.

"Maybe. Look, I appreciate your help. I'm going hard after this guy. I'm certain he's my killer."

"Anything else I can do on my side, short of questioning the entire city?"

"I don't think so. Wait, will you send me the tox report?"

"Yeah, I'll get it to you and the twenty bucks, too."

Evans said, "No worries. How about if we lay it on Wings versus Bruins the next time they play."

"Deal. I'll take that any day, as long as you keep betting on the Dead Wings."

"Fine," Evans said, hanging up.

Evans asked for Latham's military records, and for Sarah to shift her focus toward Latham.

Chapter 54

Twenty-six million passwords belonging to employees of Fortune 1,000 companies are readily available in web markets and data dumps.

Sarah felt good about what she had discovered in Abernathy's finances and was eager to delve into his emails and text messages.

She remembered from his financial statements that he took trips to Boston and Chicago. Maybe those travels linked him to Tricia in Boston and Randy in Chicago. This was good stuff, possibly what Evans was looking for. Sarah was frustrated at not being able to complete the circle by placing Abernathy in or around Grand Rapids at the time of Emily's death.

She noted that he'd sent a few emails to a COR employee named Koral Roberts. Roberts never initiated communication between the two of them. A few years ago, Abernathy sent Roberts an email with information on an experimental drug for Alzheimer's and suggested that Roberts look into purchasing the company that made the drug. Two years later, Abernathy told Roberts that the Alzheimer's study was not going well, people were not responding to the drug. The email took on an apologetic tone.

In an email sent twenty months ago, he told Roberts about an upcoming trial evaluating a promising drug for the treatment of status epilepticus. Sarah wondered whether Abernathy had provided Roberts with insider information, for example, results of drug trials, which Roberts then used to decide whether to purchase the lab or company that made a drug. Maybe the insider information was the reason behind Roberts's golden touch. He seemed to identify profitable drug companies with ease. At a minimum, Sarah found a connection between COR, Roberts, and SETTUP.

Sarah felt Evans deserved another update and called him. "I've found a few more things in Abernathy's communications which I thought you might want to know about."

"Go ahead, I was just on my way up to see you," Evans replied.

"Remember when I said that he sent a few emails to a company called COR? The emails went to one employee, a Koral Roberts."

"I know Roberts, I spoke to him the other day. Man, I'm glad I did. He's dirty, Roberts is dirty. I could see it. Feel it. Sorry to interrupt. Have you found anything that ties a guy named Clive Latham to Abernathy? Or Latham to Roberts?"

"No. But Abernathy hacked Northeastern-Jacksonville's email system and sent letters to a SETTUP patient and a big-time donor. Files of some nasty porn and Neo Nazi stuff were attached to the emails."

"Abernathy did? He sent the damning email that caused Stephen Cohen to lose his job?"

Sarah replied, "I didn't know that he lost his job, but yeah. They were sent from his email address through Abernathy's IP address."

"No shit. That's great Sarah, really great. Who's this money guy?"

"No idea. I mean, I read that he'd donated a boatload to the university, but I was hoping it'd make sense to you."

"I don't know who the money guy is, but we all know that Stephen Cohen worked as a Site Monitor on the drug trial. He was fired when they found porn on his laptop," Evans said.

"It was nasty stuff, I'm not surprised they let him go. Okay, so Abernathy gets this Stephen Cohen guy terminated, which stops him from working on the seizure drug trial," Sarah said.

"Right, then replaces him with his handpicked stand-in. Do you have any evidence linking Abernathy directly to Emily? He's the key player here, Abernathy is. He's the only one who could have known about the email that Emily sent to Tricia, Randy, and Stephen, telling them to be on the lookout for strokes in SETTUP patients. After that email went out, Emily and Tricia were murdered and Stephen and Randy are no longer working on the trial."

"Negatory. Other than he was her boss, no, not so far. But

I've still got more files to go through. These guys write a lot of emails and fortunately for us, never delete them. Who's this Latham guy? That's the first time you've mentioned him," Sarah said.

"It's this guy named Clive Latham. I'm confident he's the assassin. Long story, but he's our guy. I need you to focus on connecting Latham to Abernathy. Oh, and before I forget, I've got another search warrant for you. Can you do this one more thing for me? It will help me out a great deal."

Sarah was exhausted, she'd had a long day. She closed her laptop and reached for her coat. Evans's latest request could wait until the morning.

Damn him. He would never let something this important wait until the next day. She hung up her coat, called her babysitter, and asked whether it would be okay if she picked her son up an hour later than normal as something came up at work. The sitter said Sammy was having a blast emptying her cupboards and he could be picked up any time before seven-thirty.

Sarah opened her computer and found the TFH.net website, which required a passcode for access. Evans! He hadn't said anything about it being a secure site. Despite her frustration, she found the password in minutes. She isolated the CCTV tape from January 8 and repeatedly reviewed the images on the day that Emily died. The tape had been tampered with, portions deleted. Now for the hard part, figuring out who altered the Three Fires Hotel security film. She identified the IP address that had done the erasing, but not the person. She didn't recognize the IP address.

Finding the owner of the computer would have to wait until daylight. She had a hard time keeping her eyes open and had to pick up Sammy before she fell asleep. She closed up shop for the night.

Chapter 55

Epilepsy is derived from the Greek word epilambanein, meaning "to seize," in which the body and mind are seized from the individual.

Evans was ecstatic seeing that the judge had signed off on the warrant for Roberts's laptop and phone. Serving the warrant wouldn't make him any friends at COR but fuck me if they can't take a joke. He drove to the Grand Rapids National Bank building at 150 Pearl Street.

He got off the elevator and entered suite 719. There was no one at the reception desk. He waited for a minute before a gentleman walked in behind them.

"Can I help you?" asked a tall, physically fit male walking past Evans. He wore a black suit with no tie.

Evans flashed his ID and said, "Yes, I'm Detective Evans, GRPD. I need to see Koral Roberts."

The young man glared at Evans. "I'm his partner, Bull Zemanski. Why do you need to see Reefer?"

"Reefer?" Evans asked.

"When we learned that his parents named him after diving on some reefs, he became Reefer," Bull explained.

Evans added, "I don't need to see Reefer, himself. But I have a search and seize warrant for his laptop and phone."

"I'm not sure that he's here. He usually works from home, and I haven't seen him today. Have a seat, will ya? I'm going to talk to one of our partners, who was an attorney in his former life, about your warrant," Bull said, disappearing behind a door leading to the offices.

"Sure thing. I'm not going anywhere." Lawyering up over a warrant wouldn't amount to anything. Complete BS.

Several minutes later, Bull walked through the door. "He's here. Come on back," he said, opening the door and motioning the local lawman through.

"Lead the way," Evans said. He held the warrant in his right hand, tapping it against his thigh. Bull led him to Hamilton

Xavier's office. Xavier was visibly upset, as was Roberts.

Roberts's face flushed as he pointed a threatening finger at Evans. "What the hell is this all about?" he demanded.

"Hold on there, Roberts," Xavier said, sitting forward and resting his elbows on his desk. "Let me see the warrant, Detective."

"It's right here, Mr. Xavier," Evans said.

Xavier ripped the warrant from his hand, opened it, and read in silence. "What do you need his laptop and phone for?"

"It's part of an ongoing investigation, sir," Evans said, standing with his arms by his sides.

Roberts's hands were on his hips. Bull opened and closed his fists.

Xavier asked, "How is Roberts involved with your investigation?" He sat back.

"I can't go into any details of an ongoing investigation," Evans said.

"There's a lot of confidential information on our things. You know it's a company laptop, and phone for that matter," Xavier said, setting the document on his desk.

Evans said, "I understand. My team will only be looking for specific things. We look, but don't see what we're not supposed to."

Roberts slammed his fist on Xavier's desk saying, "You know this is bullshit. I don't know anything about your dead girl. You have no right to look at my files. They're confidential, you can't just look at them."

"Look, I get it. I do. I serve a lot of warrants, mostly to unhappy people," Evans said, trying to assure them. "I'm going to tell you the same thing I tell everyone. I'm doing my due diligence, tracking down leads. If you have nothing to worry about, then don't worry about it. I'll get the laptop and phone back to you as soon as we're through with them." He was not persuaded by Roberts's overt display of anger, who was putting on a show for his partners.

"I want your assurance that our confidential work will not be reviewed," Xavier demanded.

"I can guarantee you that we won't look at any of your confidential files," Evans exaggerated. At that point, he just wanted to get the laptop and phone and get out of there.

"Roberts, give him your stuff," Xavier said, staring at Evans.

Roberts pulled his phone from his breast coat pocket and handed it to Evans. "I don't have the laptop."

Everyone in the room looked at Roberts incredulously.

Bull nodded.

"What do you mean you don't have it?" Evans asked, reaching for the phone. "Where is it?"

"It's not here. Not here, here, as in the office, here," Roberts said, looking at Xavier.

"Well, I guess we'll have to go to your house and get it," Evans said.

"What the hell, Roberts. Give him the damn laptop," Xavier said, now staring at Roberts.

Evans smiled at Roberts's evasiveness. Xavier was not in the mood for Roberts's games and was not smiling. Bull's expression had not changed; he continued nodding.

Roberts said, "It's not at home, and it's not here in the office, either."

"Then where is it?" Evans asked, smiling at his attempt to hide the evidence which couldn't be hidden.

"My car, it's in my car," Roberts said, looking down.

"Fine, let's get to the parking lot and your car. Say, Reefer, before we leave, will you validate my ticket?" Evans flamboyantly patted his pockets, apparently looking for a parking ticket stub.

Evans followed Roberts to the parking lot and retrieved the laptop. Evans went to the ground floor, then headed to his home base.

As soon as he arrived at Headquarters, he walked to the Forensics Unit. He came across Spencer reviewing a blood splatter pattern from a recent shooting. The gunfire was fallout from the gang turf war that he was investigating.

"Hey, Spense, how's it goin'?" Evans asked.

Spencer brushed hair off his face and said, "Great, I'm working on the gang shooting which you dumped in my lap."

Evans said, “Sorry about that, but someone’s gotta do it. Have you seen Sarah?”

Spencer pointed north and said, “Check out her office. That’s usually where the Mini-Cyborg hangs out.”

“Whoa. What does Sarah think of her new moniker?”

“Loves it,” Spencer said. “Or maybe it’s me who appreciates a job well done. Anyway, check out her office.”

Evans knocked on the semi-opened door, “Sarah, got a minute?” Seeing no one, he left the empty workstation.

“Spence, she’s not here,” Evans said.

“You’re right, I completely forgot. She had to pick up Sammy. Has she shown you his latest pictures?”

“Hard to miss them, she greets everyone with her phone open to Photos. Okay, tell her I stopped by with a laptop and phone. They’re important, they belong to Roberts.”

“I’ll tell her you stopped by. Does she know who this Roberts guy is, because I don’t.”

“Yeah, she does. He’s involved with the Three Fires killing,” Evans said.

“Gotcha.”

Chapter 56

In the biomedical field alone, more than one million papers, about two per minute, are entered in the PubMed database each year.

When Abernathy first started at Solutions & Synergy, he was excited about the next chapter of his career. He enthusiastically arrived at the office early, before six. The further he distanced himself from clinical medicine, the more the excitement eroded. The void was filled with apathy.

He trudged into his office and hung up his overcoat. Sitting in darkness, he turned on his desktop. The job, the culture had worn him down. It was ten minutes before eight.

Abernathy sent an email to every SETTUP Clinical Site PI thanking them for their participation in the trial. They were closing in on their planned enrollment of 2,000 patients. He then asked the trial biostatisticians for data as soon as enrollment ended. He was anxious to put SETTUP behind him. The sooner, the better. If the study ended on a positive note, he'd keep his string of receiving five-figure end-of-year bonuses alive.

He was in the middle of two projects and decided to address the manuscript first. He wouldn't receive the final statistics for weeks, possibly months, so he decided to get a head start on writing the manuscript. He'd fill in the Results and Conclusions sections later.

Abernathy knew which trial PIs wanted to contribute to the manuscript. Publishing the results of a large clinical trial in Epilepsia or a similar peer-reviewed journal with an Impact Factor north of five offered each contributing PI a chance to buff their respective CVs. He wanted to get the initial draft out, knowing the others would be tied up with clinical duties, committee work, and teaching.

Two hours later, he was satisfied with the first draft.

Abstract

Objective: Successful treatment of status epilepticus (SE) is time dependent. The longer SE persists, the chance of developing refractory or super refractory SE increases. We compared treating SE with SGY140008-12 versus standard of care in 2,000 consecutive patients admitted with SE.

Methods: Two thousand patients, admitted with a diagnosis of SE at forty-five Clinical Sites, were randomly assigned to receive SGY140008-12 or standard of care.

Results: XX% of patients in the study group responded well to SGY140008-12. The time to stop SE in the study group was XX minutes, versus YY minutes in the standard of care cohort (p= 0.000YYY). XX% of patients treated with SGY140008-12 developed seizures within twenty-four hours following cessation of SE versus YY% in the standard of care group (p= 0.000XXX).

Conclusions: SGY140008-12 is effective in stopping SE. SGY140008-12 treated patients developed refractory SE XX% less often than the standard of care cohort (p=0.00ZZ). The treated cohort had a shorter length of stay, less morbidity, and less mortality than those in the standard of care group.

Abernathy sent the first draft to a few PIs, most of whom he had worked with on other trials. It would be weeks before he would hear back from them. Project two was more involved.

He started with the first New Drug Application (NDA) document: Application to Market a New or Abbreviated New Drug for Human Use. There were fourteen documents that needed to be completed to even get a review by the Center for Drug Evaluation and Research. The CDER Committee, the FDA's review body, was made up of scientists, clinicians, pharmacists, and statisticians. Numerous attachments were required and because he didn't have all the data, he was unable to complete the first document. And so it went. He'd start a section, fill in as much as he could, then move on to the next one. He stood up at three and stretched. He went to the bathroom and returned to his desk to hear the phone ringing.

Chapter 57

Jay Berwanger received the first Heisman Trophy in 1935 while he was a senior at the University of Chicago.

Evans called Solutions & Synergy and asked to be forwarded to Dr. Abernathy. "Hi Dr. Abernathy. Thank you for taking the time to speak with me."

"When do I get my phone and computer back?" Abernathy demanded.

"Soon, I hope. Very soon."

"Detective, your annoying habit of calling at all hours of the day interrupts my workflow. I don't have time for your bullshit, I have things to do," the oncologist said.

Evans said, "I just have a few follow-up questions about Emily. But before that, I'm computer illiterate and can't email my way out of a wet paper bag. How are your computer skills?"

"I spend most of my day on the computer. I'm capable of writing notes and letters."

"If something goes wrong with your computer, will you call IT for help, or are you able to fix it yourself?"

"What does this have to do with Emily? I just told you that my computer skills are better than most."

Evans replied, "Nothing, just wondering."

"I don't have time for your nonsense. You know what, I'm tired of your harassment, too. I should report you to your superiors."

"Harassment? I'm just doing my job, Doctor. Do you know Stephen Cohen?" Evans asked.

Abernathy hesitated. "I'm not familiar with anyone by that name."

"He works for you. Or used to work for you, I should say. He worked in Jacksonville on that SETTUP trial until you fired him. Still don't know him?"

"I do not. Solutions & Synergy has thousands of employees, and I can't possibly know all of them."

Evans said, "Well, that's interesting. You don't know Stephen

Cohen, who worked on your trial, and your computer skills are better than average, right?"

"What do my computer skills have to do with Cohen? This is ridiculous. You have no idea what you're doing Evans."

"So, it's Cohen now. You sure you don't know Stephen?"

Abernathy replied, "Positive."

Evans said, "Let me get this straight. You're insisting that you don't know someone that you recently fired. Do you terminate so many people that you can't keep them straight?"

"I told you, I've never met anyone named Cohen," Abernathy said.

"Then why did you hack his email account?"

"I don't know what you're talking about. I'm no hacker, I've never broken into anything."

"Never? That's not what my forensic cyber specialist told me."

"Where do you come up with this crap?"

"I can assure you that it's not crap. I have to caution you, Doctor. Lying gets me upset and you don't want to do that. I've been told that I'm not very nice to people who mess with me. Let's get back to Emily for a moment. Had Emily expressed concerns to you about stroke side effects that she recorded during the SETTUP trial?"

Abernathy said, "I already told you that SAEs are reported every day, during every clinical trial that I've ever been involved with over the past thirty years. Serious adverse events have been reported since we enrolled our first patient and they're still being reported. All it takes is for one person to complain of a symptom and we're obligated to document it, record it, and report it. There was nothing in Emily's reports that were alarming or of concern. Now, if you'll excuse me, I have a meeting."

Finding Abernathy adequately agitated, Evans asked, "You wrote in an email to Emily about an incident. What was the incident?"

"I don't know what you're talking about," Abernathy stammered.

"Yeah, I read it in one of Emily's emails. On December 19, you sent Emily a note that said, and I quote, 'I hope you're not jeopardizing your career over the incident.' You then reminded Emily that she had a performance review coming up."

Abernathy paused. "I don't recall any incident. It must have somehow been related to her work."

Evans wasn't going to let Abernathy off that easily and asked, "What do you mean 'related to her work?'"

Abernathy replied, "That was months ago, I don't remember the details. She must have done something wrong. It had to be something related to her position."

"How do you know that it was months ago if you can't recall the incident?"

"What? I don't know. You said it was months. What I do know, is that I don't like your insinuations. Maybe I should have my attorney present before answering any more of your questions."

"We're having a casual conversation here. How would you describe your relationship with Emily?" Evans asked.

"I was her supervisor, nothing more," Abernathy said.

Evans said, "Here's what I think. I think you tried to hit on Emily and when she gave you the Heisman, you had her killed."

"Are you crazy? I've never killed anyone. I told you that personal relationships are forbidden between Solutions & Synergy employees. My relationship with Emily was strictly professional. I'll tell you what's unprofessional, your character assassination. Do you harass and threaten everyone like this?" Abernathy said.

Evans said, "Dr. Abernathy, please don't take offense to my questions. I know they're difficult. I don't want to leave a single stone unturned in this investigation."

Abernathy replied, "I have my meeting."

"I was going through your financial records, and saw that you recently made trips to Boston and Chicago."

"Is there a question in there?" Abernathy snapped.

"What was the purpose of those trips?"

"Am I obliged to answer you?"

"You are under no legal obligation to answer any of my

questions. I was wondering if they had anything to do with the recently deceased or disabled SETTUP employees?"

Abernathy said, "You're grasping. I had nothing to do with Emily's death, or the others, nothing at all. Why aren't you out looking for the guy who killed them?"

"You know, the first time we spoke, you told me that Emily committed suicide. Now you're claiming that she was murdered. What changed your mind? And what about your other employees who abruptly stopped working on SETTUP? Why were you in Boston and Chicago, cities where your employees were killed and assaulted."

Abernathy said, "My visit to Boston was related to CME. I need to obtain so many hours per year to maintain my medical license. I attended the International Conference on Big Data Analytics in Healthcare in Boston. Chicago was purely for pleasure. My wife likes to go shopping on the Miracle Mile after Christmas, when everyone has sales going on. Nothing nefarious about either trip, Detective."

Evans asked, "And CME is what, exactly?"

"Continuing Medical Education."

"Nice. My doctor goes to conferences for the same reason, to keep up on the latest. I want to get back to Emily. How were her performance reviews?"

"She was doing okay, other than the one incident."

"So, you recall it now? The one where she shamed you for acting like the predator that you are?" Evans asked.

"Have you completely lost your mind? I already told you that I don't recall the incident, which had nothing to do with me. And how dare you call me a predator," Abernathy said tersely.

Evans said, "Doctor, where were you on January 8?"

"How the hell do I know where I was on January 8, for Christ's sake."

"Yes, I know two weeks was a long time ago. Let me help you out by telling you that a colleague of yours, Emily Naismith, was murdered in Grand Rapids on Sunday, the eighth of January."

"That doesn't help me at all," Abernathy said.

Evans asked, "Were you at home? Perhaps you were at

work? Traveling? Do you travel for your job, Doctor?"

"Yes, I travel a little, not much."

"So, you think you were at home, work, or traveling, is that right?" Evans asked.

"I don't know where I was. How is my whereabouts relevant? Is this how you conduct all your investigations? Throwing out wild accusations like this," Abernathy said.

"I'm not accusing you of anything. I'm just trying to determine your whereabouts on January 8. It's a straightforward question."

"And I've already told you that I don't know where I was on *any* day this month. Ridiculous."

Evans said, "I'm a little surprised that you're so upset by my question. My doctor asks me all kinds of questions during my physical. Asking questions is kind of a doctor's thing, isn't it?"

"I'm hanging up," Abernathy said.

"And I'm sorry you feel it's ridiculous of me to ask questions while I'm trying to solve a homicide. Maybe you can check your calendar as we speak," Evans said.

"This is bullshit. Cast a wide net and see what you catch. Any first-year medical student will tell you that's a lazy way to make a diagnosis. Probably a lazy way to catch a criminal too. No warrant, no calendar."

"I've got a question for you. What's the medical explanation for the little hairs on my neck sticking up?"

"I haven't the faintest idea of how you're wired," Abernathy said.

"Yeah, I can't explain it either. It's weird. You know what I'm talking about?"

"No, I've never experienced anything like that."

"I'm asking because, that's the feeling I get whenever someone that I'm interviewing asks for a lawyer. I get that same feeling whenever someone refuses to show me something without a warrant. Still no explanation for the phenomenon, Doctor?" Evans asked.

"You've wasted enough of my time," Abernathy said.

"Only a couple more questions. Did you, or anyone at

Solutions & Synergy, ask SGY Bioengineering for a loan?"

"You're an idiot, Evans. I would never ask them for a loan. That's what banks are for."

With one more item on his agenda, Evans asked, "Do you have a problem with Stella Murray?"

"I don't know Dr. Murray."

With pursed lips, Evans said, "Oh, but I think you do. You see, I never said she was a physician. Let me make myself perfectly clear. I'm very fond of Dr. Murray. Very. If anything, anything at all, happens to her, I'm coming for you."

Abernathy said, "Are you threatening me?"

"You're goddamn right I'm threatening you. Anything at all, Abernathy."

"That's it, we're done here."

"And you can bet your ass that I'm get—"

Abernathy ended the call before Evans was able to tell Abernathy that he was getting close to solving Emily's murder.

Evans was getting anything but the truth from Abernathy. He lied when he said he didn't know Stephen Cohen. He lied about the investigational drug causing stroke. He lied about not knowing where he was on January 8. He was so obsessive-compulsive that he knew exactly where he was every minute of every day. He lied about not knowing Stella. The only thing Abernathy wasn't lying about was his computer skills, which he downplayed.

It was late, after hours, but Evans called Sarah and asked her to confirm whether Abernathy's credit card was used in Boston and Chicago. Sarah verified the dates when his card was used at a hotel and two restaurants in Boston; she confirmed that there were several purchases made on his card in Chicago this past winter and the prior year as well.

Chapter 58

Ancient Greeks believed the cause of epilepsy involved a brain overflowing with phlegm, which, when it rushed into blood vessels, caused symptoms of the attack.

Sarah entered her office, removed her coat and boots, sat at her desk, and saw a note to call Evans. Typical Evans, he was going at the Emily case with everything he had. He had even called the previous night with credit card questions about Abernathy. Sarah was so focused on Emily's murder that she'd neglected Smitty's fraud case. She vowed to finish the fraud file before doing anything more on the Three Fires homicide.

Later that afternoon, Sarah sighed. The fraud case was exhausting. A HUD landlord had been caught submitting invoices with inflated rent for low-income clients, people with disabilities, and relatives of disabled clients. It turned out that some of the relatives of the clients with disabilities had not been living in HUD low-income apartments; housing had been provided by one of the State's Level IV Correctional Facilities. The landlord was caught when a brother of a disabled client was going through the release process from the Muskegon Correctional Facility, and an astute Social Worker noted that the soon-to-be-released prisoner had listed the low-income HUD apartment as his address for the entirety of his twenty-six month stay at MCF. Smitty investigated and found rampant abuse of the system by the HUD landlord in question. Sarah found receipts of fraudulent charges going back decades.

She signed out Roberts's laptop from Evidence and decided to look at his electronic communications, finances, and phone, in descending order. She went online and read that Roberts was a partner in COR; a venture capital group that did a good job of raising capital and an even better job of investing said capital.

Roberts's primary Inbox folder was clogged with 1,014 mucus plugging emails. He obviously didn't utilize the Delete button. Sarah found Tolonetzumab in the subject title for hundreds of emails from three years ago and researched it. Tolonetzumab was a drug that showed promise with its ability to remove amyloid, a toxic protein, from the brains of genetically engineered mice who developed Alzheimer's Disease. However, in two Phase III trials Tolonetzumab treated patients hadn't improved their memory, which meant the trial had not met its primary end point. Tolonetzumab was not approved by the FDA. Hmm. Maybe Roberts's touch wasn't a hundred percent after all.

Sarah filtered the search to include SETTUP and found he received many emails, but sent none, with SETTUP in the subject heading. She discovered an email sent to Stephanie Van Huissen gauging her interest in a career change. Was she interested in working for Solutions & Synergy? Well, that's interesting. The email was dated January 9, the day after Emily's murder.

Sarah found an email with the subject of TEST. Roberts had communicated with some guy named DB about an encrypted email. DB replied that he couldn't break the encryption. She ran a decryption program and, twenty minutes later, was able to read the cryptic note. The content was not significant, it was just a test.

She found that Roberts had a personal email account, which only family and friends used. She found nothing with COR in the subject line of his private Inbox. She then searched after applying filters of SETTUP + Emily Naismith and SETTUP + SGY Bioengineering and came up empty handed. Likewise, there was no communication with Abernathy in Roberts's personal email account.

She searched the cloud and found that Roberts had a third email account on the darknet, the dark web. WTF was a partner in a prominent venture capital group doing on the dark web. This case keeps on giving and giving. He hadn't used the dark web account often; he had only sent a few emails from it. She snapped her fingers and pointed at her laptop. That's what the TEST email he sent to DB must have been for.

Her computing skills were going to be seriously challenged by his use of the dark web. The darknet's encryption technology routes a dark web user's data through a minimum of three intermediate servers. The transmitted information can be decrypted only by the subsequent node in the scheme, and each node can only decrypt enough to enable it to send information to the next node. A node cannot detect where transmitted information came from, building in electronic rapid forgetting and thus, anonymity. And a hell of a decryption challenge. Four hours later, Sarah discovered the IP address of the email account that Roberts communicated with on the dark web. She couldn't uncover who owned the IP address; it was a dead end, which is presumably what he wanted.

She found his financial records even more interesting. He made a boatload of money, seven figures, nearly every year. She noted that Roberts frequently used automatic bill payments for two mortgages, property taxes, and monthly dues for two Country Clubs. Once she had a good handle on his monthly expenses, she isolated every payment over $5,000. There were many.

Roberts took his family on a Hawaiian vacation last winter with the flights alone costing him $7,000. Aloha. He spent a minimum of $5,000 on each of the last five Christmases. Happy Holidays. He recently purchased a BMW for $70,000. A one percenter.

She found a few payments which were not aligned with holidays or vacations. Most, but not all, went to a Swiss account. Sarah noted a pattern where each wire transfer was preceded by a Venmo exchange. Roberts initiated a Venmo transaction of $50,000 a few days prior to making a $50,000 wire transfer to Switzerland. Those deals took place a week before Emily was killed. A Venmo transfer of $15,000 took place the same day as a $150,000 wire transfer, two days after Emily was murdered. Maybe that accounted for Boston and Chicago? Holy shit. Without a preceding Venmo deal, he had recently transferred $750,000 to the same Swiss account.

She easily accessed Roberts's checking account and found each Venmo transaction went to Abernathy. Not smart guys, not smart at all. You can run, but you can't hide when you're up against the first string.

She had enough information to satisfy Evans and called him

with a critical update.

"Gordie, first off, did you know that Roberts recommended that this Stephanie Van Huissen woman should be hired by Solutions & Synergy as a Site Monitor? He specifically chose her as Emily's replacement."

"Wait a bloody minute. How did Roberts even know about the open position?" Evans asked.

"No clue. Roberts asked Stephanie about her personal life, work interests, career goals, that sort of thing. He then told her that Solutions & Synergy needed to fill an opening. Stephanie responded to him by telling him that she would consider the opportunity."

"So, Roberts specifically recommended Stephanie to Abernathy for the Grand Rapids position," Evans said.

"Yes, that's the way I read the emails," Sarah said.

"So, Abernathy and Roberts are tied at the hip, at least through Stephanie."

"Yup."

Evans said, "I know you said no last night, but are you absolutely sure that Abernathy wasn't in Grand Rapids on the day that Emily was murdered?"

"Positive. He wasn't anywhere near GR on or around January 8."

"What about Latham? Any connection between Clive Latham and those two guys?"

"Not yet. But I've got more on Roberts," Sarah said.

"Hold that thought. I've got a conference call," Evans said.

Chapter 59

Bromides were introduced in 1857 as the first medication for seizures.

Roberts was accustomed to making cold calls. He had identified two companies for the next round: Northern Biotech and SGY Bioengineering. There were similarities between the two companies. Both were well run with productive labs. Each company recently achieved marketplace success with a drug (Northern Biotech), and an imaging contrast material (SGY Bioengineering). If, or rather when, things progressed and COR purchased one of the organizations, he anticipated being named to the Board of Directors of the newly acquired business.

Northern Biotech had a reputation for forward thinking while applying novel technology, cutting edge stuff, that caught the attention of investors. They were in the final stages of developing a new class of drugs with anti-apoptotic properties, which mitigated damage from traumatic brain injuries. SGY Bioengineering's most recent success story was a contrast material (Seizural) used during PET scans as part of the presurgical evaluation of medically refractory epilepsy. The PET scan ligand bound to, and highlighted, neurons where a seizure just started. The PET hot spots provided a roadmap for surgically removing the seizure nidus.

Roberts was happy to be home after visiting Northern Biotech. He was impressed with their personnel, their lab, their scientists, and most importantly, their eagerness to work with the COR Management Team. He was entertained by Northern Biotech to the *n*th degree. He attended a Lakers game, met a retired, but still famous Laker, and dined in fine restaurants. His initial interaction with SGY Bioengineering was different.

His call to SGY Bioengineering began with him being put on hold. Eventually, their lead scientist, Scott Williams, came to the phone and without apologizing for the delay, said their CFO was recently arrested for embezzling company funds and wouldn't be available for negotiations, should things progress that far. In the next breath, the scientist said he wouldn't work for The Man. If Roberts intended on attempting a hostile takeover of SGY Bioengineering he should give up right then. The scientist eventually agreed to meet with Roberts.

He drove to SGY Bioengineering and examined the facility before entering. He stared at the brick building, which he estimated was built twenty years before. He saw no major flaws with the foundation, the roof, or the structure itself. He stomped his feet on a small mat inside the front door, removing as much snow from his Italian leather shoes as possible.

His first impression of the lobby was that it was interesting, but not in a good way. His first action, as a member of the Board of Directors of SGY Bioengineering, would be to construct an inspirational reception area. He wanted whoever walked through the front door to be impressed and the current decor didn't do it. He rang the bell and waited as instructed.

A young lab tech answered the bell and stared at Roberts, who broke the silence by saying, "I'm Koral Roberts, I have an appointment with Scott Williams and his partners."

"Right. Come on in. Watch it with those shoes, it might be slippery in here."

"Thank you, I will. Please lead the way," Roberts said, stomping his feet a second time. They walked through the lab where he recognized much of the equipment that he had seen during his forty-five-minute tour of Northern Biotech.

Scott approached Roberts and the lab tech, and without introducing himself said, "Let's go to the conference room, Mr. Roberts."

Roberts was glad to be spared another lab tour, but man, this dude was different with a capital D. No flowery, shallow bullshit greetings. And what's up with the tie-dye tee shirt splashed with yellows, greens, and blues. Dude belonged in California.

Roberts walked alongside Scott to the Conference Room where Yi and Gwen were seated at a table. Scott motioned for Roberts to sit at one end of the table, and lumbered toward his customary seat.

Gwen stood and spoke, "I'm Gwen Hopkins and this is Yi

Zhang," motioning toward her peer. "We're the G and Y of SGY Bioengineering."

Removing his outer coat before sitting, he said, "Koral Roberts. I'm pleased to meet you. Thank you for taking the time to meet with me tonight. I'm a partner in a venture capital group called COR and we've been working with small bioengineering companies, much like yourselves, for several years now. We recognize that it takes a lot to get drugs through the federal morass known as the FDA approval process. We're able to offer you financial, managerial, and operational support to help you get the seizure drug, which you've worked so hard to develop, through the regulatory process and on the market.

"As you can imagine, we do our due diligence prior to approaching companies. I've been watching the results of SETTUP for several months now and I must say that I'm impressed with your drug. And it's not just me. I recently got back from the annual American Epilepsy Society meeting in Los Angeles. The physicians involved in the trial created a buzz when they reported the preliminary results. They want the drug available to them *now*."

Scott set the latest issue of *Science* on a stack of journals. "Have you ever heard of Seizural?"

"I'm familiar with your PET scan ligand, yes. Your sales were above $5M during its first year on the market. Impressive stuff," Roberts said.

"Yeah, it works okay. Were you also aware that we sold a percentage of Seizural to another venture capital group?" Scott asked.

"May I be frank? I take my job seriously when I'm talking about partnering with someone. Yes, I know all about Seizural and Great Lakes VC. I know everything there is to know about SGY Bioengineering," Roberts said, imperceptibly thrusting his chest forward.

"Then you know that I meant it when I said we will not sell out to The Man," Scott said, pushing the pile of journals forward two inches. Not liking how it looked on the table, he returned the pile to its original position.

"Now wait a minute Scott, let's hear him out. Let's hear what he has to say. What do you think, Yi"? Gwen said, looking at Yi for confirmation.

"Brilliant, innit. I would like to hear more from Mr. Roberts himself," Yi said.

"I don't want him getting too excited, that's all. We're in a good position financially, to the point that we decide who we partner with and what help, if any, that we need. I'm not giving up ownership. That's a hard stop," Scott said. He repeatedly traced the title of the journal *Science* with his right index finger.

"I know that Scott, we all know that. I just think that it doesn't hurt to hear him out, to hear what he's proposing," Gwen said, sitting forward, resting her elbows on the table.

Roberts sat up straighter and said, "I also hear you loud and clear. We're the ones taking the risk here. Look, if your seizure drug isn't approved by the FDA, you still get a nice paycheck and we're the ones on the outside looking in. If SETTUP tanks, then we've just sunk a ton of money into your drug for nothing. Remember, it's not just the money. When you partner with COR, we offer managerial assistance and operational support. Together, we would take SGY Bioengineering to the next level. Comfortable, retirement level. Correct me if I'm wrong, but I believe you just told me about an open position in your Finance Department."

"Scott, we desperately need a CFO, which they're willing to help us out with," Gwen said.

Yi nodded saying, "Does anyone remember how last summer Albert was strutting around like a knob during our office meetings. He told me that he was diagnosed with restless leg syndrome, which caused discomfort in his legs when he had to sit for more than a few minutes. He was put on a medication which alleviated the pain. I'm wondering if the medication caused him to gamble, because his gamblings addiction began after he started on it for his miserable legs."

Roberts spoke up. "I've heard of that. A buddy of mine is a Neurologist at Northwestern. He was telling me about this guy who became addicted to porn when he took a Parkinson's drug.

He told me they usually treat restless leg syndrome with Parkinson's medications. Maybe your CFO took the same thing."

Scott looked up and said, "Albert's a good man, if what you're saying is true, we need to get him to a Neurologist. I don't want these talks to go any further until he's been checked out. Thank you for your time, Mr. Roberts."

Roberts smiled.

Yi stared.

Gwen shook her head and, clearing her throat, said, "Thank you for coming over Mr. Roberts. We're interested in hearing more about what you have to offer."

He removed business cards from his coat pocket and slid one toward each of the scientists, saying, "I understand. Please take my card and let's be in touch."

"Thank you again for meeting with us," Gwen said.

"That's fine. I'll circle back in a couple of weeks," Roberts said, standing.

Scott studied the business card and said, "Mr. Roberts, there was a detective here the other day asking if I had heard from you. A Detective Evans."

Roberts appeared stunned; a pallor emerged. "He asked about me? What did he want?"

Scott said, "Yeah, he wanted to know if you were interested in buying us or our drug. I told him the same thing I told you, I won't sell out to The Man."

Roberts's color had not returned as he walked out in silence.

Scott's glasses had migrated near the tip of his nose. Pushing them up, he asked, "Yi, didn't you communicate with a neurologist in GR about SGY140008-12?"

Yi said, "Yes. I had email communications with Dr. Murrays."

"Will you ask her to see Albert? We need our CFO back," Scott said.

"Yes, I will do that for you," Yi said.

Gwen said, "Hold on there, Scott. Maybe Albert had a reaction to a medication that caused his gambling, but he still stole from us. And what about Yi?"

"What about her?" Scott asked, staring at Yi.

"Haven't you noticed how Albert makes Yi feel uneasy? It's been going on for years. We've had enough of Albert around here," Gwen said.

"Yi?" Scott asked.

"It is true."

"I hadn't noticed. But I still want him checked out," Scott said.

"That's fine, but Albert's time here has come to an end," Gwen said.

Chapter 60

In 1713, the Council of Geneva established regulations that prohibited Swiss Banks from sharing client information with anyone except the client, unless the City Council agreed with the need to divulge information.

Sarah completed an exhaustive search of Roberts's electronic communications and turned her attention to the guy that Evans believes to be the trigger person- Clive Latham. She discovered that Latham, after fulfilling his military service, worked as a comic. She remembered seeing Latham's IP address before but couldn't recall where or when. Booting up her desktop, it hit her.

It was Roberts. She recognized Latham's IP address from her search of Roberts's laptop and his dark web communications. She had just tied Roberts to a computer owned by Clive Latham. She left a message for Evans to emergently prepare an affidavit that would allow her to examine Roberts's financial affairs, including all overseas transactions.

Later that morning, Sarah put Roberts finances under the microscope, starting with his wire transfers. She discovered that every wire transfer went to Mirabaud & Cie, a private Swiss Bank. Having secured a warrant, Sarah had an hour long conversation with the bank's Risk Manager before she was granted access to Mirabaud & Cie's internal system and from there, individual accounts. Through three transactions, Roberts had transferred $1M to a Trust named KFAP, LTD. The Trust account held assets in excess of $4M. Who are you, KFAP? Sarah followed up and found the Trustee for KFAP, LTD was none other than Clive Latham.

Working backwards through Latham's IP address, Sarah hacked his laptop and reviewed his search history, which was significant. He looked up Emily Naismith on January 3 and 4, days before her murder. Later that week, he examined the net for information on Tricia and Randy, only days before her death and his mugging. Latham had not looked at Stephen Cohen, which made sense because it was Abernathy, not Latham, who schemed to have Stephen fired. Holy shit. Over the past two days, Latham had been researching someone else.

Sarah called Evans and he failed to pick up. “Troy, where are you? Aren’t you coming to the Tower? I’ve got some critical stuff for you. Call me back.”

Not hearing from him, she closed her laptop, put on her boots and coat, and left the Department. Sammy, her eighteen-month-old toddler, was scheduled for a checkup with his pediatrician.

Chapter 61

Plato thought Sacred Disease, the name given to epilepsy, was justified because the disease disturbed the revolutions in the head, which were the most divine.

Evans ended his conference call with the Assistant Prosecutor. He listened to Sarah's message and then strode to the Forensics to get updates from her. He ran across Spence as he entered the fourth floor.

"Hey Gordie. Remember when you asked me to check out the pill bottles from the Three Fires Hotel?" Spencer said.

"Yeah, whatever happened with that? I haven't heard anything."

"These things take time. Anyway, I ran the pills through mass spectroscopy and guess what I found?"

"Fentanyl."

"Bingo. Every pill in her melatonin bottle was fentanyl. And there's something else," Spencer said.

"Something mixed in? I thought you just said they were fentanyl," Evans said.

"No, the pills were all fentanyl. What's interesting is that under the scope I could see an engraving on the side of each pill."

"Initials or a name?"

"Don't know. I found KFAP on every one of those little suckers."

"KFAP? What does that even mean?" Evans asked.

"No idea. I searched it on the net. The only thing that came up was a Korean rap song, which made my head spin and will never make Casey Kasem's Top Forty. Anyway, I sent KFAP through the Uniform Crime Reports and the National Incident-Based Reporting System and got a hit. KFAP was engraved on a .308 bullet casing that was used in a Miami shooting a couple of years ago, which I confirmed through NIBIN (National Integrated Ballistic Information Network). Probably Cartel related. Never got the shooter."

"Nice work on the melatonin. But a Cartel? What the hell. I

think Latham performs regularly in Miami, but I'm not sure how KFAP helps me."

"Who's Latham, again?"

"He's the guy I've targeted for killing Emily. Thanks for the follow up, Spence."

"We aim to please, Gordie."

"And you always deliver. Hey, Sarah said she's got something for me. Have you seen her?"

"You just missed her. She took Sammy to the pediatrician. You can try calling her."

Evans called, "Hey, it's me. I'm here and you're not. You said you've got more stuff on Roberts."

"I do. Hey asswipe! It doesn't get any redder than that. You still with me?" Sarah said.

"Yeah, I'm here. Maybe we should wait until you get back, I don't want you getting in an accident," Evans said.

"I'm good, I'm hands free. Listen, I forgot to tell you that I found a few emails between Roberts and his group concerning the purchase of SGY Bioengineering, the company that made the seizure drug. It turns out that Roberts pushed hard to buy the company. He boasted that it had shown great promise in Phase I and II trials and was 'killing it,' his words not mine, in the current Phase III trial. He suggested, demanded really, that COR buy SGY Bioengineering," Sarah said.

Evans asked, "Did Roberts say anything about Emily in those emails?"

"No mention of Emily. No mention of checking the trial up close and personal. No emails with stroke in the subject line or content. Now, he received a couple of emails from Abernathy regarding SETTUP. Most were the blast type, sent out to a host of people on the team."

"That's all you have for me, nothing on Latham?"

"No, I've got a lot more, but I'm at the pediatrician's office. I'm gonna have to let you go. I'll call you when I get back."

Chapter 62

Seizures are referenced in three of the four Gospels in the Bible: Mark 9:17-22, Matthew 17:14-20, Luke 9:38-42.

Sarah dropped Sammy off at the sitter's before returning to Headquarters. She called Evans and asked him to come up to the Tower.

Evans walked directly to Sarah's office asking, "Did you have to take Sammy in today?"

"Well, when I told my husband about Sammy's appointment this morning, he told me 'I'm out. I'm in the middle of a big project.' So, in addition to taking care of the laundry, shopping, cooking, and working full-time, my husband decided that Sammy had only one parent today. How about you? Do you help with the laundry, shopping, kids?" Sarah asked.

Evans said, "I've been told laundry isn't my strong suit and I'm not allowed in the kitchen. Sorry, I was out of line. You're busier than I'll ever be. Tell me about this critical information. I hope it's about Roberts. Have you been able to tie him to Emily? Or to Latham?"

Sarah said, "Kind of. But let's back up for a sec. When I got back, Spencer told me that he found KFAP on Emily's pills and a bullet casing. Which I thought was fascinating, because completely independently, I found KFAP on Latham's Swiss account. I think they're the same guy–KFAP and Latham are. Were you aware that Roberts paid Abernathy a ton of money, presumably for results from SETTUP?"

"This is great stuff. What else about Abernathy? Other than Emily's stroke email, do you have anything that ties Abernathy to Emily?"

"No, but he's been in communication with Latham," Sarah said.

"Abernathy? Wait, who's been talking to Latham?"

"Roberts, the venture capital guy," Sarah said.

"Roberts? Not Abernathy? Roberts has been in touch with Latham?"

"If you call paying Latham a million bucks being in touch with him, then yes, Roberts has been in touch with Latham. The timing of the payments correlates with Emily's death, the death in Boston, and the mugging in Chicago. You need to find him, find Latham."

"I will. I mean, I know about him. I know who he is," Evans said.

"You were right, you know. You told me to check out the Three Fires Hotel CCTV tapes. That's where I first found Latham. He's the one who erased the tape."

"No shit."

"That's right, Latham's definitely your guy. But that's not all," Sarah said.

"I know he's a piece of shit who needs to be put away."

"No, you don't get it. Troy, the searches for Emily, Tricia, and Randy, they're old. Latham is still researching people tied to the case."

"Jesus." Evans's heart started racing and he broke out into a sweat when she told him who Latham had been cyberstalking.

Chapter 63

Plutarch wrote, "Of all the animals, the goat is most seized with epilepsy and gives it to those who eat or touch one taken by the disease."

Evans walked back to his desk and pieced together what he had so far. Abernathy sold SETTUP results to Roberts, information which Roberts then used to decide whether to purchase SGY Bioengineering, the company that made the seizure drug. Buying the drug manufacturing company would make Roberts a chunk of change, but only if no more strokes were reported. He hires Latham to kill Emily, who reported the first, but presumably not the last, stroke to Abernathy and the FDA.

Evans wrote out arrest warrants for Roberts, Latham, and Abernathy. He submitted them to the Judge without having them reviewed by the Prosecutor's office.

He contemplated his next move while reviewing Latham's website. Latham had performed at Sisyphus Comedy Club in Minneapolis the weekend before. How would he get to Grand Rapids? Return home to Indianapolis first? Or fly directly from Minneapolis to GR?

He drove to Gerald R. Ford International Airport intending to speak to each airline about their flights from either Indianapolis or Minneapolis to GR. He started with United.

The United supervisor said, "Detective, nice to see you again."

"Listen, I haven't had time to get a warrant, but you were so helpful last time that I'm going to ask for your help again. I'm here to see if you brought a certain someone from Indy or Minneapolis."

"I've had no complaints about our last conversation, so I guess we're good to go. Let's start with Minneapolis because we have several direct flights from MSP. When did he or she travel?"

Evans said, "Probably Saturday night, Sunday morning, or anytime Monday. It's a guy, by the name of Clive Latham."

"Okay. Let's see what we have here. It looks like he last traveled with us back in December–from BOS to IND."

"Okay, thanks for your time." Evans suspected that Latham murdered Tricia just prior to taking that flight. He likely then drove to Chicago where he assaulted Randy.

Evans made his way down the line. Delta was next. He had taken several direct Delta flights to Minneapolis and hoped Delta would give him his answer. He approached the counter asking to see the supervisor. Making no headway, he brought out his shield, and was promptly taken behind the counter to the supervisor's office.

"That Detective is here to see you, again."

"Fine. Come on in, Detective."

Evans stated, "Thank you for seeing me without an appointment. I have a name for you this time. I need to know if Clive Latham flew from Minneapolis to GR within the last four days."

"Latham? Let's see. Yes and no. He arrived from IND, not MSP, on Sunday. He came in on the DL1522, which was on time, by the way."

"Perfect. That's all I needed," Evans said, standing.

"That's it? That's all you need. That was easy."

Evans walked directly past airline check-in kiosks to the car rentals booths. A customer stood at the Hertz desk; the Budget clerk was biding his time on his phone. Evans approached the Budget desk and read "Carson" on the clerk's name badge. He brought his shield to eye level and said, "Carson, I need to see the list of people that you sold cars to on Sunday."

Carson looked up from his phone and said, "Yeah, um, no. I'm not supposed to do that. I mean, Gary will, like, kill me."

"Right now, Gary is the least of your problems. If I were in your shoes, I'd address the problem standing right in front of you. All I need is to see if you gave a car to Clive Latham," he said, returning his shield to his coat pocket.

"Yeah, but we don't, like, sell cars. We rent them," Carson said, setting his phone on the counter.

"Carson, are you aware that it's a crime to obstruct an

ongoing investigation. And do you know who in the entire GRPD has made the most arrests for interfering with a police investigation? You're looking at him."

"Don't I need a warrant or something before you can see our records?"

"You don't need anything. *I* need to see whether you rented a car to Clive Latham."

"Gary's gonna kill me."

"Gary will never know a thing. Latham, Clive Latham."

Carson searched for Clive Latham and an active account popped up. "Yeah, we did," he said, spinning the monitor towards Evans.

Evans pointed at the screen saying, "Okay, a black SVU. Where's the plate number?"

"It's down here," Carson said, pointing to the lower left part of the screen.

Evans wrote down the number and said, "That wasn't so hard, was it. Do you see any Garys? I don't see any Garys. No Garys the Goat here. Well done, son."

Evans drove back to the office ruminating about Latham. It's a big city, filled with numerous hiding places. Instead of focusing on where he was, Evans was determined to figure out where Latham would be. He'd been in town for a few days now, with enough time to follow his target. He must have a good idea of their daily routines, routes, and schedule.

After returning to GRPD Headquarters Evans put out a BOLO for Clive Latham, driving a black SUV. He walked to Lieutenant Jefferson's office, and knocking on the door, asked, "Lieu, got a minute?"

Jefferson said, "Yeah, I heard you've identified someone for the Three Fires murder."

"Yeah, I've got him, I just need to get him. I mean, you know what I mean," Evans said.

"I do. When are you gonna bring him in?"

Over the next few minutes, Evans outlined the why, the where, the when, and the how of his plan. Jefferson listened without interrupting. When Evans finished speaking, he asked,

"So, Lieu, what do you think? Are you on board?"

"Evans, you can't do that. You can't just leave them on an island like that. How well do you even know this guy?" Jefferson asked.

"As much as I can, I've had a few days to deconstruct him. Obviously, I can't get in his head, but I think I know him pretty well. I'm taking appropriate precautions. No one's on an island, no one's gonna be alone."

"They damn well better be made aware of every step of your plan. If this goes south in any way, you and the Department are toast. Understand?"

"Understand."

"How can I help?" Jefferson asked.

"I need Jonesie."

"Only one guy? Mohammad, not Smitty?"

Evans said, "Yeah, no. Jonesie'll be fine. But we'll need backup."

"How many and where do you want them?" Jefferson asked.

"I'll let you know after checking out one more thing."

"Evans, I hope you're right about this."

"Thanks for the vote of confidence. And I am."

Evans went to the basement and signed out three pieces of equipment. He placed a call to Stella, who didn't pick up, and left a message asking her to call him back. He prepared the affidavit for the arrest warrant.

Evans called Mohammad. "Jonesie, thanks for volunteering to help me out tonight. Little overtime can't hurt the wallet, right?"

"Yeah, I heard. What's going on?"

Evans said, "You remember the murder at the Three Fires Hotel?" Having recounted the entire story to Jefferson, he was able to succinctly summarize the salient features of how he saw the night playing out. Mohammad had a question about logistics and the call ended shortly thereafter.

Chapter 64

January 25, 2023. IceHouse, Belknap Park. Grand Rapids, Michigan.

Mohammad finished his shift and arrived fifteen minutes before midnight. He entered the building to find the lobby nearly empty. A few thirty to fifty-year-old guys carrying large equipment bags were milling about. He ambled through the vestibule, noting that the Pro Shop and snack bar were closed.

Evans circled the parking lot. Not seeing the vehicle he was looking for, he went inside, called Lieutenant Jefferson, and told him how many backup units he needed and where he wanted them strategically placed. He greeted Mohammad in the lobby saying, "I may be wrong, I don't see his car. Here."

"Don't need it, I have my own," Mohammad said, unzipping his jacket.

Evans asked, "Do you have a license for that thing?"

Smiling, Mohammad replied, "Sure do."

Evans led the way as they walked toward the south end of the building, and into a locker room. Two locker rooms were nearly empty as most of the players from the earlier game had showered, dressed, and left. In the last dressing room, he said hello to a few of The Kids, their opponent for the night. Mohammad scanned the room and shook his head, as he'd done after looking through the first two. He went to the lobby and waited.

Evans went to the locker room that housed his Murray's Manons teammates, said his hellos, then went to the women's locker room, where a solitary figure sat. "Here."

Stella had most of her equipment on. "Are you crazy. That thing's too big for me."

"I'm not taking any chances, and neither are you."

"Fine. You sure we're going to cut his balls off tonight?"

"As sure as I can be. I'll see you out there."

Murray's Manons players stood by the door to the rink and waited for the ice to be resurfaced. Evans walked directly to the bench. The temperature inside the rink was kept around sixty-two degrees. The temperature on the benches was closer to the ice surface of twenty-three degrees. He glanced around the rink and saw Jonesie walking back and forth between the unoccupied lobby and the empty bleachers.

Evans greeted the Zamboni driver, who looked like a young Don Knotts, as he drove in front of the bench.

"Hey, Don," Evans said.

"Hey, Gordie. Not playing tonight?"

"Not tonight. Nice hat."

"Thanks, he just gave it to me." Don was wearing an orange ear flap hat with "Safe Hunter" stitched on the front. Evans wondered what's up with the ridiculous headgear.

Mohammad watched the Zamboni leave the ice surface at the north end of the rink. The game started and play was spirited for a no-check league. Murray's Manons icers found themselves behind 2-0 after one period. A deficit of two goals wasn't unexpected as their best player was in street clothes. A few players grumbled that Evans would be better utilized as a player rather than as a coach. The complaining stopped once the puck was dropped for the start of the second period.

Goal. Murray's Manons finally got on the score board. The teams lined up for the center ice face-off.

Mohammad yelled, "There!" then started running and pointing toward the north end of the rink.

Evans saw Mohammad pointing at Don, who was standing by the Zamboni entrance holding a shovel. He then realized it wasn't Don, and it wasn't a shovel. Clive Latham was holding a rifle.

As the ref dropped the puck, Stella flew backwards as if hit by a wrecking ball.

Evans jumped on the ice and ran toward his goalie. Stella was lying on her back with a gaping hole, mid chest, in her jersey. Evans saw that she was breathing and cried out, "Call 9-1-1. Tell them we've got a doctor down."

Evans ran to the Zamboni end of the rink with his gun in his hand; Mohammad opened the doors for him. They ran past Don, who was struggling to stand.

"Damn it," Evans said, not breaking stride.

Exiting the rink, they saw the red taillights of a black SUV speeding away. Evans screwed up. He hadn't searched for Latham's car behind the rink, where the Zamboni dumps snow collected during a resurfacing. He cried out, "My car!"

They holstered their Glocks and piled into his department-issued vehicle.

Evans drove as Mohammad pulled his service radio out of his pocket and called it in. "All units, all units, suspect is in a black SUV heading west on Coldbrook."

"With North Dakota plates Romeo Mike Tango 1-1-5," Evans added.

Evans turned from Coldbrook onto Division. He saw Latham rounding a corner to his right. Latham wasn't slowing down, despite driving against traffic. Evans chased Latham cautiously, swerving around cars that were speeding toward him. Some of the drivers in opposing traffic recorded the chase on their phones, all were blasting their horns.

Mohammad radioed the patrol officers stationed at the corner of Leonard and Division that they were rapidly approaching northbound on Division. Four GRPD cruisers, each parked perpendicular to the flow of traffic, blocked traffic on three sides of the Leonard and Division intersection. Spike strips covered each intersection.

Latham drove over the spikes when he turned west, onto Leonard. He drove around the right side of the roadblock, clipped a cruiser, took out a light post, and a bus stop canopy.

Latham lost his momentum after hitting the cruiser and was driving twenty mph as he approached the Grand River flowing under US-131. Evans was able to pass the roadblock on the right side without losing speed. He drove in the middle of Leonard and caught Latham before he passed under the expressway.

With his car parallel to Latham, Evans yelled, *"Hang on."*

"Wait, I'm right here. You hit him and you're gonna kill me," Mohammad yelled back.

"That ain't gonna happen," Evans said, turning the steering wheel hard to the right, ramming Latham, forcing his SUV off the road.

Latham tried to stay on the road by turning his SUV toward Evans, but he'd lost whatever size advantage his larger vehicle had after driving over the spike strips, puncturing his tires, and losing most of his speed. Latham couldn't stop his car from being pushed to the right. When he hit the curb, his car rolled on two wheels for twenty yards before flipping and plunging into the Grand River.

Evans jumped out of his car and followed Mohammad to the river's edge. They saw Latham's SUV slowly sinking under the rapidly flowing water. Latham was suspended by his seat belt and appeared to be hugging the airbag and steering wheel. He was not moving.

Evans jumped into the water while Mohammad stayed on the ice crusted, sloping bank. The shock of the frigid water took away Evans's breath, making it difficult for him to move. He struggled to open Latham's door as the icy water caused his muscles to cramp. Fighting the freezing water, cramps, and a sinking SUV, Evans faltered while trying to unclick Latham's seat belt. The SUV dipped further below the river's brim.

Evans and Latham submerged under the freezing water before Evans was able to secure a cross chest hold on Latham.

"Hang on, I got you," Mohammad yelled. With his lengthy reach and powerful grip, he held on to Evans's waterlogged coat. Mohammad was losing the tug of war with the current, which was insistent on pulling the three of them downstream. He slipped on the riverbank, causing his left leg to submerge up to his knee. He repeatedly smashed the heel of his water-filled boot against the icy riverside until he was able to gain sufficient footing. With his base secure, Mohammad had enough leverage over the rushing water to pull Evans and Latham to solid ground. Evans staggered to his feet as Mohammad secured Latham in handcuffs.

Evans and Mohammad helped two EMTs put an unconscious Latham on a gurney. Evans was hypothermic and accepted a warming blanket from the EMTs. The EMS unit that carried Evans arrived on the scene last and departed for Blanchard Hospital ED first. A rookie Patrol Officer, who knew nothing about Emily's case, rode with a handcuffed, unresponsive Latham to the hospital. Latham's vital signs were stable en route. Mohammad accepted a warming blanket from the EMTs but chose not to go to the ED for "a little water in his boot."

***

Latham didn't have time to dwell on how in the hell GRPD knew he'd be at the rink. The roadblocks meant they anticipated his being there. Improvise. Adapt. Overcome. He needed a plan. He heard the Patrol Officer and EMT talking, believing their passenger was unconscious. There was only a tiny, small window for getting out of this mess. He'd strike when they removed the handcuffs.

Latham felt the EMS unit come to a stop. The EMT removed the blood pressure cuff from his arm and shimmied past him toward the rear door. As soon as Latham felt the handcuffs being removed, he sat up, grabbed the Patrol Officer's coat, and slammed his head against the officer's face. Simultaneously, blood poured from the officer's fractured nose and Latham's forehead. The cop was unresponsive. The EMT had the presence of mind to grab the defibrillator paddles.

Latham, looking at the trembling tech, said, "Put those down. I'm not going to hurt you. I only kill for a price."

Evans heard a commotion coming from the ED entrance. Ripping off his blanket, he ran to see what caused the disturbance. Following a line of nurses and nurse techs outside, he pushed aside cops and hospital Security Officers who were focusing their attention inside an EMS rig. Evans saw a shaken EMT trying to revive an unconscious cop. Empty handcuffs and blood-splattered, rumpled sheets lie on the gurney. Latham had escaped.

Epilogue

One month later. The Store. Grand Rapids, Michigan.

With the holidays over and decorations packed up, The Store returned to its normal resting state. Evans arrived before Stella and sat in a booth under the sign indicating eggs, dairy, and cheese were available in the aisle. Despite a 4-1 victory by Murray's Manons, he was not in a celebratory mood.

Stella arrived after Evans had consumed a third of his beer. "Finally," he said.

"Piss off, you bloody wanker. I needed to call home."

"I love it when you watch British TV."

"Yeah, Ash got me hooked on *The Crowne*. Do you know how scared I was when I first stepped on the ice tonight," Stella said, sliding into the booth.

Evans said, "Why? I told you that you didn't have anything to worry about."

"That's easy for you to say. Latham didn't shoot you." She removed her gloves and camel hair coat.

"How are the ribs, by the way?" Evans asked.

"Still sore, not that you care."

"Hey, I care about all of my teammates. Look, Latham's picture has been on the news, the internet, everywhere. He's the most wanted man in the world right now. We'll find him," Evans said.

Stella straightened her wind-blown hair saying, "Why'd you let him get away?"

Evans said, "We didn't *let* him do anything. He escaped. With Abernathy and Roberts in jail, Latham has no reason to come after you again." In hindsight, he should not have placed Stella in a position where her life was at risk. He was embarrassed by his misstep and very proud of her.

"I suppose. Was there any fallout over his escape?" Stella asked.

"Not really. The officer was reprimanded for uncuffing him while they were still in the EMS van, truck, rig, or whatever you call those things. I think my Lieutenant was getting tired and was going to call it quits anyway. He announced his retirement after forty-five years of service."

"Is the great Detective Evans taking his place?" Stella asked.

"That ain't gonna happen. I recommended Smitty, who's a much better fit. He knows how to talk to politicians and suits. And I can do without all those damn meetings."

Stella said, "Say, why did you have two Kevlar vests for me?"

Evans explained, "I didn't. I signed out three earlier that day: one for Jonesie, one for you, and the last one for me. Jonesie wore his own to the rink. I knew that Latham had used a rifle in the past, and thought you could probably use two.

"Did I ever tell you that Jonesie was at the Three Fires Hotel when I was first called to the scene? He said he'd had a nice weekend, which included 'a lot of laughs.' When I found out Latham was a comedian, I asked Jonesie if he'd been at Dr. Funny Bones on Saturday night. Once he confirmed that he'd been there, that meant Jonesie had stared at Latham for an hour, without knowing that he was Latham. I mean, without knowing that Latham was the assassin. I thought Jonesie had a better chance of recognizing Latham than if I'd passed his professional head shot around the department."

Stella said, "One guy was the 'massive back up' that you promised me?"

"Yeah, but he's really good."

"I don't know how a parent can bury a child or grandchild. Emily's death must have been God-awful for her parents. I should reach out to them, to let them know that she was a wonderful person," Stella said.

Evans said, "Yeah, sorry about that. I know you were fond of Emily. I've been in touch with the Naismiths. It's been rough for them. Emily's mother told me they're surviving with counseling. Hey, I almost forgot, do you know Dr. Colson-Brown?"

"Wilma? Yeah, I love her. I've presented with her several times during Clinical Path Conferences."

"Love?" Evans said, smiling.

"You can be a real dick sometimes. How does your better

half, no, your extremely superior half put up with you?" Stella asked.

"She tells me that I was lucky to marry up. Anyway, Wilma confirmed that Emily's boyfriend was the father of her baby. When I found out that Abernathy tried to hit on Emily, I had to make sure it wasn't Abernathy who got Emily pregnant."

"Why didn't you ask me? I would have told you there's no way Emily would have gotten involved with Abernathy."

"I couldn't, you were a suspect at the time. Abernathy claims it was boredom, but I think he got greedy. Said he'd always lived a clean life, always done the right thing. One day, he decided that he was going to do the wrong thing. Roberts claimed it was never about the money for him. It was all about winning or losing, or something like that. He couldn't stand to lose at anything," Evans said.

Stella sipped her wine and said, "Yeah, those two represent the dark, unspoken side of medicine. There's so much money involved it's hard not to be tempted. Hey, were you serious? Was I honestly on your suspect list?"

"Stells, I saw the CCTV footage. You went to Emily's room after dinner at the Three Fires Hotel that night. You were the last person to see Emily alive."

"Well, take me off your little list. That stays between us. I'm serious," Stella said.

"Done."

"Thank you for that. Have you heard anything from the Bioengineers?" Stella inquired.

Evans said, "I've been in touch with them regarding their CFO's fraud deal. By the way, did you ever see Albert, he of limited gambling acumen?"

"I can neither confirm nor deny that I've met with this Albert that you speak of. But what I *can* tell you is that if someone, hypothetically speaking, were to have looked at someone's med list, they may or may not have noticed that this person was taking a med which may or may not be used to treat restless leg syndrome. That same med may or may not rarely cause compulsive behaviors, like gambling. It's a rare, but well-documented side effect. If someone were to have noticed this person's med list included this specific med and took him or her off it, the compulsive urge to gamble may have subsided," Stella said.

"Hypothetically," Evans said.

"Hypothetically. Whatever happened to his case?"

Evans replied, "He'll probably plead, promise to pay them back. Maybe spend a few weeks or months in jail. They're close to patenting their next creation . . . the scientists are. Some monoclonal antibody for Parkinson's Disease."

"Great, we need all the help we can get with Parkinson's. Oh, that reminds me, SETTUP ended. The FDA didn't approve the drug because of concerns that it causes stroke. I asked the CDC to investigate why strokes were only reported in northern latitudes. Apparently, the nanoparticle caused a cryoprecipitate in cold temperatures, which triggered thrombogenesis. So, I was right, stroke only occurred in northern regions."

Evans said, "Nice one."

They stared at the TV while paying no attention to the program. Evans peeled the label off his beer bottle. Stella spun her wine glass.

After a few minutes, Evans said, "Hey, I just remembered some good news. I interviewed this guy for the case. I thought he was full of BS and needed to speak to his fiancé to corroborate his alibi. Long story, bu-"

"All of your stories are long and boring, but go ahead," Stella said smiling.

"Anyway, she sent me an invitation to their destination wedding in Charlevoix."

Stella said, "How nice for them. Ashley and I are taking Charlie up there for a week this summer."

"I need to get back up there, it's been a few years."

"Let me know if you're up there when we are. We'd love to see your supremely better half. Did I ever tell you about Billy?" Stella asked.

"Billy, the dog you promised to name after me, but didn't? No, I haven't heard anything about him lately. What's up?"

"Yeah, Charlie named him, but whatever. What I wanted to tell you is that he's developed a new behavior, which I'm sure you'll love. He's become a little humper."

"Billy!" Evans said, clapping his hands.

"Settle down. It's not legs, or dogs, or anything like that. He takes advantage of our pillows. As in, bedroom and couch pillows. I'm pretty sure he's violated every one of them."

Evans said, "I think he's earned a new name–The Humpmeister."

"I knew you'd love it. You're such a Cro," Stella said.

"Wait a sec, crow as in fierce black bird or Crow as in Native American? You know a fighter, warrior, protector of the land and people."

"Cro as in Cro-Magnon, disheveled keeper of the fire and cave."

Laughing and tilting his head forward, Evans spit his last sip back in the bottle. "Did Dr. Murray just tell me to piss off?"

"Maybe. Listen, I've got to run, I've got an early clinic tomorrow." Stella wondered where Latham was and who'd eventually capture him: GRPD? The FBI? Interpol? She paid the bill without finishing her half-empty glass of Chardonnay.

Evans wondered when Latham would surface; it was only a matter of time. Pushing aside his half-full bottle, he wiped the spilled beer off the table and said, "Hang on. I'm coming, I'm coming."

They walked out of The Store to find three inches of freshly fallen snow had blanketed the city.

The End

www.ingramcontent.com/pod-product-compliance
Lightning Source LLC
LaVergne TN
LVHW010640110826
845149LV00014B/2903

* 9 7 8 1 9 6 0 1 0 4 8 1 6 *